R

D0423688

Contents

DREAMS AND WONDERS
Stories from the Dawn of Modern Fantasy

EDITED AND WITH A PREFACE BY
MIKE ASHLEY

DOVER PUBLICATIONS, INC.
Mineola, New York

Bibliographical Note

Dreams and Wonders: Stories from the Dawn of Modern Fantasy, first published by Dover Publications, Inc., in 2010, is a new compilation of stories from standard editions (see "Sources," pp. ix–xi, for details). A Preface has been written specially for the present edition by Mike Ashley.

Library of Congress Cataloging-in-Publication Data

Dreams and wonders : stories from the dawn of modern fantasy / edited and with a preface by Mike Ashley.
    p. cm.
  ISBN-13: 978-0-486-47775-6
  ISBN-10: 0-486-47775-4
    1. Fantasy fiction, English.   I. Ashley, Michael.
PR1309.F3D74 2010
823'.0876608—dc22

                                                                    2010004549

Manufactured in the United States by Courier Corporation
47775401
www.doverpublications.com

Preface

This anthology traces the development of modern fantasy during the nineteenth and early twentieth centuries. Fantasy is the world's oldest literature. *The Epic of Gilgamesh*, for instance, dates back to at least 2000 BCE, which makes Homer's *Iliad* and *Odyssey*, dating from around 800 BCE (though relating to events of three centuries earlier), seem almost modern. The Egyptians, Greeks, and Romans produced many tales of fantasy, though many have been lost. Apuleius's *Metamorphoses*, dating from around A.D. 160, is the only full-length fantasy to survive in its entirety from the classical period. Many of the myths and legends of the ancient world live on in our literature today and have passed into our language, such as when we refer to the labors of Hercules, the Golden Fleece, or the Gorgon's head.

There are many other fantasies from the early and late Middle Ages, including the stories later assembled as *One Thousand and One Nights*, as well as those in *The Decameron* by Boccaccio, Dante's *Inferno,* and some of Chaucer's *Canterbury Tales*. There were also the vast cycles of medieval romance, notably the various Arthurian stories relating to the exploits of King Arthur and his knights and the quest for the Holy Grail. These tales of knightly adventures were parodied brilliantly by Miguel Cervantes in his masterwork *Don Quixote*, completed in 1615—its success brought an end, for a time, to the fantastic adventure novel. But it didn't bring an end to the fantasy genre. Fantasy as a vehicle for allegory and satire had already been evident in such texts as *Reynard the Fox*, which dates from at least the twelfth century; *Gargantua and Pantagruel* by Rabelais (begun in the 1530s); John Bunyan's *Pilgrim's Progress* (completed in 1684); and Jonathan Swift's *Gulliver's Travels* (1726); and many more.

The main shift in fantasy was toward the fairy tale, although some early examples were also vehicles for satire. The tales included by

v

Madame d'Aulnoy in her seminal collection *Les Contes de fées* (*Tales of the Fairies*, 1697) were intended for adults, not children, and were recounted in her literary salons, whose attendees would have known the subversive significance of the characters and incidents. Both Madame d'Aulnoy and her contemporary, Charles Perrault (whose *Histoires ou contes du temps passé*, also appearing in 1697, included such well-known stories as "Sleeping Beauty," "Little Red Riding Hood," and "Cinderella"), drew upon earlier folktales and the oral tradition so that many of these stories were already quite well known in one form or another; it was their adaptation by d'Aulnoy and others that cemented their popularity.

For much of the eighteenth century, France was the home of the fairy tale and the center of the fantasy tradition. It was here that Antoine Galland produced his translation and compilation of *Les Mille et une nuits*, starting in 1704—better known today as *The Arabian Nights*. This led to a vogue in "Oriental" tales. The French writer and philosopher Voltaire, who claimed to have read the *Arabian Nights* fourteen times, produced several Oriental fantasies, starting with *Zadig* (1747), set in ancient Babylon, and *The White Bull* (1773), set in ancient Egypt but based on a Greek legend, and these works may be seen as the earliest sprouting of modern fantasy.

The Oriental tale soon met a rival in the gothic tale, a genre begun by Horace Walpole in *The Castle of Otranto* (1765) and popularized by Ann Radcliffe in *The Mysteries of Udolpho* (1794). Inevitably, the gothic and Oriental genres soon merged, in William Beckford's *Vathek* (1786), and there was a parallel in the rise of the Romantic movement throughout western Europe. The movement rebelled against the new scientific orthodoxy and gave vent to the power and stimulation of the imagination. It reveled in folklore and mythology and, in particular, in the wonder and significance of dreams. In the hands of the German writers Johann Wolfgang von Goethe, Novalis and Ludwig Tieck, among others, it encouraged the growth of modern fantasy through a new interpretation of classical and popular tales. All of the raw materials were now at hand: folk and fairy tales, classical mythology, Oriental tales and the gothic extravaganza. While the fairy tale gradually devolved into nursery tales, serious, more "adult" tales of the fantastic emerged from the same stock.

It is difficult to define "modern fantasy," as the phrase does not really apply to either date or content. Much modern fantasy still draws upon folktales and legend, most notably J. R. R. Tolkien's *The Lord of the Rings.* Tolkien's series is now over fifty years old, so it is scarcely modern, yet it is still the most popular of all fantasies and virtually created fantasy as a distinct marketing genre with the success of its paperback edition in the mid-sixties. The same period saw the success of Robert E. Howard's stories featuring the barbarian hero Conan the Cimmerian. Yet these stories, originally written in the early 1930s, look back to a quasi-historic age of myth and magic, giving birth to the genre of "sword and sorcery" or, more broadly, "heroic fantasy." *The Lord of the Rings* also looks back to a mythical "Middle Earth."

It was this looking back to an apparent "golden age" that really sparked the emergence of "heroic fantasy," which became a significant element of "modern fantasy," evident in the works of William Morris. Morris was one of the Pre-Raphaelite Brotherhood, a loosely knit group of artists that included Dante Gabriel Rossetti and William Holman Hunt; they had vowed, like the Romantics, to reject the modernistic approach to art and revert to the more realistic form that had existed at the time of Raphael in the early sixteenth century. Morris extended this attitude to literature. His fascination with the "Northern thing" led to a translation of the Icelandic *Volsunga Saga* (the basis for Richard Wagner's *Ring Cycle*) and subsequently to a series of historical heroic fantasies, starting with *The Story of the Glittering Plain* in 1891.

By the late nineteenth century the so-called "fairy tale" had become firmly entrenched as children's literature, but a number of writers, among them George MacDonald, Lucy Clifford, Edith Nesbit, and Laurence Housman, were reworking the fairy tale for adults and older children. MacDonald's novels *Phantastes* (1858) and *Lilith* (1895) use both fairy-tale motifs and allegory to create what many regard as the first significant works of modern fantasy. His work was a seminal influence on C. S. Lewis, J. R. R. Tolkien, and others.

The Oriental tale also returned to popularity; the fusion of Oriental and fairy tale is most evident in the works of Lafcadio Hearn and Lord Dunsany. Starting with *The Gods of Pegana* (1905), Dunsany wrote scores of fantastical short stories that were highly influential, not least in the works of the American writers H. P. Lovecraft and Clark Ashton Smith.

The dawn of the twentieth century also saw the emergence of the scientific romance—the precursor to science fiction—which used the development of technology and the new sciences but still remained within the trappings of fantasy. Abraham Merritt, Edgar

Rice Burroughs, and even H. G. Wells were key writers in this transition from fantasy to science fiction.

Thus the trail weaves its meandering route from the ancient world to the modern, and that is the basis for this anthology. I've selected a range of stories that help us follow this route from the start of the Romantic Age to the emergence of modern fantasy and the age of the scientific romance. To help define this route I have applied another factor to help us understand a key aspect of fantasy.

In simplest terms, fantasy is the opposite of reality. The real world is governed by the laws of science and nature. Anything outside those laws is supernatural, and, therefore, fantasy. Since the fantastic is thus alien to our real world, fantasies are frequently set in other worlds, be they the world of *faerie*, an ancient world of legend and myth, or a dream world. Dreams are the closest that humans come to experiencing the fantastic, and thus it is no surprise that many early fantasies explored dreams and visions as the basis for their stories. I have thus used the idea of dreams and the imagination to link most of the stories in this anthology. They are "bookended" by two stories that are closely related in theme: Goethe's "The New Paris" and H. G. Wells's "The Door in the Wall," both of which explore how we might be denied access to our dream worlds, but also show the transition from the Romantic age to modern fantasy. Between the two is Lucy Clifford's "The Story of Willie and Fancy," a tribute to the power and liberating force of the imagination, which is at the heart of this anthology.

For each story I have provided an introduction to help guide us along the route. I hope you enjoy the journey.

Mike Ashley

Sources

Anstey, F. "The Adventure of the Snowing Globe" originally appeared in *The Strand Magazine,* December 1905, and was collected in *Salted Almonds* (London: Smith, Elder, 1906), from which this text is taken.

Bangs, John Kendrick. "Charon Makes a Discovery" is the first chapter of *A House-Boat on the Styx* (New York: Harper, 1895).

Barbauld, Anna Letitia. "Sir Bertrand, A Fragment" was originally published in *Miscellaneous Pieces in Prose by John and Anna Aikin* (London: J. Johnson, 1773).

Bulwer-Lytton, Edward. "The Life of Dreams," was originally published in *The Pilgrims of the Rhine* (London: Saunders and Otley, 1834).

Burroughs, Edgar Rice. "Under the Moons of Mars" is part of the first six chapters originally published in *The All-Story,* February 1912, and subsequently reprinted in *A Princess of Mars* (Chicago: McClurg, 1917).

Clifford, Lucy Lane (Mrs. W. K.). "The Story of "Willie and Fancy" originally appeared in *Anyhow Stories: Moral and Otherwise* (London: Macmillan, 1882).

Dunsany, Lord. "Tales of Two Thieves" incorporates the following two stories: "The Distressing Tale of Thangobrind the Jeweller" was first published in *The Sketch,* 11 January 1911, and included in *The Book of Wonder* (London: Heineman, 1912); and "The Bird of the Difficult Eye," first published in *The Sketch,* 20 May 1914, and included in *The Last Book of Wonder* (London: Elkin Mathews, 1916).

Fairbridge, Charles Aken. "The Magic Mirror" is reprinted from *The Orange Fairy Book,* edited by Andrew Lang (London: Longmans, Green, 1906).

Garnett, Richard. "The Potion of Lao-Tsze" is reprinted from the first edition of *The Twilight of the Gods* (London: T. Fisher Unwin, 1888).

Von Goethe, Johann Wolfgang. "The New Paris" was originally published as "Der neue Paris" in *Aus Meinem Leben. Dichtung und Wahrheit* (Part 1, Book 2), 1811; the English translation is by John Oxenford.

Grahame, Kenneth. "The Piper at the Gates of Dawn" is a reprint of Chapter 7 of *The Wind in the Willows* (London: Methuen, 1908).

Hearn, Lafcadio. "The Fountain of Gold" originally appeared in the *New Orleans Item* for October 15, 1880 and was reprinted in *Leaves from the Diary of an Impressionist* (Boston: Houghton Mifflin, 1911) under the title "A Tropical Intermezzo." The version used here is from *Fantastics and Other Fancies* (Boston: Houghton Mifflin, 1914).

Hoffmann, E. T. A. "The Mines of Falun" was originally published as "Die Bergwerke zu Falun" in *Der Serapionsbrüder* (Part 1, Book 1), 1819. The version used here is a translation by Alexander Ewing in *The Serapion Brethren* (London: George Bell, 1886).

Housman, Laurence. "Inside Out" was first published in *Century Magazine,* August 1917, from which this text is taken. It was collected in *All-Fellows and the Cloak of Friendship* (1923).

Lovecraft, H. P. "Celephaïs" originally appeared in *The Rainbow #2* (May 1922) and was reprinted in *Marvel Tales,* May 1934 and *Weird Tales,* June/July 1939. It was included in *The Outsider and Others* (Sauk City: Arkham House, 1939).

MacDonald, George. "The Golden Key" was originally published in *Dealings with the Fairies* (London: Alexander Strahan, 1867).

De la Mare, Walter. "The Riddle" was originally published in *The Monthly Review,* February 1903 and was included in the collection *The Riddle and Other Stories* (London: Selwyn & Blount, 1923).

Merritt, A. "Through the Dragon Glass" was originally published in *All-Story Weekly,* 24 November 1917 and collected in *The Fox Woman and Other Stories* (New York: Avon, 1949).

Morris, William and Magnusson, Eirikr. "The Death of Fafnir" was originally published in *The Story of the Volsungs and Niblungs* (London: F. S. Ellis, 1870). The version used here is from Chapters 17 and 18 of the 1888 reprint, published in London by Walter Scott Press.

Nesbit, Edith. "The Poor Lovers" originally appeared in *Atalanta,* January 1892.

Poe, Edgar Allan. "Siope—A Fable" was originally published in *The Baltimore Book* (1838) and included in the first edition of *Tales of the Grotesque and Arabesque* (Philadelphia: Lea and Blanchard, 1840).

Tennyson, Alfred, Lord. "The Lady of Shalott" was originally published in *Poems* (London: Edward Moxon, 1833), and subsequently revised and reissued in *Poems* (Moxon, 1842); that version is used here.

Wells, H. G. "The Door in the Wall" was originally published in *The Daily Chronicle,* 14 July 1906 and collected in *The Country of the Blind and Other Stories* (London: Nelson, 1911).

DREAMS AND WONDERS

Johann Wolfgang von Goethe
(1749–1832)

THE NAME of the German author Johann Wolfgang von Goethe is so inextricably linked with his play *Faust* that it is easy to believe that it was his only work of literature. Yet Goethe was immensely prolific. During a career that lasted over sixty years, he produced numerous works of poetry, fiction, drama, and philosophy. A surprising amount of his fiction falls into the category of fantasy, owing much to the fact that in his youth he was enchanted by fairy tales and by the Arabian Nights.

Goethe apparently told the following story to his fellow pupils and playmates when he was just eight or nine years old, although he did not write it down until many years later, when he included it in the first part of his autobiography, *Dichtung und Wahrheit* (1811). He recalled that the story fascinated his friends because it was based on a real place in the city of Frankfurt, with the added dimension of taking the story into another world. Though often called a "fairy tale," the story is far from that. We might go so far as to say that Goethe, in his youthful precocity, invented the modern fantasy short story. The version that he recorded in print is clearly the product of his adult years, but it still beautifully captures the childhood dream of escaping from reality. It is also a fine example of what Goethe alludes to in the title of his autobiography, which translates as "Poetry and Truth," reflecting the relationship between reality and the imagination. The road to modern fantasy had begun.

The New Paris

Johann Wolfgang von Goethe

On the night before Whitsunday, not long since, I dreamed that I stood before a mirror engaged with the new summer clothes which my dear parents had given me for the holiday. The dress consisted, as you know, of shoes of polished leather, with large silver buckles, fine cotton stockings, black nether garments of serge, and a coat of green baracan with gold buttons. The waistcoat of gold cloth was cut out of my father's bridal waistcoat. My hair had been frizzled and powdered, and my curls stuck out from my head like little wings; but I could not finish dressing myself, because I kept confusing the different articles, the first always falling off as soon as I was about to put on the next. In this dilemma, a young and handsome man came to me, and greeted me in the friendliest manner. "Oh! you are welcome," said I: "I am very glad to see you here."

"Do you know me, then?" replied he, smiling.

"Why not?" was my no less smiling answer. "You are Mercury—I have often enough seen you represented in pictures."

"I am, indeed," replied he, "and am sent to you by the gods on an important errand. Do you see these three apples?" He stretched forth his hand and showed me three apples, which he could hardly hold, and which were as wonderfully beautiful as they were large, the one of a red, the other of a yellow, the third of a green, colour. One could not help thinking they were precious stones made into the form of fruit. I would have snatched them; but he drew back, and said, "You must know, in the first place, that they are not for you. You must give them to the three handsomest youths of the city, who then, each according to his lot, will find wives to the utmost of their wishes. Take them, and success to you!" said he, as he departed, leaving the apples in my open hands. They appeared to me to have become still larger. I held them up at once against the light and found them quite transparent; but soon they expanded upward, and became

2

three beautiful little ladies about as large as middle-sized dolls, whose clothes were of the colours of the apples. They glided gently up my fingers: and when I was about to catch them, to make sure of one at least, they had already soared high and far; and I had to put up with the disappointment.

I stood there all amazed and petrified, holding up my hands, and staring at my fingers as if there were still something on them to see. Suddenly I saw a most lovely girl dance upon the very tips. She was smaller, but pretty and lively; and as she did not fly away like the others, but remained dancing, now on one finger-point, now on another, I regarded her for a long while with admiration. And, as she pleased me so much, I thought in the end I could catch her, and made, as I fancied, a very adroit grasp. But at the moment I felt such a blow on my head that I fell down stunned, and did not awake from my stupor till it was time to dress myself and go to church.

During the service I often called those images to mind, and also when I was eating dinner at my grandfather's table. In the afternoon I wished to visit some friends, partly to show myself in my new dress, with my hat under my arm and my sword by my side, and partly to return their visits. I found no one at home; and, as I heard that they were gone to the gardens, I resolved to follow them, and pass the evening pleasantly.

My way led towards the town wall, and I came to the spot which is rightly called the Bad Wall, for it is never quite safe from ghosts there. I walked slowly, and thought of my three goddesses, but especially of the little nymph, and often held up my fingers in hopes she might be kind enough to balance herself there again. With such thoughts I was proceeding, when I saw in the wall on my left hand a little gate which I did not remember to have ever noticed before. It looked low, but its pointed arch would have allowed the tallest man to enter. Arch and wall had been chiselled in the handsomest way, both by mason and sculptor; but it was the door itself which first properly attracted my attention. The old brown wood, though slightly ornamented, was crossed with broad bands of brass wrought both in relief and intaglio. The foliage on these, with the most natural birds sitting in it, I could not sufficiently admire. But, what seemed most remarkable, no key-hole could be seen, no latch, no knocker; and from this I conjectured that the door could be opened only from within. I was not in error; for, when I went nearer in order to touch the ornaments, it opened inwards; and there appeared a man whose dress was somewhat long, wide, and singular. A venerable beard enveloped his chin, so that I was inclined to think him a Jew. But he, as if he had divined my thoughts, made the sign of the holy cross, by which he gave me to understand that he was a good Catholic Christian.

"Young gentleman, how came you here, and what are you doing?" he said to me, with a friendly voice and manner.

"I am admiring," I replied, "the workmanship of this door; for I have never seen anything like it, except in some small pieces in the collections of amateurs."

"I am glad," he answered, "that you like such works. The door is much more beautiful inside. Come in, if you like."

My heart, in some degree, failed me. The mysterious dress of the porter, the seclusion, and a something, I know not what, that seemed to be in the air, oppressed me. I paused, therefore, under the pretext of examining the outside still longer; and at the same time I cast stolen glances into the garden, for a garden it was which had opened before me. Just inside the door I saw a space. Old linden-trees, standing at regular distances from each other, entirely covered it with their thickly interwoven branches; so that the most numerous parties, during the hottest of the day, might have refreshed themselves in the shade. Already I had stepped upon the threshold, and the old man contrived gradually to allure me on. Properly speaking, I did not resist; for I had always heard that a prince or sultan in such a case must never ask whether there be danger at hand. I had my sword by my side too; and could I not soon have finished with the old man, in case of hostile demonstrations? I therefore entered perfectly re-assured: the keeper closed the door, which bolted so softly that I scarcely heard it. He now showed me the workmanship on the inside, which in truth was still more artistic than the outside, explained it to me, and at the same time manifested particular good will.

Being thus entirely at my ease, I let myself be guided in the shaded space by the wall, that formed a circle, where I found much to admire. Niches tastefully adorned with shells, corals, and pieces of ore, poured a profusion of water from the mouths of tritons into marble basins. Between them were aviaries and other lattice-work, in which squirrels frisked about, guinea-pigs ran hither and thither, with as many other pretty little creatures as one could wish to see. The birds called and sang to us as we advanced: the starlings, particularly, chattered the silliest stuff. One always cried, "Paris, Paris!" and the other, "Narcissus,

Narcissus!" as plainly as a schoolboy can say them. The old man seemed to continue looking at me earnestly while the birds called out thus; but I feigned not to notice it, and had in truth no time to attend to him, for I could easily perceive that we went round and round, and that this shaded space was in fact a great circle, which enclosed another much more important. Indeed, we had actually reached the small door again, and it seemed as though the old man would let me out. But my eyes remained directed towards a golden railing, which seemed to hedge round the middle of this wonderful garden, and which I had found means enough of observing in our walk; although the old man managed to keep me always close to the wall, and therefore pretty far from the centre.

Now, just as he was going to the door, I said to him, with a bow, "You have been so extremely kind to me that I would fain venture to make one more request before I part from you. Might I not look more closely at that golden railing, which appears to enclose in a very wide circle the interior of the garden?"

"Very willingly," replied he, "but in that case you must submit to some conditions."

"In what do they consist?" I asked hastily.

"You must leave here your hat and sword, and must not let go my hand while I accompany you."

"Most willingly," I replied; and laid my hat and sword on the nearest stone bench. Immediately he grasped my left hand with his right, held it fast, and led me with some force straight forwards. When we reached the railing, my wonder changed into amazement. On a high plinth of marble stood innumerable spears and partisans, ranged beneath each other, joined by their strangely ornamented points, and forming a complete circle. I looked through the intervals, and saw just behind a gently flowing piece of water, bounded on both sides by marble, and displaying in its clear depths a multitude of gold and silver fish, which moved about now slowly and now swiftly, now alone and now in shoals. I would also fain have looked beyond the canal, to see what there was in the heart of the garden. But I found, to my great sorrow, that the other side of the water was bordered by a similar railing, and with so much art, that to each interval on this side exactly fitted a spear or partisan on the other. These, and the other ornaments, rendered it impossible for one to see through, stand as he would. Besides, the old man, who still held me fast, prevented me from moving freely. My curiosity, meanwhile, after all I had seen, increased more and more; and I took heart to ask the old man whether one could not pass over.

"Why not?" returned he, "but on new conditions." When I asked him what these were, he gave me to understand that I must put on other clothes. I was satisfied to do so: he led me back towards the wall into a small, neat room, on the sides of which hung many kinds of garments, all of which seemed to approach the Oriental costume. I soon changed my dress. He confined my powdered hair under a many-coloured net, after having to my horror violently dusted it out. Now, standing before a great mirror, I found myself quite handsome in my disguise, and pleased myself better than in my formal Sunday clothes. I made gestures, and leaped, as I had seen the dancers do at the fair-theatre. In the midst of this I looked in the glass, and saw by chance the image of a niche which was behind me. On its white ground hung three green cords, each of them twisted up in a way which from the distance I could not clearly discern. I therefore turned round rather hastily, and asked the old man about the niche as well as the cords. He very courteously took a cord down, and showed it to me. It was a band of green silk of moderate thickness, the ends of which, joined by green leather with two holes in it, gave it the appearance of an instrument for no very desirable purpose. The thing struck me as suspicious, and I asked the old man the meaning. He answered me very quietly and kindly, "This is for those who abuse the confidence which is here readily shown them." He hung the cord again in its place, and immediately desired me to follow him; for this time he did not hold me, and so I walked freely beside him.

My chief curiosity now was, to discover where the gate and bridge, for passing through the railing and over the canal, might be; since as yet I had not been able to find anything of the kind. I therefore watched the golden fence very narrowly as we hastened towards it. But in a moment my sight failed: lances, spears, halberds, and partisans began unexpectedly to rattle and quiver; and the strange movement ended in all the points sinking towards each other just as if two ancient hosts, armed with pikes, were about to charge. The confusion to the eyes, the clatter to the ears, was hardly to be borne; but infinitely surprising was the sight, when, falling perfectly level, they covered the circle of the canal, and formed the most glorious bridge that one can imagine. For now a most variegated garden parterre met my sight. It was laid out in curvilinear beds, which, looked at together, formed a labyrinth of ornaments; all with green borders of a low, woolly plant, which I had never seen before; all with flowers, each division of different colours, which, being likewise low and close to the ground, allowed the plan to be easily traced. This delicious sight, which I enjoyed in the full sunshine, quite riveted my eyes. But I hardly knew where I was to set my foot; for the serpentine paths were most delicately laid with blue sand, which seemed to form upon the earth a darker sky, or a sky seen in the water: and so I walked for a while beside my conductor, with my eyes fixed upon the ground, until at last I perceived, that, in the middle of this round of beds and flowers, there was a great circle of cypresses or poplar-like trees, through which one could not see, because the lowest branches seemed to spring out of the ground. My guide, without taking me exactly the shortest way, led me nevertheless immediately towards that centre; and how was I astonished, when, on entering the circle of high trees, I saw before me the peristyle of a magnificent garden-house, which seemed to have similar prospects and entrances on the other sides! The heavenly music which streamed from the building transported me still more than this model of architecture. I fancied that I heard now a lute, now a harp, now a guitar, and now something tinkling which did not belong to any of these instruments.

The door for which we made opened soon on being lightly touched by the old man. But how amazed I was when the female porter who came out perfectly resembled the delicate girl who had danced upon my fingers in the dream! She greeted me as if we were already acquainted, and invited me to walk in. The old man stayed behind; and I went with her through a short passage, arched and finely ornamented, to the middle hall, the splendid, dome-like ceiling of which attracted my gaze on my entrance, and filled me with astonishment. Yet my eye could not dwell on this long, being allured down by a more charming spectacle. On a carpet, directly under the middle of the cupola, sat three women in a triangle, clad in three different colours,—one red, the other yellow, the third green. The seats were gilt, and the carpet was a perfect flower-bed. In their arms lay the three instruments which I had been able to distinguish from without; for, being disturbed by my arrival, they had stopped their playing.

"Welcome!" said the middle one, who sat with her face to the door, in a red dress, and with the harp. "Sit down by Alerte, and listen, if you are a lover of music."

I now saw for the first time that there was a rather long bench placed obliquely before them, on which lay a mandolin. The pretty girl took it up, sat down, and drew me to her side. Now also I looked at the second lady on my right. She wore the yellow dress, and had the guitar in her hand; and if the harp-player was dignified in form, grand in features, and majestic in her deportment, one might remark in the guitar-player an easy grace and cheerfulness. She was a slender blonde, while the other was adorned by dark-brown hair. The variety and accordance of their music could not prevent me from remarking the third beauty, in the green dress, whose lute-playing was for me at once touching and striking. She was the one who seemed to notice me the most, and to direct her music to me: only I could not make up my mind about her; for she appeared to me now tender, now whimsical, now frank, now self-willed, according as she changed her mien and mode of playing. Sometimes she seemed to wish to excite my emotions, sometimes to tease me; but, do what she would, she got little out of me; for my little neighbour, by whom I sat elbow to elbow, had gained me entirely to herself: and while I clearly saw in those three ladies the sylphides of my dream, and recognized the colours of the apples, I conceived that I had no cause to detain them. I should have liked better to lay hold of the pretty little maiden if I had not but too well remembered the blow she had given me in my dream. Hitherto she had remained quite quiet with her mandolin; but, when her mistresses had ceased, they commanded her to perform some pleasant little piece. Scarcely had she jingled off some dance-tune, in a most exciting manner, than she sprang up: I did the same. She played and danced; I was hurried on to accompany her steps; and we executed a kind of little ballet, with which the ladies seemed satisfied; for, as soon as we had done, they commanded the little girl to refresh me with something nice till supper should come in. I had indeed forgotten that there was anything in the world beyond this paradise.

Alerte led me back immediately into the passage by which I had entered. On one side of it she had two well-arranged rooms. In that in which she lived she set before me oranges, figs, peaches, and grapes; and I enjoyed with great gusto both the fruits of foreign lands and those of our own not yet in season. Confectionery there was in profusion: she filled, too, a goblet of polished crystal with foaming wine; but I had no need to drink, as I had refreshed myself with the fruits.

"Now we will play," said she, and led me into the other room. Here all looked like a Christmas fair, but such costly and exquisite things were never seen in a Christmas booth. There were all kinds of dolls, dolls' clothes, and dolls' furniture; kitchens, parlours, and shops, and single toys innumerable. She led me round to all the glass cases in which these ingenious works were preserved. But she soon closed again the first cases, and said, "That is nothing for you, I know well enough. Here," she said, "we could find building-materials, walls and towers, houses, palaces, churches, to put together a great city. But this does not entertain me. We will take something else, which will be amusing to both of us." Then she brought out some boxes, in which I saw an army of little soldiers piled one upon the other, of which I must needs confess that I had never seen anything so beautiful. She did not leave me time to examine them in detail, but took one box under her arm, while I seized the other. "We will go," she said, "to the golden bridge. There one plays best with soldiers: the lances give at once the direction in which the armies are to be opposed to each other."

We had now reached the golden, trembling floor; and below me I could hear the waters gurgle and the fishes splash, while I knelt down to range my columns. All, as I now saw, were cavalry. She boasted that she had the queen of the Amazons as leader of her female host. I, on the contrary, found Achilles and a very stately Grecian cavalry. The armies stood facing each other, and nothing could have been seen more beautiful. They were not flat, leaden horsemen like ours; but man and horse were round and solid, and most finely wrought: nor could one conceive how they kept their balance; for they stood of themselves, without a support for their feet.

Both of us had inspected our hosts with much self-complacency, when she announced the onset. We had found ordnance in our chests; viz., little boxes full of well-polished agate balls. With these we were to fight against each other from a certain distance; while, however, it was an express condition that we should not throw with more force than was necessary to upset the figures, as none of them were to be injured. Now the cannonade began on both sides, and at first it succeeded to the satisfaction of us both. But when my adversary observed that I aimed better than she, and might in the end win the victory, which depended on the majority of pieces remaining upright, she came nearer, and her girlish way of throwing had then the desired result. She prostrated a multitude of my best troops, and the more I protested the more eagerly did she throw. This at last vexed me, and I declared that I would do the same. In fact, I not only went nearer, but in my rage threw with much more violence; so that it was not long before a pair of her little centauresses flew in pieces. In her eagerness she did not instantly notice it, but I stood petrified when the broken figures joined together again of themselves: Amazon and horse became again one, and also perfectly close, set up a gallop from the golden bridge under the lime-trees, and, running swiftly backwards and forwards, were lost in their career, I know not how, in the direction of the wall. My fair opponent had hardly perceived this, when she broke out into loud weeping and lamentation, and exclaimed that I had caused her an irreparable loss, which was far greater than could be expressed. But I, by this time provoked, was glad to annoy her, and blindly flung a couple of the remaining agate balls with force into the midst of her army. Unhappily I hit the queen, who had hitherto, during our regular game, been excepted. She flew in pieces, and her nearest officers were also shivered. But they swiftly set themselves up again, and started off like the others, galloping very merrily about under the lime-trees, and disappearing against the wall. My opponent scolded and abused me; but, being now in full play, I stooped to pick up some agate balls which rolled about upon the golden lances. It was my fierce desire to destroy her whole army. She, on the other hand, not idle, sprang at me, and gave me a box on the ear, which made my head ring. Having always heard that a hearty kiss was the proper response to a girl's box of the ear, I took her by the ears, and kissed her repeatedly. But she uttered such a piercing scream as frightened even me. I let her go; and it was fortunate that I did so, for in a moment I knew not what was happening to me.

The ground beneath me began to shake and rattle. I soon remarked that the railings again set themselves in motion; but I had no time to consider, nor could I get a footing so as to fly. I feared every moment to be pierced; for the partisans and lances, which had lifted themselves up, were already tearing my clothes. It is sufficient to say, that, I know not how it was, hearing and sight failed me; and I recovered from my swoon and terror at the foot of a lime-tree, against which the pikes in springing up had thrown me. As I awoke, my anger awakened also, and violently increased when I heard from the other side the gibes and laughter of my opponent, who had probably reached the earth somewhat more softly than I. Therefore I jumped up; and as I saw the little host with its leader Achilles scattered around me, having been driven over with me by the rising of the rails, I seized the hero first, and threw him against a tree. His resuscitation and flight now pleased me doubly, a malicious pleasure combining with the prettiest sight in the world; and I was on the point of sending all the other Greeks after him, when suddenly hissing waters spurted at me on all sides, from stones and wall, from ground and branches, and, wherever I turned, dashed against me crossways. In a short time my light garment was wet through. It was already rent, and I did not hesitate to tear it entirely off my body. I cast away my slippers, and one covering after another. Nay, at last I found it very agreeable to let such a shower-bath play over me in the warm day. Now, being quite naked, I walked gravely along between these welcome waters, where I thought to enjoy myself for some time.

My anger cooled, and I wished for nothing more than a reconciliation with my little adversary. But, in a twinkling, the water stopped; and I stood drenched upon the saturated ground. The presence of the old man, who appeared before me unexpectedly, was by no means welcome. I could have wished, if not to hide, at least to clothe, myself. The shame, the shivering, the effort to cover myself in some degree, made me cut a most piteous figure. The old man employed the moment in venting the severest reproaches against me.

"What hinders me," he exclaimed, "from taking one of the green cords, and fitting it, if not to your neck, to your back?"

This threat I took in very ill part. "Refrain," I cried, "from such words, even from such thoughts; for otherwise you and your mistresses will be lost."

"Who, then, are you," he asked in defiance, "who dare speak thus?"

"A favourite of the gods," I said, "on whom it depends whether those ladies shall find worthy husbands and pass a happy life, or be left to pine and wither in their magic cell."

The old man stepped some paces back. "Who has revealed that to you?" he inquired, with astonishment and concern.

"Three apples," I said, "three jewels."

"And what reward do you require?" he exclaimed.

"Before all things, the little creature," I replied, "who has brought me into this accursed state."

The old man cast himself down before me, without shrinking from the wet and miry soil: then he rose without being wetted, took me kindly by the hand, led me into the hall, clad me again quickly; and I was soon once more decked out and frizzled in my Sunday fashion as before. The porter did not speak another word; but, before he let me pass the entrance, he stopped me, and showed me some objects on the wall over the way, while, at the same time, he pointed backwards to the door. I understood him: he wished to imprint the objects on my mind, that I might the more certainly find the door, which had unexpectedly closed behind me.

I now took good notice of what was opposite me. Above a high wall rose the boughs of extremely old nut-trees, and partly covered the cornice at the top. The branches reached down to a stone tablet, the ornamented border of which I could perfectly recognize, though I could not read the inscription. It rested on the top-stone of a niche, in which a finely wrought fountain poured water from cup to cup into a great basin, that formed, as it were, a little pond, and disappeared in the earth. Fountain, inscription, nut-trees, all stood perpendicularly, one above another: I would paint it as I saw it.

Now, it may easily be conceived how I passed this evening, and many following days, and how often I repeated to myself this story, which even I could hardly believe. As soon as it was in any degree possible, I went again to the Bad Wall, at least to refresh my remembrance of these signs, and to look at the precious door. But, to my great amazement, I found all changed. Nut-trees, indeed, overtopped the wall; but they did not stand immediately in contact. A tablet also was inserted in the wall, but far to the right of the trees, without ornament, and with a legible inscription. A niche with a fountain was found far to the left, but with no resemblance whatever to that which I had seen; so that I almost believed that the second adventure was, like the first, a dream, for of the door there is not the slightest trace. The only thing that consoles me is the observation, that these three objects seem always to change their places. For, in repeated visits to the spot, I think I have noticed that the nut-trees have moved somewhat nearer together, and that the tablet and the fountain seem likewise to approach each other. Probably, when all is brought together again, the door, too, will once more be visible; and I will do my best to take up the thread of the adventure. Whether I shall be able to tell you what further happens, or whether I shall be expressly forbidden to do so, I cannot say.

Anna Letitia Barbauld (1743–1825)

GOTHIC FICTION usually is associated with horror and the super-natural rather than the wider field of fantasy, but the historical Gothic had much in common. Many gothic novels were set in the Middle Ages or earlier, and, when incorporating ghosts, wizards, or knightly quests, bore comparison with the chivalric romances of old.

This is especially evident in the following incomplete piece by Anna Letitia Barbauld. It may have been composed as a fragment because it was used as an example to demonstrate her ideas and those of her younger brother, John Aikin, on why people seemed to delight in tales of horror. In their essay "On the Pleasure Derived from Objects of Terror," the Aikins remarked, "the apparent delight with which we dwell upon objects of pure terror, where our moral feelings are not in the least concerned, and no passion seems to be excited but the depressing one of fear, is a paradox of the heart." They further observed that "the more wild, fanciful and extraordinary are the circumstances of a scene of horror, the more pleasure we receive from it." Anna Letitia Barbauld saw psychological, even therapeutic, value in tales of terror and fantasy long before such psychoanalytical uses were developed.

Surprisingly, then, "Sir Bertrand," which was appended to that essay, was her only venture into gothic fantasy. Aikin earned an early reputation as a poet, but, after her marriage in 1774 to Rochemont Barbauld, she and her husband ran a school for boys. She occasion-ally returned to literature and became well known for her essays and poems supporting political and social reform. She also pro-duced several books for children. It was through these works that her reputation, after her death, was soured by an ungrateful Samuel Taylor Coleridge (to whom Mrs. Barbauld had been something of a mentor), who regarded her writing as too moralistic. Edith Nesbit perpetuated that attitude in her children's book *Wet Magic* (1913), in which Mrs. Barbauld is included amongst the malicious Book People.

Anna Barbauld deserved a better fate. One can only imagine what might have happened had she persevered with "Sir Bertrand," and what effect this might have had on the evolution of modern fantasy.

Sir Bertrand, A Fragment

Anna Letitia Barbauld

Sir Bertrand turned his steed towards the wolds, hoping to cross these dreary moors before the curfew. But ere he had proceeded half his journey, he was bewildered by the different tracks, and not being able, as far as the eye could reach, to espy any object but the brown heath surrounding him, he was at length quite uncertain which way he should direct his course.

Night overtook him in this situation. It was one of those nights when the moon gives a faint glimmering of light through the thick black clouds of a lowering sky. Now and then she suddenly emerged in full splendor from her veil; and then instantly retired behind it, having just served to give the forlorn Sir Bertrand a wide extended prospect over the desolate waste. Hope and native courage a while urged him to push forwards, but at length the increasing darkness and fatigue of body and mind overcame him; he dreaded moving from the ground he stood on, for fear of unknown pits and bogs, and alighting; from his horse in despair, he threw himself on the ground.

He had not long continued in that posture the sullen toll of a distant bell struck his ears—he started up, and turning towards the sound discerned a dim twinkling light. Instantly he seized his horse's bridle, and with cautious steps advanced towards it. After a painful march he was stopt by a moated ditch surrounding the place from whence the light proceeded; and by a momentary glimpse of moonlight he had a full view of a large antique mansion, with turrets at the corners, and an ample porch in the centre. The injuries of time were strongly marked on everything about it. The roof in various places was fallen in, the battlements were half demolished, and the windows broken and dismantled. A drawbridge, with a ruinous gateway at each end, led to the court before the building.

He entered, and instantly the light, which proceeded from a window in one of the turrets, glided along and vanished; at the same

15

moment the moon sunk beneath a black cloud, and the night was darker than ever. All was silent—Sir Bertrand fastened his steed under a shed, and approaching the house traversed its whole front with light and slow footsteps—All was still as death—He looked in at the lower windows, but could not distinguish a single object through the impenetrable gloom. After a short parley with himself, he entered the porch, and seizing a massy iron knocker at the gate, lifted it up, and hesitating, at length struck a loud stroke. The noise resounded through the whole mansion with hollow echoes. All was still again. He repeated the strokes more boldly and louder. Another interval of silence ensued. A third time he knocked, and a third time all was still.

He then fell back to some distance that he might discern whether any light could be seen in the whole front. It again appeared in the same place and quickly glided away as before—at the same instant a deep sullen toll sounded from the turret. Sir Bertrand's heart made a fearful stop. He was a while motionless; then terror impelled him to make some hasty steps toward his steed, but shame stopt his flight; and urged by honour, and a resistless desire of finishing the adventure, he returned to the porch and, working up his soul to a full steadiness of resolution, he drew forth his sword with one hand, and with the other lifted up the latch of the gate. The heavy door, creaking upon its hinges, reluctantly yielded to his hand. He applied his shoulder to it and forced it open. He quitted it and stept forward. The door instantly shut with a thundering clap. Sir Bertrand's blood was chilled. He turned back to find the door, and it was long ere his trembling hands could seize it, but his utmost strength could not open it again.

After several ineffectual attempts, he looked behind him, and beheld, across a hall, upon a large staircase, a pale bluish flame which cast a dismal gleam of light around. He again summoned forth his courage and advanced towards it. It retired. He came to the foot of the stairs, and after a moment's deliberation ascended. He went slowly up, the flame retiring before him, till he came to a wide gallery. The flame proceeded along it, and he followed in silent horrors, treading lightly, for the echoes of his footsteps startled him. It led him to the foot of another staircase, and then vanished.

At the same instant another toll sounded from the turret. Sir Bertrand felt it strike upon his heart. He was now in total darkness, and with his arms extended, began to ascend the second staircase. A dead cold hand met his left hand and firmly grasped it, drawing him forcibly forwards. He endeavoured to disengage himself, but could not. He made a furious blow with his sword, and instantly a loud shriek pierced his ears, and the dead hand was left powerless in his. He dropt it, and rushed forwards with a desperate valour. The stairs were narrow and winding, and interrupted by frequent breaches, and loose fragments of stone. The staircase grew narrower and narrower and at length terminated in a low iron grate. Sir Bertrand pushed it open. It led to an intricate winding passage, just large enough to admit a person upon his hands and knees. A faint glimmering of light served to show the nature of the place. Sir Bertrand entered. A deep hollow groan resounded from a distance through the vault. He went forwards, and proceeding beyond the first turning, discerned the same blue flame which had before conducted him. He followed it. The vault, at length, suddenly opened into a lofty gallery, in the midst of which a figure appeared, compleatly armed, with a terrible frown and menacing gesture, and brandishing a sword in his hand. Sir Bertrand undauntedly sprung forwards; and aiming a fierce blow at the figure, it instantly vanished, letting fall a massy iron key. The flame now rested upon a pair of ample folding doors at the end of the gallery. Sir Bertrand went up to it, and applied the key to a brazen lock. With difficulty he turned the bolt.

Instantly the doors flew open, and discovered a large apartment, at the end of which was a coffin rested upon a bier, with a taper burning on each side of it. Along the room on both sides were gigantic statues of black marble, attired in the Moorish habits, and holding enormous sabres in their right hands. Each of them reared his arm, and advanced one leg forwards, as the knight entered; at the same moment the lid of the coffin flew open, and the bell tolled. The flame still glided forwards, and Sir Bertrand resolutely followed, till he arrived within six paces of the coffin. Suddenly, a lady in a shroud and black veil rose up in it, and stretched out her arms towards him. At the same time the statues clashed their sabres and advanced. Sir Bertrand flew to the lady and clasped her in his arms. She threw up her veil and kissed his lips; and instantly the whole building shook as with an earthquake, and fell asunder with a horrible crash.

Sir Bertrand was thrown into a sudden trance, and on recovering, found himself seated on a velvet sofa, in the most magnificent room he had ever seen, lighted with innumerable tapers, in lustres of pure crystal. A sumptuous banquet was set in the middle. The doors opening to soft music, a lady of incomparable beauty, attired with amazing splendour entered, surrounded by a troop of gay nymphs far more fair than the Graces. She advanced on the knight, and falling on her knees thanked him as her deliverer. The nymphs placed a garland of laurel on his head, and the lady led him by the hand to the banquet, and sat beside him. The nymphs placed themselves at the table, and a numerous train of servants entering, served up the feast; delicious music playing all the time. Sir Bertrand could not speak for astonishment. He could only return their honours by courteous looks and gestures.

E. T. A. Hoffmann (1776–1822)

THE NAME ERNST THEODOR AMADEUS HOFFMANN lives on in Offenbach's opera *Tales of Hoffmann* (1881), which was based on three of his stories, including "The Sandman" (1816). But his best-known work must surely be "The Nutcracker," or, more properly, "The Nutcracker and the Mouse-King" (1819), immortalized in Tchaikovsky's 1892 ballet. Though classified today as a fairy tale, the "Nutcracker," in its full original version, is a deeply sinister allegory with dark undertones. Hoffmann did not write it for children, and it is a shame that it is usually consigned to the children's market in an abbreviated form. It is, alas, too long to include in this anthology, but it is one of the fundamental stories marking the transition from the fairy tale to modern fantasy. Throughout his fantasies, Hoffmann sought to revolutionize the fairy tale by blending fantasy or illusion with reality. Time and again his stories make us question our concepts of reality and perception.

"The Mines of Falun" (1819) is an intriguing example of reality versus fantasy because it was based on a real incident. In 1670, a mine in Falun, Sweden, collapsed. It wasn't until 1719, when the mine was drained, that the body of a missing miner was discovered in a remarkable state of preservation. The body was put on show, and an elderly woman recognized her fiancé, who had vanished almost fifty years before. Hoffmann's story transcends the original account by creating one world above ground and another one below where imagination, dreams, and desires take on a new perspective.

"The Mines of Falun" appeared in Hoffmann's collection *Die Serapionsbrüder,* or *The Serapion Brethren.* The title referred to a gathering of friends, all of whom were part of the Romantic movement, who shared stories. Yet Hoffmann was not regarded as one of the Romantics. Goethe declared that his stories were "sickly and diseased." Over time, Hoffmann was dismissed as an alcoholic (which probably contributed to his liver problems, leading to an early death at the age of forty-six). However, his mind remained sharp—otherwise he could not have performed his duties as a special investigator within the Prussian Intelligence Service. Hoffmann trained as a lawyer but had always been interested in music and literature. Thankfully, he is remembered today in both of those artistic endeavours.

The Mines of Falun

E. T. A. Hoffmann

One bright, sunny day in July the whole population of Goethaborg was assembled at the harbour. A fine East-Indiaman, happily returned from her long voyage, was lying at anchor, with her long, homeward-bound pennant, and the Swedish flag fluttering gaily in the azure sky. Hundreds of boats, skiffs, and other small craft, thronged with rejoicing seafolk, were going to and fro on the mirroring waters of the Goethaelf, and the cannon of Masthuggetorg thundered their far-echoing greeting out to sea. The gentlemen of the East-India Company were walking up and down on the quay, reckoning up, with smiling faces, the plentiful profits they had netted, and rejoicing their hearts at the yearly increasing success of their hazardous enterprise, and at the growing commercial importance of their good town of Goethaborg. For the same reasons everybody looked at these brave adventurers with pleasure and pride, and shared their rejoicing; for their success brought sap and vigour into the whole life of the place.

The crew of the East-Indiaman, about a hundred strong, landed in a number of boats (gaily dressed with flags for the occasion) and prepared to hold their Hoensning. That is the name of the feast which the sailors hold on such occasions; it often goes on for several days. Musicians went before them, in strange, gay dresses, playing lustily on violins, oboes, fifes and drums, whilst others sung merry songs; after them came the crew, walking two and two; some, with gay ribbons on their hats and jackets, waved fluttering streamers; others danced and skipped; and all of them shouted and cheered at the tops of their voices, till the sounds of merriment rang far and wide.

Thus the gay procession passed through the streets, and on to the Haga suburb, where a feast of eating and drinking was ready for them in a tavern.

Here the best of *Oel* flowed in rivers and bumper after bumper was quaffed. Numbers of women joined them, as is always the case when

21

sailors come home from a long voyage; dancing began, and wilder and wilder grew the revel, and louder and louder the din.

One sailor only—a slender, handsome lad of about twenty, or scarcely so much—had slipped away from the revel, and was sitting alone outside, on the bench at the door of the tavern.

Two or three of his shipmates came out to him, and cried, laughing loudly:

"Now then, Elis Froebom! are you going to be a donkey, as usual, and sit out here in the sulks, instead of joining the sport like a man? Why, you might as well part company from the old ship altogether, and set sail on your own hook, as fight shy of the Hoensning. One would think you were a regular long-shore land-lubber, and had never been afloat on blue water. All the same, you've got as good pluck as any sailor that walks a deck, ay, and as cool and steady a head in a gale of wind as ever I came athwart; but, you see, you can't take your liquor! You'd sooner keep the ducats in your pocket than serve them out to the land-sharks ashore here. There, lad! take a drink of that; or Naecken, the sea-devil, and all the Troll will be foul of your hawse before you know where you are!"

Elis Froebom jumped up quickly from the bench; glared angrily at his shipmates; took the tumbler which was filled to the brim with brandy and emptied it at a draught; then he said:

"You see I can take my glass with any man of you, Ivens; and you can ask the captain if I'm a good sailorman, or not; so stow away that long tongue of yours, and sheer off! I don't care about all this drink and row here; and what I'm doing out here by myself is no business of yours; you have nothing to do with it."

"All right, my hearty!" answered Ivens. "I know all about it. You're one of these Nerica men and a moony lot the whole cargo of them are too. They're the sort of chaps that would rather sit and pipe their eye about nothing particular, than take a good glass, and see what the pretty lasses at home are made of, after a twelve-month's cruise! But just you belay there a bit. Steer full and bye, and stand off and on, and I'll send somebody out to you that'll cut you adrift, in a pig's whisper, from that old bench where you've cast your anchor."

They went; and presently a very pretty, rather refined-looking girl came out of the tavern, and sat down beside the melancholy Elis, who was still sitting, silent and thoughtful, on the bench. From her dress and general appearance there could be no doubt as to her terrible calling. But the life she was leading had not yet quite marred the delicacy of the wonderfully tender features of her beautiful face; there was no trace of repulsive boldness about the expression of her dark eyes rather a quiet, melancholy longing.

"Aren't you coming to join your shipmates, Elis?" she said. "Now that you're back safe and sound, after all you've gone through on your long voyage, aren't you glad to be home in the old country again?"

The girl spoke in a soft, gentle voice, putting her arms about him. Elis Froebom looked into her eyes, as if roused from a dream. He took her hand; he pressed her to his breast. It was evident that what she had said had made its way to his heart.

"Ah!" he said, as if collecting his thoughts, "it's no use talking about my enjoying myself. I can't join in all that riot and uproar; there's no pleasure in it, for me. You go away, my dear child! Sing and shout like the rest of them, if you can, and let the gloomy, melancholy Elis stay out here by himself; he would only spoil your pleasure. Wait a minute, though! I like you, and I should wish you to think of me sometimes, when I'm away on the sea again."

With that he took two shining ducats out of his pocket, and a beautiful Indian handkerchief from his breast, and gave them to the girl. But her eyes streamed with tears; she rose, laid the money on the bench, and said: "Oh, keep your ducats; they only make me miserable; but I'll wear the handkerchief in dear remembrance of you. You're not likely to find me next year when you hold your Hoensning in the Haga." And she crept slowly away down the street, with her hands pressed to her face.

Elis fell back into his gloomy reveries. At length, as the uproar in the tavern grew loud and wild, he cried: "Oh, that I were lying deep, deep beneath the sea! for there's nobody left in the wide, wide world that I can be happy with now!"

A deep, harsh voice spoke, close behind him: "You must have been most unfortunate, youngster, to wish to die, just when life should be opening before you."

Elis looked round, and saw an old miner standing leaning against the boarded wall of the tavern, with folded arms, looking down at him with a grave, penetrating glance.

As Elis looked at him, a feeling came to him as if some familiar figure had suddenly come into the deep, wild solitude in which he had thought himself lost. He pulled himself together, and told the old miner that his father had been a stout sailor, but had perished in the storm from which he himself had been saved as by a miracle; that his two soldier brothers had died in battle, and he had supported his mother with the liberal pay he drew for sailing to the East Indies. He said he had been obliged to follow the life of a sailor, having been brought up to it from childhood, and it had been a great piece of good fortune that he got into the service of the East-India Company. This voyage, the profits had been greater than usual, and each of the crew had been given a sum of money over and above his pay; so that he had hastened, in the highest spirits, with his pockets full of ducats, to the little cottage where his mother lived. But strange faces looked at him from the windows, and a young woman who opened the door to him at last told him, in a cold, harsh tone, that his mother had died three months before, and that he would find the few bits of things that were left, after paying the funeral expenses, waiting for him at the Town Hall. The death of his mother broke his heart. He felt alone in the world as much so as if he had been wrecked on some lonely reef, helpless and miserable. All his life at sea seemed to him to have been a mistaken, purposeless driving. And when he thought of his mother, perhaps badly looked after by strangers, he thought it a wrong and horrible thing that he should have gone to sea at all, instead of staying at home and taking proper care of her. His comrades had dragged him to the Hoensning in spite of himself, and he had thought, too, that the uproar, and even the drink, might have deadened his pain; but instead of that, all the veins in his breast seemed to be bursting, and he felt as if he must bleed to death.

"Well," said the old miner, "you'll soon be off to sea again, Elis, and then your sorrow will soon be over. Old folks must die; there's no help for that: she has only gone from this miserable world to a better."

"Ah!" said Elis, "it is just because nobody believes in my sorrow, and that they all think me a fool to feel it I say it's that which is driving me out of the world! I shall go to sea no more; I'm sick of existence altogether. When the ship used to go flying along through the water, with all sail set, spreading like glorious wings, the waves playing and dashing in exquisite music, and the wind singing in the rigging, my heart used to bound. Then I could hurrah and shout on deck like the best of them. And when I was on look-out duty of dark, quiet nights, I used to think about getting home, and how glad my dear old mother would be to have me back. I could enjoy a Hoensning like the rest of them, then. And when I had shaken the ducats into mother's lap, and given her the handkerchiefs and all the other pretty things I had brought home, her eyes would sparkle with pleasure, and she would clap her hands for joy, and run out and in, and fetch me the "Aehl" which she had kept for my home-coming. And when I sat with her of an evening, I would tell her of all the strange folks I had seen, and their ways and customs, and about the wonderful things I had come across in my long voyages. This delighted her; and she would tell me of my father's wonderful cruises in the far North, and serve me up lots of strange, sailor's yarns, which I had heard a hundred times, but never could hear too often. Ah! who will give me that happiness back again? No, no! never more on land! Never more at sea! What should I do among my shipmates? They would only laugh at me. Where should I find any heart for my work? It would be nothing but an objectless striving."

"It gives me real satisfaction to listen to you, youngster," said the old miner. "I have been observing you, without your knowledge, for the last hour or two, and have had my own enjoyment in so doing. All that you have said and done has shown me that you possess a profoundly thoughtful mind, and a character and nature pious, simple, and sincere. Heaven could have given you no more precious gifts; but you were never in all your born days in the least cut out for a sailor. How should the wild, unsettled sailor's life suit a meditative, melancholy Neriker like you? For I can see that you come from Nerica by your features, and whole appearance. You are right to say good-bye to that life for ever. But you're not going to walk about idle, with your hands in your pockets? Take my advice, Elis Froebom. Go to Falun, and be a miner. You are young and strong. You'll soon be a first-class pick-hand; then a hewer; presently a surveyor, and so get higher and higher. You have a lot of ducats in your pocket. Take care of them; invest them; add more to them. Very likely you'll soon get a Hemmans of your own, and then a share in the works. Take my advice, Elis Froebom; be a miner."

The old man's words caused him a sort of fear.

"What?" he cried. "Would you have me leave the bright, sunny sky that revives and refreshes me, and go down into that dreadful, hell-like abyss, and dig and tunnel like a mole for metals and ores, merely to gain a few wretched ducats? Oh, never!"

"The usual thing," said the old man. "People despise what they have had no chance of knowing anything about! As if all the constant wearing, petty anxieties inseparable from business up here on the surface, were nobler than the miner's work. To his skill, knowledge, and untiring industry Nature lays bare her most secret treasures. You speak of gain with contempt, Elis Froebom. Well, there's something infinitely higher in question here, perhaps: the mole tunnels the ground from blind instinct; but, it may be, in the deepest depths, by the pale glimmer of the mine candle, men's eyes get to see clearer, and at length, growing stronger and stronger, acquire the power of reading in the stones, the gems, and the minerals, the mirroring of secrets which are hidden above the clouds. You know nothing about mining, Elis. Let me tell you a little."

He sat down on the bench beside Elis, and began to describe the various processes minutely, placing all the details before him in the clearest and brightest colours. He talked of the Mines of Falun, in which he said he had worked since he was a boy; he described the great main-shaft, with its dark brown sides; he told how incalculably rich the mine was in gems of the finest water. More and more vivid grew his words, more and more glowing his face. He went, in his description, through the different shafts as if they had been the alleys of some enchanted garden. The jewels came to life, the fossils began to move; the wondrous Pyrosmalite and the Almandine flashed in the light of the miner's candles; the Rock-Crystals glittered, and darted their rays.

Elis listened intently. The old man's strange way of speaking of all these subterranean marvels as if he were standing in the midst of them, impressed him deeply. His breast felt stifled; it seemed to him as if he were already down in these depths with the old man, and would never more look upon the friendly light of day. And yet it seemed as though the old man were opening to him a new and unknown world, to which he really properly belonged, and that he had somehow felt all the magic of that world, in mystic forebodings, since his boyhood.

"Elis Froebom," said the old man at length, "I have laid before you all the glories of a calling for which Nature really destined you. Think the subject well over with yourself, and then act as your better judgment counsels you."

He rose quickly from the bench, and strode away without any goodbye to Elis, without looking at him even. Soon he disappeared from his sight.

Meanwhile quietness had set in in the tavern. The strong *Aehl* and brandy had got the upper hand. Many of the sailors had gone away with the girls; others were lying snoring in corners. Elis who could go no more to his old home asked for, and was given, a little room to sleep in.

Scarcely had he thrown himself, worn and weary as he was, upon his bed, when dreams began to wave their pinions over him. He thought he was sailing in a beautiful vessel on a sea calm and clear as a mirror, with a dark, cloudy sky vaulted overhead. But when he looked down into the sea he presently saw that what he had thought was water was a firm, transparent, sparkling substance, in the shimmer of which the ship, in a wonderful manner, melted away, so that he found himself standing upon this floor of crystal, with a vault of black rock above him, for that was rock which he had taken at first for clouds. Impelled by some power unknown to him he stepped onwards, but, at that moment, every thing around him began to move, and wonderful plants and flowers, of glittering metal, came shooting up out of the crystal mass he was standing on, and entwined their leaves and blossoms in the loveliest manner. The crystal floor was so transparent that Elis could distinctly see the roots of these plants. But soon, as his glance penetrated deeper and deeper, he saw, far, far down in the depths, innumerable beautiful maidens, holding each other embraced with white, gleaming arms; and it was from their hearts that the roots, plants, and flowers were growing. And when these maidens smiled, a sweet sound rang all through the vault above, and the wonderful metal-flowers shot up higher, and waved their leaves and branches in joy. An indescribable sense of rapture came upon the lad; a world of love and passionate longing awoke in his heart.

"Down, down to you!" he cried, and threw himself with outstretched arras down upon the crystal ground. But it gave way under him, and he seemed to be floating in shimmering æther.

"Ha! Elis Froebom; what think you of this world of glory?" a strong voice cried. It was the old miner. But as Elis looked at him, he seemed to expand into gigantic size, and to be made of glowing metal. Elis was beginning to be terrified; but a brilliant light came darting, like a sudden lightning-flash, out of the depths of the abyss, and the earnest face of a grand, majestic woman appeared. Elis felt the rapture of his heart swelling and swelling into destroying pain. The old man had hold of him, and cried: "Take care, Elis Froebom! That is the queen. You may look up now."

He turned his head involuntarily, and saw the stars of the night sky shining through a cleft in the vault overhead. A gentle voice called his name as if in inconsolable sorrow. It was his mother's. He thought he saw her form up at the cleft. But it was a young and beautiful woman who was calling him, and stretching her hands down into the vault.

"Take me up!" he cried to the old man. "I tell you I belong to the upper world, and its familiar, friendly sky."

"Take care, Froebom," said the old man solemnly; "be faithful to the queen, whom you have devoted yourself to."

But now, when he looked down again into the immobile face of the majestic woman, he felt that his personality dissolved away into glowing molten stone. He screamed aloud, in nameless fear, and awoke from this dream of wonder, whose rapture and terror echoed deep within his being.

"I suppose I could scarcely help dreaming all this extraordinary stuff," he said to himself, as he collected his senses with difficulty; "the old miner told me so much about the glories of the subterranean world that of course my head's quite full of it. But I never in my life felt as I do now. Perhaps I'm dreaming still. No, no; I suppose I must be a little out of sorts. Let's get into the open air. The fresh sea-breeze will soon set me all right."

He pulled himself together, and ran to the Klippa Haven, where the uproar of the Hoensning was breaking out again. But he soon found that all enjoyment passed him by, that he couldn't hold any thought fast in his mind, that presages and wishes, to which he could give no name, went crossing each other in his mind. He thought of his dead mother with the bitterest sorrow; but then, again, it seemed to him that what he most longed for was to see that girl again—the one whom he gave the handkerchief to—who had spoken so nicely to him the evening before. And yet he was afraid that if she were to come meeting him out of some street she would turn out to be the old miner in the end. And he was afraid of *him;* though, at the same time, he would have liked to hear more from him of the wonders of the mine.

Driven hither and thither by all these fancies, he looked down into the water, and then he thought he saw the silver ripples hardening into the sparkling glimmer in which the grand ships melted away, while the dark clouds, which were beginning to gather and obscure the blue sky, seemed to sink down and thicken into a vault of rock. He was in his dream again, gazing into the immobile face of the majestic woman, and the devouring pain of passionate longing took possession of him as before.

His shipmates roused him from his reverie to go and join one of their processions, but an unknown voice seemed to whisper in his ear: "What are you doing here? Away, away! Your home is in the Mines of Falun. There all the glories which you saw in your dream are waiting for you. Away, away to Falun!"

For three days Elis hung and loitered about the streets of Goethaborg, constantly haunted by the wonderful imagery of his dream, continually urged by the unknown voice. On the fourth day he was standing at the gate through which the road to Gefle goes, when a tall man walked through it, passing him. Elis fancied he recognized in this man the old miner, and he hastened on after him, but could not overtake him.

He followed him on and on, without stopping.

He knew he was on the road to Falun, and this circumstance quieted him in a curious way; for he felt certain that the voice of destiny had spoken to him through the old miner, and that it was he who was now leading him on to his appointed place and fate.

And, in fact, he many times—particularly if there was any uncertainty about the road—saw the old man suddenly appear out of some ravine, or from thick bushes, or gloomy rocks, stalk away before him, without looking round, and then disappear again.

At last, after journeying for many weary days, Elis saw, in the distance, two great lakes, with a thick vapour rising between them. As he mounted the hill to westward, he saw some towers and black roofs rising through the smoke. The old man appeared before him, grown to gigantic size, pointed with outstretched hand towards the vapour, and disappeared again amongst the rocks.

"There lies Falun," said Elis, "the end of my journey."

He was right; for people, coming up from behind him, said the town of Falun lay between the lakes Runn and Warhann, and that the hill he was ascending was the Guffrisberg, where the main-shaft of the mine was.

He went bravely on. But when he came to the enormous gulf, like the jaws of hell itself, the blood curdled in his veins, and he stood as if turned to stone at the sight of this colossal work of destruction.

The main-shaft of the Falun mines is some twelve hundred feet long, six hundred feet broad, and a hundred and eighty feet deep. Its dark brown sides go, at first for the most part, perpendicularly down, till about half way they are sloped inwards towards the centre by enormous accumulations of stones and refuse. In these, and on the sides, there peeped out here and there timberings of old shafts, formed of strong shores set close together and strongly rabbeted at the ends, in the way that block-houses are built. Not a tree, not a blade of grass to be seen in all the bare, blank, crumbling congeries of stony chasms; the pointed, jagged, indented masses of rock tower aloft all round in wonderful forms, often like monstrous animals turned to stone, often like colossal human beings. In the abyss itself lie, in wild confusion—pell-mell—stones, slag, and scoria, and an eternal, stupefying sulphury vapour rises from the depths, as if the hell-broth, whose reek poisons and kills all the green gladsomeness of nature, were being brewed down below. One would think this was where Dante went down and saw the Inferno, with all its horror and immitigable pain.

As Elis looked down into this monstrous abyss, he remembered what an old sailor, one of his shipmates, had told him once. This shipmate of his, at a time when he was down with fever, thought the sea had suddenly all gone dry, and the boundless depths of the abyss had opened under him, so that he saw all the horrible creatures of the deep twining and writhing about amongst thousands of extraordinary shells, and groves of coral, in dreadful contortions, till they died, and lay dead, with their mouths all gaping. The old sailor said that to see such a vision meant death, ere long, in the waves; and in fact he did very soon after fall overboard, no one knew exactly how, and was drowned without possibility of rescue. Elis thought of that: for indeed the abyss seemed to him to be a good deal like the bottom of the sea run dry; and the black rocks, and the blue and red slag and scoria, were like horrible monsters shooting out polyp-arms at him. Two or three miners happened, just then, to be coming up from work in the mine, and in their dark mining clothes, with their black, grimy faces, they were much like ugly, diabolical creatures of some sort, slowly and painfully crawling, and forcing their way up to the surface.

Elis felt a shudder of dread go through him, and—what he had never experienced in all his career as a sailor—his head got giddy. Unseen hands seemed to be dragging him down into the abyss.

He closed his eyes and ran a few steps away from it; and it was not till he began climbing up the Guffrisberg again, far from the shaft, and could look up at the bright, sunny sky, that he quite lost the feeling of terror which had taken possession of him. He breathed freely once more, and cried, from the depths of his heart:

"Lord of my Life! what are the dangers of the sea compared with the horror which dwells in that awful abyss of rock? The storm may rage, the black clouds may come whirling down upon the breaking billows, but the beautiful, glorious sun soon gets the mastery again, and the storm is past. But never does the sun penetrate into these black, gloomy caverns; never a freshening breeze of spring can revive the heart down there. No! I shall not join you, black earthworms that you are! Never could I bring myself to lead that terrible life."

He resolved to spend that night in Falun, and set off back to Goethaborg the first thing in the morning.

When he got to the market-place, he found a crowd of people there. A train of miners with their mine-candles in their hands, and musicians before them, was halted before a handsome house. A tall, slightly built man, of middle age, came out, looking round him with kindly smiles. It was easy to see, by his frank manner, his open brow, and his bright, dark-blue eyes, that he was a genuine Dalkarl. The miners formed a circle round him, and he shook them each cordially by the hand, saying kindly words to them all.

Elis learned that this was Pehrson Dahlsjoe, Alderman, and owner of a fine "Fraelse" at Stora-Kopparberg. "Fraelse" is the name given in Sweden to landed property leased out for the working of the lodes of copper and silver contained in it. The owners of these lands have shares in the mines and are responsible for their management.

Elis was told, further, that the Assizes were just over that day, and that then the miners went round in procession to the houses of the aldermen, the chief engineers and the minemasters, and were hospitably entertained.

When he looked at these fine, handsome fellows, with their kindly, frank faces, he forgot all about the earthworms he had seen coming up the shaft. The healthy gladsomeness which broke out afresh in the whole circle, as if new-fanned by a spring breeze, when Pehrson Dahlsjoe came out, was of a different kidney to the senseless noise and uproar of the sailors' Hoensning. The manner in which these miners enjoyed themselves went straight to the serious Elis's heart. He felt indescribably happy; but he could scarce restrain his tears when some of the young pickmen sang an ancient ditty in praise of the miner's calling, and of the happiness of his lot, to a simple melody which touched his heart and soul.

When this song was ended, Pehrson Dahlsjoe opened his door, and the miners all went into his house one after another. Elis followed involuntarily, and stood at the threshold, so that he overlooked the spacious floor, where the miners took their places on benches. Then the doors at the side opposite to him opened, and a beautiful young lady, in evening dress, came in. She was in the full glory of the freshest bloom of youth, tall and slight, with dark hair in many curls, and a bodice fastened with rich clasps. The miners all stood up, and a low murmur of pleasure ran through their ranks. "Ulla Dahlsjoe!" they said. "What a blessing Heaven has bestowed on our hearty alderman in her!" Even the oldest miners' eyes sparkled when she gave them her hand in kindly greeting, as she did to them all. Then she brought beautiful silver tankards, filled them with splendid Aehl (such as Falun is famous for), and handed them to the guests with a face beaming with kindness and hospitality.

When Elis saw her a lightning flash seemed to go through his heart, kindling all the heavenly bliss, the love-longings, the passionate ardour lying hidden and imprisoned there. For it was Ulla Dahlsjoe who had held out the hand of rescue to him in his mysterious dream. He thought he understood, now, the deep significance of that dream, and, forgetting the old miner, praised the stroke of fortune which had brought him to Falun.

Alas! he felt he was but an unknown, unnoticed stranger, standing there on the doorstep miserable, comfortless, alone and he wished he had died before he saw Ulla, as he now must perish for love and longing. He could not move his eyes from the beautiful creature, and, as she passed close to him, he pronounced her name in a low, trembling voice. She turned, and saw him standing there with a face as red as fire, unable to utter a syllable. So she went up to him, and said, with a sweet smile: "I suppose you are a stranger, friend, as you are dressed as a sailor. Well, why are you standing at the door? Come in and join us."

Elis felt as if in the blissful paradise of some happy dream, from which he would presently waken to inexpressible wretchedness. He emptied the tankard which she had given him; and Pehrson Dahlsjoe came up, and, after kindly shaking hands with him, asked him where he came from, and what had brought him to Falun.

Elis felt the warming power of the noble liquor in his veins, and, looking the hearty Dahlsjoe in the eyes, he felt happy and courageous. He told him he was a sailor's son and had been at sea since his childhood, had just come home from the East Indies and found his mother dead; that he was now alone in the world; that the wild sea life had become altogether distasteful to him; that his keenest inclination led him to a miner's calling, and that he wished to get employment as a miner here in Falun. The latter statement, quite the reverse of his recent determination, escaped him involuntarily; it was

THE MINES OF FALUN

as if he could not have said anything else to the alderman, nay as if it were the most ardent desire of his soul, although he had not known it till now, himself.

Pehrson Dahlsjoe looked at him long and carefully, as if he would read his heart; then he said: "I cannot suppose, Elis Froebom, that it is mere thoughtless fickleness and the love of change that lead you to give up the calling you have followed hitherto, nor that you have omitted to maturely weigh and consider all the difficulties and hardships of the miner's life before making up your mind to take to it. It is an old belief with us that the mighty elements with which the miner has to deal, and which he controls so bravely, destroy him unless he strains all his being to keep command of them if he gives place to other thoughts which weaken that vigour which he has to reserve wholly for his constant conflict with Earth and Fire. But if you have properly tested the sincerity of your inward call, and it has withstood the trial, you are come in a good hour. Workmen are wanted in my part of the mine. If you like, you can stay here with me, from now, and tomorrow the Captain will take you down with him, and show you what to set about."

Elis's heart swelled with gladness at this. He thought no more of the terror of the awful, hell-like abyss into which he had looked. The thought that he was going to see Ulla every day, and live under the same roof with her, filled him with rapture and delight. He gave way to the sweetest hopes.

Pehrson Dahlsjoe told the miners that a young hand had applied for employment, and presented him to them then and there. They all looked approvingly at the well-knit lad, and thought he was quite cut out for a miner, as regarded his light, powerful figure, having no doubt that he would not fail in industry and straight-forwardness, either.

One of the men, well advanced in years, came and shook hands with him cordially, saying he was Head-Captain in Pehrson Dahlsjoe's part of the mine, and would be very glad to give him any help and instruction in his power. Elis had to sit down beside this man, who at once began, over his tankard of Aehl, to describe with much minuteness the sort of work which Elis would have to commence with.

Elis remembered the old miner whom he had seen at Goethaborg, and, strangely enough, found he was able to repeat nearly all that he had told him.

"Ay," cried the Head-Captain. "Where can you have learned all that? It's most surprising! There can't be a doubt that you will be the finest pickman in the mine in a very short time."

Ulla, going backwards and forwards amongst the guests and attending to them, often nodded kindly to Elis and told him to be sure and enjoy himself. "You're not a stranger now, you know," she said, "but one of the household. You have nothing more to do with the treacherous sea—the rich mines of Falun are your home."

A heaven of bliss and rapture dawned upon Elis at these words of Ulla's. It was evident that she liked to be near him; and Pehrson Dahlsjoe watched his quiet earnestness of character with manifest approval.

But Elis's heart beat violently when he stood again by the reeking hell-mouth, and went down the mine with the Captain, in his miner's clothes, with the heavy, iron-shod Dalkarl shoes on his feet. Hot vapours soon threatened to suffocate him; and then, presently, the candles flickered in the cutting draughts of cold air that blew in the lower levels. They went down deeper and deeper, on iron ladders at last scarcely a foot wide; and Elis found that his sailor's adroitness at climbing was not of the slightest service to him there.

They got to the lowest depths of the mine at last, and the Captain showed him what work he was to set about.

Elis thought of Ulla. Like some bright angel he saw her hovering over him, and he forgot all the terror of the abyss, and the hardness of the toilsome labour.

It was clear in all his thoughts that it was only if he devoted himself with all the power of his mind, and with all the exertion which his body would endure, to mining work here with Pehrson Dahlsjoe, that there was any possibility of his fondest hopes being someday realized. Wherefore it came about that he was as good at his work as the most practised hand, in an incredibly short space of time.

Staunch Pehrson Dahlsjoe got to like this good, industrious lad better and better every day, and often told him plainly that he had found in him one whom he regarded as a dear son, as well as a first-class mine-hand. Also Ulla's regard for him became more and more unmistakeable. Often, when he was going to his work, and there was any prospect of danger, she would enjoin him to be sure to take care of himself, with tears in her eyes. And she would come running to meet him when he came back, and always had the finest of Aehl, or some other refreshment, ready for him. His heart danced for joy one day when Pehrson said to him that as he had brought a good sum of money with him, there could be no doubt that, with his habits of economy and industry, he would soon have a Hemmans, or perhaps even a Fraelse; and then not a mineowner in all Falun would say him nay if he asked for his daughter. Fain would Elis have told him at once how unspeakably he loved Ulla, and how all his hopes of happiness were based upon her. But unconquerable shyness, and the doubt whether Ulla really liked him—though he often thought she did—sealed his lips.

One day it chanced that Elis was at work in the lowest depths of the mine, shrouded in thick, sulphurous vapour, so that his candle only shed a feeble glimmer, and he could scarcely distinguish the run of the lode. Suddenly he heard as if coming from some still deeper cutting a knocking resounding, as if somebody was at work with a pick-hammer. As that sort of work was scarcely possible at such a depth, and as he knew nobody was down there that day but himself—because the Captain had got all the men employed in another part of the mine—this knocking and hammering struck him as strange and uncanny. He stopped working, and listened to the hollow sounds, which seemed to come nearer and nearer. All at once he saw, close by him, a black shadow and—as a keen draught of air blew away the sulphur vapour—the old miner whom he had seen in Goethaborg.

"Good luck," he cried, "good luck to Elis Froebom, down here among the stones! What think you of the life, comrade?"

Elis would fain have asked in what wonderful way the old man had got into the mine; but he kept striking his hammer on the rocks with such force that the fire-sparks went whirling all round, and the mine rang as if with distant thunder. Then he cried, in a terrible voice: "There's a grand run of trap just here; but a scurvy, ignorant scoundrel like you sees nothing in it but a narrow streak of Trumm not worth a beanstalk. Down here you're a sightless mole, and you'll always be a mere abomination to the Metal Prince. You're of no use up above either trying to get hold of the pure Regulus; which you never will. Hey! You want to marry Pehrson Dahlsjoe's daughter; that's what you've taken to mine work for, not from any love of your own for the thing. Mind what you're after, double-face; take care that the Metal Prince, whom you are trying to deceive, doesn't take you and dash you down so that the sharp rocks tear you limb from limb. And Ulla will never be your wife; that much I tell you."

Elis's anger was kindled at the old man's insulting words.

"What are you about," he cried, "here in my master, Herr Pehrson Dahlsjoe's shaft, where I am doing my duty, and working as hard at it as I can? Be off out of this the way you came, or we'll see which of us two will dash the other's brains out down here."

With which he placed himself in a threatening attitude, and swung his hammer about the old man's ears; who only gave a sneering laugh, and Elis saw with terror how he swarmed up the narrow ladder rungs like a squirrel, and disappeared amongst the black labyrinths of the chasms.

The young man felt paralyzed in all his limbs; he could not go on with his work, but went up. When the old Head-Captain who had been busy in another part of the mine saw him, he cried: "For God's sake, Elis, what has happened to you? You're as pale as death. I suppose it's the sulphur gas; you're not accustomed to it yet. Here, take a drink, my lad; that'll do you good."

Elis took a good mouthful of brandy out of the flask which the Head-Captain handed to him; and then, feeling better, told him what had happened down in the mine, as also how he had made the uncanny old miner's acquaintance in Goethaborg.

The Head-Captain listened silently; then dubiously shook his head and said: "That must have been old Torbern that you met with, Elis; and I see, now, that there really is something in the tales that people tell about him. More than one hundred years ago, there was a miner here of the name of Torbern. He seems to have been one of the first to bring mining into a flourishing condition at Falun here, and in his time the profits far exceeded anything that we know of now. Nobody at that time knew so much about mining as Torbern, who had great scientific skill, and thoroughly understood all the ins and outs of the business. The richest lodes seemed to disclose themselves to him, as if he had been endowed with higher powers peculiar to himself; and as he was a gloomy, meditative man, without wife or child—with no regular home, indeed—and very seldom came up to the surface, it couldn't fail that a story soon went about that he was in compact with the mysterious power which dwells in the bowels of the earth, and fuses the metals. Disregarding Torbern's solemn warnings—for he always prophesied that some calamity would happen as soon as the miners' impulse to work ceased to be sincere love for the marvellous metals and ores people—went on enlarging the excavations more and more for the sake of mere profit, till, on St. John's Day of the year 1678, came the terrible landslip and subsidence which formed our present enormous main-shaft, laying waste the whole of the works, as they were then, in the process. It was only after many months' labour that several of the shafts were, with much difficulty, got into workable order again. Nothing was seen or heard of Torbern. There seemed to

be no doubt that he had been at work down below at the time of
the catastrophe, so that there could be no question what his fate had
been. But not long after, and particularly when the work was beginning to go on better again, the miners said they had seen old Torbern
in the mine, and that he had given them valuable advice, and pointed
out rich lodes to them. Others had come across him at the top of
the main-shaft, walking round it, sometimes lamenting, sometimes
shouting in wild anger. Other young fellows have come here in the
way you yourself did, saying that an old miner had advised them to
take to mining, and shewn them the way to Falun. This always happened when there was a scarcity of hands; very likely it was Torbern's
way of helping on the cause. But if it really was he whom you had
those words with in the mine, and if he spoke of a fine run of trap,
there isn't a doubt that there must be a grand vein of ore thereabouts,
and we must see, to-morrow, if we can come across it. Of course you
remember that we call rich veins of the kind 'trap-runs,' and that a
'Trumm' is a vein which goes sub-dividing into several smaller ones,
and probably gets lost altogether."

When Elis, tossed hither and thither by various thoughts, went
into Pehrson Dahlsjoe's, Ulla did not come meeting him as usual. She
was sitting with downcast looks, and as he thought eyes which had
been weeping; and beside her was a handsome young fellow, holding
her hand, and trying to say all sorts of kind and amusing things, to
which she seemed to pay little attention. Pehrson Dahlsjoe took Elis
who, seized by gloomy presentiments, was keeping a darksome glance
riveted on the pair into another room, and said:

"Well, Elis, you will soon have it in your power to give me a proof
of your regard and sincerity. I have always looked upon you as a son,
but you will soon take the place of one altogether. The man whom
you see in there is a well-to-do merchant, Eric Olavsen by name,
from Goethaborg. I am giving him my daughter for his wife, at his
desire. He will take her to Goethaborg, and then you will be left
alone with me, my only support in my declining years. Well, you say
nothing? You turn pale? I trust this step doesn't displease you, and that
now that I'm going to lose my daughter you are not going to leave
me too? But I hear Olavsen mentioning my name; I must go in."

With which he went back to the room.

Elis felt a thousand red-hot irons tearing at his heart. He could find
no words, no tears. In wild despair he ran out, out of the house, away
to the great mine-shaft.

That monstrous chasm had a terrible appearance by day; but now, when night had fallen, and the moon was just peeping down into it, the desolate crags looked like a numberless horde of horrible monsters, the direful brood of hell, rolling and writhing, in wildest confusion, all about its reeking sides and clefts, and flashing up fiery eyes, and shooting forth glowing claws to clutch the race of mortals.

"Torbern, Torbern," Elis cried, in a terrible voice, which made the rocks re-echo. "Torbern, I am here; you were not wrong. I was a wretched fool to fix my hopes on any earthly love, up on the surface here. My treasure, and my life, my all-in-all, are down below. Torbern! take me down with you! Show me the richest veins, the lodes of ore, the glowing metal! I will dig and bore, and toil and labour. Never, never more will I come back to see the light of day. Torbern! Torbern! take me down to you!"

He took his flint and steel from his pocket, lighted his candle, and went quickly down the shaft, into the deep cutting where he had been on the previous day, without seeing anything of the old man. But what was his amazement when, at the deepest point, he saw the vein of metal with the utmost clearness and distinctness, so that he could trace every one of its ramifications, and its risings and fallings. But as he kept his gaze fixed more and more firmly on this wonderful vein, a dazzling light seemed to come shining through the shaft, and the walls of rock grew transparent as crystal. That mysterious dream which he had had in Goethaborg came back upon him. He was looking upon those Elysian Fields of glorious metallic trees and plants, on which, by way of fruits, buds, and blossoms, hung jewels streaming with fire. He saw the maidens, and he looked upon the face of the mighty queen. She put out her arms, drew him to her, and pressed him to her breast, Then a burning ray darted through his heart, and all his consciousness was merged in a feeling of floating in waves of some blue, transparent, glittering mist.

"Elis Froebom! Elis Froebom!" a powerful voice from above cried out, and the reflection of torches began shining in the shaft. It was Pehrson Dahlsjoe come down with the Captain to search for the lad, who had been seen running in the direction of the main-shaft like a mad creature.

They found him standing as if turned to stone, with his face pressed against the cold, hard rock.

"What are you doing down here in the night-time, you foolish fellow?" cried Pehrson. "Pull yourself together, and come up with us. Who knows what good news you may hear."

Elis went up in profound silence after Dahlsjoe, who did not cease to rate him soundly for exposing himself to such danger. It was broad daylight in the morning when they got to the house.

Ulla threw herself into Elis's arms with a great cry, and called him by the fondest names, and Pehrson said to him: "You foolish fellow! How could I help seeing, long ago, that you were in love with Ulla, and that it was on her account, in all probability, that you were working so hard in the mine? Neither could I help seeing that she was just as fond of you. Could I wish for a better son-in-law than a fine, hearty, hard-working, honest miner than just yourself, Elis? What vexed me was that you never would speak."

"We scarcely knew ourselves," said Ulla, "how fond we were of each other."

"However that may be," said Pehrson, "I was annoyed that Elis didn't tell me openly and candidly of his love for you, and that was why I made up the story about Eric Olavsen, which was so nearly being the death of you, you silly fellow. Not but what I wished to try you, Ulla, into the bargain. Eric Olavsen has been married for many a day, and I give my daughter to you, Elis Froebom, for, I say it again, I couldn't wish for a better son-in-law."

Tears of joy and happiness ran down Elis's cheeks. The highest bliss which his imagination had pictured had come to pass so suddenly and unexpectedly that he could scarce believe it was anything but another blissful dream. The workpeople came to dinner, by Dahlsjoe's invitation, in honour of the event. Ulla had dressed in her prettiest attire, and looked more charming than ever, so that they all cried, over and over again, "Ey! What a sweet and charming creature Elis has got for a betrothed! May God bless them and make them happy!"

Yet the terror of the past night still lay upon Elis's pale face, and he often stared about him as if he were far away from all that was going on round him. "Elis, darling, what is the matter?" Ulla asked anxiously. He pressed her to his heart and said, "Yes, yes, you are my own, and all is well." But in the midst of all his happiness he often felt as though an icy hand clutched at his heart, and a dismal voice asked him, "Is it your highest ideal, then, to be betrothed to Ulla? Wretched fool! Have you not looked upon the face of the queen?"

He felt himself overpowered by an indescribable, anxious alarm. He was haunted and tortured by the thought that one of the workmen would suddenly assume gigantic proportions, and to his horror he would recognize in him Torbern, come to remind him, in a terrible manner, of the subterranean realm of gems and metals to which he had devoted himself.

And yet he could see no reason why the spectral old man should be hostile to him, or what connection there was between his mining work and his love.

Pehrson, seeing Elis's disordered condition, attributed it to the trouble he had gone through, and his nocturnal visit to the mine. Not so, Ulla, who, seized by a secret presentiment, implored her lover to tell her what terrible thing had happened to him to tear him away from her so entirely. This almost broke his heart. It was in vain that he tried to tell her of the wonderful face which had revealed itself to him in the depths of the mine. Some unknown power seemed to seal his lips forcibly; he felt as though the terrible face of the queen were looking out from his heart, so that if he mentioned her everything about him would turn to stone, to dark, black rock, as at the sight of the Medusa's frightful head. All the glory and magnificence which had filled him with rapture in the abyss appeared to him now as a pandemonium of immitigable torture, deceptively decked out to allure him to his ruin.

Dahlsjoe told him he must stay at home for a few days, so as to shake off the sickness which he seemed to have fallen into. And during this time Ulla's affection, which now streamed bright and clear from her candid, child-like heart, drove away the memory of his fateful adventure in the mine-depths. Joy and happiness brought him back to life, and to belief in his good fortune, and in the impossibility of its being ever interfered with by any evil power.

When he went down the pit again, everything appeared quite different to what it used to be. The most glorious veins lay clear and distinct before his eyes. He worked twice as zealously as before; he forgot everything else. When he got to the surface again, it cost him an effort of thought to remember about Pehrson Dahlsjoe, about his Ulla, even. He felt as if divided into two halves, as if his better self, his real personality, went down to the central point of the earth, and there rested in bliss in the queen's arms, whilst *he* went to his darksome dwelling in Falun. When Ulla spoke of their love, and the happiness of their future life together, he would begin to talk of the splendours of the depths, and the inestimably precious treasures that lay hidden there, and in so doing would get entangled in such wonderful, incomprehensible sayings, that alarm and terrible anxiety took possession of the poor child, who could not divine why Elis should be so completely altered from his former self. He kept telling the Captain, and Dahlsjoe himself, with the greatest delight, that he had discovered the richest veins and the most magnificent trap-runs, and when these turned out to be nothing but unproductive rock, he would laugh contemptuously and say that none but he understood the secret signs, the significant writing, fraught with hidden meaning, which the queen's own hand had inscribed on the rocks, and that it was sufficient to understand those signs without bringing to light what they indicated.

The old Captain looked sorrowfully at Elis, who spoke, with wild gleaming eyes, of the glorious paradise which glowed down in the depths of the earth. "That terrible old Torbern has been at him," he whispered in Dahlsjoe's ear.

"Pshaw! Don't believe these miners' yarns," cried Dahlsjoe. "He's a deep-thinking serious fellow, and love has turned his head, that's all. Wait till the marriage is over, then we'll hear no more of the trap-runs, the treasures, and the subterranean paradise."

The wedding-day, fixed by Dahlsjoe, came at last. For a few days previously Elis had been more tranquil, more serious, more sunk in deep reflection than ever. But, on the other hand, never had he shown such affection for Ulla as at this time. He could not leave her for a moment, and never went down the mine at all. He seemed to have forgotten his restless excitement about mining work, and never a word of the subterranean kingdom crossed his lips. Ulla was all rapture. Her fear lest the dangerous powers of the subterranean world, of which she had heard old miners speak, had been luring him to his destruction, had left her; and Dahlsjoe, too, said, laughing to the Captain, "You see, Elis was only a little light-headed for love of my Ulla."

Early on the morning of the wedding-day, which was St. John's Day as it chanced, Elis knocked at the door of Ulla's room. She opened it, and started back terrified at the sight of Elis, dressed in his wedding clothes already, deadly pale, with dark gloomy fire sparkling in his eyes.

"I only want to tell you, my beloved Ulla," he said, in a faint, trembling voice, "that we are just arrived at the summit of the highest good fortune which it is possible for mortals to attain. Everything has been revealed to me in the night which is just over. Down in the depths below, hidden in chlorite and mica, lies the cherry-coloured sparkling almandine, on which the tablet of our lives is graven. I have to give it to you as a wedding present. It is more splendid than the most glorious blood-red carbuncle, and when, united in truest affection, we look into its streaming splendour together, we shall see and understand the peculiar manner in which our hearts and souls have grown together into the wonderful branch which shoots from the queen's heart, at the central point of the globe. All that is necessary is that I go and bring this stone to the surface, and that I will do now, as fast as I can. Take care of yourself meanwhile, beloved darling. I will be back to you directly."

Ulla implored him, with bitter tears, to give up all idea of such a dream-like undertaking, for she felt a strong presentiment of disaster; but Elis declared that without this stone he should never know a moment's peace or happiness, and that there was not the slightest danger of any kind. He pressed her fondly to his heart, and was gone.

The guests were all assembled to accompany the bridal pair to the church of Copparberg, where they were to be married, and a crowd of girls, who were to be the bridesmaids and walk in procession before the bride (as is the custom of the place), were laughing and playing round Ulla. The musicians were tuning their instruments to begin a wedding march. It was almost noon, but Ellis had not made his appearance. Suddenly some miners came running up, horror in their pale faces, with the news that there had been a terrible catastrophe, a subsidence of the earth, which had destroyed the whole of Pehrson Dahlsjoe's part of the mine.

"Elis! oh, Elis! you are gone!" screamed Ulla, wildly, and fell as if dead. Then only, for the first time, Dahlsjoe learned from the Captain that Elis had gone down the main-shaft in the morning. Nobody else had been in the mine, the rest of the men having been invited to the wedding. Dahlsjoe and all the others hurried off to search, at the imminent danger of their own lives. In vain! Elis Froebom was not to be found. There could be no question that the earth-fall had buried him in the rock. And thus came desolation and mourning upon the house of brave Pehrson Dahlsjoe, at the moment when he thought he was assured of peace and happiness for the remainder of his days.

*

Long had stout Pehrson Dahlsjoe been dead, his daughter Ulla long lost sight of and forgotten. Nobody in Falun remembered them. More than fifty years had gone by since Froebom's luckless wedding-day, when it chanced that some miners who were making a connection-passage between two shafts, found, at a depth of three hundred yards, buried in vitriolated water, the body of a young miner, which seemed, when they brought it to the daylight, to be turned to stone.

The young man looked as if he were lying in a deep sleep, so perfectly preserved were the features of his face, so wholly without trace of decay his new suit of miner's clothes, and even the flowers in his breast. The people of the neighbourhood all collected round the young man, but no one recognized him or could say who he had been, and none of the workmen missed any comrade.

The body was going to be taken to Falun, when out of the distance an old, old woman came creeping slowly and painfully up on crutches.

"Here's the old St. John's Day grandmother!" the miners said. They had given her this name because they had noticed that she came always every year on St. John's Day up to the main shaft, and looked down into its depths, weeping, lamenting, and wringing her hands as she crept round it, then going away again.

The moment she saw the body she threw away her crutches, lifted her arms to Heaven, and cried, in the most heartrending accents of the deepest lamentation: "Oh! Elis Froebom! Oh, my sweet, sweet bridegroom!"

And she cowered down beside the body, took the stony hands and pressed them to her heart, chilled with age, but throbbing still with the fondest love, like some naphtha flame under the surface ice.

"Ah!" she said, looking round at the spectators, "nobody, nobody among you all, remembers poor Ulla Dahlsjoe, this poor boy's happy bride fifty long years ago. When I went away, in my terrible sorrow and despair, to Ornaes, old Torbern comforted me, and told me I should see my poor Elis, who was buried in the rock upon our wedding-day, yet once more here upon earth. And I have come every year and looked for him, all longing and faithful love. And now this blessed meeting has been granted me this day. Oh, Elis! Elis! my beloved husband!"

She wound her arms about him as if she would never part from him more, and the people all stood round in the deepest emotion.

Fainter and fainter grew her sobs and sighs, till they ceased to be audible.

The miners closed round. They would have raised poor Ulla, but she had breathed out her life upon her bridegroom's body. The spectators noticed now that it was beginning to crumble into dust. The appearance of petrifaction had been deceptive.

In the church of Copparberg, where they were to have been married fifty years before, they laid in the earth the ashes of Elis Froebom, and with them the body of her who had been thus "Faithful unto death."

Edward Bulwer-Lytton (1803–1873)

EDWARD BULWER, better known as Lord Bulwer-Lytton, did not inherit that aristocratic title until 1843; by then he had over twenty years of literary experience and considerable success as one of the best-selling authors of his day. Bulwer-Lytton undoubtedly was one of the best-educated and intelligent writers of his day. His fame was founded, for the most part, on what was termed "Newgate fiction," because it dealt with the underbelly of society as depicted in the *Newgate Calendar,* a graphic account of criminality used to promote moral behavior. Similar books included *Paul Clifford* (1830) and *Eugene Aram* (1832). Bulwer-Lytton went on to become a popular historical novelist with *The Last Days of Pompeii* (1834) and *Harold, the Last of the Saxons* (1848). He also achieved a reputation for his occult fiction, including *Zanoni* (1842) and the classic ghost story "The Haunted and the Haunters" (1859).

Bulwer-Lytton had always been interested in the occult and the bizarre. His very first book, *Ismael* (1820), was subtitled "An Oriental Tale." *Asmodeus at Large* (1833) is a rambling novel in which the narrator learns about the world with the help of the demon Asmodeus. Tucked within this novel is the short story "The Tale of Kosem Kesamim, the Magician," which tells the history of Kesamim, who passes through death in pursuit of the ultimate source of knowledge. It includes much occult background, yet Bulwer-Lytton reveals in a footnote that this story was based on jottings he made during his school days, revealing that he had an innate occult understanding. He later reworked the theme of that story first as "Zicci" (1841) and then as *Zanoni,* one of the seminal novels of the occult.

The present tale is from *The Pilgrims of the Rhine,* an episodic novel published in 1834. It follows the young Gertrude Vane on a journey along the Rhine, accompanied by her father, her fiancé, and her physician. Gertrude is dying of consumption, and a party of fairies decides to help make her final days as pleasant as possible. En route, the group relates several stories, of which the following is the most fascinating, bringing us back to the theme of other worlds encountered within dreams.

45

The Life of Dreams

Edward Bulwer-Lytton

There are two lives to each of us, gliding on at the same time, scarcely connected with each other,—the life of our actions, the life of our minds; the external and the inward history; the movements of the frame, the deep and ever-restless workings of the heart! They who have loved know that there is a diary of the affections, which we might keep for years without having occasion even to touch upon the exterior surface of life, our busy occupations, the mechanical progress of our existence; yet by the last are we judged, the first is never known. History reveals men's deeds, men's outward character, but *not themselves*. There is a secret self that hath its own life "rounded by a dream," unpenetrated, unguessed. What passed within Trevylyan, hour after hour, as he watched over the declining health of the only being in the world whom his proud heart had been ever destined to love? His real record of the time was marked by every cloud upon Gertrude's brow, every smile of her countenance, every—the faintest—alteration in her disease; yet, to the outward seeming, all this vast current of varying eventful emotion lay dark and unconjectured. He filled up with wonted regularity the colourings of existence, and smiled and moved as other men. For still, in the heroism with which devotion conquers self, he sought only to cheer and gladden the young heart on which he had embarked his all; and he kept the dark tempest of his anguish for the solitude of night.

That was a peculiar doom which Fate had reserved for him; and casting him, in after years, on the great sea of public strife, it seemed as if she were resolved to tear from his heart all yearnings for the land. For him there was to be no green or sequestered spot in the valley of household peace. His bark was to know no haven, and his soul not even the desire of rest. For action is that Lethe in which alone we forget our former dreams, and the mind that, too stern not to wrestle with its emotions, seeks to conquer regret, must leave itself no leisure

46

to look behind. Who knows what benefits to the world may have
sprung from the sorrows of the benefactor? As the harvest that gladdens mankind in the suns of autumn was called forth by the rains of
spring, so the griefs of youth may make the fame of maturity.

Gertrude, charmed by the beauties of the river, desired to continue
the voyage to Mayence. The rich Trevylyan persuaded the physician
who had attended her to accompany them, and they once more pursued their way along the banks of the feudal Rhine. For what the
Tiber is to the classic, the Rhine is to the chivalric age. The steep
rock and the gray dismantled tower, the massive and rude picturesque
of the feudal days, constitute the great features of the scene; and you
might almost fancy, as you glide along, that you are sailing back adown
the river of Time, and the monuments of the pomp and power of old,
rising, one after one, upon its shores!

Vane and Du——e, the physician, at the farther end of the vessel,
conversed upon stones and strata, in that singular pedantry of science
which strips nature to a skeleton, and prowls among the dead bones
of the world, unconscious of its living beauty.

They left Gertrude and Trevylyan to themselves; and, "bending
o'er the vessel's laving side," they indulged in silence the melancholy
with which each was imbued. For Gertrude began to waken, though
doubtingly and at intervals, to a sense of the short span that was
granted to her life; and over the loveliness around her there floated
that sad and ineffable interest which springs from the presentiment
of our own death. They passed the rich island of Oberwerth, and
Hochheim, famous for its ruby grape, and saw, from his mountain
bed, the Lahn bear his tribute of fruits and corn into the treasury of
the Rhine. Proudly rose the tower of Niederlahnstein, and deeply lay
its shadow along the stream. It was late noon; the cattle had sought
the shade from the slanting sun, and, far beyond, the holy castle of
Marksburg raised its battlements above mountains covered with the
vine. On the water two boats had been drawn alongside each other;
and from one, now moving to the land, the splash of oars broke the
general stillness of the tide. Fast by an old tower the fishermen were
busied in their craft, but the sound of their voices did not reach the
ear. It was life, but a silent life, suited to the tranquillity of noon.

"There is something in travel," said Gertrude, "which constantly,
even amidst the most retired spots, impresses us with the exuberance
of life. We come to those quiet nooks and find a race whose existence
we never dreamed of. In their humble path they know the same

passions and tread the same career as ourselves. The mountains shut them out from the great world, but their village is a world in itself. And they know and heed no more of the turbulent scenes of remote cities than our own planet of the inhabitants of the distant stars. What then is death, but the forgetfulness of some few hearts added to the general unconsciousness of our existence that pervades the universe? The bubble breaks in the vast desert of the air without a sound."

"Why talk of death?" said Trevylyan, with a writhing smile. "These sunny scenes should not call forth such melancholy images."

"Melancholy," repeated Gertrude, mechanically. "Yes, death is indeed melancholy when we are loved!"

They stayed a short time at Niederlahnstein, for Vane was anxious to examine the minerals that the Lahn brings into the Rhine; and the sun was waning towards its close as they renewed their voyage. As they sailed slowly on, Gertrude said, "How like a dream is this sentiment of existence, when, without labour or motion, every change of scene is brought before us; and if I am with you, dearest, I do not feel it less resembling a dream, for I have dreamed of you lately more than ever; and dreams have become a part of my life itself."

"Speaking of dreams," said Trevylyan, as they pursued that mysterious subject, "I once during my former residence in Germany fell in with a singular enthusiast, who had taught himself what he termed "A System of Dreaming.' When he first spoke to me upon it I asked him to explain what he meant, which he did somewhat in the following words."

"I was born," said he, "with many of the sentiments of the poet, but without the language to express them; my feelings were constantly chilled by the intercourse of the actual world. My family, mere Germans, dull and unimpassioned, had nothing in common with me; nor did I out of my family find those with whom I could better sympathize. I was revolted by friendships,—for they were susceptible to every change; I was disappointed in love,—for the truth never approached to my ideal. Nursed early in the lap of Romance, enamoured of the wild and the adventurous, the commonplaces of life were to me inexpressibly tame and joyless. And yet indolence, which belongs to the poetical character, was more inviting than that eager and uncontemplative action which can alone wring enterprise from life. Meditation was my natural element. I loved to spend the noon reclined by some shady stream, and in a half sleep to shape images from the glancing sunbeams. A dim and unreal order of philosophy, that belongs to our nation, was my favourite intellectual pursuit; and I sought amongst the Obscure and the Recondite the variety and emotion I could not find in the Familiar. Thus constantly watching the operations of the inner mind, it occurred to me at last that sleep having its own world, but as yet a rude and fragmentary one, it might be possible to shape from its chaos all those combinations of beauty, of power, of glory, and of love, which were denied to me in the world in which my frame walked and had its being. So soon as this idea came upon me, I nursed and cherished and mused over it, till I found that the imagination began to effect the miracle I desired. By brooding ardently, intensely, before I retired to rest, over any especial train of thought, over any ideal creations; by keeping the body utterly still and quiescent during the whole day; by shutting out all living adventure, the memory of which might perplex and interfere with the stream of events that I desired to pour forth into the wilds of sleep, I discovered at last that I could lead in dreams a life solely their own, and utterly distinct from the life of day. Towers and palaces, all my heritage and seigneury, rose before me from the depths of night; I quaffed from jewelled cups the Falernian of imperial vaults; music from harps of celestial tone filled up the crevices of air; and the smiles of immortal beauty flushed like sunlight over all. Thus the adventure and the glory that I could not for my waking life obtain, was obtained for me in sleep. I wandered with the gryphon and the gnome; I sounded the horn at enchanted portals; I conquered in the knightly lists; I planted my standard over battlements huge as the painter's birth of Babylon itself.

"But I was afraid to call forth one shape on whose loveliness to pour all the hidden passion of my soul. I trembled lest my sleep should present me some image which it could never restore, and, waking from which, even the new world I had created might be left desolate forever. I shuddered lest I should adore a vision which the first ray of morning could smite to the grave.

"In this train of mind I began to wonder whether it might not be possible to connect dreams together; to supply the thread that was wanting; to make one night continue the history of the other, so as to bring together the same shapes and the same scenes, and thus lead a connected and harmonious life, not only in the one half of existence, but in the other, the richer and more glorious half. No sooner did this idea present itself to me, than I burned to accomplish it. I had before taught myself that Faith is the great creator; that to believe fervently is to make belief true. So I would not suffer my mind to doubt the practicability of its scheme. I shut myself up then entirely by day, refused books, and hated the very sun, and compelled all my thoughts (and sleep is the mirror of thought) to glide in one direction,—the direction of my dreams,—so that from night to night the imagination might keep up the thread of action, and I might thus lie down full of the past dream and confident of the sequel. Not for one day only, or for one month, did I pursue this system, but I continued it zealously and sternly till at length it began to succeed. "Who shall tell,' cried the enthusiast,—I see him now with his deep, bright, sunken eyes, and his wild hair thrown backward from his brow,—"the rapture I experienced, when first, faintly and half distinct, I perceived the harmony I had invoked dawn upon my dreams? At first there was only a partial and desultory connection between them; my eye recognized certain shapes, my ear certain tones common to each; by degrees these augmented in number, and were more defined in outline. At length one fair face broke forth from among the ruder forms, and night after night appeared mixing with them for a moment and then vanishing, just as the mariner watches, in a clouded sky, the moon shining through the drifting rack, and quickly gone. My curiosity was now vividly excited; the face, with its lustrous eyes and seraph features, roused all the emotions that no living shape had called forth. I became enamoured of a dream, and as the statue to the Cyprian was my creation to me; so from this intent and unceasing passion I at length worked out my reward. My dream became more palpable; I spoke with it; I knelt to it; my lips were pressed to its own; we exchanged the vows of love, and morning only separated us with the certainty that at night we should meet again.

"'Thus then,' continued my visionary, "I commenced a history utterly separate from the history of the world, and it went on alternately with my harsh and chilling history of the day, equally regular and equally continuous. And what, you ask, was that history? Methought I was a prince in some Eastern island that had no features in common with the colder north of my native home. By day I looked upon the dull walls of a German town, and saw homely or squalid forms passing before me; the sky was dim and the sun cheerless. Night came on with her thousand stars, and brought me the dews of sleep. Then suddenly there was a new world; the richest fruits hung from the trees in clusters of gold and purple. Palaces of the quaint fashion of the sunnier climes, with spiral minarets and glittering cupolas, were mirrored upon vast lakes sheltered by the palm-tree and banana.

The sun seemed a different orb, so mellow and gorgeous were his beams; birds and winged things of all hues fluttered in the shining air; the faces and garments of men were not of the northern regions of the world, and their voices spoke a tongue which, strange at first, by degrees I interpreted. Sometimes I made war upon neighbouring kings; sometimes I chased the spotted pard through the vast gloom of immemorial forests; my life was at once a life of enterprise and pomp. But above all there was the history of my love! I thought there were a thousand difficulties in the way of attaining its possession. Many were the rocks I had to scale, and the battles to wage, and the fortresses to storm, in order to win her as my bride. But at last' (continued the enthusiast), 'she *is* won, she is my own! Time in that wild world, which I visit nightly, passes not so slowly as in this, and yet an hour may be the same as a year. This continuity of existence, this successive series of dreams, so different from the broken incoherence of other men's sleep, at times bewilders me with strange and suspicious thoughts. What if this glorious sleep be a real life, and this dull waking the true repose? Why not? What is there more faithful in the one than in the other? And there have I garnered and collected all of pleasure that I am capable of feeling. I seek no joy in this world; I form no ties, I feast not, nor love, nor make merry; I am only impatient till the hour when I may re-enter my royal realms and pour my renewed delight into the bosom of my bright Ideal. There then have I found all that the world denied me; there have I realized the yearning and the aspiration within me; there have I coined the untold poetry into the Felt, the Seen!'

"I found," continued Trevylyan, "that this tale was corroborated by inquiry into the visionary's habits. He shunned society; avoided all unnecessary movement or excitement. He fared with rigid abstemiousness, and only appeared to feel pleasure as the day departed, and the hour of return to his imaginary kingdom approached. He always retired to rest punctually at a certain hour, and would sleep so soundly that a cannon fired under his window would not arouse him. He never, which may seem singular, spoke or moved much in his sleep, but was peculiarly calm, almost to the appearance of lifelessness; but, discovering once that he had been watched in sleep, he was wont afterwards carefully to secure the chamber from intrusion. His victory over the natural incoherence of sleep had, when I first knew him, lasted for some years; possibly what imagination first produced was afterwards continued by habit.

"I saw him again a few months subsequent to this confession, and he seemed to me much changed. His health was broken, and his abstraction had deepened into gloom. I questioned him of the cause of the alteration, and he answered me with great reluctance,—

"'She is dead,' said he; "my realms are desolate! A serpent stung her, and she died in these very arms. Vainly, when I started from my sleep in horror and despair, vainly did I say to myself,—This is but a dream. I shall see her again. A vision cannot die! Hath it flesh that decays; is it not a spirit,—bodiless, indissoluble? With what terrible anxiety I awaited the night! Again I slept, and the dream lay again before me, dead and withered. Even the ideal can vanish. I assisted in the burial; I laid her in the earth; I heaped the monumental mockery over her form. And never since hath she, or ought like her, revisited my dreams. I see her only when I wake; thus to wake is indeed to dream! But,' continued the visionary in a solemn voice, 'I feel myself departing from this world, and with a fearful joy; for I think there may be a land beyond even the land of sleep where I shall see her again,—a land in which a vision itself may be restored.'

"And in truth," concluded Trevylyan, "the dreamer died shortly afterwards, suddenly, and in his sleep. And never before, perhaps, had Fate so literally made of a living man (with his passions and his powers, his ambition and his love) the plaything and puppet of a dream!"

"Ah," said Vane, who had heard the latter part of Trevylyan's story, "could the German have bequeathed to us his secret, what a refuge should we possess from the ills of earth! The dungeon and disease, poverty, affliction, shame, would cease to be the tyrants of our lot; and to Sleep we should confine our history and transfer our emotions."

"Gertrude," whispered the lover, "what his kingdom and his bride were to the Dreamer art thou to me!"

Edgar Allan Poe (1809–1849)

EDGAR ALLAN POE was greatly influenced by both E. T. A. Hoffmann (and indeed the entire German Gothic and Romantic movements) and the works of Edward Bulwer-Lytton. Poe's first published story, "Metzengerstein" (1832) has all the gothic paraphernalia. A blending of all of these influences distinguish what is arguably Poe's best story—certainly one of his most atmospheric—"The Fall of the House of Usher" (1839). When Poe first planned to assemble a volume of stories for publication, he called the work *Tales of the Folio Club,* emulating Hoffmann's Serapion Brethren.

Poe's literary output was remarkable, considering his brief career of just seventeen years. He did not limit himself to horror stories but produced a wide range of crime, mystery, and strange and fanciful tales. The one that bears the most direct influence of Bulwer-Lytton is the following, originally called "Siope" when published in the *Baltimore Book* in 1838 and included in the first edition of *Tales of the Grotesque and Arabesque* in 1840. The story was later revised and retitled "Silence—a Fable," the name under which it usually is reprinted.

Poe was a devotee of Bulwer-Lytton's work. When he reviewed Bulwer-Lytton's historical novel *Rienzi* in 1836, Poe wrote, "We take up any production of his pen with a positive certainty that, in reading it, the wildest passions of our nature, the most profound of our thoughts, the brightest visions of our fancy, and the most ennobling and lofty of our aspirations will, in due turn, be enkindled within us. We feel sure of rising from the perusal a wiser if not a better man."

"Siope" is a clear imitation of Bulwer-Lytton's "Tale of Kosem Kesamim," though far shorter. It has the same basic scenario of the demon conducting the narrator on a visitation, as well as the dreamlike quality and theme of Man vs. Nature. But Poe focuses on just one image and one message, and because of this the story has a far stronger potency.

53

Siope—A Fable

Edgar Allan Poe

Ours is a world of words: Quiet we call *Silence*—which is the merest word of all.

Al Aaraaf

"Listen to *me*," said the Demon, as he placed his hand upon my head. "There is a spot upon this accursed earth which thou hast never yet beheld. And if by any chance thou *hast* beheld it, it must have been in one of those vigorous dreams which come like the Simoon upon the brain of the sleeper who hath lain down to sleep among the forbidden sunbeams—among the sunbeams, I say, which slide from off the solemn columns of the melancholy temples in the wilderness. The region of which I speak is a dreary region in Libya, by the borders of the river Zaire. And there is no quiet there, nor silence.

"The waters of the river have a saffron and sickly hue—and they flow not onwards to the sea, but palpitate forever and forever beneath the red eye of the sun with a tumultuous and convulsive motion. For many miles on either side of the river's oozy bed is a pale desert of gigantic water-lilies. They sigh one unto the other in that solitude, and stretch towards the heaven their long ghastly necks, and nod to and fro their everlasting heads. And there is an indistinct murmur which cometh out from among them like the rushing of subterrene water. And they sigh one unto the other.

"But there is a boundary to their realm—the boundary of the dark, horrible, lofty forest. There, like the waves about the Hebrides, the low underwood is agitated continually. But there is no wind throughout the heaven. And the tall primœval trees rock eternally hither and thither with a crashing and mighty sound. And from their high summits, one by one, drop everlasting dews. And at the roots strange poisonous flowers lie writhing in perturbed slumber. And overhead, with a rustling and loud noise, the grey clouds rush westwardly forever, until they roll, a cataract, over the fiery wall of the horizon. But there is no wind throughout the heaven. And by the shores of the river Zaire there is neither quiet nor silence.

"It was night, and the rain fell; and, falling, it was rain, but, having fallen, it was blood. And I stood in the morass among the tall lilies, and the rain fell upon my head—and the lilies sighed one unto the other in the solemnity of their desolation.

"And, all at once, the moon arose through the thin ghastly mist, and was crimson in color. And mine eyes fell upon a huge grey rock which stood by the shore of the river, and was litten by the light of the moon. And the rock was grey, and ghastly, and tall,—and the rock was grey. Upon its front were characters engraven in the stone; and I walked through the morass of water-lilies, until I came close unto the shore, that I might read the characters upon the stone. But I could not decypher the characters. And I was going back into the morass, when the moon shone with a fuller red, and I turned and looked again upon the rock, and upon the characters—and the characters were DESOLATION.

"And I looked upwards, and there stood a man upon the summit of the rock, and I hid myself among the water-lilies that I might discover the actions of the man. And the man was tall and stately in form, and was wrapped up from his shoulders to his feet in the toga of old Rome. And the outlines of his figure were indistinct—but his features were the features of a Deity; for the mantle of the night, and of the mist, and of the moon, and of the dew, had left uncovered the features of his face. And his brow was lofty with thought, and his eye wild with care; and, in the few furrows upon his cheek I read the fables of sorrow, and weariness, and disgust with mankind, and a longing after solitude. And the moon shone upon his face, and upon the features of his face, and oh! they were more beautiful than the airy dreams which hovered about the souls of the daughters of Delos!

"And the man sat down upon the rock, and leaned his head upon his hand, and looked out upon the desolation. He looked down into the low unquiet shrubbery, and up into the tall primœval trees, and up higher at the rustling heaven, and into the crimson moon. And I lay close within shelter of the lilies, and observed the actions of the man. And the man trembled in the solitude—but the night waned and he sat upon the rock.

"And the man turned his attention from the heaven, and looked out upon the dreary river Zaire, and upon the yellow ghastly waters, and upon the pale legions of the water-lilies. And the man listened to the sighs of the water-lilies, and of the murmur that came up from among them. And I lay close within my covert and observed the actions of the man. And the man trembled in the solitude—but the night waned and he sat upon the rock.

"Then I went down into the recesses of the morass, and waded afar in among the wilderness of the lilies, and called unto the hippopotami which dwelt among the fens in the recesses of the morass. And the hippopotami heard my call, and came, with the behemoth, unto the foot of the rock, and roared loudly and fearfully beneath the moon. And I lay close within my covert and observed the actions of the man. And the man trembled in the solitude—but the night waned and he sat upon the rock.

"Then I cursed the elements with the curse of tumult; and a frightful tempest gathered in the heaven where before there had been no wind. And the heaven became livid with the violence of the tempest—and the rain beat upon the head of the man—and the floods of the river came down—and the river was tormented into foam—and the water-lilies shrieked within their beds—and the forest crumbled before the wind—and the thunder rolled,—and the lightning fell—and the rock rocked to its foundation. And I lay close within my covert and observed the actions of the man. And the man trembled in the solitude—but the night waned and he sat upon the rock.

"Then I grew angry and cursed, with the curse of silence, the river, and the lilies, and the wind, and the forest, and the heaven, and the thunder, and the sighs of the water-lilies. And they became accursed and *were still*. And the moon ceased to totter in its pathway up the heaven—and the thunder died away—and the lightning did not flash—and the clouds hung motionless—and the waters sunk to their level and remained—and the trees ceased to rock—and the water-lilies sighed no more—and the murmur was heard no longer from among them, nor any shadow of sound throughout the vast illimitable desert. And I looked upon the characters of the rock, and they were changed—and the characters were SILENCE.

"And mine eyes fell upon the countenance of the man, and his countenance was wan with terror. And, hurriedly, he raised his head from his hand, and stood forth upon the rock, and listened. But there was no voice throughout the vast illimitable desert, and the characters upon the rock were SILENCE. And the man shuddered, and turned his face away, and fled afar off, and I beheld him no more."

★

Now there are fine tales in the volumes of the Magi—in the iron-bound, melancholy volumes of the Magi. Therein, I say, are glorious histories of the Heaven, and of the Earth, and of the mighty Sea—and of the Genii that over-ruled the sea, and the earth, and the lofty heaven. There was much lore too in the sayings which were said by the sybils; and holy, holy things were heard of old by the dim leaves that trembled around Dodona—but, as Allah liveth, that fable which the Demon told me as he sat by my side in the shadow of the tomb, I hold to be the most wonderful of all! And as the Demon made an end of his story, he fell back within the cavity of the tomb and laughed. And I could not laugh with the Demon, and he cursed me because I could not laugh. And the lynx which dwelleth forever in the tomb, came out therefrom, and lay down at the feet of the Demon, and looked at him steadily in the face.

Alfred, Lord Tennyson (1809–1892)

No DOUBT the poem that helped generate the re-emergence of the fantasy tradition is "The Lady of Shalott" (1832), one of Tennyson's best known poems.

Alfred, Lord Tennyson, who was Britain's Poet Laureate for more than forty years, had a lifelong fascination with the Arthur legends. The Arthurian cycle of stories and romances had begun with Geoffrey of Monmouth's *History of the Kings of Britain* (1138); it grew to incorporate the Knights of the Round Table and the Quest for the Holy Grail, and culminated in Thomas Malory's *Le Mort Darthur,* first printed in 1485. Malory's magnum opus was considered to be definitive, and Arthurian literature lay dormant for over three hundred years.

With the birth of the Romantic movement, the genre of Arthurian legend revived: Christopher Wieland wrote *Merlin der Zauberer* ("Merlin the Magician") in 1777; Walter Scott produced a new edition of Sir Tristrem in 1804; and Robert Southey prepared a new edition of *Le Mort Darthur* in 1817. Tennyson encountered Southey's edition while still a child, and it made a deep impression. "The Lady of Shalott," which gave us the image of "many tower'd Camelot," was Tennyson's first published Arthurian poem. He produced others over the next few years, leading to the first edition of *Idylls of the King* in 1859. He continued to write and revise poems, concluding with "Merlin and the Gleam" in 1889. "The Lady of Shalott" and *Idylls of the King* inspired the Pre-Raphaelites, who painted many images based on the works and led the way to the Victorian fascination with the fantastic.

The Lady of Shalott

Alfred, Lord Tennyson

PART I

On either side the river lie
Long fields of barley and of rye,
That clothe the wold and meet the sky;
And thro' the field the road runs by
    To many-tower'd Camelot;
And up and down the people go,
Gazing where the lilies blow
Round an island there below,
    The island of Shalott.

Willows whiten, aspens quiver,
Little breezes dusk and shiver
Thro' the wave that runs for ever
By the island in the river
    Flowing down to Camelot.
Four grey walls, and four grey towers,
Overlook a space of flowers,
And the silent isle imbowers
    The Lady of Shalott.

By the margin, willow veil'd,
Slide the heavy barges trail'd
By slow horses; and unhail'd
The shallop flitteth silken-sail'd
    Skimming down to Camelot:
But who hath seen her wave her hand?
Or at the casement seen her stand?
Or is she known in all the land,
    The Lady of Shalott?

Only reapers, reaping early,
In among the bearded barley,
Hear a song that echoes cheerly
From the river winding clearly;
    Down to tower'd Camelot;
And by the moon the reaper weary,
Piling sheaves in uplands airy,
Listening, whispers, " 'Tis the fairy
    Lady of Shalott."

PART II

There she weaves by night and day
A magic web with colours gay.
She has heard a whisper say,
A curse is on her if she stay
    To look down to Camelot.
She knows not what the curse may be,
And so she weaveth steadily,
And little other care hath she,
    The Lady of Shalott.

And moving thro' a mirror clear
That hangs before her all the year,
Shadows of the world appear.
There she sees the highway near
    Winding down to Camelot;
There the river eddy whirls,
And there the surly village-churls,
And the red cloaks of market girls,
    Pass onward from Shalott.

Sometimes a troop of damsels glad,
An abbot on an ambling pad,
Sometimes a curly shepherd-lad,
Or long-hair'd page in crimson clad
    Goes by to tower'd Camelot;
And sometimes thro' the mirror blue
The knights come riding two and two:
She hath no loyal knight and true,
    The Lady of Shalott.

But in her web she still delights
To weave the mirror's magic sights,
For often thro' the silent nights
A funeral, with plumes and lights
   And music, went to Camelot;
Or when the moon was overhead,
Came two young lovers lately wed:
"I am half sick of shadows," said
   The Lady of Shalott.

PART III

A bow-shot from her bower-eaves,
He rode between the barley-sheaves.
The sun came dazzling thro' the leaves,
And flamed upon the brazen greaves
   Of bold Sir Lancelot.
A red-cross knight for ever kneel'd
To a lady in his shield,
That sparkled on the yellow field,
   Beside remote Shalott.

The gemmy bridle glitter'd free,
Like to some branch of stars we see
Hung in the golden Galaxy.
The bridle bells rang merrily
   As he rode down to Camelot;
And from his blazon'd baldric slung
A mighty silver bugle hung,
And as he rode his armor rung,
   Beside remote Shalott.

All in the blue unclouded weather
Thick-jewell'd shone the saddle-leather,
The helmet and the helmet-feather
Burn'd like one burning flame together,
   As he rode down to Camelot;
As often thro' the purple night,
Below the starry clusters bright,
Some bearded meteor, trailing light,
   Moves over still Shalott.

His broad clear brow in sunlight glow'd;
On burnish'd hooves his war-horse trode;
From underneath his helmet flow'd
His coal-black curls as on he rode,
    As he rode down to Camelot.
From the bank and from the river
He flash'd into the crystal mirror,
"Tirra lirra," by the river
    Sang Sir Lancelot.

She left the web, she left the loom,
She made three paces thro' the room,
She saw the water-lily bloom,
She saw the helmet and the plume,
    She look'd down to Camelot.
Out flew the web and floated wide;
The mirror crack'd from side to side;
"The curse is come upon me," cried
    The Lady of Shalott.

PART IV

In the stormy east-wind straining,
The pale yellow woods were waning,
The broad stream in his banks complaining,
Heavily the low sky raining
    Over tower'd Camelot;
Down she came and found a boat
Beneath a willow left afloat,
And around about the prow she wrote
    The Lady of Shalott.

And down the river's dim expanse
Like some bold seër in a trance,
Seeing all his own mischance—
With a glassy countenance
    Did she look to Camelot.
And at the closing of the day
She loosed the chain, and down she lay;
The broad stream bore her far away,
    The Lady of Shalott.

Lying, robed in snowy white
That loosely flew to left and right—
The leaves upon her falling light—
Thro' the noises of the night
    She floated down to Camelot;
And as the boat-head wound along
The willowy hills and fields among,
They heard her singing her last song,
    The Lady of Shalott.

Heard a carol, mournful, holy,
Chanted loudly, chanted lowly,
Till her blood was frozen slowly,
And her eyes were darkened wholly,
    Turn'd to tower'd Camelot.
For ere she reach'd upon the tide
The first house by the water-side,
Singing in her song she died,
    The Lady of Shalott.

Under tower and balcony,
By garden-wall and gallery,
A gleaming shape she floated by,
Dead-pale between the houses high,
    Silent into Camelot.
Out upon the wharfs they came,
Knight and burgher, lord and dame,
And around the prow they read her name,
    The Lady of Shalott.

Who is this? And what is here?
And in the lighted palace near
Died the sound of royal cheer;
And they cross'd themselves for fear,
    All the knights at Camelot:
But Lancelot mused a little space;
He said, "She has a lovely face;
God in his mercy lend her grace,
    The Lady of Shalott."

William Morris (1834–1896)

WILLIAM MORRIS discovered the lore of King Arthur as a result of reading Tennyson's "Lady of Shalott" and Robert Southey's translation of *Mort Darthur* while he was studying at Oxford (1853 to 1855). Morris developed his own view of the Arthurian world and composed a suite of poems published as *The Defence of Guenevere and Other Poems* in 1858. Morris was a key member of the Pre-Raphaelite art movement, which included Edward Burne-Jones, John Everett Millais, and Dante Gabriel Rossetti. Morris was a pioneer socialist, fascinated with an idealized past, who dreamed of a social and political utopia—ideas that he expressed in his epic poem *The Earthly Paradise* (1870), and in the novels *A Dream of John Bull* (1888) and *News from Nowhere* (1890).

Morris also was intrigued by Scandinavian lore. He had already written several stories for the *Oxford and Cambridge Magazine* in 1856, such as "Lindenborg Pool" and "Svend and His Brethren," as well as the novella *The Hollow Land,* in which the narrator falls into a "lost land" or dream world which he thereafter perpetually seeks. He developed an interest in the ancient sagas and, with the help of Eirikr Magnusson, translated several, including the *Völsunga Saga* (1870).

Morris wasn't solely a writer—his talents covered a wide range of arts and crafts. In 1861 he started a company to produce decorative art for buildings, including stained glass, carpets, and wallpapers; many of his designs are used today. In 1891 he established the Kelmscott Press to print books in the style of the fifteenth century. Towards the end of his life he returned to writing; in a highly productive period he produced a stream of novels in the style of the old sagas and romances. The first was *A Tale of the House of the Wolfings* (1889) which, along with *The Roots of the Mountains* (1890), were extravagant historical novels. In *The Story of the Glittering Plain* (1891)—the first book printed by the Kelmscott Press—he added a fantastic dimension: the Glittering Plain is a halfway house where people may find eternal life. There followed, in quick succession, *The Wood Beyond the*

World (1894), *Child Christopher and Goldilind the Fair* (1895), *The Well at the World's End* (1896), *The Water of the Wondrous Isles* (1897), and *The Sundering Flood* (1898).

Morris's novels are far too long and unwieldy to tease out an extract to stand alone, and the early stories are either too long or not sufficiently fantastic. Therefore, I turned to his retelling of the *Völsunga Saga*—in particular, to an episode that also fascinated J. R. R. Tolkien. The climax of *The Hobbit* is the battle against the dragon Smaug. The following story, "The Death of Fafnir," is its literary source.

The Death of Fafnir

William Morris and Eirikr Magnusson

Now Sigurd went to the kings and spake thus—

"Here have I abode a space with you, and I owe you thanks and reward, for great love and many gifts and all due honour; but now will I away from the land and go meet the sons of Hunding, and do them to wit that the Volsungs are not all dead; and your might would I have to strengthen me therein."

So the kings said that they would give him all things soever that he desired, and therewith was a great army got ready, and all things wrought in the most heedful wise, ships and all war-gear, so that his journey might be of the stateliest: but Sigurd himself steered the dragon-keel which was the greatest and noblest; richly wrought were their sails, and glorious to look on.

So they sail and have wind at will; but when a few days were overpast, there arose a great storm on the sea, and the waves were to behold even as the foam of men's blood, but Sigurd bade take in no sail, howsoever they might be riven, but rather to lay on higher than heretofore. But as they sailed past the rocks of a ness, a certain man hailed the ships, and asked who was captain over that navy; then was it told him that the chief and lord was Sigurd, the son of Sigmund, the most famed of all the young men who now are.

Then said the man, "Naught but one thing, certes do all say of him, that none among the sons of kings may be likened unto him; now fain were I that ye would shorten sail on some of the ships, and take me aboard."

Then they asked him of his name, and he sang—

"Hnikar I hight,
When I gladdened Huginn,
And went to battle,
Bright son of Volsung;

Now may ye call
The carl on the cliff top,
Feng or Fjolnir:
Fain would I with you."
They made for land therewith, and took that man aboard.
Then quoth Sigurd, as the song says—
"Tell me this, O Hnikar,
Since full well thou knowest
Fate of Gods, good and ill of mankind,
What best our hap foresheweth,
When amid the battle
About us sweeps the sword edge."
Quoth Hnikar—
"Good are many tokens
If thereof men wotted
When the swords are sweeping:
Fair fellow deem I
The dark-winged raven,
In war, to weapon-wielder.
"The second good thing:
When abroad thou goest
For the long road well arrayed,
Good if thou seest
Two men standing,
Fain of fame within the forecourt.
"A third thing:
Good hearing,
The wolf a howling
Abroad under ash boughs;
Good hap shalt thou have
Dealing with helm-staves,
If thou seest these fare before thee.
"No man in fight
His face shall turn
Against the moon's sister
Low, late-shining,
For he winneth battle
Who best beholdeth
Through the midmost sword-play,
And the sloping ranks best shapeth.

"Great is the trouble
Of foot ill-tripping,
When arrayed for fight thou farest,
For on both sides about
Are the Disir
Guileful, wishful of thy wounding.
"Fair-combed, well washen
Let each warrior be,
Nor lack meat in the morning,
For who can rule
The eve's returning,
And base to fall before fate grovelling."

Then the storm abated, and on they fared till they came aland in the realm of Hunding's sons, and then Fjolnir vanished away.

Then they let loose fire and sword, and slew men and burnt their abodes, and did waste all before them: a great company of folk fled before the face of them to Lyngi the King, and tell him that men of war are in the land, and are faring with such rage and fury that the like has never been heard of; and that the sons of King Hunding had no great forecast in that they said they would never fear the Volsungs more, for here was come Sigurd, the son of Sigmund, as captain over this army.

So King Lyngi let send the war-message all throughout his realm, and has no will to flee, but summons to him all such as would give him aid. So he came against Sigurd with a great army, he and his brothers with him, and an exceeding fierce fight befell; many a spear and many an arrow might men see there raised aloft, axes hard driven, shields cleft and byrnies torn, helmets were shivered, skulls split atwain, and many a man felled to the cold earth.

And now when the fight has long dured in such wise, Sigurd goes forth before the banners, and has the good sword Gram in his hand, and smites down both men and horses, and goes through the thickest of the throng with both arms red with blood to the shoulder; and folk shrank aback before him wheresoever he went, nor would either helm or byrny hold before him, and no man deemed he had ever seen his like. So a long while the battle lasted, and many a man was slain, and furious was the onset; till at last it befell, even as seldom comes to hand, when a land army falls on, that, do whatso they might, naught was brought about; but so many men fell of the sons of Hunding that the tale of them may not be told; and now whenas Sigurd was among the foremost, came the sons of Hunding against him, and Sigurd smote therewith at Lyngi the king, and clave him down, both helm and head, and mail-clad body, and thereafter he smote Hjorward his brother atwain, and then slew all the other sons of Hunding who were yet alive, and the more part of their folk withal.

Now home goes Sigurd with fair victory won, and plenteous wealth and great honour, which he had gotten to him in this journey, and feasts were made for him against he came back to the realm.

But when Sigurd had been at home but a little, came Regin to talk with him, and said—

"Belike thou wilt now have good will to bow down Fafnir's crest according to thy word plighted, since thou hast thus revenged thy father and the others of thy kin."

Sigurd answered, "That will we hold to, even as we have promised, nor did it ever fall from our memory."

★

Now Sigurd and Regin rode up the heath along that same way wherein Fafnir was wont to creep when he fared to the water; and folk say that thirty fathoms was the height of that cliff along which he lay when he drank of the water below. Then Sigurd spake—

"How sayedst thou, Regin, that this drake was no greater than other lingworms; methinks the track of him is marvellous great?"

Then said Regin, "Make thee a hole, and sit down therein, and whenas the worm comes to the water, smite him into the heart, and so do him to death, and win thee great fame thereby."

But Sigurd said, "What will betide me if I be before the blood of the worm?"

Says Regin, "Of what avail to counsel thee if thou art still afeard of everything? Little art thou like thy kin in stoutness of heart."

Then Sigurd rides right over the heath; but Regin gets him gone, sore afeard.

But Sigurd fell to digging him a pit, and whiles he was at that work, there came to him an old man with a long beard, and asked what he wrought there, and he told him.

Then answered the old man and said, "Thou doest after sorry counsel: rather dig thee many pits, and let the blood run therein; but sit thee down in one thereof, and so thrust the worm's heart through."

And therewithal he vanished away; but Sigurd made the pits even as it was shown to him.

Now crept the worm down to his place of watering, and the earth shook all about him, and he snorted forth venom on all the way before him as he went; but Sigurd neither trembled nor was adrad at the roaring of him. So whenas the worm crept over the pits, Sigurd thrust his sword under his left shoulder, so that it sank in up to the hilts; then up leapt Sigurd from the pit and drew the sword back again unto him, and therewith was his arm all bloody, up to the very shoulder.

Now when that mighty worm was ware that he had his death-wound, then he lashed out head and tail, so that all things soever that were before him were broken to pieces.

So whenas Fafnir had his death-wound, he asked "Who art thou? And who is thy father? And what thy kin, that thou wert so hardy as to bear weapons against me?"

Sigurd answered, "Unknown to men is my kin. I am called a noble beast: neither father have I nor mother, and all alone have I fared hither."

Said Fafnir, "Whereas thou hast neither father nor mother, of what wonder weft thou born then? But now, though thou tellest me not thy name on this my death-day, yet thou knowest verily that thou liest unto me."

He answered, "Sigurd am I called, and my father was Sigmund."

Says Fafnir, "Who egged thee on to this deed, and why wouldst thou be driven to it? Hadst thou never heard how that all folk were adrad of me, and of the awe of my countenance? But an eager father thou hadst, O bright eyed swain!"

Sigurd answered, "A hardy heart urged me on hereto, and a strong hand and this sharp sword, which well thou knowest now, stood me in stead in the doing of the deed. "Seldom hath hardy eld a faint-heart youth.'"

Fafnir said, "Well, I wot that hadst thou waxed amid thy kin, thou mightest have good skill to slay folk in thine anger; but more of a marvel is it, that thou, a bondsman taken in war, shouldst have the heart to set on me, "for few among bondsmen have heart for the fight.'"

Said Sigurd, "Wilt thou then cast it in my teeth that I am far away from my kin? Albeit I was a bondsman, yet was I never shackled. God wot thou hast found me free enow."

Fafnir answered, "In angry wise dost thou take my speech; but hearken, for that same gold which I have owned shall be thy bane too."

Quoth Sigurd, "Fain would we keep all our wealth til that day of days; yet shall each man die once for all."

Said Fafnir, "Few things wilt thou do after my counsel, but take heed that thou shalt be drowned if thou farest unwarily over the sea; so bide thou rather on the dry land for the coming of the calm tide."

Then said Sigurd, "Speak, Fafnir, and say, if thou art so exceeding wise, who are the Norns who rule the lot of all mothers' sons."

Fafnir answers, "Many there be and wide apart; for some are of the kin of the Aesir, and some are of Elfin kin, and some there are who are daughters of Dvalin."

Said Sigurd, "How namest thou the holm whereon Surt and the Aesir mix and mingle the water of the sword?"

"Unshapen is that holm hight," said Fafnir.

And yet again he said, "Regin, my brother, has brought about my end, and it gladdens my heart that thine too he bringeth about; for thus will things be according to his will."

And once again he spake, "A countenance of terror I bore up before all folk, after that I brooded over the heritage of my brother, and on every side did I spout out poison, so that none durst come anigh me, and of no weapon was I adrad, nor ever had I so many men before me, as that I deemed myself not stronger than all; for all men were sore afeard of me."

Sigurd answered and said, "Few may have victory by means of that same countenance of terror, for whoso comes amongst many shall one day find that no one man is by so far the mightiest of all."

Then says Fafnir, "Such counsel I give thee, that thou take thy horse and ride away at thy speediest, for ofttimes it fails out so, that he who gets a death-wound avenges himself none the less."

Sigurd answered, "Such as thy redes are I will nowise do after them; nay, I will ride now to thy lair and take to me that great treasure of thy kin."

"Ride there then," said Fafnir, "and thou shalt find gold enow to suffice thee for all thy life-days; yet shall that gold be thy bane, and the bane of every one soever who owns it."

Then up stood Sigurd, and said, "Home would I ride and lose all that wealth, if I deemed that by the losing thereof I should never die; but every brave and true man will fain have his hand on wealth till that last day that thou, Fafnir, wallow in the death-pain til Death and Hell have thee."

And therewithal Fafnir died.

George MacDonald (1824–1905)

MYTHS AND SAGAS were one source of the new interest in fantasy fiction, as were the Romantic and gothic movements, but fairy tales were also an inspiration. Unfortunately, from the start of the nineteenth century, most stories identified as fairy tales were increasingly marketed for children. The Brothers Grimm had much to do with this, since their early collection recast folktales as moral stories suitable for the young, as in the 1812 collection *Kinder und Hausmärchen* ("Tales for Children and the Home"). Other classic fairy tales were similarly expurgated and adapted for children—thereby losing much of their original purpose and power—and ended up neutralized in collections such as *Crowquill's Fairy Book* (1840) and Mrs. Craik's *Fairy Book* (1863). Unfortunately, it is an attitude that is still all too prevalent, and the wonder of the true fairy tale is lost to many.

One person who did much to counter that trend and produce literary fairy tales that could be appreciated by all ages was the Scottish minister, poet, and author George MacDonald. In his youth, MacDonald was fascinated by the German Romantics, especially Hoffmann and Novalis. When he wrote his first full-length fantasy, *Phantastes* (1858), which he called "A Faerie Romance for Men and Women," he modeled it on *Heinrich von Ofterdingen* (1802) by Novalis; in this work, the travels of a young boy are influenced by a dream, and MacDonald quoted from Novalis in the preface to the book. He saw the fairy tale as a vehicle for escape from reality into a world of dreams where it was possible to explore the human subconscious using both allegory and imagery. Thus MacDonald returned to the roots of the fairy tale, showing its potential for opening the reader's awareness to what may motivate us and to what directs the world. MacDonald's work was highly influential, not least on C. S. Lewis and J. R. R. Tolkien. Lewis revealed that reading *Phantastes* was "to convert, even to baptize, my imagination," adding:"I have never concealed the fact that I regarded him as my master."Tolkien was not quite as effusive and, indeed, in later years found his taste in MacDonald had faded, though he retained a fondness for "The Golden Key." Nevertheless it was MacDonald's portrayal of the goblins in *The Princess and the Goblin* (1872), which Tolkien had read as a child, that stayed with him and shaped the orcs.

"The Golden Key" is a beautiful allegorical tale—perhaps the most delightful fairy tale ever written. I never tire of reading it.

The Golden Key

George MacDonald

There was a boy who used to sit in the twilight and listen to his great-aunt's stories. She told him that if he could reach the place where the end of the rainbow stands he would find there a golden key.

"And what is the key for?" the boy would ask. "What is it the key of? What will it open?"

"That nobody knows," his aunt would reply. "He has to find that out."

"I suppose, being gold," the boy once said, thoughtfully, "that I could get a good deal of money for it if I sold it."

"Better never find it than sell it," returned his aunt.

And the boy went to bed and dreamed about the golden key.

Now all that his great-aunt told the boy about the golden key would have been nonsense, had it not been that their little house stood on the borders of Fairyland. For it is perfectly well known that out of Fairyland nobody ever can find where the rainbow stands. The creature takes such good care of its golden key, always flitting from place to place, lest anyone should find it! But in Fairyland it is quite different. Things that look real in this country look very thin indeed in Fairyland, while some of the things that here cannot stand still for a moment, will not move there. So it was not in the least absurd of the old lady to tell her nephew such things about the golden key.

"Did you ever know anybody to find it?" he asked, one evening.

"Yes. Your father, I believe, found it."

"And what did he do with it, can you tell me?"

"He never told me."

"What was it like?"

"He never showed it to me."

"How does a new key come there always?"

"I don't know. There it is."

"Perhaps it is the rainbow's egg."

75

"Perhaps it is. You will be a happy boy if you find the nest."

"Perhaps it comes tumbling down the rainbow from the sky."

"Perhaps it does."

One evening, in summer, he went into his own room and stood at the lattice-window, and gazed into the forest which fringed the outskirts of Fairyland. It came close up to his great-aunt's garden, and, indeed, sent some straggling trees into it. The forest lay to the east, and the sun, which was setting behind the cottage, looked straight into the dark wood with his level red eye. The trees were all old, and had few branches below, so that the sun could see a great way into the forest and the boy, being keen-sighted, could see almost as far as the sun. The trunks stood like rows of red columns in the shine of the red sun, and he could see down aisle after aisle in the vanishing distance. And as he gazed into the forest he began to feel as if the trees were all waiting for him, and had something they could not go on with till he came to them. But he was hungry and wanted his supper. So he lingered.

Suddenly, far among the trees, as far as the sun could shine, he saw a glorious thing. It was the end of a rainbow, large and brilliant. He could count all seven colours, and could see shade after shade beyond the violet; while before the red stood a colour more gorgeous and mysterious still. It was a colour he had never seen before. Only the spring of the rainbow-arch was visible. He could see nothing of it above the trees.

"The golden key!" he said to himself, and darted out of the house, and into the wood.

He had not gone far before the sun set. But the rainbow only glowed the brighter. For the rainbow of Fairyland is not dependent upon the sun, as ours is. The trees welcomed him. The bushes made way for him. The rainbow grew larger and brighter; and at length he found himself within two trees of it.

It was a grand sight, burning away there in silence, with its gorgeous, its lovely, its delicate colours, each distinct, all combining. He could now see a great deal more of it. It rose high into the blue heavens, but bent so little that he could not tell how high the crown of the arch must reach. It was still only a small portion of a huge bow.

He stood gazing at it till he forgot himself with delight—even forgot the key which he had come to seek. And as he stood it grew more wonderful still. For in each of the colours, which was as large as the column of a church, he could faintly see beautiful forms slowly ascending as if by the steps of a winding stair. The forms appeared irregularly—now one, now many, now several, now none—men and women and children—all different, all beautiful.

He drew nearer to the rainbow. It vanished. He started back a step in dismay. It was there again, as beautiful as ever. So he contented himself with standing as near it as he might, and watching the forms that ascended the glorious colours towards the unknown height of the arch, which did not end abruptly but faded away in the blue air, so gradually that he could not say where it ceased.

When the thought of the golden key returned, the boy very wisely proceeded to mark out in his mind the space covered by the foundation of the rainbow, in order that he might know where to search, should the rainbow disappear. It was based chiefly upon a bed of moss.

Meantime it had grown quite dark in the wood. The rainbow alone was visible by its own light. But the moment the moon rose the rainbow vanished. Nor could any change of place restore the vision to the boy's eyes. So he threw himself down upon the mossy bed, to wait till the sunlight would give him a chance of finding the key. There he fell fast asleep.

When he woke in the morning the sun was looking straight into his eyes. He turned away from it, and the same moment saw a brilliant little thing lying on the moss within a foot of his face. It was the golden key. The pipe of it was of plain gold, as bright as gold could be. The handle was curiously wrought and set with sapphires. In a terror of delight he put out his hand and took it, and had it.

He lay for a while, turning it over and over, and feeding his eyes upon its beauty. Then he jumped to his feet, remembering that the pretty thing was of no use to him yet. Where was the lock to which the key belonged? It must be somewhere, for how could anybody be so silly as make a key for which there was no lock? Where should he go to look for it? He gazed about him, up into the air, down to the earth, but saw no keyhole in the clouds, in the grass, or in the trees.

Just as he began to grow disconsolate, however, he saw something glimmering in the wood. It was a mere glimmer that he saw, but he took it for a glimmer of rainbow, and went towards it.—And now I will go back to the borders of the forest.

Not far from the house where the boy had lived, there was another house, the owner of which was a merchant, who was much away from home. He had lost his wife some years before, and had only one child, a little girl, whom he left to the charge of two servants, who were very idle and careless. So she was neglected and left untidy, and was sometimes ill-used besides.

Now it is well known that the little creatures commonly known as fairies, though there are many different kinds of fairies in Fairyland, have an exceeding dislike to untidiness. Indeed, they are quite spiteful to slovenly people. Being used to all the lovely ways of the trees and flowers, and to the neatness of the birds and all woodland creatures, it makes them feel miserable, even in their deep woods and on their grassy carpets, to think that within the same moonlight lies a dirty, uncomfortable, slovenly house. And this makes them angry with the people that live in it, and they would gladly drive them out of the world if they could. They want the whole earth nice and clean. So they pinch the maids black and blue and play them all manner of uncomfortable tricks.

But this house was quite a shame, and the fairies in the forest could not endure it. They tried everything on the maids without effect, and at last resolved upon making a clean riddance, beginning with the child. They ought to have known that it was not her fault, but they have little principle and much mischief in them, and they thought that if they got rid of her the maids would be sure to be turned away.

So one evening, the poor little girl having been put to bed early, before the sun was down, the servants went off to the village, locking the door behind them. The child did not know she was alone, and lay contentedly looking out of her window towards the forest, of which, however, she could not see much, because of the ivy and other creeping plants which had straggled across her window. All at once she saw an ape making faces at her out of the mirror, and the heads carved upon a great old wardrobe grinning fearfully. Then two old spider-legged chairs came forward into the middle of the room, and began to dance a queer, old-fashioned dance. This set her laughing and she forgot the ape and the grinning heads. So the fairies saw they had made a mistake, and sent the chairs back to their places. But they knew that she had been reading the story of Silverhair all day. So the next moment she heard the voices of the three bears upon the stair, big voice, middle voice, and little voice, and she heard their soft, heavy tread, as if they had stockings over their boots, coming nearer and nearer to the door of her room, till she could bear it no longer. She did just as Silverhair did, and as the fairies wanted her to do; she darted to the window, pulled it open, got upon the ivy, and so scrambled to the ground. She then fled to the forest as fast as she could run.

Now, although she did not know it, this was the very best way she could have gone; for nothing is ever so mischievous in its own place as it is out of it; and, besides, these mischievous creatures were only the children of Fairyland, as it were, and there are many other beings there as well; and if a wanderer gets in among them, the good ones will always help him more than the evil ones will be able to hurt him.

The sun was now set, and the darkness coming on, but the child thought of no danger but the bears behind her. If she had looked round, however, she would have seen that she was followed by a very different creature from a bear. It was a curious creature, made like a fish, but covered, instead of scales, with feathers of all colours, sparkling like those of a humming-bird. It had fins, not wings, and swam through the air as a fish does through the water. Its head was like the head of a small owl.

After running a long way, and as the last of the light was disappearing, she passed under a tree with drooping branches. It dropped its branches to the ground all about her, and caught her as in a trap. She struggled to get out, but the branches pressed her closer and closer to the trunk. She was in great terror and distress, when the air-fish, swimming into the thicket of branches, began tearing them with its beak. They loosened their hold at once, and the creature went on attacking them, till at length they let the child go. Then the air-fish came from behind her, and swam on in front, glittering and sparkling all lovely colours; and she followed.

It led her gently along till all at once it swam in at a cottage door. The child followed still. There was a bright fire in the middle of the floor, upon which stood a pot without a lid, full of water that boiled and bubbled furiously. The air-fish swam straight to the pot and into the boiling water, where it lay quiet. A beautiful woman rose from the opposite side of the fire and came to meet the girl. She took her up in her arms, and said,—

"Ah, you are come at last! I have been looking for you a long time."

She sat down with her on her lap, and there the girl sat staring at her. She had never seen anything so beautiful. She was tall and strong, with white arms and neck, and a delicate flush on her face. The child

could not tell what was the colour of her hair, but could not help
thinking it had a tinge of dark green. She had not one ornament upon
her, but she looked as if she had just put off quantities of diamonds
and emeralds. Yet here she was in the simplest, poorest little cottage,
where she was evidently at home. She was dressed in shining green.

The girl looked at the lady, and the lady looked at the girl.

"What is your name?" asked the lady.

"The servants always called me Tangle."

"Ah, that was because your hair was so untidy. But that was their
fault, the naughty women! Still it is a pretty name, and I will call you
Tangle too. You must not mind my asking you questions, for you may
ask me the same questions, every one of them, and any others that
you like. How old are you?"

"Ten," answered Tangle.

"You don't look like it," said the lady.

"How old are you. please?" returned Tangle.

"Thousands of years old," answered the lady.

"You don't look like it," said Tangle.

"Don't I? I think I do. Don't you see how beautiful I am!"

And her great blue eyes looked down on the little Tangle, as if all
the stars in the sky were melted in them to make their brightness.

"Ah! but," said Tangle, "when people live long they grow old. At
least I always thought so."

"I have no time to grow old," said the lady. "I am too busy for that.
It is very idle to grow old.—but I cannot have my little girl so untidy.
Do you know I can't find a clean spot on your face to kiss!"

"Perhaps," suggested Tangle, feeling ashamed, but not too much
so to say a word for herself,—"perhaps that is because the tree made
me cry so."

"My poor darling!" said the lady, looking now as if the moon were
melted in her eyes, and kissing her little face, dirty as it was, "the
naughty tree must suffer for making a girl cry."

"And what is your name, please?" asked Tangle.

"Grandmother," answered the lady.

"Is it really?"

"Yes, indeed. I never tell stories, even in fun."

"How good of you!"

"I couldn't if I tried. It would come true if I said it, and then I
should be punished enough." And she smiled like the sun through a
summer shower.

"But now," she went on, "I must get you washed and dressed, and then we shall have some supper."

"Oh! I had supper long ago," said Tangle.

"Yes, indeed you had," answered the lady,—"three years ago. You don't know that it is three years since you ran away from the bears. You are thirteen and more now."

Tangle could only stare. She felt quite sure it was true.

"You will not be afraid of anything I do with you—will you?" said the lady.

"I will try very hard not to be; but I can't be certain, you know," replied Tangle.

"I like your saying so, and I shall be quite satisfied," answered the lady.

She took off the girl's night-gown, rose with her in her arms, and going to the wall of the cottage, opened a door. Then Tangle saw a deep tank, the sides of which were filled with green plants, which had flowers of all colours. There was a roof over it like the roof of the cottage. It was filled with beautiful clear water, in which swam a multitude of such fishes as the one that had led her to the cottage. It was the light their colours gave that showed the place in which they were.

The lady spoke some words Tangle could not understand, and threw her into the tank.

The fishes came crowding about her. Two or three of them got under her head and kept it up. The rest of them rubbed themselves all over her, and with their wet feathers washed her quite clean. Then the lady, who had been looking on all the time, spoke again; whereupon some thirty or forty of the fishes rose out of the water underneath Tangle, and so bore her up to the arms the lady held out to take her. She carried her back to the fire, and, having dried her well, opened a chest, and taking out the finest linen garments, smelling of grass and lavender, put them upon her, and over all a green dress, just like her own, shining like hers, and soft like hers, and going into just such lovely folds from the waist, where it was tied with a brown cord, to her bare feet.

"Won't you give me a pair of shoes too, Grandmother?" said Tangle.

"No, my dear; no shoes. Look here. I wear no shoes."

So saying she lifted her dress a little, and there were the loveliest white feet, but no shoes. Then Tangle was content to go without shoes too. And the lady sat down with her again, and combed her hair, and brushed it, and then left it to dry while she got the supper.

First she got bread out of one hole in the wall; then milk out of another; then several kinds of fruit out of a third; and then she went to the pot on the fire, and took out of the fish, now nicely cooked, and, as soon as she had pulled off its feathered skin, ready to be eaten.

"But," exclaimed Tangle. And she stared at the fish, and could say no more.

"I know what you mean," returned the lady. "You do not like to eat the messenger that brought you home. But it is the kindest return you can make. The creature was afraid to go until it saw me put the pot on, and heard me promise it should be boiled the moment it returned with you. Then it darted out of the door at once. You saw it go into the pot of itself the moment it entered, did you not?"

"I did," answered Tangle, "and I thought it very strange; but then I saw you, and forgot all about the fish."

"In Fairyland," resumed the lady, as they sat down to the table, "the ambition of the animals is to be eaten by the people; for that is their highest end in that condition. But they are not therefore destroyed. Out of that pot comes something more than the dead fish, you will see."

Tangle now remarked that the lid was on the pot. But the lady took no further notice of it till they had eaten the fish, which Tangle found nicer than any fish she had ever tasted before. It was as white as snow, and as delicate as cream. And the moment she had swallowed a mouthful of it, a change she could not describe began to take place in her. She heard a murmuring all about her, which became more and more articulate, and at length, as she went on eating, grew intelligible. By the time she had finished her share, the sounds of all the animals in the forest came crowding through the door to her ears; for the door still stood wide open, though it was pitch-dark outside; and they were no longer sounds only; they were speech, and speech that she could understand. She could tell what the insects in the cottage were saying to each other too. She had even a suspicion that the trees and flowers all about the cottage were holding midnight communications with each other; but what they said she could not hear.

As soon as the fish was eaten, the lady went to the fire and took the lid off the pot. A lovely little creature in human shape, with large white wings, rose out of it, and flew round and round the roof of the cottage; then dropped, fluttering, and nestled in the lap of the lady.

She spoke to it some strange words, carried it to the door, and threw it out into the darkness. Tangle heard the flapping of its wings die away in the distance.

"Now have we done the fish any harm?" she said, returning.

"No," answered Tangle, "I do not think we have. I should not mind eating one every day."

"They must wait their time, like you and me too, my little Tangle."

And she smiled a smile which the sadness in it made more lovely.

"But," she continued, "I think we may have one for supper to-morrow."

So saying she went to the door of the tank, and spoke; and now Tangle understood her perfectly.

"I want one of you," she said,—"the wisest."

Thereupon the fishes got together in the middle of the tank, with their heads forming a circle above the water, and their tails a larger circle beneath it. They were holding a council, in which their relative wisdom should be determined. At length one of them flew up into the lady's hand, looking lively and ready.

"You know where the rainbow stands?" she asked.

"Yes, mother, quite well," answered the fish.

"Bring home a young man you will find there, who does not know where to go."

The fish was out of the door in a moment. Then the lady told Tangle it was time to go to bed; and, opening another door in the side of the cottage, showed her a little arbour, cool and green, with a bed of purple heath growing in it, upon which she threw a large wrapper made of the feathered skins of the wise fishes, shining gorgeous in the firelight. Tangle was soon lost in the strangest, loveliest dreams. And the beautiful lady was in every one of her dreams.

In the morning she woke to the rustling of leaves over her head, and the sound of running water. But, to her surprise, she could find no door—nothing but the moss grown wall of the cottage. So she crept through an opening in the arbour, and stood in the forest. Then she bathed in a stream that ran merrily through the trees, and felt happier; for having once been in her grandmother's pond, she must be clean and tidy ever after; and, having put on her green dress, felt like a lady.

She spent that day in the wood, listening to the birds and beasts and creeping things. She understood all that they said, though she

could not repeat a word of it; and every kind had a different language, while there was a common though more limited understanding between all the inhabitants of the forest. She saw nothing of the
beautiful lady, but she felt that she was near her all the time; and she
took care not to go out of sight of the cottage. It was round, like a
snow-hut or a wigwam; and she could see neither door nor window
in it. The fact was, it had no windows; and though it was full of
doors, they all opened from the inside, and could not even be seen
from the outside.

She was standing at the foot of a tree in the twilight, listening
to a quarrel between a mole and a squirrel, in which the mole told
the squirrel that the tail was the best of him, and the squirrel called
the mole Spade-fists, when, the darkness having deepened around
her, she became aware of something shining in her face, and looking
round, saw that the door of the cottage was open, and the red light
of the fire flowing from it like a river through the darkness. She left
Mole and Squirrel to settle matters as they might, and darted off to
the cottage. Entering, she found the pot boiling on the fire, and the
grand, lovely lady sitting on the other side of it.

"I've been watching you all day," said the lady. "You shall have
something to eat by-and-by, but we must wait till our supper comes
home."

She took Tangle on her knee, and began to sing to her—such songs
as made her wish she could listen to them for ever. But at length in
rushed the shining fish, and snuggled down in the pot. It was followed by a youth who had outgrown his worn garments. His face
was ruddy with health, and in his hand he carried a little jewel, which
sparkled in the firelight.

The first words the lady said were—

"What is that in your hand, Mossy?"

Now Mossy was the name his companions had given him, because
he had a favourite stone covered with moss, on which he used to sit
whole days reading; and they said the moss had begun to grow upon
him too.

Mossy held out his hand. The moment the lady saw that it was the
golden key, she rose from her chair, kissed Mossy on the forehead,
made him sit down on her seat, and stood before him like a servant.
Mossy could not bear this, and rose at once. But the lady begged him,
with tears in her beautiful eyes, to sit, and let her wait on him.

"But you are a great, splendid, beautiful lady," said Mossy.

"Yes, I am. But I work all day long—that is my pleasure; and you will have to leave me so soon!"

"How do you know that, if you please, madam?" asked Mossy.

"Because you have got the golden key."

"But I don't know what it is for. I can't find the keyhole. Will you tell me what to do?"

"You must look for the keyhole. That is your work. I cannot help you. I can only tell you that if you look for it you will find it."

"What kind of box will it open? What is there inside?"

"I do not know. I dream about it, but I know nothing."

"Must I go at once?"

"You may stop here tonight, and have some of my supper. But you must go in the morning. All I can do for you is to give you clothes. Here is a girl called Tangle, whom you must take with you."

"That *will* be nice," said Mossy.

"No, no!" said Tangle. "I don't want to leave you, please, grandmother."

"You must go with him, Tangle. I am sorry to lose you, but it will be the best thing for you. Even the fishes, you see, have to go into the pot, and then out into the dark. If you fall in with the Old Man of the Sea, mind you ask him whether he has not got some more fishes ready for me. My tank is getting thin."

So saying, she took the fish from the pot, and put the lid on as before. They sat down and ate the fish, and then the winged creature rose from the pot, circled the roof, and settled on the lady's lap. She talked to it, carried it to the door, and threw it out into the dark. They heard the flap of its wings die away in the distance.

The lady then showed Mossy into just such another chamber as that of Tangle; and in the morning he found a suit of clothes laid beside him. He looked very handsome in them. But the wearer of Grandmother's clothes never thinks about how he or she looks, but thinks always how handsome other people are.

Tangle was very unwilling to go.

"Why should I leave you? I don't know the young man," she said to the lady.

"I am never allowed to keep my children long. You need not go with him except you please, but you must go some day; and I should like you to go with him, for he has the golden key. No girl need be afraid to go with a youth that has the golden key. You will take care of her, Mossy, will you not?"

"That I will," said Mossy.

And Tangle cast a glance at him, and thought she should like to go with him.

"And," said the lady, "If you should lose each other as you go through the—the—I never can remember the name of that country,—do not be afraid, but go on and on."

She kissed Tangle on the mouth and Mossy on the forehead, led them to the door, and waved her hand eastward. Mossy and Tangle took each other's hand and walked away into the depth of the forest. In his right hand Mossy held the golden key.

They wandered thus a long way, with endless amusement from the talk of the animals. They soon learned enough of their language to ask them necessary questions. The squirrels were always friendly, and gave them nuts out of their own hoards; but the bees were selfish and rude, justifying themselves on the ground that Tangle and Mossy were not subjects of their queen, and charity must begin at home, though indeed they had not one drone in their poorhouse at the time. Even the blinking moles would fetch them an earth-nut or a truffle now and then, talking as if their mouths, as well as their eyes and ears, were full of cotton wool, or their own velvety fur. By the time they got out of the forest they were very fond of each other, and Tangle was not in the least sorry that her grandmother had sent her away with Mossy.

At length the trees grew smaller, and stood farther apart, and the ground began to rise, and it got more and more steep, till the trees were all left behind, and the two were climbing a narrow path with rocks on each side. Suddenly they came upon a rude doorway, by which they entered a narrow gallery cut in the rock. It grew darker and darker, till it was pitch dark, and they had to feel their way. At length the light began to return, and at last they came out upon a narrow path on the face of a lofty precipice. This path went winding down the rock to a wide plain, circular in shape, and surrounded on all sides by mountains. Those opposite to them were a great way off, and towered to an awful height, shooting up sharp, blue, ice-enamelled pinnacles. An utter silence reigned where they stood. Not even the sound of water reached them.

Looking down, they could not tell whether the valley below was a grassy plain or a great still lake. They had never seen any place look like it. The way to it was difficult and dangerous, but down the narrow path they went, and reached the bottom in safety. They found it composed of smooth, light-coloured sandstone, undulating in parts, but mostly level. It was no wonder to them now that they had not been able to tell what it was, for this surface was everywhere crowded with shadows. It was a sea of shadows. The mass was chiefly made up of the shadows of leaves innumerable, of all lovely and imaginative forms, waving to and fro, floating and quivering in the breath of a breeze whose motion was unfelt, whose sound was unheard. No forests clothed the mountain-sides, no trees were anywhere to be seen, and yet the shadows of the leaves, branches, and stems of all various trees covered the valley as far as their eyes could reach. They soon spied the shadows of flowers mingled with those of the leaves, and now and then the shadow of a bird with open beak, and throat distended with song. At times would appear the forms of strange, graceful creatures, running up and down the shadow-boles and along the branches, to disappear in the wind-tossed foliage. As they walked they waded knee-deep in the lovely lake. For the shadows were not merely lying on the surface of the ground, but heaped up above it like substantial forms of darkness, as if they had been cast upon a thousand different planes of the air. Tangle and Mossy often lifted their heads and gazed upwards to descry whence the shadows came; but they could see nothing more than a bright mist spread above them, higher than the tops of the mountains, which stood clear against it. No forests, no leaves, no birds were visible.

After a while, they reached more open spaces, where the shadows were thinner; and came even to portions over which shadows only flitted, leaving them clear for such as might follow. Now a wonderful form, half bird-like half human, would float across on outspread sailing pinions. Anon an exquisite shadow group of gambolling children would be followed by the loveliest female form, and that again by the grand stride of a Titanic shape, each disappearing in the surrounding press of shadowy foliage. Sometimes a profile of unspeakable beauty or grandeur would appear for a moment and vanish. Sometimes they seemed lovers that passed linked arm in arm, sometimes father and son, sometimes brothers in loving contest, sometimes sisters entwined in gracefullest community of complex form. Sometimes wild horses would tear across, free, or bestrode by noble shadows of ruling men. But some of the things which pleased them most they never knew how to describe.

About the middle of the plain they sat down to rest in the heart of a heap of shadows. After sitting for a while, each, looking up, saw the other in tears: they were each longing after the country whence the shadows fell.

"We MUST find the country from which the shadows come," said Mossy.

"We must, dear Mossy," responded Tangle. "What if your golden key should be the key to it?"

"Ah! that would be grand," returned Mossy.—"But we must rest here for a little, and then we shall be able to cross the plain before night."

So he lay down on the ground, and about him on every side, and over his head, was the constant play of the wonderful shadows. He could look through them, and see the one behind the other, till they mixed in a mass of darkness. Tangle, too, lay admiring, and wondering, and longing after the country whence the shadows came. When they were rested they rose and pursued their journey.

How long they were in crossing this plain I cannot tell; but before night Mossy's hair was streaked with grey, and Tangle had got wrinkles on her forehead.

As evening drew on, the shadows fell deeper and rose higher. At length they reached a place where they rose above their heads, and made all dark around them. Then they took hold of each other's hand, and walked on in silence and in some dismay. They felt the gathering darkness, and something strangely solemn besides, and the beauty of the shadows ceased to delight them. All at once Tangle found that she had not a hold of Mossy's hand, though when she lost it she could not tell.

"Mossy, Mossy!" she cried aloud in terror.

But no Mossy replied.

A moment after, the shadows sank to her feet, and down under her feet, and the mountains rose before her. She turned towards the gloomy region she had left, and called once more upon Mossy. There the gloom lay tossing and heaving, a dark stormy, foamless sea of shadows, but no Mossy rose out of it, or came climbing up the hill on which she stood. She threw herself down and wept in despair.

Suddenly she remembered that the beautiful lady had told them, if they lost each other in a country of which she could not remember the name, they were not to be afraid, but to go straight on.

"And besides," she said to herself, "Mossy has the golden key, and so no harm will come to him, I do believe."

She rose from the ground, and went on.

Before long she arrived at a precipice, in the face of which a stair was cut. When she had ascended halfway, the stair ceased, and the path led straight into the mountain. She was afraid to enter, and turning again towards the stair, grew giddy at the sight of the depth beneath her, and was forced to throw herself down in the mouth of the cave.

When she opened her eyes, she saw a beautiful little creature with wings standing beside her, waiting.

"I know you," said Tangle. "You are my fish."

"Yes. But I am a fish no longer. I am an aëranth now."

"What is that?" asked Tangle.

"What you see I am," answered the shape. "And I am come to lead you through the mountain."

"Oh! thank you, dear fish—aëranth, I mean," returned Tangle, rising.

Thereupon the aëranth took to his wings, and flew on through the long narrow passage, reminding Tangle very much of the way he had swum on before her when he was a fish. And the moment his white wings moved, they began to throw off a continuous shower of sparks of all colours, which lighted up the passage before them. All at once he vanished, and Tangle heard a low, sweet sound, quite different from the rush and crackle of his wings. Before her was an open arch, and through it came light, mixed with the sound of sea-waves.

She hurried out, and fell, tired and happy, upon the yellow sand of the shore. There she lay, half asleep with weariness and rest, listening to the low plash and retreat of the tiny waves, which seemed ever enticing the land to leave off being land, and become sea. And as she lay, her eyes were fixed upon the foot of a great rainbow standing far away against the sky on the other side of the sea. At length she fell fast asleep.

When she awoke, she saw an old man with long white hair down to his shoulders, leaning upon a stick covered with green buds, and so bending over her.

"What do you want here, beautiful woman?" he said.

"Am I beautiful? I am so glad!" answered Tangle, rising. "My grandmother is beautiful."

"Yes. But what do you want?" he repeated, kindly.

"I think I want you. Are not you the Old Man of the Sea?"

"I am."

"Then grandmother says, have you any more fishes ready for her?"

"We will go and see, my dear," answered the old man, speaking yet more kindly than before. "And I can do something for you, can I not?"

"Yes—show me the way up to the country from which the shadows fall," said Tangle. For there she hoped to find Mossy again.

"Ah! indeed, that would be worth doing," said the old man. "But I cannot, for I do not know the way myself. But I will send you to the Old Man of the Earth. Perhaps he can tell you. He is much older than I am."

Leaning on his staff, he conducted her along the shore to a steep rock, that looked like a petrified ship turned upside down. The door of it was the rudder of a great vessel, ages ago at the bottom of the sea. Immediately within the door was a stair in the rock, down which the old man went, and Tangle followed. At the bottom, the old man had his house, and there he lived.

As soon as she entered it, Tangle heard a strange noise, unlike anything she had ever heard before. She soon found that it was the fishes talking. She tried to understand what they said; but their speech was so old-fashioned, and rude, and undefined, that she could not make much of it.

"I will go and see about those fishes for my daughter," said the Old Man of the Sea.

And moving a slide in the wall of his house, he first looked out, and then tapped upon a thick piece of crystal that filled the round opening. Tangle came up behind him, and peeping through the window into the heart of the great deep green ocean, saw the most curious creatures, some very ugly, all very odd, and with especially queer mouths, swimming about everywhere, above and below, but all coming towards the window in answer to the tap of the Old Man of the Sea. Only a few could get their mouths against the glass; but those who were floating miles away yet turned their heads towards it. The Old Man looked through the whole flock carefully for some minutes, and then turning to Tangle, said,—

"I am sorry I have not got one ready yet. I want more time than she does. But I will send some as soon as I can."

He then shut the slide.

Presently a great noise arose in the sea. The old man opened the slide again, and tapped on the glass, whereupon the fishes were all as still as sleep.

"They were only talking about you," he said. "And they do speak such nonsense!—Tomorrow," he continued, "I must show you the way to the Old Man of the Earth. He lives a long way from here."

"Do let me go at once," said Tangle.

"No. That is not possible. You must come this way first."

He led her to a hole in the wall, which she had not observed before. It was covered with the green leaves and white blossoms of a creeping plant.

"Only white-blossoming plants can grow under the sea," said the old man. "In there you will find a bath, in which you must lie till I call you."

Tangle went in, and found a smaller room or cave, in the further corner of which was a great basin hollowed out of a rock, and half full of the clearest sea-water. Little streams were constantly running into it from cracks in the wall of the cavern. It was polished quite smooth inside, and had a carpet of yellow sand in the bottom of it. Large green leaves and white flowers of various plants crowded up and over it, draping and covering it almost entirely.

No sooner was she undressed and lying in the bath, than she began to feel as if the water were sinking into her, and she was receiving all the good of sleep without undergoing its forgetfulness. She felt the good coming all the time. And she grew happier and more hopeful than she had been since she lost Mossy. But she could not help thinking how very sad it was for a poor old man to live there all alone, and have to take care of a whole seaful of stupid and riotous fishes.

After about an hour, as she thought, she heard his voice calling her, and rose out of the bath. All the fatigue and aching of her long journey had vanished. She was as whole, and strong, and well as if she had slept for seven days.

Returning to the opening that led into the other part of the house, she started back with amazement, for through it she saw the form of a grand man, with a majestic and beautiful face, waiting for her.

"Come," he said; "I see you are ready."

She entered with reverence.

"Where is the Old Man of the Sea?" she asked, humbly.

"There is no one here but me," he answered, smiling. "Some people call me the Old Man of the Sea. Others have another name for me, and are terribly frightened when they meet me taking a walk by the shore. Therefore I avoid being seen by them, for they are so afraid, that they never see what I really am. You see me now. But I must show you the way to the Old Man of the Earth."

He led her into the cave where the bath was, and there she saw, in the opposite corner, a second opening in the rock.

"Go down that stair, and it will bring you to him," said the Old Man of the Sea.

With humble thanks Tangle took her leave. She went down the winding-stair, till she began to fear there was no end to it. Still down and down it went, rough and broken, with springs of water bursting out of the rocks and running down the steps beside her. It was quite dark about her, and yet she could see. For after being in that bath, people's eyes always give out a light they can see by. There were no creeping things in the way. All was safe and pleasant though so dark and damp and deep.

At last there was not one step more, and she found herself in a glimmering cave. On a stone in the middle of it sat a figure with its back towards her—the figure of an old man bent double with age. From behind she could see his white beard spread out on the rocky floor in front of him. He did not move as she entered, so she passed round that she might stand before him and speak to him. The moment she looked in his face, she saw that he was a youth of marvellous beauty. He sat entranced with the delight of what he beheld in a mirror of something like silver, which lay on the floor at his feet, and which from behind she had taken for his white beard. He sat on, heedless of her presence, pale with the joy of his vision. She stood and watched him. At length, all trembling, she spoke. But her voice made no sound. Yet the youth lifted up his head. He showed no surprise, however, at seeing her—only smiled a welcome.

"Are you the Old Man of the Earth?" Tangle had said.

And the youth answered, and Tangle heard him, though not with her ears:—

"I am. What can I do for you?"

"Tell me the way to the country whence the shadows fall."

"Ah! that I do not know. I only dream about it myself. I see its shadows sometimes in my mirror: the way to it I do not know. But I think the Old Man of the Fire must know. He is much older than I am. He is the oldest man of all."

"Where does he live?"

"I will show you the way to his place. I never saw him myself."

So saying, the young man rose, and then stood for a while gazing at Tangle.

"I wish I could see that country too," he said. "But I must mind my work."

He led her to the side of the cave, and told her to lay her ear against the wall.

"What do you hear?" he asked.

"I hear," answered Tangle, "the sound of a great water running inside the rock."

"That river runs down to the dwelling of the oldest man of all— the Old Man of the Fire. I wish I could go to see him. But I must mind my work. That river is the only way to him."

Then the Old Man of the Earth stooped over the floor of the cave, raised a huge stone from it, and left it leaning. It disclosed a great hole that went plumb-down.

"That is the way," he said.

"But there are no stairs."

"You must throw yourself in. There is no other way."

She turned and looked him full in the face—stood so for a whole minute, as she thought: it was a whole year—then threw herself headlong into the hole.

When she came to herself, she found herself gliding down fast and deep. Her head was under water, but that did not signify, for, when she thought about it, she could not remember that she had breathed once since her bath in the cave of the Old Man of the Sea. When she lifted up her head a sudden and fierce heat struck her, and she sank in again instantly, and went sweeping on.

Gradually the stream grew shallower. At length she could hardly keep her head under. Then the water could carry her no farther. She rose from the channel, and went step for step down the burning descent. The water ceased altogether. The heat was terrible. She felt scorched to the bone, but it did not touch her strength. It grew hotter and hotter. She said, "I can bear it no longer." Yet she went on.

At the long last, the stair ended at a rude archway in an all but glowing rock. Through this archway Tangle fell exhausted into a cool mossy cave. The floor and walls were covered with moss—green, soft, and damp. A little stream spouted from a rent in the rock and fell into a basin of moss. She plunged her face into it and drank. Then she lifted her head and looked around. Then she rose and looked again.

She saw no one in the cave. But the moment she stood upright she
had a marvellous sense that she was in the secret of the earth and
all its ways. Everything she had seen, or learned from books; all that
her grandmother had said or sung to her; all the talk of the beasts,
birds, and fishes; all that had happened to her on her journey with
Mossy, and since then in the heart of the earth with the Old man
and the Older man—all was plain: she understood it all, and saw that
everything meant the same thing, though she could not have put it
into words again.

The next moment she descried, in a corner of the cave, a little
naked child, sitting on the moss. He was playing with balls of various
colours and sizes, which he disposed in strange figures upon the
floor beside him. And now Tangle felt that there was something in
her knowledge which was not in her understanding. For she knew
there must be an infinite meaning in the change and sequence and
individual forms of the figures into which the child arranged the
balls, as well as in the varied harmonies of their colours, but what it
all meant she could not tell. He went on busily, tirelessly, playing his
solitary game, without looking up, or seeming to know that there
was a stranger in his deep-withdrawn cell. Diligently as a lace-maker
shifts her bobbins, he shifted and arranged his balls. Flashes of meaning would now pass from them to Tangle, and now again all would
be not merely obscure, but utterly dark. She stood looking for a
long time, for there was fascination in the sight; and the longer she
looked the more an indescribable vague intelligence went on rous-
ing itself in her mind. For seven years she had stood there watching
the naked child with his coloured balls, and it seemed to her like
seven hours, when all at once the shape the balls took, she knew not
why, reminded her of the Valley of Shadows, and she spoke:—

"Where is the Old Man of the Fire?" she said.

"Here I am," answered the child, rising and leaving his balls on the
moss. "What can I do for you?"

There was such an awfulness of absolute repose on the face of the
child that Tangle stood dumb before him. He had no smile, but the
love in his large grey eyes was deep as the centre. And with the repose
there lay on his face a shimmer as of moonlight, which seemed as
if any moment it might break into such a ravishing smile as would
cause the beholder to weep himself to death. But the smile never
came, and the moonlight lay there unbroken. For the heart of the
child was too deep for any smile to reach from it to his face.

"Are you the oldest man of all?" Tangle at length, although filled with awe, ventured to ask.

"Yes, I am. I am very, very old. I am able to help you, I know. I can help everybody."

And the child drew near and looked up in her face so that she burst into tears.

"Can you tell me the way to the country the shadows fall from?" she sobbed.

"Yes. I know the way quite well. I go there myself sometimes. But you could not go my way; you are not old enough. I will show you how you can go."

"Do not send me out into the great heat again," prayed Tangle.

"I will not," answered the child.

And he reached up, and put his little cool hand on her heart.

"Now," he said, "you can go. The fire will not burn you. Come."

He led her from the cave, and following him through another archway, she found herself in a vast desert of sand and rock. The sky of it was of rock, lowering over them like solid thunderclouds; and the whole place was so hot that she saw, in bright rivulets, the yellow gold and white silver and red copper trickling molten from the rocks. But the heat never came near her.

When they had gone some distance, the child turned up a great stone, and took something like an egg from under it. He next drew a long curved line in the sand with his finger, and laid the egg in it. He then spoke something Tangle could not understand. The egg broke, a small snake came out, and, lying in the line in the sand, grew and grew till he filled it. The moment he was thus full-grown, he began to glide away, undulating like a sea-wave.

"Follow that serpent," said the child. "He will lead you the right way."

Tangle followed the serpent. But she could not go far without looking back at the marvellous Child. He stood alone in the midst of the glowing desert, beside a fountain of red flame that had burst forth at his feet, his naked whiteness glimmering a pale rosy red in the torrid fire. There he stood, looking after her, till, from the lengthening distance, she could see him no more. The serpent went straight on, turning neither to the right nor left.

Meantime Mossy had got out of the lake of shadows and, following his mournful, lonely way, had reached the seashore. It was a dark, stormy evening. The sun had set. The wind was blowing from the sea.

The waves had surrounded the rock within which lay the Old Man's house. A deep water rolled between it and the shore, upon which a majestic figure was walking alone.

Mossy went up to him and said,—

"Will you tell me where to find the Old Man of the Sea?"

"I am the Old Man of the Sea," the figure answered.

"I see a strong kingly man of middle age," returned Mossy.

Then the Old Man looked at him more intently, and said,—

"Your sight, young man, is better than that of most who take this way. The night is stormy: come to my house and tell me what I can do for you."

Mossy followed him. The waves flew from before the footsteps of the Old Man of the Sea, and Mossy followed upon dry sand.

When they had reached the cave, they sat down and gazed at each other.

Now Mossy was an old man by this time. He looked much older than the Old Man of the Sea, and his feet were very weary.

After looking at him for a moment, the Old Man took him by the hand and led him into his inner cave. There he helped him to undress, and laid him in the bath. And he saw that one of his hands Mossy did not open.

"What have you got in that hand?" he asked.

Mossy opened his hand, and there lay the golden key.

"Ah!" said the Old Man, "that accounts for your knowing me. And I know the way you have to go."

"I want to find the country whence the shadows fall," said Mossy.

"I dare say you do. So do I. But meantime, one thing is certain.— what is that key for, do you think?"

"For a keyhole somewhere. But I don't know why I keep it. I never could find the keyhole. And I have lived a good while, I believe," said Mossy, sadly. "I'm not sure that I'm not old. I know my feet ache."

"Do they?" said the Old Man, as if he really meant to ask the question; and Mossy, who was still lying in the bath, watched his feet for a moment before he replied.

"No, they do not," he answered. "Perhaps I am not old either."

"Get up and look at yourself in the water."

He rose and looked at himself in the water, and there was not a grey hair on his head or a wrinkle on his skin.

"You have tasted of death now," said the Old Man. "Is it good?"

"It is good," said Mossy. "It is better than life."

"No," said the Old Man, "it is only more life.—Your feet will make no holes in the water now."

"What do you mean?"

"I will show you that presently."

They returned to the outer cave, and sat and talked together for a long time. At length the Old Man of the Sea rose, and said to Mossy,—

"Follow me."

He led him up the stair again, and opened another door. They stood on the level of the raging sea, looking towards the east. Across the waste of waters, against the bosom of a fierce black cloud, stood the foot of a rainbow, glowing in the dark.

"This indeed is my way," said Mossy, as soon as he saw the rainbow, and stepped out upon the sea. His feet made no holes in the water. He fought the wind, and climbed the waves, and went on towards the rainbow.

The storm died away. A lovely day and a lovelier night followed. A cool wind blew over the wide plain of the quiet ocean. And still Mossy journeyed eastward. But the rainbow had vanished with the storm.

Day after day he held on, and he thought he had no guide. He did not see how a shining fish under the waters directed his steps. He crossed the sea, and came to a great precipice of rock, up which he could discover but one path. Nor did this lead him farther than half-way up the rock, where it ended on a platform. Here he stood and pondered.—It could not be that the way stopped here, else what was the path for? It was a rough path, not very plain, yet certainly a path.—He examined the face of the rock. It was smooth as glass. But as his eyes kept roving hopelessly over it, something glittered, and he caught sight of a row of small sapphires. They bordered a little hole in the rock.

"The keyhole!" he cried.

He tried the key. It fitted. It turned. A great clang and clash, as of iron bolts on huge brazen caldrons, echoed thunderously within. He drew out the key. The rock in front of him began to fall. He retreated from it as far as the breadth of the platform would allow. A great slab fell at his feet. In front was still the solid rock, with this one slab fallen forward out of it. But the moment he stepped upon it, a second fell, just short of the edge of the first, making the next step of a stair, which thus kept dropping itself before him as he ascended into the heart of the precipice. It led him into a hall fit for such an approach—irregular and rude in formation, but floor, sides, pillars, and vaulted roof, all one mass of shining stones of every colour that light can show. In the centre stood seven columns, ranged from red to violet. And on the pedestal of one of them sat a woman, motionless, with her face bowed upon her knees. Seven years had she sat there waiting. She lifted her head as Mossy drew near. It was Tangle. Her hair had grown to her feet, and was rippled like the windless sea on broad sands. Her face was beautiful, like her grandmother's, and as still and peaceful as that of the Old Man of the Fire. Her form was tall and noble. Yet Mossy knew her at once.

"How beautiful you are, Tangle!" he said, in delight and astonishment.

"Am I?" she returned. "Oh, I have waited for you so long! But you, you are the Old Man of the Sea. No. You are like the Old Man of the Earth. No, no. You are like the oldest man of all. You are like them all. And yet you are my own old Mossy! How did you come here? What did you do after I lost you? Did you find the keyhole? Have you got the key still?"

She had a hundred questions to ask him, and he a hundred more to ask her. They told each other all their adventures, and were as happy as man and woman could be. For they were younger and better and stronger and wiser than they had ever been before.

It began to grow dark. And they wanted more than ever to reach the country whence the shadows fall. So they looked about them for a way out of the cave. The door by which Mossy entered had closed again, and there was half a mile of rock between them and the sea. Neither could Tangle find the opening in the floor by which the serpent had led her thither. They searched till it grew so dark that they could see nothing, and gave it up.

After a while, however, the cave began to glimmer again. The light came from the moon, but it did not look like moon light, for it gleamed through those seven pillars in the middle, and filled the place with all colours. And now Mossy saw that there was a pillar beside the red one, which he had not observed before. And it was of the same new colour that he had seen in the rainbow when he saw it first in the fairy forest. And on it he saw a sparkle of blue. It was the sapphires round the keyhole.

He took his key. It turned in the lock to the sounds of Aeolian music. A door opened upon slow hinges, and disclosed a winding stair within. The key vanished from his fingers. Tangle went up. Mossy followed. The door closed behind them. They climbed out of the earth; and, still climbing, rose above it. They were in the rainbow. Far abroad, over ocean and land, they could see through its transparent walls the earth beneath their feet. Stairs beside stairs wound up together, and beautiful beings of all ages climbed along with them.

They knew that they were going up to the country whence the shadows fall.

And by this time I think they must have got there.

Lucy Lane Clifford (1846–1929)

THE REPUTATION OF Lucy Lane Clifford is at last being restored and enhanced with the rediscovery of her stories for children. The 1984 edition of *The Oxford Companion to Children's Literature* has no entry on Clifford; it does include one for her collection *Anyhow Stories* (1882), stating that the tales "have elements of almost gratuitous horror." Yet just a few years later, Jack Zipes, writing in *Victorian Fairy Tales* (1987), referred to these same stories as "unusual tales with psychological sophistication." Their power continues to be appreciated. Singled out is "The New Mother," a frightening story of Victorian strictness and child abuse that raises questions concerning Lucy's own childhood, about which she would never speak. A later "Anyhow" story is "Wooden Tony" (from *The Last Touches,* 1892, a collection written for adults), about a lazy, introspective boy who wants to escape from this world and become like the puppets his father carves. Writing in *The Guardian* in 2002, Charlotte Moore demonstrated how close Tony's condition is to that of autism, a condition not to be identified for another sixty years.

Clifford, born Sophia Lucy Lane, married the noted mathematician and philosopher William Kingdon Clifford in 1875. The couple were devoted, but their happiness was soon cut short when Clifford died of consumption in 1879, at the age of thirty-three. Lucy was left to support herself and her young children on her own, although her friends rallied around her. She came to know many literary lights; she was already friends with George Eliot and would later become friends with Rudyard Kipling, Henry James, Somerset Maugham, and F. Anstey.

In a letter she wrote shortly after her husband's death, Clifford said: "Supposing there is after-consciousness . . . could it be possible for many forms of intellect and beauty to take refuge in one physical frame until they made up a perfect whole, worthy of standing alone; so that Willie represented the former consciousness of many and is

101

after all living still or carrying on in some other world what is just going on in this—the survival of the fittest."

The following story was written soon after that letter, and it is clear that the "Willie" of the story represents the author's own husband; it is both a love story and a tribute to how the imagination can liberate the soul. As such, this story is a paean to the fantastic.

The Story of Willie and Fancy

Lucy Lane Clifford

It always seemed to Willie as if other children knew so many more things than he did, as if they played at some game at which he was left out, as if they had some clue to life and its enjoyment which he had somehow missed. Perhaps it was only because he had never known any children of his own age. His father and mother were dead, and he lived with his grandparents in a little cottage at the top of the hill, just about a mile from the village. There were two other cottages adjoining his grandfather's but no one had lived in them since he could remember, and all three cottages were nearly tumbling down and yet never quite tumbled. The grandfather used to say it was a bad thing to live in a broken-to-bits cottage, but he never thought of leaving it. Willie was left to do just as he liked, for his grandparents were very old, and did not know how to amuse a little boy. His grandmother, to be sure, cut up her husband's old clothes for him, and made him a seedcake once a fortnight, but that was all. The cut-up clothes were very funny; the trousers were generally too short, and the jacket sleeves too long, and the pockets were never in the right place; but somehow they always seemed to go well with Willie's grave little face, and large blue eyes, and soft hair, that was brown in the shade and gold in the sun.

He was very lonely in the winter-time, for his grandmother was very old and nervous, and did not like his wandering about in the cold or when the snow was on the ground.

"You might fall and break your leg," she said; "and then what would you do? Wooden legs are dear to buy and awkward to walk with; besides boots are always bought in pairs, and one boot would be wasted if you had no foot to put it on, so it is real economy to stay at home and keep two legs, my dear!" And Willie looked up with his big blue eyes at his grandmother, and said—

"Yes, granny, dear; but the odd boots would do to throw at the sparrows in the cherry-tree."

"It would never do to throw new boots at them," his grandmother answered; "it would frighten the poor little sparrows, for they have been used to old ones so long."

And so all through the winter Willie seldom went far from the cottage; but he amused himself by getting over the fence into the next-door gardens, and then by the unbolted doors into the empty cottages. He was never tired of going through and through the deserted rooms. He looked in all the empty cupboards, and stood before all the rusty little fireplaces, trying to imagine what the people, who had dwelt there once, had been like; the people who had lived, and laughed, and worked, and wept, between the mouldy grimy walls; who had sat over the damp fireplaces, and kept their good things in the bare cupboards, and who had died or journeyed on to other places.

"Perhaps there were children," he thought once, "and perhaps they ran in and out, and sang, and danced, and gathered the fruit in the garden in the summer, and played at snowball in the winter. I would give the world to have seen them."

In the summer-time he was not nearly so lonely, for then he could go off for the whole day if he pleased, and wander about in the fields and woods, or over the brow of the hill to look at the long straight road beyond,—he never knew where that road led to,—and in the evening he went home past the blacksmith's shop. The blacksmith lived just half-way between the village and the cottage, and there was generally a little group of children round the door of the forge; and Willie used to stand too, and watch the sparks fly upwards, and listen to the sound of the blacksmith's hammer; but he always stood a little way off from the others, for they were strange to him, and he was shy. The blacksmith's little daughter was generally sitting by the door sewing; it seemed as if she stitched away at the same piece of blue-checked linen forever. She was evidently making something, but Willie often though it had had no beginning and would have no end, that forever the blacksmith would be hammering at his anvil, and forever his little daughter would be sitting by the door, stitching away at the same piece of coarse blue linen.

"Grandfather," Willie asked one day, "is it far to the rest of the world?"

"The rest of the world?" his grandfather said looking up; "why, what are you thinking of, lad?"

"I want to see it, that is all; is it far?"

"It depends what part you want to see, it's a long way from end to end of the world, if that is what you mean; and a vast deal lies between."

"Shall I ever see it all, grandfather?"

"No, I should say not. I have seen little enough myself, and I don't know how you are going to see more. By and by you'll have to learn, and when you have done learning you'll have to work, and when you have done working, and maybe before, you'll have to die. That's what life is for most of us, lad—one after another, one after another; little enough difference there is in the lives of us, take them all round."

"But some work in one way and some in another," the old man's wife said, looking up quickly; "and it's the business of some to travel far, and of some to stay at home."

"Tell me more, granny dear," the boy said eagerly. His grandmother thought about more things than his grandfather did, or at any rate talked about more, and Willie liked best to listen to her. "What does one do if one wants to travel?"

"Get ready—ready for what one means to do."

"Get what ready, dear granny?"

The old woman took her knitting, put on her glasses, and looking up into her little grandson's face, said quickly, "Oneself."

He waited a minute and then he asked, "What shall I be when I am a man, dear granny?"

"How can I tell, lad? you are only a boy yet. Bless me," she said suddenly, "but you are eight years old, and it is time you took to getting ready to be a man." Then she turned to her husband. "Tom, the boy is eight years old. We must write to the city and ask John what we shall do with him." The old woman's eldest son, who was a lawyer, lived in the city. He was a clever man, who had taught himself nearly all he knew and had made money, for people were glad to get his advice. "Yes, we must write John. He will tell us what to do with the lad. What would you like to be, Willie, some day when you are a man?"

Then Willie thought for a few minutes.

"Granny, dear, I should like to be something that should take me right to the end of the world; I want to see what there is there. And I should like to go to sea in a ship and to be wrecked; oh granny, I should like it so; and to escape in a little boat while the waves tossed and tossed all about, and we rode over them and over them ever so high."

The old woman laid down her knitting, and took off her spectacles and wiped them well, and put them on again. "Willie, my little lad," she said, "you have been reading books. Now, where did you get them?"

"It is only the book up on grandfather's shelf, grandmother. I looked at the picture, and then I thought I should like to be one of the people in the boat."

"Ah, well, people are safe enough once they are in a picture, but no one knows what they have had to go through before they got there. Don't let pictures unsettle your mind, lad, and set you hankering after dangerous things that do you no good till they are past and gone, and maybe have taken you with them."

"Oh, grandmother, but I am tired of seeing so little and being so little; I want to see more."

"Ah, it's wonderful the things one wants and never gets. It takes a long time to understand how little it is one ever gets of what one wants," the grandfather said. "One grows used to doing without at last and so content."

"More's the pity if one's young," the old woman answered; and then she turned to Willie again and said, "Learn to do without things, lad; but never to be content not to get them while you have hands to work, and feet to run, and a head to think. Try after all things, but not to keep them, for they are better worth winning for others than for oneself. Remember that, dear, as long as you live."

"But I don't know anyone to do things for, except you and grandfather," the boy said, puzzled. He often wondered how it was that his grandmother talked so strangely. After the first few minutes she sometimes said things that seemed to belong not to the old woman who lived in the cottage and knitted day in and day out, and who thought of nothing save the chickens and the cherry-tree and the making of cakes and clothes for Willie and the keeping of the cottage tidy, but to some past life, and to some world in which she lived no longer, and of whose ways some knowledge lingered unknown to her memory; it was almost as if some past self awoke, a self of which the present one was unconscious.

"I don't know anyone but you and grandfather to do things for, and even then I don't know how to do them, or how to begin, granny dear."

"You won't have far to look. There'll be a crowd waiting when you lift up your eyes, dear. One has never far to seek when one has a mind to help—learn how to do first, and the chance to do will be at your elbow."

"Ah, but, grandmother, I want to see so much, and first of all, I want to go right to the end of the world."

"Well, well," she said, and took up her knitting again, "we'll ask your uncle John. There's little that he cannot give one advice about. Your grandfather shall write soon enough. Go out and see that the chickens are gone to roost, and take a little run over the brow, and maybe you'll think less of the end of the world for tonight."

Then Willie went out and looked at the chickens. They fluttered their wings and flew past him as he entered the fowl-house, for they were just settling down to roost and did not want to be disturbed. He pulled-to the door of the fowl-house, and then he went out at the little wooden gate by the side of the cottage, and ran along the road that led over the hill. "If I could only run to the end of the world," he thought, "or to the great sea, and hear the waves. I don't want to do things," he went on. "I want to see them."

There was a little grassy bank at the side of the road; he sat down to think, and rested his face in his hand so long, wondering and wondering, that he did not notice the twilight gather closer and closer around him, or the mist rise up from the river and the fields, and wrap the trees in a soft gray cloak and hide all things before him. It was odd, but as he sat there, it seemed as if he could hear a soft voice singing the words that were running in his head—

"Right to the end of the world, my dear;
Right to the end of the world."

"It isn't a song," he said to himself. "It is only what I was saying to myself and yet I thought I heard someone else singing it." He looked up, but there was no one near. He saw the mist then. He felt it softly touching his face and hair. It made him think of the waves and the sailors. "If I could but see them just once," he cried.

"I will take you Willie; come with me," he heard a voice say; and looking up quickly, he saw that on the dewy green bank beside him a little girl was sitting. He looked at her face long and gravely. He could see it well in the dim light. It was very beautiful, and he had never seen it before; but yet he felt that he and she knew each other. He remembered her as one remembers some sweet dream, forgetting when one dreamt it. She had soft restless eyes that seemed to have a thousand things to say; her hair was like threads of gold and fell down to her waist, and her mouth was sweet, and her smile was bright. Oh, she was lovely, and never was any one half so sweet as Fancy when Willie first saw her.

"Dear Fancy," he said, for he knew her name quite well, "have you come to me?" Then she crept up closer to him.

"We will go so far together," she said softly. "Oh, Willie, you are not afraid, are you? The sea is creeping up to us. It has overtaken the river. It is sweeping over the meadows. Are you afraid?" she whispered. Then he held her tight and close, and her face was pale, and he saw no longer the gold upon her hair or the sweetness in her eyes, for the night had grown dark and the wind had risen and cried out shrilly from tree to tree, and slowly and surely the great sea was coming with many a leap and many a roar over the meadows and over the hill towards them. And yet he knew that somewhere, afar off in some still corner that fled back and back as the sea came on, the cottage was safe; the danger was only for him and for Fancy, and he was brave for both. And still the waves came madly on till suddenly they were at his feet, and then he ran, holding Fancy close, so that no harm should come to her.

"Perhaps we could ride on the waves," she whispered. "See, there is a great ship; the wind is driving it on. Oh, we are going already; hold my hand; hold fast, lest we be lost." But he could hear no more, for they were riding on and on, over and over the great waves, faster and faster than the ship, and nowhere was anything to be seen save the blackness and the sea and the sky and the great ship being driven on. Soon they overtook the ship. They saw the man at the wheel. They knew that he was not thinking of the storm and the waves, but of a little cottage high up upon a cliff, and of the sunshine falling down upon it, and of a woman shading her eyes with her hands and forever turning her face southwards and watching, while the children played among the flowers and asked, "When will he come home, dear mother? when will he come home?" On went Willie and Fancy, on and on. There was a little boat, tossing higher and higher while Death rode on in front, but, oh so slowly! Willie could have cried out with fear, for he knew the boat would overtake it, and he saw the wild eyes and the scared white faces of the wrecked as they with their last hope passed by. On went Willie and Fancy, on and on, till far above them shone one little star, and the water became suddenly smooth, and the waves rocked them as a mother rocks her child to sleep, and gently carried them home to the cottage-gate, and in a minute Fancy had waved her hand to him, and Willie had climbed the narrow stairs that led to the little room in which he slept.

He heard Fancy's voice long after she had left him. He heard it in his dreams that night. "We will go so far," she whispered. "We will see the end of the world together."

II

"WHERE shall we go?" Fancy asked; "where shall we go to-day? The sun is in the sky, the flowers are all in bloom, and the birds are singing. Where shall we go to-day?" She did not wait for an answer, but danced all down the wood, taking the strangest flights and singing the wildest songs, telling Willie a hundred things he had never heard before, teaching him to hear where till now he had heard no sound, and to see where formerly he had seen nothing. He never knew how they went, how high they climbed, or the names of the places he passed, or of the people he met, but none of them were strange to him, for Fancy knew them well, and made them all known to him.

"Dear Fancy," he said, "why did you not come before? I have been alone so long; till you came I had no companion."

"You did not call me," she cried. "You did not want me till the days when you went through and through the empty cottages thinking of all the people who once dwelt there; and then, though you said no word, I heard your voice calling me faintly, and I came a little nearer and a little nearer until at last I was sitting by you on the grassy bank."

"And when shall we go to the end of the world?" he asked. "Let it be soon, for I am always thinking of it."

"We will go to-night," she said, "this very night. I will tap at the window-pane when you have slept one single hour, and then you must wake up and open wide the window, and there on the window-ledge I will be waiting."

"How shall we get down?"

"We will climb down by the cherry-tree, and soon we will be far away."

"Is it very far?" he asked; "for what will grandmother say?"

"It is very far, but we shall soon be there"; and then Fancy skipped away.

He saw her at the end of the wood, the sun still shining on her hair, and he held out his hands and called, "Come back for a little while now, and sing me one song more, dear Fancy"; but she laughed a merry mocking laugh, and was gone.

"Where have you been, my little lad?" his grandmother asked, "and what have you been doing?"

"Oh, grandmother," he said, "I am so happy. I shall never be lonely more"; but his grandmother had no desire to listen.

"Ah, well, you will have to go to school soon and learn, and then you'll have less time on your hands," was all she said.

"Am I to go to school?" he asked.

"Your grandfather has written to uncle John about it. The blacksmith's little daughter is going to school, and she is younger than you. She is going to learn some day how to teach others. It is time you were thinking of your books too." And then the grandmother took up her knitting. "A great man is your uncle John," she said presently, "a very great man; and all his greatness is his own doing. We never thought he'd be the man he is." Then suddenly she said, "There's a large cake in the oven, dear lad; do you think you could go and turn it?"

So Willie went and turned the cake, and then sat down on the rug and looked at the great tabby cat fast asleep, and listened to the ticking of the clock, and thought how much he longed to see all the world before he did any work in it; and then he smelt the cake, and remembered how kind his grandmother was to him; yet here was he, who had never done anything in the world, grumbling and discontented because some day he would have to make a beginning. He got up and went back to his grandmother, and put his arms round her neck and his little face close to hers.

"Dear granny," he said, "I will be a great man some day if I can. I will try to be like uncle John. Perhaps Fancy will teach me."

"Fancy! Fancy will teach you nothing," she said. "Don't waste your time on Fancy"; and then she looked into the little lad's blue eyes and grave pale face. "It is by your own head and your own heart that you will be great, my dear, if you have the will to mind them."

III

"Willie, Willie," called Fancy, "are you ready? I am waiting"; and in a minute Willie sprang up and opened the window; he was dressed, and had been listening for her tap. He clambered on to the window-ledge, and then together they jumped into the cherry-tree and down to the garden beneath. He stopped for a moment and looked round—at the cottage, and his own little window wide open, and the fowl-house, and the empty cottages beyond, and at the cherry-tree above him, and at Fancy—Fancy with her golden hair and restless eyes and eager bright face beside him.

"Are we going to the end of the world?" he asked with a sigh, for he had longed so much for this strange journey.

"Yes, we are going," answered Fancy; "are you ready?"

"Yes, I am ready; but wait a minute," he said, and picked a rose. It fell to pieces as he held it, and the rose leaves fluttered to his feet. He looked down at it, and something like a sob was in his throat, though he did not know why. It is long years since that summer night, and he has travelled far, and seen much, and many things are known to him now, yet no memory of past days stays with him more faithfully or is sweeter than the memory of this one evening when he stood beneath the cherry-tree with Fancy by his side and the rose leaves at his feet, waiting to start for the end of the world, he and Fancy hand in hand together.

"Come," said Fancy, "come"; and looking into her eyes, and giving himself up to her guidance, they started. Slowly down the garden they went, over the fence at the bottom, then quickly across the field. They passed the blacksmith's cottage; there was a light in the window, for the blacksmith's wife was stitching at new clothes for her little daughter. On through the village they went; they heard the neighbours talking in the doorway, but they did not stay to listen. "We must run," said Fancy. "Hold my hand tighter"; and through the woods and along the roads and over the great high hills, faster and faster they ran; they saw the twinkling lights of the city, and in a minute they were there; they heard a mother weeping, for her little one had died; they heard some merrymakers singing till the voices grew faint in the distance. "Quicker, quicker," cried Fancy, "for we must journey faster than the wind and faster than time, and as yet we have not overtaken the middle of the night; the city is not sleeping yet: faster—faster—faster!" she cried, and on they went beyond the city and over the moors. They saw the mountains in the distance; the moon was slowly climbing them. On and on through the dense forest; on and on through the villages, and over the shining waters, past great cities, with their high buildings and their towers and their steeples; past the scattered houses around and beyond them—the houses that seemed as if they would have crept into the throng had their courage been great enough; past every habitation in which man could live, on and on, faster and faster went Willie and Fancy, till fewer and fewer became the landmarks, and farther and farther apart all things that the hand of man had placed, and taller and thicker were the trees, and vaster and vaster the great bare tracks of land, and then at last amid mighty stones that seemed hurled from some unseen height,— mountains and forest and sea and cities all far behind; then at last Willie and Fancy stood at the end of the world. Before them were only the clouds and the great moon shining, and the little stars that seemed like golden stairs leading up higher and higher; and beyond and above all towered two mountains in the midst of the stars and the clouds; the one bathed in golden light; the other dark and drear, wild and rugged with strange masses of blackness clinging to it.

"Come up higher, come up higher," he could hear Fancy calling. "The little stars shall be your steps; come up higher." And with his eyes still straining upwards, he went on climbing, up and up, treading on the stars till they were far beneath his feet and even the moon was behind, until at last he halted and saw the world afar off beneath him.

"Fancy," he cried, "Fancy, where are you?"

"I am here beside you," she whispered, for she was half afraid.

"There is a woman up there; tell me what she is doing?" Then Fancy looked up and laughed a wild strange laugh; it almost made Willie shudder, it seemed so out of place.

"She is there to rub up the world," laughed Fancy. "Oh, it takes a great deal of rubbing, so many people make it dull, so few make it bright; and there she sits for ever working away, but it is little enough she can do, so little that few besides the children find the bright places."

"What are the two hills over there? why is one dark and one so bright?"

"They are the sunshine and the storms. The one is made of laughter and gladness, of all the good that people do; the other of tears and sorrow and misery and vice; from the one the sunbeams and the warm sweet days of summer journey; from the other is hurled the storms, and from it steals the darkness. Every smile you cause, every good thing you do, makes the one hill taller, and is given back as sunshine into the world. Every tear you cause others to shed, every wrong you do, is heaped on to the dark hill there, and helps to make the sad days and stormy ones. Of joy and sorrow, of light and darkness, is the whole world made."

IV

"GET up," called the grandmother; "it is the first day of school; get up, lad and feed the chickens, and hurry away to the village."

"Oh, grandmother, but I like the woods so well," Willie answered.

"Uncle John says you are to learn, learn on until he comes in the spring, and then he will see what you are fit for." So Willie got up and fed the chickens, and took his books and went to school. He passed the blacksmith's shop, but the blacksmith's daughter was learning too, and no longer sat by the door of the forge. All down the road Fancy went by his side, singing to him in the fresh sweet morning; but he had no time to listen to her, he had to think of all he was going to do.

The first day and the first week and the first month went by, and every morning saw Willie going to the village; at first Fancy always went by his side, but he found that her songs came between him and his books, and he turned his head away and would not hear her, and would not see her, until at last she troubled him no more.

The days were not so sweet when she had ceased to sing him songs, and to take him breathless journeys, and tell him of the strange things that were or that might be between the earth and sky. He went on day after day trying to do his best, making his happiness in seeing his grandmother's face light up when he was first in his class, or in hearing his grandfather say, "Ah, he's a good lad; he'll be as great as his uncle John some day." At night, when he had learned his lessons, he went to sleep quickly lest Fancy should come and carry him off on some strange journey, and so unfit him for the next day's work. Yet how he sometimes thought of her, and longed for her, and dreamt for a little while of those days that would surely come, when he and she would once more be companions!

At last the winter came; and with it the holidays; and Willie, being older, was allowed to walk about as he pleased, and so he wandered through the leafless woods, and over the brow of the hill, and looked again and again at the long straight road, wondering to what strange city it might lead.

One day, when the snow was on the ground, he went in the woods, and sat down beneath a tree, to think a while. The few leaves that lingered were sere and yellow, but as he looked down the pathway he thought, as he shivered, that they would look like gold, if the sun would but shine through the trees. And as he thought this, suddenly he looked up, and there was Fancy. But, ah! how she was changed!

All the colour had gone from her face, her eyes were sad, her hair was dull.

"Fancy," he said, "is it you?" and his heart smote him for forgetting her.

"Yes, it is I," she answered, sadly and bitterly.

"But how you are changed!" he said. "The blue is gone from your eyes, and the gold from your hair. Oh, Fancy, you are not so bright as you used to be."

"How can I be?" she cried. "You will not hear me, you will not see me, you will not listen if I sing, or follow if I lead. How can I be the same?"

Then the tears came into Willie's eyes.

"Sing to me," he said; "sing one of your old sweet songs, dear Fancy, and let me wander with you again." Then Fancy tried to sing, but her voice was weak and faltering, and she broke down in the middle of her song and sobbed.

"Oh, I cannot," she cried, "for I am starved."

"And I am almost frozen," said Willie, his teeth chattering with cold. "But come closer, Fancy, and tell me what I can do to help you. Oh, my sweet Fancy," he cried, "how happy we have been together!"

"But you are frozen," she said; "what is the use of you? Is your heart cold too?"

"Oh no," he answered, "that is very warm; it always is."

"Let me creep in there," she whispered, "and make it my home; and I will grow bright again, and make the world bright for you; and I will tell you strange stories, and sing you sweet songs, which you shall hear in your sleep, and call dreams. Take me into your heart, dear Willie, and let me rest there."

"Fancy, oh Fancy," he cried, "there is no one so sweet as you, even now"; and he held out his arms, and she nestled down in them, and found her home at last. For many a day was she there; many a lonely hour did she beguile for Willie; many a song she sang to him, and many a tale she told him; and sometimes, when he had worked hard and yet could not accomplish what he wished, she would whisper some sound to him, that helped him, he hardly knew how, to do what before he had given up as hopeless.

But the months went on, and Willie had so much to do that, though Fancy still stayed in his heart, he had no time to listen her; and then sorrow came to him, for his grandfather died; and his heart was so full of grief there was no room in it for Fancy.

"I must work hard and learn all things, so that I may know how to comfort you, dear granny," he said; "and by and by we will live together in the cottage again."

But she answered, "Oh, no, dear lad, you will be great when you are a man, and the people will want you to go and live among them, to make their lives better."

And still Fancy stayed by his side, half hoping that one day he would turn from his work, and see her, and once again go journeying with her. She had grown small and thin, and sad and grave, and her steps were slow and soft, and she was afraid to whisper to him lest he should tell her that the time for play had passed and the time for work had come, and send her from him.

At last there came the day on which she left him. Willie had grown tall and strong, and had to choose what he would be when he should be a man; and then his uncle sat down and talked to him of all the things that he might do. When Willie had listened, he looked up and said, "Uncle John, I should like to be a lawyer." And when Fancy heard that sad word she fled away from him swiftly and forever.

She went back again to the cottage and the woods, and the fields where she and Willie had been so happy, and sadly roamed alone, until the blacksmith's little daughter, dreaming over her poetry books one day, went fast asleep, and Fancy, stealing up to her crept into her life and held fast to it forever.

Long afterwards, when the blacksmith's little daughter had become a woman, and was a teacher of others, and lived in a schoolhouse, Willie met her and wondered why it was he found some new beauty in her face. In her eyes there seemed to be some strange history that was half his own, and he thought that life with her would be sweeter than any life without her.

At last he fell to wondering if she would marry him, so that he might have her with him always; and when she said "Yes," and everything around seemed changed and brighter far than it had since he had wandered away from the cherry-tree, he never for a moment thought that the reason was just this—that the blacksmith's daughter had taken his Fancy.

Edith Nesbit (1858–1924)

EDITH NESBIT is best remembered for her children's books, especially *The Railway Children* (1906) but also *Five Children and It* (1902), *The Phoenix and the Carpet* (1904), and *The Story of the Amulet* (1906). Yet by then she had been writing for almost twenty years and her early works are considerably different.

Nesbit, who became Mrs. Hubert Bland with her marriage in 1880, was always a non-conformist. She became a socialist and, with her husband, founded the Fabian Society in 1884. This was a debating society that became one of the stimuli for the formation of the political Independent Labour Party in 1893. The Society attracted many free-thinkers and reformists, including William Morris. As a child, Nesbit had known Morris, who was friends with her elder sister, Mary. Morris's idealized view of the past would influence Edith, who used similar images in *The Story of the Amulet* and other children's books. Her first published book, however, *The Prophet's Mantle* (1885), written with her husband and published under the pen name Fabian Bland, was far removed from her children's books—it dealt with the growing threat of Russian anarchists in Britain.

When not organizing socialist meetings or assisting in editing the social newspaper *To-Day,* Nesbit wrote poetry, producing several books of verse before turning to short fiction after 1890. She produced stories for adults and children alike, including supernatural horror stories collected in *Grim Tales* and *Something Wrong* (both 1893). This dichotomy between stories for different age groups was most manifest in those that she contributed to *Atalanta,* a magazine aimed at young ladies. The following may read superficially like a fairy tale, but it has much deeper connotations. The same tragedy that befalls the couple would, eight years after its publication, haunt Edith and her husband. To my knowledge this story hasn't been reprinted since its first appearance; its publication might have been too much for her to bear.

117

The Poor Lovers

Edith Nesbit

There were once two poor lovers who loved each other very dearly.
They wanted to give each other a keepsake, but they were poor—
poor—poor,—so poor that they had nothing to give. One evening,
walking through the meadows when the grass was down and the
hedges were pink with wild roses, they talked of this and each wept
to think that neither could give a gift to the other; but as they were
kissing away each other's tears, a little fairy saw them. The fairy was
riding by on a sunbeam, and he was rather in a hurry, because of
course the sunbeam had to be home before dusk. However, the fairy
stopped a moment to see what was the matter. Then he whispered
in their ears, and the lovers looked into each other's eyes and smiled
through their tears, and said, "Yes; we will!"

So they were married. Having nothing else to give, they gave
themselves to each other and each one thought the gift the most
precious in the world.

And they went to London to seek their fortunes.

Their friends gave them a little money to start with, and when
they got to London they were so fortunate as to get work—the work
for which the public thought their talents fitted them.

He was a poet—but poetry is not marketable unless you are a
lord, or have a friend who is a critic of the *Daily News*. So he had
to write notices of other people's poetry, and to "interview" people
who had made money by oil and nitrates and money-lending and
other unpoetic methods. She painted beautifully, but pictures are not
marketable unless you take a room in Bond Street, and hang the walls
with sage-green satin, and give afternoon tea to possible purchasers.
So she had to paint birthday cards, and fans, and handkerchief boxes,
which is tiring work and badly paid. Thus they were still poor, but
they were foolishly happy, and thought the world a very beautiful
place indeed.

But when they had been in London about two years troubles began, worse than they had ever dreamed of. First they had a little dear baby, with a round, soft, dark head and bright eyes, and little pink hands and feet. This, of course, was not a trouble, but the greatest joy in the world, greater than any joy they had ever dreamed of. Their little shabby sitting-room was quite beautiful now the cradle was in it. He used to look up from his writing and see her sitting by the little window trying to make the baby notice the dusty London sparrows, and his eyes used to prick and smart with tears of joy that never fell.

But a day came, a cruel sunshiny day, when he and she had to kiss the little round head for the last time, to close the dear eyes, to cover up the little pink fingers and feet, to leave the baby alone in a strange garden, and go home to the empty cradle and the silent rooms.

He and she never spoke of the baby, and she never cried when he could see her because she loved him so. But when he was out "interviewing," or at night when he was asleep, she used to cry and cry and cry.

And it grew more and more difficult for her to paint, and at last she went to a doctor, who understood about people's eyes. And he told her very kindly and gently that she had painted too much and cried too much and that she would soon be quite blind, but she did not tell *him*.

That night he came home very tired and sad and sat down at her feet and put his head in her lap and said: "Wife, you'll have to keep us both, for I've lost my place as reporter, and they say my interviews are badly done, and so they are."

And she put her arms round his neck and leaned over him and said sweet foolish things to him till he forgot all his troubles and laughed and was glad. And she did not tell him her secret because she loved him so.

The next day came some money, two pounds, which she had earned.

"Dear sweetheart," she said to him, "I am ill. I can work no more. Let us with this two pounds go home again."

"But—" he began.

"I want to go home," she sobbed, leaning on his shoulder and rubbing her cheek against his, so that he felt her tears for the first time since he and she covered up the little brown head and the little pink hands and feet. "I want to go home, the noise tires me. I am ill.

You are ill. Everything is a mistake; let us go home. At least, we can
die there—"

"My love, my dear," he answered, "we will go home for a day. One
whole, long, happy day. Not to see any of the people—they have
forgotten us: but the church, where we were married, and the wood
where I used to kiss you."

"Yes," she answered, "that is what I wish."

"So next day they went very early, for it was a long journey, and
they walked together through the meadows, gray with hay, and by
hedges where the wild roses were pink and sweet.

There never was such a day. They forgot all their sorrows, and only
remembered each other, and the summer and the sunlight, and their
love. They wandered through the woods, and heard the thrushes and
nightingales, and they saw a squirrel and two rabbits.

By and by they strayed down to the sea, and saw the great jewel
blazing in the sun, and they sat down on the sand and held each
other's hands. They were so happy that they fell asleep.

While they lay there on the sand asleep they both dreamed a beautiful dream. That he was writing songs that made men's hearts beat
high, and their souls thrill to noble aims; that she was painting pictures
which mothers brought their children to see, and stood before with
tears and smiles, saying, "It is more beautiful than life."

The sun sank red behind the sea, and still they dreamed this dream, and
they dreamed further that they were always together, each always lover
and beloved, and that their little lost baby had come back to them.

Now, as they lay there asleep, the Queen of the Water-fairies came
by. She is the most potent enchantress in the world and can do almost
anything. But she can't make roses grow on a bramble, and she can't
put pretty dreams in the place of ugly ones. But where she finds
pretty dreams she can fix them. She came up out of the blue water
with her little babies laughing and leaping round her. It's the greatest
mistake to suppose that water-fairies have tails. Mermaids have, of
course; but that has nothing to do with the story.

Well, when the sea-fairy came to where the poor lovers were
sleeping, she stopped and looked at them. Her merry white babies
stopped too.

"Who are these?" they asked.

The Queen of the Sea-fairies (who knows everything) sighed and
said: "They are two poor lovers and when they wake they will be
very sad, because this is their last pretty day. The rest is all sadness."

The smallest, whitest sea-baby stooped to look closely at them. "Why are they sad?"

"They have lost their little dear baby; they are ill, and they are poor."

"What is poor."

"A kind of illness these land-creatures have."

"Can't you help them?" asked the children.

"Only in one way," the great queen answered.

"Oh, mother, darling, help them," cried all the little sea-babies, clinging round her. "Do, do, do help them, because they have no nice babies as you have."

The Sea Queen sighed and smiled and the two poor lovers also smiled and sighed, for their dreams were growing more and more beautiful. Yet through it all, some thread of their thoughts still clung to the bitter truth of life, and so they sighed.

"Help them, dear mother, do!"

"Hush!" the Sea Queen answered, and she raised her hand and beckoned.

The sea answered her. A great blue wave, rising like a wall of sapphire, swept up the beach and bore her and her children back into the depths of the sea. In its breast the great blue wave bore also the two poor lovers and their dream.

Lafcadio Hearn (1850–1904)

THE LIFE OF Lafcadio Hearn was never conventional—nor was his name. His first name was Patrick, but for his writing he always used Lafcadio, derived from the island of his birth, Lefkada, one of the Greek Ionian islands. His father, who was Irish, was stationed there as a surgeon in the British Army. Hearn's mother was a renowned Greek beauty, and Lafcadio appears to have inherited her restless spirit.

His childhood was unsettled. His father was reposted to the West Indies, but Lafcadio and his mother remained on Lefkada until he was two and then they travelled to the paternal home in Dublin. This sudden change from the bright, warm sunshine of Greece to the dull, rainy skies of Ireland clearly affected Lafcadio. He was forever on the move, traveling first to the United States in 1869 (to Cincinnati and then, in 1877, to New Orleans); then to the West Indies, in 1887; and finally, in 1890, to Japan, where he remained for the rest of his life.

Yet that childhood memory of eternal summer stayed with him and was expressed, most poignantly, in the story "The Dream of a Summer Day" (1894), in which he wrote, "I have memory of a place and a magical time in which the Sun and the Moon were larger and brighter than now. Whether it was of this life or of some life before, I cannot tell. But I know the sky was very much more blue, and nearer to the world."

It may be that Hearn's later fascination with the legend of the Fountain of Youth owes something to this desire to recapture a lost childhood. He used the idea in several stories, including "The Dream of a Summer Day" and the following tale, which dates from 1880 and may be his first use of the theme.

When Hearn settled in the United States, he became a newspaper reporter, rapidly establishing a reputation not only for his quick ability to write highly readable journalism, but for his way of describing the bizarre and the grotesque. His items, signed or unsigned, helped sell

123

the papers. When he moved to New Orleans he became the assistant editor and feature writer for the daily newspaper, the *Item*. Hearn did not just report on news stories, he happily invented stories as well. These "hoaxes" were a long-standing tradition in American newspapers and gave life to many "urban myths" of later years. The following story was one of these, though at its core it bears comparison with other stories set in the land of faerie.

The Fountain of Gold

Lafcadio Hearn

(This is the tale told in the last hours of a summer night to the old Spanish priest in the Hotel Dieu, by an aged wanderer from the Spanish Americas; and I write it almost as I heard it from the priest's lips.)

★

"I could not sleep. The strange odors of the flowers; the sense of romantic excitement which fills a vivid imagination in a new land; the sight of a new heaven illuminated by unfamiliar constellations, and a new world which seemed to me a very garden of Eden, perhaps all of these added to beget the spirit of unrest which consumed me as with a fever. I rose and went out under the stars. I heard the heavy breathing of the soldiers, whose steel corselets glimmered in the ghostly light; the occasional snorting of the horses; the regular tread of the sentries guarding the sleep of their comrades. An inexplicable longing came upon me to wander alone into the deep forest beyond, such a longing as in summer days in Seville had seized me when I heard the bearded soldiers tell of the enchantment of the New World. I did not dream of danger; for in those days I feared neither God nor devil, and the Commander held me the most desperate of that desperate band of men. I strode out beyond the lines; the grizzled sentry growled out a rough protest as I received his greeting in sullen silence; I cursed him and passed on.

"The deep sapphire of that marvelous southern night paled to pale amethyst; then the horizon brightened into yellow behind the crests of the palm trees; and at last the diamond-fires of the Southern Cross faded out. Far behind me I heard the Spanish bugles, ringing their call through the odorous air of that tropical morning, quaveringly sweet in the distance, faint as music from another world. Yet I did not dream of retracing my steps. As in a dream I wandered on under the same strange impulse, and the bugle-call again rang out,

125

but fainter than before. I do not know if it was the strange perfume
of the strange flowers, or the odors of the spice-bearing trees, or the
caressing warmth of the tropical air, or witchcraft; but a new sense
of feeling came to me. I would have given worlds to have been able
to weep: I felt the old fierceness die out of my heart; wild doves flew
down from the trees and perched upon my shoulders, and I laughed
to find myself caressing them, I whose hands were red with blood,
and whose heart was black with crime.

"And the day broadened and brightened into a paradise of emerald
and gold; birds no larger than bees, but painted with strange metallic fires of color, hummed about me; parrots chattered in the trees;
apes swung themselves with fantastic agility from branch to branch;
a million million blossoms of inexpressible beauty opened their silky
hearts to the sun; and the drowsy perfume of the dreamy woods
became more intoxicating. It seemed to me a land of witchcraft, such
as the Moors told us of in Spain, when they spoke of countries lying
near the rising of the sun. And it came to pass that I found myself
dreaming of the Fountain of Gold which Ponce de Leon sought.

"Then it seemed to me that the trees became loftier. The palms
looked older than the deluge, and their cacique-plumes seemed to
touch the azure of heaven. And suddenly I found myself within a
great clear space, ringed in by the primeval trees so lofty that all
within their circle was bathed in verdant shadow. The ground was
carpeted with moss and odorous herbs and flowers, so thickly growing that the foot made no sound upon their elastic leaves and petals;
and from the circle of the trees on every side the land sloped down
to a vast basin filled with sparkling water, and there was a lofty jet
in the midst of the basin, such as I had seen in the Moorish courts
of Granada. The water was deep and clear as the eyes of a woman
in her first hours of love; I saw gold-sprinkled sands far below, and
rainbow lights where the rain of the fountain made ripples. It seemed
strange to me that the jet leaped from nothing formed by the hand
of man; it was as though a mighty underflow forced it upward in a
gush above the bright level of the basin. I unbuckled my armor and
doffed my clothing, and plunged into the fountain with delight. It
was far deeper than I expected; the crystalline purity of the water had
deceived me; I could not even dive to the bottom. I swam over to
the fountain jet and found to my astonishment that while the waters
of the basin were cool as the flow of a mountain spring, the leaping
column of living crystal in its centre was warm as blood!

"I felt an inexpressible exhilaration from my strange bath; I gamboled in the water like a boy; I even cried aloud to the woods and the birds; and the parrots shouted back my cries from the heights of the palms. And, leaving the fountain, I felt no fatigue or hunger; but when I lay down a deep and leaden sleep came upon me, such a sleep as a child sleeps in the arms of its mother.

"When I awoke a woman was bending over me. She was wholly unclad, and with her perfect beauty, and the tropical tint of her skin, she looked like a statue of amber. Her flowing black hair was interwoven with white flowers; her eyes were very large, and dark and deep, and fringed with silky lashes. She wore no ornaments of gold, like the Indian girls I had seen, only the white flowers in her hair. I looked at her wonderingly as upon an angel; and with her tall and slender grace she seemed to me, indeed, of another world. For the first time in all that dark life of mine, I felt fear in the presence of a woman; but a fear not unmixed with pleasure. I spoke to her in Spanish; but she only opened her dark eyes more widely, and smiled. I made signs; she brought me fruits and clear water in a gourd; and as she bent over me again, I kissed her.

"Why should I tell of our love, Padre? Let me only say that those were the happiest years of my life. Earth and heaven seemed to have embraced in that strange land; it was Eden; it was paradise; never wearying love, eternal youth! No other mortal ever knew such happiness as I; yet none ever suffered so agonizing a loss. We lived upon fruits and the water of the Fountain; our bed was the moss and the flowers; the doves were our play-mates; the stars our lamps. Never storm or cloud; never rain or heat; only the tepid summer drowsy with sweet odors, the songs of birds and murmuring water; the waving palms, the jewel-breasted minstrels of the woods who chanted to us through the night. And we never left the little valley. My armor and my good rapier rusted away; my garments were soon worn out; but there we needed no raiment, it was all warmth and light and repose.

"'We shall never grow old here,' she whispered. But when I asked her if that was, indeed, the Fountain of Youth, she only smiled and placed her finger upon her lips. Neither could I ever learn her name. I could not acquire her tongue; yet she had learned mine with marvelous quickness. We never had a quarrel; I could never find heart to even frown upon her. She was all gentleness, playfulness, loveliness but what do you care, Padre, to hear all these things?

"Did I say our happiness was perfect? No: there was one strange cause of anxiety which regularly troubled me. Each night, while lying in her arms, I heard the Spanish bugle-call, far and faint and ghostly as a voice from the dead. It seemed like a melancholy voice calling to me. And whenever the sound floated to us, I felt that she trembled, and wound her arms faster about me, and she would weep until I kissed away her tears. And through all those years I heard the bugle-call. Did I say years? Nay, centuries, for in that land one never grows old; I heard it through centuries after all my companions were dead.

The priest crossed himself under the lamplight, and murmured a prayer. "Continue, *hijo mio,*" he said at last; "tell me all."

"It was anger, Padre; I wished to see for myself where the sounds came from that tortured my life. And I know not why she slept so deeply that night. As I bent over to kiss her, she moaned in her dreams, and I saw a crystal tear glimmer on the dark fringe of her eyes and then that cursed bugle-call."

The old man's voice failed a moment. He gave a feeble cough, spat blood, and went on:

"I have little time to tell you more, Padre. I never could find my way back again to the valley. I lost her forever. When I wandered out among men, they spoke another language that I could not speak; and the world was changed. When I met Spaniards at last, they spoke a tongue unlike what I heard in my youth. I did not dare to tell my story. They would have confined me with madmen. I speak the Spanish of other centuries; and the men of my own nation mock my quaint ways. Had I lived much in this new world of yours, I should have been regarded as mad, for my thoughts and ways are not of to-day; but I have spent my life among the swamps of the tropics, with the python and the cayman, in the heart of untrodden forests and by the shores of rivers that have no names, and the ruins of dead Indian cities, until my strength died and my hair became white in looking for her."

"My son," cried the old priest, "banish these evil thoughts. I have heard your story; and any, save a priest, would believe you mad. I believe all you have told me; the legends of the Church contain much that is equally strange. You have been a great sinner in your youth; and God has punished you by making your sins the very instrument of your punishment. Yet has He not preserved you through the centuries that you might repent? Banish all thoughts of the demon who still tempts you in the shape of a woman; repent and commend your soul to God, that I may absolve you."

"Repent!" said the dying man, fixing upon the priest's face his great black eyes, which flamed up again as with the fierce fires of his youth; "repent, father? I cannot repent! I love her! I love her! And if there be a life beyond death, I shall love her through all time and eternity: more than my own soul I love her! more than my hope of heaven! more than my fear of death and hell!"

The priest fell on his knees, and, covering his face, prayed fervently. When he lifted his eyes again, the soul had passed away unabsolved; but there was such a smile upon the dead face that the priest wondered, and, forgetting the Miserere upon his lips, involuntarily muttered: "He hath found Her at last." And the east brightened; and touched by the magic of the rising sun, the mists above the place of his rising formed themselves into a Fountain of Gold.

Richard Garnett (1835–1906)

WHEN LAFCADIO HEARN settled in Japan he soon established himself as a writer, retelling Japanese and other "Oriental" folk tales and creating a few of his own. The interest in Oriental tales may have faded slightly during the mid-eighteenth century, but improved political relations between Britain and Japan towards the end of the nineteenth century revived an interest. A Japanese village exhibition held in Knightsbridge, London, in 1885 caused a considerable stir and gave W. S. Gilbert the inspiration for *The Mikado* (1885). Hearn's books *Some Chinese Ghosts* (1887), *Out of the East* (1895), *In Ghostly Japan* (1899) and particularly *Kwaidan* (1904) were hugely popular in the United States as well as in Japan. In fact, Hearn became one of Japan's most popular writers and is still remembered there today.

Several British writers, including Richard Garnett, turned to the interest in the Orient. Ernest Bramah produced his Kai Lung stories, which, as we shall see, inspired Lord Dunsany to create his own fantasies. Perhaps one of the more surprising contributors was Richard Garnett, the Keeper of the Printed Books at the British Museum from 1890 through1899. His knowledge of books and literary subjects was prodigious: many regarded him as omniscient, as well, for he was reputed to remember the location of every book in the British Museum. Garnett was fluent in many languages, translating books from Greek, Italian, Spanish, and German, and was well acquainted with Asian manuscripts. His collection *The Twilight of the Gods* (1888; expanded in 1903) used legends and folktales from various countries as a basis for exploring and comparing moral and philosophical issues. They were often lighthearted, though shaped by a subtle and intelligent wit.

The Potion of Lao-Tsze

Richard Garnett

And there the body lay, age after age,
Mute, breathing, beating, warm, and undecaying,
Like one asleep in a green hermitage,
With gentle sleep about its eyelids playing,
And living in its dreams beyond the rage
Of death or life; while they were still arraying
In liveries ever new the rapid, blind,
And fleeting generations of mankind.

In the days of the Tang dynasty, China was long happy under the sceptre of a good Emperor, named Sin-Woo. He had overcome the enemies of the land, confirmed the friendship of its allies, augmented the wealth of the rich, and mitigated the wretchedness of the poor. But most especially was he admired and beloved for his persecution of the impious sect of Lao-tsze, which he had well nigh exterminated.

It was but natural that such an Emperor should congratulate himself upon his goodness and worth; yet, as no human bliss is perfect, sorrow could not fail to enter his mind.

"It is grievous to reflect," said he to his courtiers, "that if, as ye all affirm, there hath not been any Emperor of equal merit with myself before my time, neither will any such arise after me, my subjects must inevitably be sufferers by my death."

To which the courtiers unanimously responded, "O Emperor, live for ever!"

"Happy thought!" exclaimed the Emperor; "but wherewithal shall it be executed?"

The Prime Minister looked at the Chancellor, the Chancellor looked at the Treasurer, the Treasurer looked at the Chamberlain, the Chamberlain looked at the Principal Bonze, the Principal Bonze looked at the Second Bonze, who, to his great surprise, looked at him in return.

132

"When the turn comes to me," murmured the inferior function-ary, "I would say somewhat."

"Speak!" commanded the Emperor.

"O Uncle of the stars," said the Bonze, "there are those in your Majesty's dominions who possess the power of lengthening life, who have, in fact, discovered the Elixir of Immortality."

"Let them be immediately brought hither," commanded the Emperor.

"Unhappily," returned the Bonze, "these persons, without excep-tion, belong to the abominable sect of Lao-tsze, whose members your Majesty long ago commanded to cease from existence, with which august order they have for the most part complied. In my own diocese, where for some years after your Majesty's happy accession we were accustomed to impale twenty thousand annually, it is now difficult to find twenty, with the utmost diligence on the part of the executioners."

"It has of late sometimes appeared to me," said the Emperor, "that there may be more good in that sect than I have been led to believe by my counsellors."

"I have always thought," said the Prime Minister, "that they were rather misguided than wilfully wicked."

"They are a kind of harmless lunatics," said the Chancellor; "they should, I think, be made wards in Chancery."

"Their money does not appear different from other men's," said the Treasurer.

"I," said the Chamberlain, "have known an old woman who had known another old woman who belonged to this sect, and who assured her that she had been very good when she was a little girl."

"If," said the Emperor, "it appears that his Grace the Principal Bonze hath in any respect misled us, his property will necessarily be confiscated to the Imperial Treasury, and the Second Bonze will succeed to his office. It is needful, however, to ascertain before all things whether this sect does really possess the Elixir of Immortality, for on that the entire question of its deserts obviously depends. Our counsellor the Second Bonze having, next to myself, the greatest interest in the matter, I desire him to make due inquiries and report to us at the next council, when I shall be prepared to state what fine will be imposed upon him, should he not have succeeded."

That night all the members of the Lao-tsze sect inhabiting prisons under the jurisdiction of the Principal Bonze were decapitated, and the P. B. laid his own head upon his pillow with some approach to peace of mind, trusting that the knowledge of the Elixir of Immortality had perished with them.

The Second Bonze, having a different object to obtain, proceeded in a different manner. He sent for his captives, and discoursed to them touching the evil arts of unprincipled courtiers, and the facility with which they mislead even the best-intentioned princes. For years had he, the Second Bonze, pleaded the cause of toleration at court; and had at length succeeded in enlightening his Majesty to such an extent that there was every prospect of an edict of indulgence being shortly promulgated, provided always that the Elixir of Life was previously forthcoming.

The unfortunate heretics would have been only too thankful to prolong the Emperor's life indefinitely in consideration of securing peace for their own, but they could only inform the Bonze of the general tradition of their sect. This was that the knowledge of Lao-tsze's secret was confined to certain adepts, most of whom were plunged into so deep a trance that any communication with them was impossible. For the administration of the miraculous draught, it appeared, was attended with this inconvenience, that it threw the partaker into a deep sleep, lasting any time between ten years and eternity, according to the depth of his potation. During its continuance the ordinary operations of nature were suspended, and the patient awoke with precisely the same bodily constitution, old or young, as he had possessed on falling into his lethargy; and though still liable to wounds and accidents, he or she continued to enjoy undiminished health and vigour for a period equal to the duration of the trance, after which he sank back into the ranks of mortality, unless he could repeat the potion. All the adepts who had come to life under his present Majesty's most clement reign had immediately emigrated: the only persons, therefore, capable of giving information were now buried in slumber, and of course would speak only when they should awake. They were mostly concealed in the recesses of caverns, those inhabited by wild beasts being usually preferred for the sake of better security, as no tiger or bear would harm a follower of Lao-tsze. The witnesses, therefore, advised the Bonze to ascertain the residences of the most ferocious tigers in his diocese, and to wait upon them personally, in the hope of thus discovering what he sought.

This suggestion was exceedingly unpalatable to the Bonze, who felt almost equally unwilling to venture himself into a wild beast's den or to give any other person the chance of making the discovery. While he hesitated in unspeakable perplexity he was informed that an old man, about to expire at the age of an hundred and twenty years, desired to have speech with him. Thinking so venerable a personage likely to have at least a glimmering of the great secret, the Bonze hurried to his bedside.

"Our master, Lao-tsze," began the old man, "forbids us to leave this world without anything undisclosed which may contribute to the advantage of our fellow-creatures. Whether he deemed the knowledge of the cup of immortality conducive to this end I cannot say, but the question doth not arise, for I do not possess it. Hear my tale, nevertheless. Ninety years ago, being a hunter, it was my hap to fall into the jaws of an enormous tiger, who bore me off to his cavern. I there found myself in the presence of two ladies, one youthful and of surpassing loveliness, the other haggard and wrinkled. The younger lady expostulated with the tiger, and he forthwith released me. My gratitude won the women's confidence, and I learned that they were disciples of Lao-tsze who had repaired to the cavern to partake of the miraculous draught, which they were just about to do. They were, it appeared, mother and daughter, and I distinctly remember that the composition of the beverage was known to the daughter only. This impressed me, for I should naturally have expected the contrary. The tiger escorted me home. I forswore hunting, and became, and have secretly continued, a disciple of Lao-tsze. I will now indicate the position of the cavern to thee: whether the ladies will still be found in it is beyond my power to say."

And having pointed out the direction of the cavern, he expired.

The thing had to be done. The Bonze dressed himself up as much like a votary of Lao-tsze as possible, provided himself with a body-guard of *bona fide* disciples, and, accompanied by a small army of huntsmen and warriors as well, marched in quest of the den of the tiger. It was discovered about nightfall, and, having tethered a small boy near the entrance, that his screams when being devoured might give notice of the tiger's issue from or return to his habitation, the Bonze and his myrmidons took up a flank position and awaited the dawn. The distant howls of roaming beasts of prey entirely deprived the holy man of his rest, but nothing worse befell him, and when in the morning the small boy, instead of providing the tiger with a breakfast, was heard crying for his own, the besiegers mustered up courage to enter the cavern. The glare of their torches revealed no tiger: but, to the Bonze's inexpressible delight, two females lay on the floor of the cave, corresponding in all respects to the description of the old man. Their costume was that of the preceeding century. One was wrinkled and hoary; the inexpressible loveliness of the other, who might have seen seventeen or eighteen summers, extorted a universal cry of admiration, followed by a hush of enraptured silence. Warm, flexible, fresh in colour, breathing naturally as in slumber, the figures lay, the younger woman's arm underneath the elder woman's neck, and her chin nestling on the other's shoulder. The countenance of each seemed to indicate happy dreams.

"Can this indeed be but a trance?" simultaneously questioned several of the Bonze's followers.

"*Fiat experimentum in corpore vili!*"[1] exclaimed the Bonze; and he thrust his long hunting-spear into the elder woman's bosom. Blood poured forth freely, but there was no change in the expression of the countenance. No struggle announced dissolution; not until the body grew chill and the limbs stiff could they be sure the old woman was indeed dead.

"Carry the young woman like porcelain," ordered the priest, and like the most fragile porcelain the exquisite young beauty was borne from the cavern smiling in her trance and utterly unconscious, while the corpse of her aged companion was abandoned to the hyaenas. So often did the bearers pause to look on her beauty that it was found necessary to drape the countenance entirely, until reaching the closed sedan in which, vigilantly watched by the Bonze, she was transported to the Imperial palace.

And so she was brought to the Emperor, and he worshipped her. She was laid on a couch of cloth of gold in the Imperial apartments. Wonderful was the contrast between her youthful beauty, so still in its repose, and the old Emperor, fevered with the lust of beauty and love of life.

"O Majesty," said his wisest counsellor, "is there any sect in thy dominions that possesses the secret of perpetual youth?"

And the Emperor made proclamation, but no such sect could be found. And he mourned exceedingly, and caused strong perfumes to be burned around the sleeper, and conches to be blown and gongs beaten in her ears, hoping that she would awake ere he was dead or

---

[1]"Let an experiment be made on a worthless subject!"

wholly decrepit. But she stirred not. And he shut himself up with her and passed his time praying to Fo for her awakening.

But one day the door of the chamber was beaten down, and his old wife came in passionately upbraiding him.

"Sin-Woo," she cried, "thou hast not the heart of a man! Thou wouldest be deathless, leaving me to die! I shall be laid in the grave, and thou wilt reign with another! Wherefore have I been true to thee, if not that our ashes might mingle at the last? Thou hoary sensualist!"

"Su-Ti," said the Emperor, with feeling, "thou dost grievously misjudge me. I am no heartless sensualist, no butterfly sipper at the lips of beauty. Is not my soul entirely possessed by this divine creature, whom I love with an affection infinitely exceeding that which I have entertained for thee at any period? And knowest thou," added he, striving to soothe her, "that I will not give thee to drink of the miraculous potion?"

"And keep my grey hairs and wrinkles through all time! Nay, Sin-Woo, I am no fool like thee, and were I so, I am not in love with any youth. And know I not that even if I would accept the boon, thou wouldst never give it?"

And she rushed away in fury and hanged herself by her Imperial girdle. Whereupon all the other wives and concubines of the Emperor did likewise, as custom and reason prescribe. All the palace was filled with lamentation and funerals. But the Emperor lamented not, nor turned his gaze from the sleeper, nor did the sleeper waken.

And his son came to him angry with exceeding wrath.

"Thou hast murdered my mother. Thou wouldst rob me of the crown that is rightfully mine. I, born to be an Emperor, shall die a subject! Nay, but I will save thee from thyself. I will pierce thy leman with the sword, or burn her with fire."

And the Emperor, fearing he would do as he threatened, commanded him to be slain, as also his brothers and sisters. And he paid no heed to the affairs of State, but gave all into the hand of the Second, now the Principal Bonze. And the laws ceased to be observed, and rebellions broke out in the provinces, and enemies invaded the country, and there was famine in the land.

And now the Emperor was well nigh ten years nearer to the gates of death than when the Sleeping Beauty had been brought to his court. The love of beauty was nearly quenched in him, but the longing for life grew more intense. He became angry with the sleeper, that she awakened not, and with his little remaining strength smote her fiercely on the cheeks, but she gave no sign of reviving. Remembering that if he gained the potion of immortality he would himself be plunged into a trance, he made all preparations for the interregnum. He decreed that he was to be seated erect on his throne, with all his imperial insignia, and it was to be death to anyone who should presume to remove any of them. His slumbering figure was to preside at all councils, and to be consulted on every act of State, and all ministers and officers were to do homage daily. The revived Sleeping Beauty was to partake of the draught anew, at the same time and in the same manner as himself, that she might awake with him, and that he might find her charms unimpaired. All the ministers swore solemnly to observe these regulations; firmly purposing to burn the sleeper, if sleep he ever did, at the very first opportunity, and scatter his ashes to the winds. Then they would fight for the Empire among themselves; each, meanwhile, was mainly occupied in striving to gain the rebels over to his interest, insomuch that the people grew more miserable day by day.

And as the aged Emperor waxed more and more feeble, he began to see visions. Legions of little black imps surrounded him, crying, "We are thy sins, and would be punished—wouldst thou, by living for ever, deprive us of our due?" And fair female forms came veiled with drooping heads, and murmured, "We are thy virtues, and would be rewarded—wouldst thou cheat us?" And other figures came, dark but lovely, and whispered, "We are thy dead friends who have long waited for thee—wouldst thou take to thyself new friends, and forget us?" And others said, "We are thy memories—wilt thou live on till we are all withered in thy heart?" And others said, "We are thy strength and thy beauty, thy memory and thy wit—canst thou live, knowing thou wilt never see us more?" And at last came two warders, officers of the King of Death, and one of them was laughing. And the other asked why he laughed, and he replied:

"I laugh at the Emperor, who thinks to escape our master, not knowing that the moment of his decease was engraved with a pen of iron upon a rock of adamant a million, million years or ever this world was."

"And when comes it?" asked the other.

"In ten minutes," said the first.

When the Emperor heard this he was wild with terror, and tottered to the couch on which the Sleeping Beauty lay. "Oh, awake!"

he cried, "awake and save me ere it is too late!" And, oh wonder! the sleeper stirred, and opened her eyes.

If she had been so beautiful while sleeping, what was she when awake! But the love of life had overcome the love of beauty in the Emperor's bosom, and he saw not the eyes like stars, and the bloom as of peaches and lilies, nor the aspect grand and smiling as daybreak. He could only cry, "Give me the potion, lest I die, give me the potion!"

"That cannot I," she said. "The secret was known only to my daughter."

"Who is thy daughter?"

"The hoary woman, she who slept with me in the cavern."

"That aged crone thy daughter, daughter to thee so youthful and fresh?"

"Even so," she said. "I bore her at sixteen, and slumbered for seventy years. When I awoke she was withered and decrepit: I youthful as when I closed my eyes. But she had learned the secret, which I never knew."

"The Bonze shall be crucified!" yelled the Emperor.

"It is too late," said she; "he is torn in pieces already."

"By whom?"

"By the multitude that are now coming to treat thee in like manner."

And as she spoke the doors were burst open, and in rushed the people, headed by the most pious Bonze in the Empire (after the late Principal Bonze), who plunged a sword into the Emperor's breast, exclaiming:

"He who despises this life in comparison with another deserves to lose the life which he has." Words, saith the historian Li, which have been thought worthy to be inscribed in letters of gold in the Hall of Confucius.

And the people were crying, "Kill the sorceress!" But she looked upon them, and they cried, "Be our Empress!"

"Remember," said she, "that ye will have to bear with me for a hundred years!"

"Would," said they, "that it might be a hundred thousand!"

So she took the sceptre, and reigned gloriously. Among her good acts is enumerated her toleration of the followers of Lao-tsze. Since, however, they have ceased to be persecuted by man, it is observed that wild beasts have lost their respect for them, and devour them with no less appetite than the members of other sects and denominations.

John Kendrick Bangs (1862–1922)

THE USE OF humor in fantasy, especially through satire, was a feature used as far back as Francois Rabelais' *Gargantua and Pantagruel* (1532), and, of course, Jonathan Swift's *Gulliver's Travels* (1726). Fantastic humor took a giant leap forward in the Alice books by Lewis Carroll and the various nonsense rhymes by Edward Lear, and with growing sophistication it was incorporated in adult fiction by writers such as W. S. Gilbert, Mark Twain, Frank R. Stockton, and the next two authors in this anthology, John Kendrick Bangs and F. Anstey.

Bangs was a regular contributor to and assistant editor of *Life*, *Harper's Bazaar* and, later, full editor of *Harper's Weekly* and *Puck*. He was a noted humorist and parodist, starting with *New Waggings for Old Tales* (1888). He found fantasy and the supernatural an especially good field for his humor which he used to great effect in "The Water Ghost of Harrowby Hall" (1891), *Over the Plum Pudding* (1901), *Alice in Blunderland* (1907), and his best known books, *A House-Boat on the Styx* (1895) and its sequels, *The Pursuit of the House-Boat* (1897) and *The Enchanted Typewriter* (1899). In this final sequence he used characters from throughout history who are trapped in the after-life and consider the state of the world as it was in Bangs's day. Alas, humor can be a fickle thing, easily dated. Although he was highly popular in his day, few people read Bangs today except for his ghost stories. The best parts of the *House-Boat* sequence are those that don't rely on parody, but create a scene of general amusement. That is how the book begins, with Charon, the overworked boatman of the Styx, who ferries the souls of the dead to Hades. He is suddenly confronted by a newly established committee of souls and their great plans.

Charon Makes a Discovery

John Kendrick Bangs

Charon, the ferryman of renown, was cruising slowly along the Styx one pleasant Friday morning not long ago, and as he paddled idly on he chuckled mildly to himself as he thought of the monopoly in ferriage which in the course of years he had managed to build up.

"It's a great thing," he said, with a smirk of satisfaction—"it's a great thing to be the go-between between two states of being; to have the exclusive franchise to export and import shades from one state to the other, and withal to have had as clean a record as mine has been. Valuable as is my franchise, I never corrupted a public official in my life, and—"

Here Charon stopped his soliloquy and his boat simultaneously. As he rounded one of the many turns in the river a singular object met his gaze, and one, too, that filled him with misgiving. It was another craft, and that was a thing not to be tolerated. Had he, Charon, owned the exclusive right of way on the Styx all these years to have it disputed here in the closing decade of the Nineteenth Century? Had not he dealt satisfactorily with all, whether it was in the line of ferriage or in the providing of boats for pleasure-trips up the river? Had he not received expressions of satisfaction, indeed, from the most exclusive families of Hades with the very select series of picnics he had given at Charon's Glen Island? No wonder, then, that the queer-looking boat that met his gaze, moored in a shady nook on the dark side of the river, filled him with dismay.

"Blow me for a landlubber if I like that!" he said, in a hardly audible whisper. "And shiver my timbers if I don't find out what she's there for. If anybody thinks he can run an opposition line to mine on this river he's mightily mistaken. If it comes to competition, I can carry shades for nothing and still quaff the B. & G. yellow-label benzine three times a day without experiencing a financial panic. I'll show

142

'em a thing or two if they attempt to rival me. And what a boat! It looks for all the world like a Florentine barn on a canal-boat."

Charon paddled up to the side of the craft, and, standing up in the middle of his boat, cried out,

"Ship ahoy!"

There was no answer, and the Ferryman hailed her again. Receiving no response to his second call, he resolved to investigate for himself; so, fastening his own boat to the stern-post of the stranger, he clambered on board. If he was astonished as he sat in his ferry-boat, he was paralyzed when he cast his eye over the unwelcome vessel he had boarded. He stood for at least two minutes rooted to the spot. His eye swept over a long, broad deck, the polish of which resembled that of a ball-room floor. Amidships, running from three-quarters aft to three-quarters forward, stood a structure that in its lines resembled, as Charon had intimated, a barn, designed by an architect enamoured of Florentine simplicity; but in its construction the richest of woods had been used, and in its interior arrangement and adornment nothing more palatial could be conceived.

"What's the blooming thing for?" said Charon, more dismayed than ever. "If they start another line with a craft like this, I'm very much afraid I'm done for after all. I wouldn't take a boat like mine myself if there was a floating palace like this going the same way. I'll have to see the Commissioners about this, and find out what it all means. I suppose it'll cost me a pretty penny, too, confound them!"

A prey to these unhappy reflections, Charon investigated further, and the more he saw the less he liked it. He was about to encounter opposition, and an opposition which was apparently backed by persons of great wealth—perhaps the Commissioners themselves. It was a consoling thought that he had saved enough money in the course of his career to enable him to live in comfort all his days, but this was not really what Charon was after. He wished to acquire enough to retire and become one of the smart set. It had been done in that section of the universe which lay on the bright side of the Styx, why not, therefore, on the other, he asked.

"I'm pretty well connected even if I am a boatman," he had been known to say. "With Chaos for a grandfather, and Erebus and Nox for parents, I've just as good blood in my veins as anybody in Hades. The Noxes are a mighty fine family, not as bright as the Days, but older; and we're poor—that's it, poor—and it's money makes caste these days. If I had millions, and owned a railroad, they'd call me a yacht-owner. As I haven't, I'm only a boatman. Bah! Wait and see! I'll be giving swell functions myself some day, and these upstarts will be on their knees before me begging to be asked. Then I'll get up a little aristocracy of my own, and I won't let a soul into it whose name isn't mentioned in the Grecian mythologies. Mention in Burke's peerage and the Elite directories of America won't admit anybody to Commodore Charon's house unless there's some other mighty good reason for it."

Foreseeing an unhappy ending to all his hopes, the old man clambered sadly back into his ancient vessel and paddled off into the darkness. Some hours later, returning with a large company of new arrivals, while counting up the profits of the day Charon again caught sight of the new craft, and saw that it was brilliantly lighted and thronged with the most famous citizens of the Erebean country. Up in the bow was a spirit band discoursing music of the sweetest sort. Merry peals of laughter rang out over the dark waters of the Styx. The clink of glasses and the popping of corks punctuated the music with a frequency which would have delighted the soul of the most ardent lover of commas, all of which so overpowered the grand master boatman of the Stygian Ferry Company that he dropped three oboli and an American dime, which he carried as a pocket-piece, overboard. This, of course, added to his woe; but it was forgotten in an instant, for some one on the new boat had turned a search-light directly upon Charon himself, and simultaneously hailed the master of the ferry-boat.

"Charon!" cried the shade in charge of the light. "Charon, ahoy!"

"Ahoy yourself!" returned the old man, paddling his craft close up to the stranger. "What do you want?"

"You," said the shade. "The house committee want to see you right away."

"What for?" asked Charon, cautiously.

"I'm sure I don't know. I'm only a member of the club, and house committees never let mere members know anything about their plans. All I know is that you are wanted," said the other.

"Who are the house committee?" queried the Ferryman.

"Sir Walter Raleigh, Cassius, Demosthenes, Blackstone, Doctor Johnson, and Confucius," replied the shade.

"Tell 'em I'll be back in an hour," said Charon, pushing off. "I've got a cargo of shades on board consigned to various places up the river. I've promised to get 'em all through to-night, but I'll put on a couple of extra paddles—two of the new arrivals are working their passage this trip—and it won't take as long as usual. What boat is this, anyhow?"

"The *Nancy Nox,* of Erebus."

"Thunder!" cried Charon, as he pushed off and proceeded on his way up the river. "Named after my mother! Perhaps it'll come out all right yet."

More hopeful of mood, Charon, aided by the two dead-head passengers, soon got through with his evening's work, and in less than an hour was back seeking admittance, as requested, to the company of Sir Walter Raleigh and his fellow-members on the house committee. He was received by these worthies with considerable effusiveness, considering his position in society, and it warmed the cockles of his aged heart to note that Sir Walter, who had always been rather distant to him since he had carelessly upset that worthy and Queen Elizabeth in the middle of the Styx far back in the last century, permitted him to shake three fingers of his left hand when he entered the committee-room.

"How do you do, Charon?" said Sir Walter, affably. "We are very glad to see you."

"Thank you, kindly, Sir Walter," said the boatman. "I'm glad to hear those words, your honor, for I've been feeling very bad since I had the misfortune to drop your Excellency and her Majesty overboard. I never knew how it happened, sir, but happen it did, and but for her Majesty's kind assistance it might have been the worse for us. Eh, Sir Walter?"

The knight shook his head menacingly at Charon. Hitherto he had managed to keep it a secret that the Queen had rescued him from drowning upon that occasion by swimming ashore herself first and throwing Sir Walter her ruff as soon as she landed, which he had used as a life-preserver.

"'Sh!" he said, *sotto voce.* "Don't say anything about that, my man."

"Very well, Sir Walter, I won't," said the boatman; but he made a mental note of the knight's agitation, and perceived a means by which that illustrious courtier could be made useful to him in his scheming for social advancement.

"I understood you had something to say to me," said Charon, after he had greeted the others.

"We have," said Sir Walter. "We want you to assume command of this boat."

The old fellow's eyes lighted up with pleasure.

"You want a captain, eh?" he said.

"No," said Confucius, tapping the table with a diamond-studded chop-stick. "No. We want a—er—what the deuce is it they call the functionary, Cassius?"

"Senator, I think," said Cassius.

Demosthenes gave a loud laugh.

"Your mind is still running on Senatorships, my dear Cassius. That is quite evident," he said. "This is not one of them, however. The title we wish Charon to assume is neither Captain nor Senator; it is Janitor."

"What's that?" asked Charon, a little disappointed. "What does a Janitor have to do?"

"He has to look after things in the house," explained Sir Walter. "He's a sort of proprietor by proxy. We want you to take charge of the house, and see to it that the boat is kept shipshape."

"Where is the house?" queried the astonished boatman.

"This is it," said Sir Walter. "This is the house, and the boat too. In fact, it is a house-boat."

"Then it isn't a new-fangled scheme to drive me out of business?" said Charon, warily.

"Not at all," returned Sir Walter. "It's a new-fangled scheme to set you up in business. We'll pay you a large salary, and there won't be much to do. You are the best man for the place, because, while you don't know much about houses, you do know a great deal about boats, and the boat part is the most important part of a house-boat. If the boat sinks, you can't save the house; but if the house burns, you may be able to save the boat. See?"

"I think I do, sir," said Charon.

"Another reason why we want to employ you for Janitor," said Confucius, "is that our club wants to be in direct communication with both sides of the Styx; and we think you as Janitor would be able to make better arrangements for transportation with yourself as boatman, than some other man as Janitor could make with you."

"Spoken like a sage," said Demosthenes.

"Furthermore," said Cassius, "occasionally we shall want to have this boat towed up or down the river, according to the house committee's pleasure, and we think it would be well to have a Janitor who has some influence with the towing company which you represent."

"Can't this boat be moved without towing?" asked Charon.

"No," said Cassius.

"And I'm the only man who can tow it, eh?"

"You are," said Blackstone. "Worse luck."

"And you want me to be Janitor on a salary of what?"

"A hundred oboli a month," said Sir Walter, uneasily.

"Very well, gentlemen," said Charon. "I'll accept the office on a salary of two hundred oboli a month, with Saturdays off."

The committee went into executive session for five minutes, and on their return informed Charon that in behalf of the Associated Shades they accepted his offer.

"In behalf of what?" the old man asked.

"The Associated Shades," said Sir Walter. "The swellest organization in Hades, whose new house-boat you are now on board of. When shall you be ready to begin work?"

"Right away," said Charon, noting by the clock that it was the hour of midnight. "I'll start in right away, and as it is now Saturday morning, I'll begin by taking my day off."

F. Anstey (1856–1934)

THOMAS ANSTEY GUTHRIE, a regular contributor to *Punch,* was probably, more than any other writer of his period, the most successful at creating comic fantasy novels and stories. Some of his work, most notably *Vice Versa* (1885), where a young man and his father exchange identities, is still remembered today.

When Guthrie decided to use a pseudonym he chose "T. Anstey," but because he wrote the "T" in cursive on his manuscript, it was mistaken for an "F," and his name was printed as "F. Anstey." This proved singularly appropriate, as the name could easily be read as "Fantasy," and one might argue that Anstey's popularity actually created the modern genre of fantasy, or at least comic fantasy. When an omnibus volume of his works was published in 1931, it was called, rather aptly, *Humour and Fantasy.*

Anstey's best known works include *The Tinted Venus* (1885), in which a magic ring brings a statue to life; *The Brass Bottle* (1900), in which an overly zealous genie grants an increasingly embarrassing series of wishes; and "The Talking Horse" (1891)—the forerunner of Mr. Ed—in which a loquacious horse becomes a nuisance. His best work still stands up today, mostly because of his wry observations on unchanging human nature. The following story, which lampoons the traditional fairy tale, pokes fun at the legal profession.

The Adventure of the Snowing Globe

F. Anstey

Before beginning to relate an experience which, I am fully aware, will seem to many so singular as to be almost, if not quite, incredible, it is perhaps as well to state that I am a solicitor of several years' standing, and that I do not regard myself—nor, to the best of my knowledge and belief, have I ever been regarded—as a person in whom the imaginative faculty is at all unduly prominent.

It was in Christmas week of last year. I was walking home from my office in New Square, Lincoln's Inn, as my habit is—except on occasions when the state of the weather renders such open-air exercise too imprudent—and on my way I went into a toy-shop, with a view to purchasing some seasonable present for a small godchild of mine.

As was only to be expected at that time of year, the shop was crowded with customers, and I had to wait until one of the assistants should be at liberty. While waiting, my attention was attracted to a toy on the counter before me.

It was a glass globe, about the size of a moderately large orange. Inside it was a representation of what appeared to be the façade of a castle, before which stood a figure holding by a thread a small pear-shaped air-ball striped red and blue. The globe was full of water containing a white sediment in solution, which, when agitated, produced the effect of a miniature snowstorm.

I cannot account for such a childish proceeding, except by the circumstance that I had nothing better to occupy me at the moment, but I employed myself in shaking the globe and watching the tiny snowflakes circulating in the fluid, till I became so engrossed as to be altogether oblivious of my surroundings. So that I was not particularly surprised when I found, as I presently did, that the flakes were falling and melting on my coat-sleeve. Before me was a heavy gateway belonging to a grim, castellated edifice, which I thought at first must be Holloway Gaol, though how I could have wandered so far out of my way was more than I could understand.

But on looking round I saw no signs of any suburban residences, and recognised that I had somehow strayed into a locality with which I was totally unacquainted, but which was evidently considerably beyond the Metropolitan radius. It seemed to me that my best plan would be to knock at the gate and ask the lodge-keeper where I was and my way to the nearest railway-station; but before I could carry out my intention a wicket in one of the gates was cautiously opened by a person of ancient and venerable appearance. He did not look like an ordinary porter, but was in a peculiar livery, which I took to be a seneschal's—not that I have ever seen a seneschal, but that was my impression of him. Whoever he was, he appeared distinctly pleased to see me. "You are right welcome, fair sir!" he said, in a high, cracked voice. "Well knew I that my hapless lady would not lack a protector in her sad plight, though she had well-nigh abandoned all hope of your coming!"

I explained that I had not called by appointment, but was simply a stranger who found himself in the neighbourhood by the merest chance.

" 'Tis no matter," he replied, in his old-fashioned diction, "seeing that you have come, for truly, sir, she is in sore need of any one who is ready to undertake her cause!"

I said that I happened to be a member of the legal profession, and that if, as I gathered, his mistress was in any difficulty in which she desired my assistance, I was quite prepared to advise her to the best of my ability, and to act for her, should her case be one which, in my opinion, required it.

"That does it, indeed!" he said; "but I pray you stand no longer parleying without, which, since I perceive you are but ill-protected at present," he added fussily, "may be fraught with unnecessary danger. Come within without further delay!"

I did not think there was any real risk of catching cold, but I did wonder why it had not occurred to me to put up my umbrella, until I discovered that my right hand was already engaged in holding a cord to which was attached a gaudily-coloured balloon that floated above my head.

This was so unsuitable an appendage to any solicitor, especially to one about to offer his services in an affair which was apparently serious, that I was somewhat disconcerted for the moment. But I soon recollected having gone into a toy-shop some time previously, and concluded that I must have purchased this air-ball as a present for my godchild.

I was about to explain this to the old man, when he pulled me suddenly through the wicket-gate, shutting the door so sharply that it snapped the string of the balloon. I saw it soaring up on the other side of the wall till a whirl of snow hid it from my sight.

"Trouble not for its loss," said the seneschal; "it has fulfilled its purpose in bringing you to our gates."

If he really supposed that anybody was at all likely to adopt so eccentric a means of conveyance, he must, I thought, be in his dotage, and I began to have a misgiving that, by accepting his invitation to step in, I might have placed myself in a false position.

However, I had gone too far to retract now, so I allowed him to conduct me to his mistress. He took me across a vast courtyard to a side entrance, and then up a winding stair, along deserted corridors, and through empty ante-chambers, until we came into a great hall, poorly lighted from above, and hung with dim tapestries. There he left me, saying that he would inform his mistress of my arrival.

I had not long to wait before she entered by an opposite archway.

I regret my inability—owing partly to the indifferent manner in which the apartment was lit—to describe her with anything like precision. She was quite young—not much, I should be inclined to say, over eighteen; she was richly but fantastically dressed in some shimmering kind of robe, and her long hair was let down and flowing loose about her shoulders, which (although I am bound to say that the effect, in her case, was not unbecoming) always has, to my mind at least, a certain air of untidiness in a grown-up person, and almost made me doubt for a moment whether she was quite in her right senses.

But, while she was evidently in a highly emotional state, I could detect nothing in her manner or speech that indicated any actual mental aberration. Her personal appearance, too, was distinctly pleasing, and altogether I cannot remember ever to have felt so interested at first sight in any female client.

"Tell me," she cried, "is it really true? Have you indeed come to my deliverance?"

"My dear young lady," I said, perceiving that any apology for what I had feared must seem a highly irregular intrusion was unnecessary,

"I have been given to understand that you have some occasion for my services, and if that is correct I can only say that they are entirely at your disposal. Just try to compose yourself and tell me, as clearly and concisely as you can, the material facts of your case."

"Alas! sir," she said, wringing her hands, which I remember noticing were of quite remarkable beauty, "I am the unhappiest Princess in the whole world."

I trust I am as free from snobbishness as most people, but I admit to feeling some gratification in the fact that I was honoured by the confidence of a lady of so exalted a rank.

"I am extremely sorry to hear it, ma'am," I said, recollecting that that was the proper way to address a Princess. "But I am afraid," I added, as I prepared to take her instructions, "that I can be but of little assistance to you unless you can bring yourself to furnish me with somewhat fuller particulars."

"Surely," she said, "you cannot be ignorant that I am in the power of a wicked and tyrannous uncle?"

I might have explained that I was far too busy a man to have leisure to keep up with the latest Court scandals, but I refrained.

"I may take it, then," I said, "that you are an orphan, and that the relative you refer to is your sole guardian?"

She implied by a gesture that both these inferences were correct. "He has shut me up a close prisoner in this gloomy place," she declared, "and deprived me of all my attendants one by one, save the aged but faithful retainer whom you have beheld."

I replied, of course, that this was an unwarrantable abuse of his authority, and inquired whether she could assign any motive for such a proceeding on his part.

"He is determined that I shall marry his son," she explained, "whom I detest with an unutterable loathing!"

"Possibly," I ventured to hint, "there is someone else who—"

"There is none," she said, "since I have never been permitted to look upon any other suitor, and here I am held in durance until I consent to this hated union—and I will die sooner! But you will save me from so terrible a fate! For what else are you here?"

"I should be incompetent indeed, ma'am," I assured her, "if I could not see a way out of what is really a very ordinary predicament. By attempting to force you into a marriage against your will your guardian has obviously shown himself a totally unfit person to have you in his custody. You have the law entirely on your side."

"Unfit is he, truly!" she agreed. "But I care not who else is on my side, so long as you will be my champion. Only, how will you achieve my rescue?"

"Under all the circumstances," I told her, "I think our best course would be to apply for a *habeas corpus*. You will then be brought up to the Courts of Justice, and the judge could make any order he thought advisable. In all probability he would remove your uncle from his position and have you made a ward of court."

There is always a difficulty in getting ladies to understand even the simplest details of legal procedure, and my Princess was no exception to the rule. She did not seem in the least to realise the power which every court possesses of enforcing its own decrees.

"Sir, you forget," she said, "that my uncle, who has great renown in these parts as a sorcerer and magician, will assuredly laugh any such order to scorn."

"In that case, ma'am," said I, "he will render himself liable for contempt of court. Besides, should his local reputation answer your description, we have another hold on him. If we can only prove that he has been using any subtle craft, means, or device to impose on any of his Majesty's subjects, he could be prosecuted under the Vagrancy Act of 1824 as a rogue and a vagabond. He might get as much as six months for it!"

"Ah, sir," she cried—rather peevishly, I thought—"we do but waste precious time in idle talk such as this, of which I comprehend scarce a word! And the hour is nigh when I must meet my uncle face to face, and should I still refuse to obey his will, his wrath will be dire indeed!"

"All you have to do is to refer him to *me*," I said. "I think I shall be able, in the course of a personal interview, to bring him to take a more reasonable view of his position. If you are expecting him shortly, perhaps I had better remain here till he arrives?"

"Happily for us both," she replied, "he is still many leagues distant from here! Can you not see that, if my rescue is to be accomplished at all, it must be ere his return, or else am I all undone? Is it possible that, after coming thus far, you can tarry here doing naught?"

I took a little time for reflection before answering. "After careful consideration," I said at last, "I have come to the conclusion that, as you are evidently under grave apprehension of some personal vio-lence from your uncle in the event of his finding you on the premises, I should be fully justified in dispensing with the usual formalities and removing you from his custody at once. At all events, I will take that responsibility on myself—whatever risk I may incur."

"I crave your pardon for my seeming petulance," she said, with a pretty humility. "I should have known right well that I might safely rely on the protection of so gallant and fearless a knight!"

"You will understand, I am sure, ma'am," I said, "that I cannot, as a bachelor, offer you shelter under my own roof. What I propose (subject, of course, to your approval) is that I should place you under the care of an old aunt of mine at Croydon until some other arrangement can be made. I presume it will not take you long to make your preparations for the journey?"

"What need of preparation?" she cried. "Let us delay no longer, but fly this instant!"

"I should recommend you to take at least a dressing-bag," I said; "you will have time to pack all you may require while your retainer is fetching us a fly. Then I know of nothing to hinder us from leaving at once."

"Nothing?" she exclaimed. "Do you dread a dragon so little, then, that you can speak thus lightly?"

I could not help smiling; it was so surprising to find a Princess of her age who still retained a belief in fairy tales. "I think, ma'am," I said, "that at this time of day a dragon is not an obstacle which we need take into serious consideration. You have evidently not been informed that such a monster has long since ceased to exist. In other words, it is undoubtedly extinct."

"And you have slain it!" she cried, and her eyes blazed with admiration. "I might have guessed as much! It is slain—and now even my uncle has no longer power to detain me here! For many a long month I have not dared to look from out my casements, but now I may behold the light of day once more without shrinking!" She drew back some hangings as she spoke, disclosing a large oriel window, and the next moment she cowered away with a cry of abject terror.

"Why have you deceived me?" she demanded, with indignant reproach. "It is not extinct. It is still there. Look for yourself!"

I did look; the window commanded the rear of the castle, which I had not hitherto seen, and now I saw something else so utterly unexpected that I could hardly trust the evidence of my own eyesight.

Towering above the battlemented outer wall I saw a huge horny head, poised upon a long and flexible neck, and oscillating slowly from side to side with a sinister vigilance. Although the rest of the brute was hidden by the wall, I saw quite enough to convince me that it could not well be anything else than a dragon—and a formidable one at that. I thought I understood now why the seneschal had been so anxious to get me inside, though I wished he had been rather more explicit.

I stood there staring at it—but I made no remark. To tell the truth, I did not feel equal to one just then.

The Princess spoke first. "You seem astonished, sir," she said "yet you can hardly have been in ignorance that my uncle has set this ferocious monster to guard these walls, and devour me should I strive to make my escape."

"I can only say, ma'am," I replied, "that this is the first intimation I have had of the fact."

"Still, you are wise and strong," she said. "You will surely devise some means whereby to rid me of this baleful thing!"

"If you will permit me to draw the curtain again," I said, "I will endeavour to think of something. . . . Am I right in assuming that the brute is the property of your uncle?"

She replied that that was so.

"Then I think I see a way," I said. "Your uncle could be summoned for allowing such a dangerous animal to be at large, since it is clearly not under proper control. And if an application were made to a magistrate, under the Act of 1871, he might be ordered to destroy it at once."

"You little know my uncle," she said, with a touch of scorn, "if you deem that he would destroy his sole remaining dragon at the bidding of any person whatever!"

"He will incur a penalty of twenty shillings a day till he does," I replied. "In any case, I can promise you that, if I can only manage to get out of this place, you shall not be exposed to this annoyance very much longer."

"You will?" she cried. "Are you quite sure that you will succeed?"

"Practically I am," I said. "I shall apply—always supposing I can get home safely—the first thing to-morrow morning, and, if I can only convince the Bench that the terms of the Act are wide enough to include not only dogs, but any other unmanageable quadrupeds, why, the thing is as good as done!"

"Tomorrow! tomorrow!" she repeated impatiently. "Must I tell you once more that this is no time to delay? Indeed, sir, if I am to be rescued at all, your hand alone can deliver me from this loathly worm!"

I confess I considered she was taking an altogether extravagant view of the relations between solicitor and client.

"If," I said, "it could be described with any accuracy as a worm, I should not feel the slightest hesitation about attacking it."

"Then you will?" she said, entirely missing my point, as usual. "Tell me you will—for *my* sake!"

She looked so engaging whilst making this appeal that 1 really had not the heart to pain her by a direct refusal.

"There is nothing," I said, "that is, nothing in reason, that I would not do cheerfully for your sake. But if you will only reflect, you will see at once that, in a tall hat and overcoat, and with absolutely no weapon but an umbrella, I should not stand the ghost of a chance against a dragon. I should be too hopelessly overmatched."

"You say truth," she replied, much to my satisfaction. "I could not desire any champion of mine to engage in so unequal a contest. So have no uneasiness on that score."

On this she clapped her hands as a summons to the seneschal, who appeared so promptly that I fancy he could not have been very far from the keyhole. "This gallant gentleman," she explained to him, "has undertaken to go forth and encounter the dragon without our walls, provided that he is fitly furnished for so deadly a fray."

I tried to protest that she had placed a construction on my remarks which they were not intended to bear—but the old man was so voluble in thanks and blessings that I could not get in a single word.

"You will conduct him to the armoury," the Princess continued, "and see him arrayed in harness meet for so knightly an endeavour. Sir," she added to me, "words fail me at such an hour as this. I cannot even thank you as I would. But I know you will do your utmost on my behalf. Should you fall—"

She broke off here, being evidently unable to complete her sentence, but that was unnecessary. I knew what would happen if I fell.

"But fall you will not," she resumed. "Something tells me that you will return to me victorious; and then—and then—should you demand any guerdon of me—yea" (and here she blushed divinely) "even to this hand of mine, it shall not be denied you."

Never in the whole course of my professional career had I been placed in a position of greater difficulty. My common sense told me that it was perfectly preposterous on her part to expect such services as these from one who was merely acting as her legal adviser. Even if I performed them successfully—which was, to say the least of it, doubtful—my practice would probably be injuriously affected should my connection with such an affair become known. As for the special fee she had so generously suggested, that, of course, was out of the question. At my time of life marriage with a flighty young woman of eighteen—and a Princess into the bargain—would be rather too hazardous an experiment.

And yet, whether it is that, middle-aged bachelor as I am, I have still a strain of unsuspected romance and chivalry in my nature, or for some other cause that I cannot explain, somehow I found myself kissing the little hand she extended to me, and going forth without another word to make as good a fight of it as I could for her against such an infernal beast as a dragon. I cannot say that I felt cheerful over it, but, anyhow, I went.

I followed the seneschal, who led me down by a different staircase from that I had come up, and through an enormous vaulted kitchen, untenanted by all but black-beetles, which were swarming. Merely for the sake of conversation, I made some remark on their numbers and pertinacity, and inquired why no steps had apparently been taken to abate so obvious a nuisance. "Alas! noble sir," he replied, as he sadly shook his old white head, "'twas the scullions' office to clear the place of these pests, and the last minion has long since vanished from our halls!"

I felt inclined to ask him where they had vanished to—but I did not. I thought the answer might prove discouraging. Even as it was, I would have given something for a whisky-and-soda just then—but he did not offer it, and I did not like to suggest it for fear of being misunderstood. And presently we entered the armoury.

Only a limited number of suits were hanging on the walls, and all of them were in a deplorably rusty and decayed condition, but the seneschal took them down one by one, and made fumbling attempts to buckle and hook me into them. Most unfortunately, not a single suit proved what I should call workmanlike, for I defy any man to fight a dragon in armour which is too tight even to move about in with any approach to comfort.

"I'm afraid it's no use," I told the seneschal, as I reluctantly resumed my ordinary garments.

"You can see for yourself that there's nothing here that comes near my size!"

"But you cannot engage in combat with the dragon in your present habiliments!" he remonstrated. "That were stark madness!"

I was glad that the old man had sufficient sense to see *that.* "I am quite of your opinion," I replied; "and believe me, my good old friend, nothing is farther from my thoughts. My idea is that if—I do not ask you to expose yourself to any unnecessary risk—but if you *could* contrive to divert the dragon's attention by a demonstration of some sort on one side of the castle, I might manage to slip quietly out of some door on the other."

"Are you but a caitiff, then, after all," he exclaimed, "that you can abandon so lovely a lady to certain doom?"

"There is no occasion for addressing me in offensive terms," I replied. "I have no intention whatever of abandoning your mistress. You will be good enough to inform her that I shall return to-morrow without fail with a weapon that will settle this dragon's business more effectually than any of your obsolete lances and battle-axes!"

For I had already decided on this as the only course that was now open to me. I had a friend who spent most of the year abroad in the pursuit of big game, but who chanced by good luck to be in town just then. He would, I knew, willingly lend me an express rifle and some expansive bullets, and, as an ex-volunteer and marksman, I felt that the odds would then be slightly in my favour, even if I could not, as I hoped I could, persuade my friend to join me in the expedition.

But the seneschal took a less sanguine view of my prospects.

"You forget, sir," he remarked lugubriously, "that, in order to return hither, you must first quit the shelter of these walls—which, all unarmed as you are, would be but to court instant death!"

"I don't quite see that," I argued. "After all, as the dragon made no effort to prevent me from coming in, it is at least possible that it may not object to my going out."

"For aught I can say," he replied, "it may have no orders to hinder any from entrance. As to that I know naught. But of this I am very sure—it suffers no one to depart hence undevoured."

"But could I not contrive to get out of its reach before it was aware that I had even started?" I suggested.

"I fear me, sir," he said despondently, "that the creature would not fail to follow up your tracks ere the snow could cover them."

"That had not occurred to me," I said. "But now you mention it, it does not seem altogether unlikely. In your opinion, then, I should do better in remaining where I am?"

"Only until the enchanter return," was his reply, "as, if I mistake not, he may do at any moment, after which your stay here will assuredly be but brief."

"You can't mean," I said, "that he would have the inhumanity to turn me out to be devoured by his beastly dragon? For that is what it would come to."

"Unless, perchance, by dint of strength or cunning you were to overcome the monster," he said. "And methought you had come hither with that very intent."

"My good man," I replied, "I've no idea why or how I came here, but it was certainly with no desire or expectation of meeting a dragon. However, I begin to see very clearly that if I can't find some way of putting an end to the brute—and promptly, too—he will make an end of me. The question is, how the deuce am I to set about it?"

And then, all at once, I had an inspiration. I recollected the black-beetles, and something the seneschal had said about its being the scullions' duty to keep them down. I asked him what methods they had employed for this purpose, but, such humble details being naturally outside his province, he was unable to inform me. So I returned to the kitchen, where I began a careful search, not without some hope of success.

For awhile I searched in vain, but at last, just when I had begun to despair, I found on a dusty shelf in the buttery the identical thing I had been looking for. It was an earthen vessel containing a paste, which, in spite of the fungoid growth that had collected on its surface, I instantly recognised as a composition warranted to prove fatal to every description of vermin.

I called to the seneschal and asked if he could oblige me with a loaf of white bread, which he brought in evident bewilderment. I cut a slice from the middle and was proceeding to spread the paste thickly upon it when he grasped my arm. "Hold!" he cried. "Would you rashly seek your death ere it is due?"

"You need not be alarmed," I told him; "this is not for myself. And now will you kindly show me a way out to some part of the roof where I can have access to the dragon?"

Trembling from head to foot he indicated a turret-stair, up which, however, he did not offer to accompany me; it brought me out on the leads of what appeared to be a kind of bastion. I crept cautiously to the parapet and peeped over it, and then for the first time I had a full view of the brute, which was crouching immediately below me.

I know how prone the most accurate are to exaggeration in matters of this kind, but, after making every allowance for my excited condition at the time, I do not think I am far out in estimating that the dimensions of the beast could not have been much, if at all, less than those of the "Diplodocus Carnegii," a model of which is exhibited at the Natural History Museum, while its appearance was infinitely more terrific.

I do not mind admitting frankly that the sight so unmanned me for the moment that I was seized with an almost irresistible impulse to retire by the way I had come before the creature had observed me. And yet it was not without a certain beauty of its own; I should say, indeed, that it was rather an unusually handsome specimen of its class, and I was especially struck by the magnificent colouring of its scales, which surpassed that of even the largest pythons. Still, to an unaccustomed eye there must always be something about a dragon that inspires more horror than admiration, and I was in no mood just then to enjoy the spectacle. It was hunched up together, with its head laid back, like a fowl's, between its wings, and seemed to be enjoying a short nap. I suppose I must unconsciously have given some sign of my presence, for suddenly I saw the horny films roll back like shutters from its lidless eyes, which it fixed on me with a cold glare of curiosity.

And then it shambled on to its feet, and slowly elongated its neck till it brought its horrible head on a level with the battlements. I need not say that on this I promptly retreated to a spot where I judged I should be out of immediate danger. But I had sufficient presence of mind to remember the purpose for which I was there, and, fixing the prepared slice on the ferrule of my umbrella, I extended it as far as my arm would reach in the creature's direction.

I fancy it had not been fed very lately. The head made a lightning dart across the parapet, and a voracious snap—and the next moment both bread and umbrella had disappeared down its great red gullet.

The head was then withdrawn. I could hear a hideous champing sound, as of the ribs of the umbrella being slowly crunched. After that came silence.

Again I crawled to the parapet and looked down. The huge brute was licking its plated jaws with apparent gusto, as though—which was likely enough—an umbrella came as an unaccustomed snack to its jaded palate. It was peacefully engaged now in digesting this *hors d'œuvre*.

But my heart only sank the lower at the sight. For if an alpaca umbrella with an ebony handle could be so easily assimilated, what possible chance was there that beetle-paste would produce any deleterious effect? I had been a fool to place the faintest hope on so desperate a hazard. Presently he would be coming for more—and I had nothing for him!

But by-and-by, as I gazed in a sort of fascinated repulsion, I fancied I detected some slight symptoms of uneasiness in the reptile's demeanour.

It was almost nothing at first—a restless twitch at times, and a squint in its stony eyes that I had not previously noticed—but it gave me a gleam of hope. Presently I saw the great crest along its spine slowly begin to erect itself, and the filaments that fringed its jaws bristling, as it proceeded to deal a succession of vicious pecks at its distended olive-green paunch, which it evidently regarded as responsible for the disturbance.

Little as I knew about dragons, a child could have seen that this one was feeling somewhat seriously indisposed. Only—was it due to the umbrella or the vermin-killer? As to that I could only attempt to speculate, and my fate—and the Princess's, too—hung upon which was the correct diagnosis!

However, I was not kept long in suspense. Suddenly the beast uttered a kind of bellowing roar—the most appalling sound I think I ever heard—and after that I scarcely know what happened exactly.

I fancy it had some kind of fit. It writhed and rolled over and over, thrashing the air with its big leathery wings, and tangling itself up to a degree that, unless I had seen it, I should have thought impossible, even for a dragon.

After this had gone on for some time, it untied itself and seemed calmer again, till all at once it curved into an immense arch, and remained perfectly rigid with wings outspread for nearly half a minute. Then it suddenly collapsed on its side, panting, snorting, and quivering like some monstrous automobile, after which it stretched itself out to its full length once or twice, and then lay stiff and still. Its gorgeous hues gradually faded into a dull, leaden-grey tint. . . . All was over—the vermin-destroyer had done its work after all.

I cannot say that I was much elated. I am not sure that I did not even feel a pang of self-reproach. I had slain the dragon, it was true, but by a method which I could not think would have commended

itself to St. George as entirely sportsmanlike, even though the circumstances left me no other alternative.

However, I had saved the Princess, which, after all, was the main
point, and there was no actual necessity for her to know more than
the bare fact that the dragon was dead.

I was just about to go down and inform her that she was now
free to leave the castle, when I heard a whirring noise in the air, and,
glancing back, I saw, flying towards me through the still falling snow,
an elderly gentleman of forbidding aspect, who was evidently in a
highly exasperated state. It was the Princess's uncle.

I don't know how it was, but till that moment I had never realised the extremely unprofessional proceeding into which I had
been betrayed by my own impulsiveness. But I saw now, though
too late, that, in taking the law into my own hands and adminis-
tering a poisonous drug to an animal which, however furious it
might be, was still the property of another, I had been guilty of
conduct unworthy of any respectable solicitor. It was undoubtedly
an actionable tort, if not a trespass—while he might even treat it as
a criminal offence.

So, as the magician landed on the roof, his face distorted with fury, I
felt that nothing would meet the case but the most ample apology. But,
feeling that it was better to allow the first remark to come from him, I
merely raised my hat and waited to hear what he had to say. . . .

"*Are you being attended to, sir?*" was the remark that actually came—
and both words and tone were so different from what I had expected
that I could not repress a start.

And then, to my utter astonishment, I discovered that battlements
and magician had all disappeared. I was back again in the toyshop,
staring into the glass globe, in which the snow was still languidly
circling.

"Like to take one of these shilling snowstorms, sir?" continued
the assistant, who seemed to be addressing me; "we're selling a great
quantity of them just now. Very suitable and acceptable present for a
child, sir, and only a shilling in that size, though we have them larger
in stock."

I bought the globe I had first taken up—but I have not given it to
my godchild. I preferred to keep it myself.

Of course, my adventure may have been merely a kind of day-
dream; though, if so, it is rather odd that it should have taken that
form, when, even at night, my dreams—on the rare occasions when

I do dream—never turn upon such subjects as castles, princesses, or dragons.

A scientific friend, to whom I related the experience, pronounces it to be an ordinary case of auto-hypnotism, induced by staring into a crystal globe for a prolonged period.

But I don't know. I cannot help thinking that there is something more in it than that.

I still gaze into the globe at times, when I am alone of an evening; but while I have occasionally found myself back in the snowstorm again, I have never, so far, succeeded in getting into the castle.

Perhaps it is as well; for, although I should not at all object to see something more of the Princess, she has most probably, thanks to my instrumentality, long since left the premises—and I cannot say that I have any particular desire to meet the magician.

Charles Aken Fairbridge (1824–1893)

F. ANSTEY was great friends with Andrew Lang, the compiler of the "colour" fairy books. Indeed, it was partly due to Lang's enthusiastic recommendation of *Vice Versa* in manuscript to his publisher that the book was published, and Lang's equally enthusiastic review helped cement the book's popularity. As an editor and reviewer, Lang was always generous to new authors—it was he who set Robert Louis Stevenson on the road to fame. His lifelong fascination with folklore played a significant role in promoting and encouraging the fairy tale and its place in the greater world of fantasy. Lang felt that although not all of romantic fiction dealt with the impossible, "it is only the impossible that can satisfy human aspirations." He saw fantasy as humanity's greatest source of escape.

Lang (1844–1912) was a significant writer both for children—in *Princess Nobody* (1884), *The Gold of Fairnilee* (1888) and *Prince Prigio* (1889)—and for adults; he wrote a parody of F. Rider Haggard's *She*, called *He, by the Author of It* (1887); collaborated with Haggard on *The World's Desire* (1890); and produced several worthy collections of stories, such as *In the Wrong Paradise* (1886). The "colour" fairy tale collections not only included traditional stories, but also brought tales from all over the globe, including Japan, Polynesia, India, and Africa. The following story, from Lang's *Orange Fairy Book* (1907), is based on a story from Senna in what is now Zimbabwe (then Rhodesia).

Lang credited the source for this story to "Mr. Fairbridge,"— Charles Aken Fairbridge, a South African attorney who amassed a huge library of books on South African literature and history. I have not seen the original of this story so I do not know how much it may have been altered either by Fairbridge or, more probably, by Andrew Lang, or his wife Leonora, who did most of the adaptations of the story texts for the *Fairy* books. Even so, in this form the story not only demonstrates a remarkable similarity to traditional European folktales, but also emphasises how fantasy was used as an escape valve (as Lang observed) by those peoples who had been invaded and subjugated by an alien power.

The Magic Mirror

Charles Aken Fairbridge

A long, long while ago, before ever the White Men were seen in Senna, there lived a man called Gopani-Kufa.

One day, as he was out hunting, he came upon a strange sight. An enormous python had caught an antelope and coiled itself around it; the antelope, striking out in despair with its horns, had pinned the python's neck to a tree, and so deeply had its horns sunk in the soft wood that neither creature could get away.

"Help!" cried the antelope, "for I was doing no harm, yet I have been caught, and would have been eaten, had I not defended myself."

"Help me," said the python, "for I am Insato, King of all the Reptiles, and will reward you well!"

Gopani-Kufa considered for a moment, then stabbing the antelope with his assegai, he set the python free.

"I thank you," said the python; "come back here with the new moon, when I shall have eaten the antelope, and I will reward you as I promised."

"Yes," said the dying antelope, "he will reward you, and lo! your reward shall be your own undoing!"

Gopani-Kufa went back to his kraal, and with the new moon he returned again to the spot where he had saved the python.

Insato was lying upon the ground, still sleepy from the effects of his huge meal, and when he saw the man he thanked him again, and said: "Come with me now to Pita, which is my own country, and I will give you what you will of all my possessions."

Gopani-Kufa at first was afraid, thinking of what the antelope had said, but finally he consented and followed Insato into the forest.

For several days they travelled, and at last they came to a hole leading deep into the earth. It was not very wide, but large enough to admit a man. "Hold on to my tail," said Insato, "and I will go down first, drawing you after me." The man did so, and Insato entered.

Down, down, down they went for days, all the while getting deeper and deeper into the earth, until at last the darkness ended and they dropped into a beautiful country; around them grew short green grass, on which browsed herds of cattle and sheep and goats. In the distance Gopani-Kufa saw a great collection of houses all square, built of stone and very tall, and their roofs were shining with gold and burnished iron.

Gopani-Kufa turned to Insato, but found, in the place of the python, a man, strong and handsome, with the great snake's skin wrapped round him for covering; and on his arms and neck were rings of pure gold.

The man smiled. "I am Insato," said he, "but in my own country I take man's shape—even as you see me—for this is Pita, the land over which I am king." He then took Gopani-Kufa by the hand and led him towards the town.

On the way they passed rivers in which men and women were bathing and fishing and boating; and farther on they came to gardens covered with heavy crops of rice and maize, and many other grains which Gopani-Kufa did not even know the name of. And as they passed, the people who were singing at their work in the fields, abandoned their labours and saluted Insato with delight, bringing also palm wine and green cocoanuts for refreshment, as to one returned from a long journey.

"These are my children!" said Insato, waving his hand towards the people. Gopani-Kufa was much astonished at all that he saw, but he said nothing. Presently they came to the town; everything here, too, was beautiful, and everything that a man might desire he could obtain. Even the grains of dust in the streets were of gold and silver.

Insato conducted Gopani-Kufa to the palace, and showing him his rooms, and the maidens who would wait upon him, told him that they would have a great feast that night, and on the morrow he might name his choice of the riches of Pita and it should be given him. Then he was away.

Now Gopani-Kufa had a wasp called Zengi-mizi. Zengi-mizi was not an ordinary wasp, for the spirit of the father of Gopani-Kufa had entered it, so that it was exceedingly wise. In times of doubt Gopani-Kufa always consulted the wasp as to what had better be done, so on this occasion he took it out of the little rush basket in which he carried it, saying: "Zengi-mizi, what gift shall I ask of Insato to-morrow when he would know the reward he shall bestow on me for saving his life?"

"Biz-z-z," hummed Zengi-mizi, "ask him for Sipao the Mirror." And it flew back into its basket.

Gopani-Kufa was astonished at this answer; but knowing that the words of Zengi-mizi were true words, he determined to make the request. So that night they feasted, and on the morrow Insato came to Gopani-Kufa and, giving him greeting joyfully, he said:

"Now, O my friend, name your choice amongst my possessions and you shall have it!"

"O king!" answered Gopani-Kufa, "out of all your possessions I will have the Mirror, Sipao."

The king started. "O friend, Gopani-Kufa," he said, "ask anything but that! I did not think that you would request that which is most precious to me."

"Let me think over it again then, O king," said Gopani-Kufa, "and to-morrow I will let you know if I change my mind."

But the king was still much troubled, fearing the loss of Sipao, for the mirror had magic powers, so that he who owned it had but to ask and his wish would be fulfilled; to it Insato owed all that he possessed.

As soon as the king left him, Gopani-Kufa again took Zengi-mizi, out of his basket. "Zengi-mizi," he said, "the king seems loth to grant my request for the Mirror—is there not some other thing of equal value for which I might ask?"

And the wasp answered: "There is nothing in the world, O Gopani-Kufa, which is of such value as this Mirror, for it is a Wishing Mirror, and accomplishes the desires of him who owns it. If the king hesitates, go to him the next day, and the day after, and in the end he will bestow the Mirror upon you, for you saved his life."

And it was even so. For three days Gopani-Kufa returned the same answer to the king, and, at last, with tears in his eyes, Insato gave him the Mirror, which was of polished iron, saying: "Take Sipao, then, O Gopani-Kufa, and may thy wishes come true. Go back now to thine own country; Sipao will show you the way."

Gopani-Kufa was greatly rejoiced, and, taking farewell of the king, said to the Mirror:

"Sipao, Sipao, I wish to be back upon the Earth again!"

Instantly he found himself standing upon the upper earth; but, not knowing the spot, he said again to the Mirror:

"Sipao, Sipao, I want the path to my own kraal!"

And behold! right before him lay the path!

When he arrived home he found his wife and daughter mourning for him, for they thought that he had been eaten by lions; but he comforted them, saying that while following a wounded antelope he had missed his way and had wandered for a long time before he had found the path again.

That night he asked Zengi-mizi, in whom sat the spirit of his father, what he had better ask Sipao for next?

"Biz-z-z," said the wasp, "would you not like to be as great a chief as Insato?"

And Gopani-Kufa smiled, and took the Mirror and said to it:

"Sipao, Sipao, I want a town as great as that of Insato, the King of Pita; and I wish to be chief over it!"

Then all along the banks of the Zambesi river, which flowed nearby, sprang up streets of stone buildings, and their roofs shone with gold and burnished iron like those in Pita; and in the streets men and women were walking, and young boys were driving out the sheep and cattle to pasture; and from the river came shouts and laughter from the young men and maidens who had launched their canoes and were fishing. And when the people of the new town beheld Gopani-Kufa they rejoiced greatly and hailed him as chief.

Gopani-Kufa was now as powerful as Insato the King of the Reptiles had been, and he and his family moved into the palace that stood high above the other buildings right in the middle of the town. His wife was too astonished at all these wonders to ask any questions, but his daughter Shasasa kept begging him to tell her how he had suddenly become so great; so at last he revealed the whole secret, and even entrusted Sipao the Mirror to her care, saying:

"It will be safer with you, my daughter, for you dwell apart; whereas men come to consult me on affairs of state, and the Mirror might be stolen."

Then Shasasa took the Magic Mirror and hid it beneath her pillow, and after that for many years Gopani-Kufa ruled his people both well and wisely, so that all men loved him, and never once did he need to ask Sipao to grant him a wish.

Now it happened that, after many years, when the hair of Gopani-Kufa was turning grey with age, there came white men to that country. Up the Zambesi they came, and they fought long and fiercely with Gopani-Kufa; but, because of the power of the Magic Mirror, he beat them, and they fled to the sea-coast. Chief among them was one Rei, a man of much cunning, who sought to discover whence sprang Gopani-Kufa's power. So one day he called to him a trusty servant named Butou, and said: "Go you to the town and find out for me what is the secret of its greatness."

And Butou, dressing himself in rags, set out, and when he came to Gopani-Kufa's town he asked for the chief; and the people took him into the presence of Gopani-Kufa. When the white man saw him he humbled himself, and said: "O Chief! take pity on me, for I have no home! When Rei marched against you I alone stood apart, for I knew that all the strength of the Zambesi lay in your hands, and because I would not fight against you he turned me forth into the forest to starve!"

And Gopani-Kufa believed the white man's story, and he took him in and feasted him, and gave him a house.

In this way the end came. For the heart of Shasasa, the daughter of Gopani-Kufa, went forth to Butou the traitor, and from her he learnt the secret of the Magic Mirror. One night, when all the town slept, he felt beneath her pillow and, finding the Mirror, he stole it and fled back with it to Rei, the chief of the white men.

So it befell that, one day, as Gopani-Kufa was gazing up at the river from a window of the palace he again saw the war-canoes of the white men; and at the sight his spirit misgave him.

"Shasasa! my daughter!" he cried wildly, "go fetch me the mirror, for the white men are at hand."

"Woe is me, my father!" she sobbed. "The Mirror is gone! For I loved Butou the traitor, and he has stolen Sipao from me!"

Then Gopani-Kufa calmed himself, and drew out Zengi-mizi from its rush basket.

"O spirit of my father!" he said, "what now shall I do?"

"O Gopani-Kufa!" hummed the wasp, "there is nothing now that can be done, for the words of the antelope which you slew are being fulfilled."

"Alas! I am an old man—I had forgotten!" cried the chief. "The words of the antelope were true words—my reward shall be my undoing—they are being fulfilled!"

Then the white men fell upon the people of Gopani-Kufa and slew them together with the chief and his daughter Shasasa; and since then all the power of the Earth has rested in the hands of the white men, for they have in their possession Sipao, the Magic Mirror.

Walter de la Mare (1873–1956)

IN THE STORIES of Walter de la Mare, there can be little doubt that fantasy, and not just children's fantasy, was coming of age. Today de la Mare is remembered chiefly for his poetry and perhaps for one or two ghost stories, such as "Seaton's Aunt" (1922), but thankfully his other writings are not entirely forgotten. Yet although his fantasy novels, with the possible exception of *The Three Mulla-Mulgars* (1910), are regarded as works for adults—especially *The Return* (1910)—his short fiction tends to be classified for children, and as a consequence it is all too often overlooked by adults.

It is in his short fiction that his best work may be found—certainly his most enigmatic. De la Mare's world view, as expressed through his fiction, is that life and death are one huge mystery that we are unable to understand but for which, occasionally, we may get clues (too few of which are we capable of interpreting). In other words, throughout life we only ever see a part of things and never the whole. As C. S. Lewis remarked about de la Mare, he "succeeds, partly by style and partly by never laying the cards on the table." Thus his stories are often puzzling and unresolved; perhaps none is more enigmatic than "The Riddle" (1903), which has been the subject of many interpretations but still retains its secrets. A story for children or a fabulation for adults? You decide.

171

The Riddle

Walter de la Mare

So these seven children, Ann and Matilda, James, William and Henry, Harriet and Dorothea, came to live with their grandmother. The house in which their grandmother had lived since her childhood was built in the time of the Georges. It was not a pretty house, but roomy, substantial, and square; and a great cedar tree outstretched its branches almost to the windows.

When the children were come out of the cab (five sitting inside and two beside the driver), they were shown into their grandmother's presence. They stood in a little black group before the old lady, seated in her bow-window. And she asked them each their names, and repeated each name in her kind, quavering voice. Then to one she gave a work-box, to William a jack-knife, to Dorothea a painted ball; to each a present according to age. And she kissed all her grand-children to the youngest.

"My dears," she said, "I wish to see all of you bright and gay in my house. I am an old woman, so that I cannot romp with you; but Ann must look to you, and Mrs. Fenn too. And every morning and every evening you must all come in to see your granny; and bring me smiling faces, that call back to my mind my own son Harry. But all the rest of the day, when school is done, you shall do just as you please, my dears. And there is only one thing, just one, I would have you remember. In the large spare bedroom that looks out on the slate roof there stands in the corner an old oak chest; aye, older than I, my dears, a great deal older; older than my grandmother. Play anywhere else in the house, but not there." She spoke kindly to them all, smiling at them; but she was very old, and her eyes seemed to see nothing of this world.

And the seven children, though at first they were gloomy and strange, soon began to be happy and at home in the great house. There was much to interest and to amuse them there; all was new to them. Twice every day, morning and evening, they came in to see their grandmother, who every day seemed more feeble; and she spoke pleasantly to them of her mother, and her childhood, but never forgetting to visit her store of sugar-plums. And so the weeks passed by. . . .

It was evening twilight when Henry went upstairs from the nursery by himself to look at the oak chest. He pressed his fingers into the carved fruit and flowers, and spoke to the dark-smiling heads at the corners; and then, with a glance over his shoulder, he opened the lid and looked in. But the chest concealed no treasure, neither gold nor baubles, nor was there anything to alarm the eye. The chest was empty, except that it was lined with silk of old-rose, seeming darker in the dusk, and smelling sweet of pot-pourri. And while Henry was looking in, he heard the softened laughter and the clinking of the cups downstairs in the nursery; and out at the window he saw the day darkening. These things brought strangely to his memory his mother who in her glimmering white dress used to read to him in the dusk; and he climbed into the chest; and the lid closed gently down over him.

When the other six children were tired with their playing, they filed into their grandmother's room for her good-night and her sugar-plums. She looked out between the candles at them as if she were uncertain of something in her thoughts. The next day Ann told her grandmother that Henry was not anywhere to be found.

"Dearie me, child. Then he must be gone away for a time," said the old lady. She paused. "But remember, all of you, do not meddle with the oak chest."

But Matilda could not forget her brother Henry, finding no pleasure in playing without him. So she would loiter in the house thinking where he might be. And she carried her wooden doll in her bare arms, singing under her breath all she could make up about it. And when one bright morning she peeped in on the chest, so sweet-scented and secret it seemed that she took her doll with her into it—just as Henry himself had done.

So Ann, and James, and William, Harriet and Dorothea were left at home to play together. "Some day maybe they will come back to you, my dears," said their grandmother, "or maybe you will go to them. Heed my warning as best you may."

Now Harriet and William were friends together, pretending to be sweethearts; while James and Dorothea liked wild games of hunting, and fishing, and battles.

On a silent afternoon in October, Harriet and William were talking softly together, looking out over the slate roof at the green fields, and they heard the squeak and frisking of a mouse behind them in the room. They went together and searched for the small, dark hole from whence it had come out. But finding no hole, they began to finger the carving of the chest, and to give names to the dark-smiling heads, just as Henry had done. "*I* know! let's pretend you are Sleeping Beauty, Harriet," said William, "and I'll be the Prince that squeezes through the thorns and comes in." Harriet looked gently and strangely at her brother but she got into the box and lay down, pretending to be fast asleep, and on tiptoe William leaned over, and seeing how big was the chest, he stepped in to kiss the Sleeping Beauty and to wake her from her quiet sleep. Slowly the carved lid turned on its noiseless hinges. And only the clatter of James and Dorothea came in sometimes to recall Ann from her book.

But their old grandmother was very feeble, and her sight dim, and her hearing extremely difficult.

Snow was falling through the still air upon the roof; and Dorothea was a fish in the oak chest, and James stood over the hole in the ice, brandishing a walking-stick for a harpoon, pretending to be an Esquimau. Dorothea's face was red, and her wild eyes sparkled through her tousled hair. And James had a crooked scratch upon his cheek. "You must struggle, Dorothea, and then I shall swim back and drag you out. Be quick now!" He shouted with laughter as he was drawn into the open chest. And the lid closed softly and gently down as before.

Ann, left to herself, was too old to care overmuch for sugar-plums, but she would go solitary to bid her grandmother good-night; and the old lady looked wistfully at her over her spectacles. "Well, my dear," she said with trembling head; and she squeezed Ann's fingers between her own knuckled finger and thumb. "What lonely old people, we two are, to be sure!" Ann kissed her grandmother's soft, loose cheek. She left the old lady sitting in her easy chair, her hands upon her knees, and her head turned sidelong towards her.

When Ann was gone to bed she used to sit reading her book by candlelight. She drew up her knees under the sheets, resting her book upon them. Her story was about fairies and gnomes, and the gently-flowing moonlight of the narrative seemed to illumine the white pages, and she could hear in fancy fairy voices, so silent was the great many-roomed house, and so mellifluent were the words of the story. Presently she put out her candle, and, with a confused babel of voices close to her ear, and faint swift pictures before her eyes, she fell asleep.

And in the dead of night she rose out of her bed in a dream, and with eyes wide open yet seeing nothing of reality, moved silently through the vacant house. Past the room where her grandmother was snoring in brief, heavy slumber, she stepped lightly and surely, and down the wide staircase. And Vega the far-shining stood over against the window above the slate roof. Ann walked into the strange room beneath as if she were being guided by the hand towards the oak chest. There, just as if she were dreaming it was her bed, she laid herself down in the old rose silk, in the fragrant place. But it was so dark in the room that the movement of the lid was indistinguishable.

Through the long day, the grandmother sat in her bow-window. Her lips were pursed, and she looked with dim, inquisitive scrutiny upon the street where people passed to and fro, and vehicles rolled by. At evening she climbed the stair and stood in the doorway of the large spare bedroom. The ascent had shortened her breath. Her magnifying spectacles rested upon her nose. Leaning her hand on the doorpost she peered in towards the glimmering square of window in the quiet gloom. But she could not see far, because her sight was dim and the light of day feeble. Nor could she detect the faint fragrance as of autumnal leaves. But in her mind was a tangled skein of memories—laughter and tears, and children long ago become old-fashioned, and the advent of friends, and last farewells. And gossiping fitfully, inarticulately, with herself, the old lady went down again to her window-seat.

Kenneth Grahame (1859–1932)

THE NOVEL *The Wind in the Willows* (1908) is one of the classic children's books, yet it includes a chapter which, like de la Mare's "The Riddle," seems to convey a message that goes beyond a simple tale for children, striking at the very soul of all humans. In some of the most beautiful and evocative passages ever written, it opens up our hearts to our relationship with Nature: the beauty and the mystery of the world about us. And what more stirring title can it have than "The Piper at the Gates of Dawn"?

It may seem all the more remarkable that the tale was written by the Secretary of the Bank of England, Kenneth Grahame. But Grahame had already shown where his true interests lay with his earlier books for children, *The Golden Age* (1895) and *Dream Days* (1898). The titles of both books reveal a yearning for those lost days of childhood, the inspiration for so much fantasy. Yet while basking in the wonder of childhood dreams, this story transcends imagination and approaches that glory that so many of us hope for, that there really is "Something" out there, almost within reach.

177

The Piper at the Gates of Dawn

Kenneth Grahame

The Willow-Wren was twittering his thin little song, hidden himself in the dark selvedge of the river bank. Though it was past ten o'clock at night, the sky still clung to and retained some lingering skirts of light from the departed day; and the sullen heats of the torrid afternoon broke up and rolled away at the dispersing touch of the cool fingers of the short midsummer night. Mole lay stretched on the bank, still panting from the stress of the fierce day that had been cloudless from dawn to late sunset, and waited for his friend to return. He had been on the river with some companions, leaving the Water Rat free to keep an engagement of long standing with Otter; and he had come back to find the house dark and deserted, and no sign of Rat, who was doubtless keeping it up late with his old comrade. It was still too hot to think of staying indoors, so he lay on some cool dock-leaves, and thought over the past day and its doings, and how very good they all had been.

The Rat's light footfall was presently heard approaching over the parched grass. "O, the blessed coolness!" he said, and sat down, gazing thoughtfully into the river, silent and preoccupied.

"You stayed to supper, of course?" said the Mole presently.

"Simply had to," said the Rat. "They wouldn't hear of my going before. You know how kind they always are. And they made things as jolly for me as ever they could, right up to the moment I left. But I felt a brute all the time, as it was clear to me they were very unhappy, though they tried to hide it. Mole, I'm afraid they're in trouble. Little Portly is missing again; and you know what a lot his father thinks of him, though he never says much about it."

"What, that child?" said the Mole lightly. "Well, suppose he is; why worry about it? He's always straying off and getting lost, and turning up again; he's so adventurous. But no harm ever happens to him. Everybody hereabouts knows him and likes him, just as they do old

178

Otter, and you may be sure some animal or other will come across him and bring him back again all right. Why, we've found him ourselves, miles from home, and quite self-possessed and cheerful!"

"Yes; but this time it's more serious," said the Rat gravely. "He's been missing for some days now, and the Otters have hunted everywhere, high and low, without finding the slightest trace. And they've asked every animal, too, for miles around, and no one knows anything about him. Otter's evidently more anxious than he'll admit. I got out of him that young Portly hasn't learnt to swim very well yet, and I can see he's thinking of the weir. There's a lot of water coming down still, considering the time of the year, and the place always had a fascination for the child. And then there are—well, traps and things—*you* know. Otter's not the fellow to be nervous about any son of his before it's time. And now he *is* nervous. When I left, he came out with me—said he wanted some air, and talked about stretching his legs. But I could see it wasn't that, so I drew him out and pumped him, and got it all from him at last. He was going to spend the night watching by the ford. You know the place where the old ford used to be, in by gone days before they built the bridge?"

"I know it well," said the Mole. "But why should Otter choose to watch there?"

"Well, it seems that it was there he gave Portly his first swimming-lesson," continued the Rat. "From that shallow, gravelly spit near the bank. And it was there he used to teach him fishing, and there young Portly caught his first fish, of which he was so very proud. The child loved the spot, and Otter thinks that if he came wandering back from wherever he is—if he *is* anywhere by this time, poor little chap—he might make for the ford he was so fond of; or if he came across it he'd remember it well, and stop there and play, perhaps. So Otter goes there every night and watches—on the chance, you know, just on the chance!"

They were silent for a time, both thinking of the same thing—the lonely, heart-sore animal, crouched by the ford, watching and waiting, the long night through—on the chance.

"Well, well," said the Rat presently, "I suppose we ought to be thinking about turning in." But he never offered to move.

"Rat," said the Mole, "I simply can't go and turn in, and go to sleep, and *do* nothing, even though there doesn't seem to be anything to be done. We'll get the boat out, and paddle up stream. The moon will be up in an hour or so, and then we will search as well as we can—anyhow, it will be better than going to bed and doing *nothing*."

"Just what I was thinking myself," said the Rat. "It's not the sort of night for bed anyhow; and daybreak is not so very far off, and then we may pick up some news of him from early risers as we go along."

They got the boat out, and the Rat took the sculls, paddling with caution. Out in midstream, there was a clear, narrow track that faintly reflected the sky; but wherever shadows fell on the water from bank, bush, or tree, they were as solid to all appearance as the banks themselves, and the Mole had to steer with judgment accordingly. Dark and deserted as it was, the night was full of small noises, song and chatter and rustling, telling of the busy little population who were up and about, plying their trades and vocations through the night till sunshine should fall on them at last and send them off to their well-earned repose. The water's own noises, too, were more apparent than by day, its gurglings and "cloops" more unexpected and near at hand; and constantly they started at what seemed a sudden clear call from an actual articulate voice.

The line of the horizon was clear and hard against the sky, and in one particular quarter it showed black against a silvery climbing phosphorescence that grew and grew. At last, over the rim of the waiting earth the moon lifted with slow majesty till it swung clear of the horizon and rode off, free of moorings; and once more they began to see surfaces—meadows widespread, and quiet gardens, and the river itself from bank to bank, all softly disclosed, all washed clean of mystery and terror, all radiant again as by day, but with a difference that was tremendous. Their old haunts greeted them again in other raiment, as if they had slipped away and put on this pure new apparel and come quietly back, smiling as they shyly waited to see if they would be recognised again under it.

Fastening their boat to a willow, the friends landed in this silent, silver kingdom, and patiently explored the hedges, the hollow trees, the runnels and their little culverts, the ditches and dry water-ways. Embarking again and crossing over, they worked their way up the stream in this manner, while the moon, serene and detached in a cloudless sky, did what she could, though so far off, to help them in their quest; till her hour came and she sank earthwards reluctantly, and left them, and mystery once more held field and river.

Then a change began slowly to declare itself. The horizon became clearer, field and tree came more into sight, and somehow with a different look; the mystery began to drop away from them. A bird piped suddenly, and was still; and a light breeze sprang up and set the reeds and bulrushes rustling. Rat, who was in the stern of the boat, while Mole sculled, sat up suddenly and listened with a passionate intentness. Mole, who with gentle strokes was just keeping the boat moving while he scanned the banks with care, looked at him with curiosity.

"It's gone!" sighed the Rat, sinking back in his seat again. "So beautiful and strange and new. Since it was to end so soon, I almost wish I had never heard it. For it has roused a longing in me that is pain, and nothing seems worth while but just to hear that sound once more and go on listening to it forever. No! There it is again!" he cried, alert once more. Entranced, he was silent for a long space, spellbound.

"Now it passes on and I begin to lose it," he said presently. "O Mole! the beauty of it! The merry bubble and joy, the thin, clear, happy call of the distant piping! Such music I never dreamed of, and the call in it is stronger even than the music is sweet! Row on, Mole, row! For the music and the call must be for us."

The Mole, greatly wondering, obeyed. "I hear nothing myself," he said, "but the wind playing in the reeds and rushes and osiers."

The Rat never answered, if indeed he heard. Rapt, transported, trembling, he was possessed in all his senses by this new divine thing that caught up his helpless soul and swung and dandled it, a powerless but happy infant in a strong sustaining grasp.

In silence Mole rowed steadily, and soon they came to a point where the river divided, a long backwater branching off to one side. With a slight movement of his head Rat, who had long dropped the rudder-lines, directed the rower to take the backwater. The creeping tide of light gained and gained, and now they could see the colour of the flowers that gemmed the water's edge.

"Clearer and nearer still," cried the Rat joyously. "Now you must surely hear it! Ah—at last—I see you do!"

Breathless and transfixed the Mole stopped rowing as the liquid run of that glad piping broke on him like a wave, caught him up, and possessed him utterly. He saw the tears on his comrade's cheeks, and bowed his head and understood. For a space they hung there, brushed by the purple loosestrife that fringed the bank; then the clear imperious summons that marched hand-in-hand with the intoxicating melody imposed its will on Mole, and mechanically he bent to his oars again. And the light grew steadily stronger, but no birds sang as they were wont to do at the approach of dawn; and but for the heavenly music all was marvellously still.

On either side of them, as they glided onwards, the rich meadow-grass seemed that morning of a freshness and a greenness unsurpassable. Never had they noticed the roses so vivid, the willow-herb so riotous, the meadow-sweet so odorous and pervading. Then the murmur of the approaching weir began to hold the air, and they felt a consciousness that they were nearing the end, whatever it might be, that surely awaited their expedition.

A wide half-circle of foam and glinting lights and shining shoulders of green water, the great weir closed the backwater from bank to bank, troubled all the quiet surface with twirling eddies and floating foam-streaks, and deadened all other sounds with its solemn and soothing rumble. In midmost of the stream, embraced in the weir's shimmering armspread, a small island lay anchored, fringed close with willow and silver birch and alder. Reserved, shy, but full of significance, it hid whatever it might hold behind a veil, keeping it till the hour should come, and, with the hour, those who were called and chosen.

Slowly, but with no doubt or hesitation whatever, and in something of a solemn expectancy, the two animals passed through the broken tumultuous water and moored their boat at the flowery margin of the island. In silence they landed, and pushed through the blossom and scented herbage and undergrowth that led up to the level ground, till they stood on a little lawn of a marvellous green, set round with Nature's own orchard-trees—crabapple, wild cherry, and sloe.

"This is the place of my song-dream, the place the music played to me," whispered the Rat, as if in a trance. "Here, in this holy place, here if anywhere, surely we shall find Him!"

Then suddenly the Mole felt a great Awe fall upon him, an awe that turned his muscles to water, bowed his head, and rooted his feet to the ground. It was no panic terror—indeed he felt wonderfully at peace and happy—but it was an awe that smote and held him and, without seeing, he knew it could only mean that some august Presence was very, very near. With difficulty he turned to look for his friend, and saw him at his side cowed, stricken, and trembling violently. And still there was utter silence in the populous bird-haunted branches around them; and still the light grew and grew.

Perhaps he would never have dared to raise his eyes, but that, though the piping was now hushed, the call and the summons seemed still dominant and imperious. He might not refuse, were Death himself waiting to strike him instantly, once he had looked with mortal eye on things rightly kept hidden. Trembling he obeyed, and raised his humble head; and then, in that utter clearness of the imminent dawn, while Nature, flushed with fulness of incredible colour, seemed to hold her breath for the event, he looked in the very eyes of the Friend and Helper; saw the backward sweep of the curved horns, gleaming in the growing daylight; saw the stern, hooked nose between the kindly eyes that were looking down on them humorously, while the bearded mouth broke into a half-smile at the corners; saw the rippling muscles on the arm that lay across the broad chest, the long supple hand still holding the pan-pipes only just fallen away from the parted lips; saw the splendid curves of the shaggy limbs disposed in majestic ease on the sward; saw, last of all, nestling between his very hooves, sleeping soundly in entire peace and contentment, the little, round, podgy, childish form of the baby otter. All this, he saw, for one moment breathless and intense, vivid on the morning sky; and still, as he looked, he lived; and still, as he lived, he wondered.

"Rat!" he found breath to whisper, shaking. "Are you afraid?"

"Afraid?" murmured the Rat, his eyes shining with unutterable love. "Afraid! Of *Him*? O, never, never! And yet—and yet—O, Mole, I am afraid!"

Then the two animals, crouching to the earth, bowed their heads and did worship.

Sudden and magnificent, the sun's broad golden disc showed itself over the horizon facing them; and the first rays, shooting across the level water-meadows, took the animals full in the eyes and dazzled them. When they were able to look once more, the Vision had vanished, and the air was full of the carol of birds that hailed the dawn.

As they stared blankly, in dumb misery deepening as they slowly realised all they had seen and all they had lost, a capricious little breeze, dancing up from the surface of the water, tossed the aspens, shook the dewy roses and blew lightly and caressingly in their faces; and with its soft touch came instant oblivion. For this is the last best gift that the kindly demigod is careful to bestow on those to whom he has revealed himself in their helping: the gift of forgetfulness. Lest the awful remembrance should remain and grow, and overshadow mirth and pleasure, and the great haunting memory should spoil all the after-lives of little animals helped out of difficulties, in order that they should be happy and lighthearted as before.

Mole rubbed his eyes and stared at Rat, who was looking about him in a puzzled sort of way. "I beg your pardon; what did you say, Rat?" he asked.

"I think I was only remarking," said Rat slowly, "that this was the right sort of place, and that here, if anywhere, we should find him. And look! Why, there he is, the little fellow!" And with a cry of delight he ran towards the slumbering Portly.

But Mole stood still a moment, held in thought. As one wakened suddenly from a beautiful dream, who struggles to recall it, and can recapture nothing but a dim sense of the beauty of it, the beauty! Till that, too, fades away in its turn, and the dreamer bitterly accepts the hard, cold waking and all its penalties; so Mole, after struggling with his memory for a brief space, shook his head sadly and followed the Rat.

Portly woke up with a joyous squeak, and wriggled with pleasure at the sight of his father's friends, who had played with him so often in past days. In a moment, however, his face grew blank, and he fell to hunting round in a circle with pleading whine. As a child that has fallen happily asleep in its nurse's arms, and wakes to find itself alone and laid in a strange place, and searches corners and cupboards, and runs from room to room, despair growing silently in its heart, even so Portly searched the island and searched, dogged and unwearying, till at last the black moment came for giving it up, and sitting down and crying bitterly.

The Mole ran quickly to comfort the little animal; but Rat, lingering, looked long and doubtfully at certain hoof-marks deep in the sward.

"Some—great—animal—has been here," he murmured slowly and thoughtfully; and stood musing, musing; his mind strangely stirred.

"Come along, Rat!" called the Mole. "Think of poor Otter, waiting up there by the ford!"

Portly had soon been comforted by the promise of a treat—a jaunt on the river in Mr. Rat's real boat; and the two animals conducted him to the water's side, placed him securely between them in the bottom of the boat, and paddled off down the backwater. The sun was fully up by now, and hot on them, birds sang lustily and without restraint, and flowers smiled and nodded from either bank, but somehow—so thought the animals—with less of richness and blaze of colour than they seemed to remember seeing quite recently somewhere—they wondered where.

The main river reached again, they turned the boat's head upstream, towards the point where they knew their friend was keeping his lonely vigil. As they drew near the familiar ford, the Mole took the boat in to the bank, and they lifted Portly out and set him on his legs on the tow-path, gave him his marching orders and a friendly fare-well pat on the back, and shoved out into midstream. They watched the little animal as he waddled along the path contentedly and with importance; watched him till they saw his muzzle suddenly lift and his waddle break into a clumsy amble as he quickened his pace with shrill whines and wriggles of recognition. Looking up the river, they could see Otter start up, tense and rigid, from out of the shallows where he crouched in dumb patience, and could hear his amazed and joyous bark as he bounded up through the osiers on to the path. Then the Mole, with a strong pull on one oar, swung the boat round and let the full stream bear them down again whither it would, their quest now happily ended.

"I feel strangely tired, Rat," said the Mole, leaning wearily over his oars as the boat drifted. "It's being up all night, you'll say, perhaps; but that's nothing. We do as much half the nights of the week, at this time of the year. No; I feel as if I had been through something very exciting and rather terrible, and it was just over; and yet nothing particular has happened."

"Or something very surprising and splendid and beautiful," mur-mured the Rat, leaning back and closing his eyes. "I feel just as you do, Mole; simply dead tired, though not body tired. It's lucky we've got the stream with us, to take us home. Isn't it jolly to feel the sun again, soaking into one's bones! And hark to the wind playing in the reeds!"

"It's like music—far away music," said the Mole nodding drowsily.

"So I was thinking," murmured the Rat, dreamful and languid. "Dance-music—the lilting sort that runs on without a stop—but with words in it, too—it passes into words and out of them again—I catch them at intervals—then it is dance-music once more, and then nothing but the reeds' soft thin whispering."

"You hear better than I," said the Mole sadly. "I cannot catch the words."

"Let me try and give you them," said the Rat softly, his eyes still closed. "Now it is turning into words again—faint but clear—*Lest the awe should dwell—And turn your frolic to fret—You shall look on my power at the helping hour—But then you shall forget!* Now the reeds take it up—*forget, forget,* they sigh, and it dies away in a rustle and a whisper. Then the voice returns—

"*Lest limbs be reddened and rent—I spring the trap that is set—As I loose the snare you may glimpse me there—For surely you shall forget!* Row nearer, Mole, nearer to the reeds! It is hard to catch, and grows each minute fainter."

"*Helper and healer, I cheer—Small waifs in the woodland wet—Strays I find in it, wounds I bind in it—Bidding them all forget!* Nearer, Mole, nearer! No, it is no good; the song has died away into reed-talk."

"But what do the words mean?" asked the wondering Mole.

"That I do not know," said the Rat simply. "I passed them on to you as they reached me. Ah! now they return again, and this time full and clear! This time, at last, it is the real, the unmistakable thing, simple—passionate—perfect——"

"Well, let's have it, then," said the Mole, after he had waited patiently for a few minutes, half-dozing in the hot sun.

But no answer came. He looked, and understood the silence. With a smile of much happiness on his face, and something of a listening look still lingering there, the weary Rat was fast asleep.

Laurence Housman (1865–1959)

LAURENCE HOUSMAN is in danger of becoming the forgotten fantasist, overshadowed as a poet by his eldest brother, A. E. Housman, and perhaps also by his elder sister Clemence, a fantasist writing at the same time and in much the same vogue as Lord Dunsany. This, despite the fact that Housman was very much his own man, holding strong views—particularly in his battles with the censor—which he had no qualms about making public. The *London Times* labelled him an "Idealist and Iconoclast" at the time of his death, also calling him "the last of the Victorians."

Perhaps Housman was too talented to be remembered for any one accomplishment. He was a productive artist, associated with the Pre-Raphaelites and illustrating Christina Rossetti's *Goblin Market* in 1893. He often illustrated his own and his sister's books. Housman also was a playwright, a poet, an essayist, a novelist, and a short-story writer, both for adults and for children. Some of his early fairy tales are perhaps a bit affected and some, such as those in *All-Fellows* (1896), are sanctimonious, but as he developed his art, the fantasies became sharper and more pertinent. Housman's best work may be found in *Gods and Their Makers* (1897), which anticipated Dunsany, and in *Ironical Tales* (1926), *Strange Ends and Discoveries* (1948), and *The Kind and the Foolish* (1952).

A good example of his later work is "Inside-Out," first published in 1917 during the years of the Great War; like the Senna story, recorded by Fairbridge, it considers oppression and how, through imagination, it may be escaped.

Inside-Out
The Story of Bunder-Runder, the Jailbird
Laurence Housman

Bunder-Runder was in jail. He was there for having talked too much, for saying things which the owners of the jail did not at all like, and which those who did not own the jail liked only too well.

The people of the country did not own the jail; that you must quite understand. It was owned by those of another country; the natives only paid for it. That was Bunder-Runder's complaint, or one of them. He did not yet know how good it was for a people not to own jails at all, and how much better it was to be in a jail than to own one. Would he ever find that out, do you think? What can a jail teach one?

In this jail Bunder-Runder was to remain for ten years. He was a young man, strong, rather beautiful. Women loved to look at him. They laughed when they saw him put forth his strength easily to do them a service; they laughed more when they put their children into his arms for him to play with. He had not yet any children of his own. That was soon to have been—love, marriage, and home. The vision he had long had of them was then to become a dear, kind, foolish reality, a little world of his own to shape and cherish and make grow, sweeter and more beautiful than all the bigger world around him. But now, no. That little world, on the making of which his mind had been bent, had fallen from his hand, shattered.

Ten years!

"When I come out," Bunder-Runder said to himself, "I shall be old. Everyone will have forgotten me. It will be like another world; my thoughts will not have gone into it, or anything I have done; I shall not belong to it. I shall be old, but I shall have made nothing." And as he thought thus, his very blood seemed to be weeping—the warm, swift blood which ran strenuously through him, touching as with tears the heart and head and feet and hands, which henceforth were to be useless.

Every time he began thinking, grief took hold of his thoughts and drew them to the same end.

"I am shut up in walls," he cried. "It were better that I were dead." Just as his blood went weeping through his body, so through his brain his thoughts went weeping from place to place; round and round wearily they went, beating a high-road for grief to travel by.

After he had been in prison for a while, food was brought to him, and he ate; but he did not know why he ate.

"I am eating only to become old," he said to himself. "What good is that to me?" He left off eating.

But presently he grew so hungry that food seemed good to him again, and time not so long or so vain a thing as dying without having learned all that there was to learn.

So when food was again brought to him he ate, sitting to it in seemly fashion, with thoughts turned aside from grief for a while to the strange beauty and brotherhood of things which grew and were serviceable to man.

Then his mind went out to the ricefields, green and waving and changing color toward ripeness from day to day; changing, too, as the light fell on them, morning or evening, from east or west; and at night, under moon and stars, more wonderfully changed still, and always different, yet always inwardly the same.

But as soon as he had finished eating, his thoughts came back to him with a shock, and he remembered that he was a prisoner.

"I shall see the rice-fields shining no more," he said, "till I am old. Then they will have ceased to shine, for then with my old eyes I shall no longer see them." And turning his face to the wall, he wept. It was always the same wall his thoughts came back to.

The same wall! How long had that wall been there? How had it come? Who were the men that had built it? He began to look at and to examine it. It was strong, but it was not very old; not so old, he thought, as his own father. Yet it seemed older, for already within its narrow space many young lives had pined and faded and grown old waiting for freedom.

Then, as he bethought him, he knew how it had come, and what men had had the building of it. They were his own brothers, his countrymen; and they, not gladly or willingly, but being ordered to it and for payment, had built this wall to be a prison for themselves and others. They had drawn clay from the beds of dried rivers, they had made bricks, they had hewn stone and timber, they had mixed plaster and mortar, they had reared up beam and roof, cutting off light and air from the space below, dividing it into cells; and now into this space below he, their brother, had come to be kept, wasted and useless, to bury bit by bit, one day at a time, with nothing of change to make one seem different from another, the ten most beautiful years of his life, with all their gladness taken out of them.

"Oh, Brothers, why have you done this to me?" he cried.

And suddenly his own thoughts answered for them. "Because we could not help ourselves; because we are all broken parts of that which was meant to be one whole. All over the world men are building walls, dividing themselves each from each, through ignorance and cruelty and fear. Because they don't know, that is why people are afraid of one another; and being afraid, they become cruel. That is why they build walls, not here only. All over the world it is the same—walls, walls. As walls grow rotten and old, as long as fear lasts, they will make us build others in place of them."

Bunder-Runder laid his hand on his prison-wall; he felt the strength and the depth of it, how well it was built, what a lot of brick and stone lay there, imprisoned like himself, but for much longer a time. Of that imprisonment not ten or twenty or fifty years would see the end.

"Brothers," said Bunder-Runder, "I am sorry for you. For your setting free is further away than mine; before you even begin to be old I shall be dead. Old age is good, is it not? But it is so far away."

Thus to his prison-wall he spoke, pitying it.

Suddenly he had a thought: it stood up and looked at him. It seemed to be standing only on one foot, on the very point of a toe, as if to show, even without motion, how light and quick and alert it could be. Then it seemed as though it lifted a hand and beckoned to him.

"Let us go out!" it said.

"How can one go out through this wall?" said Bunder-Runder. "We are in prison."

"There is no wall that *I* cannot get through," said his thought. It gave a flick of its foot, and was gone.

A moment later, and it was back again.

"Outside there is sunshine," it said.

"Yes," said Bunder-Runder, very attentive.

"There has been rain," his thought went on. "The wells are all full, the streams are running down from the hills; the frogs are singing in the marshes, and the rice-fields are beginning to look green."

"I know," said Bunder-Runder.

Other thoughts began cropping up thick and fast; in and out they went. It was quite true that there was no wall they could not get through.

They began to crowd in on him. Bunder-Runder let them come and go again just as they liked. He made them all welcome. If they wished to stay, they stayed; if they wished to go, they went.

Bunder-Runder sat in a sort of dream.

"This wall is wearing thin," he said to himself and laughed, while quicker and quicker his thoughts went in and out.

Presently he began singing. First he began imitating the song of the frogs, then of the birds. Hearing so much noise going on within, one of the jailers looked in on him. But Bunder-Runder was outside, and did not see him; Bunder-Runder was up in the hills. He had climbed quite high; he was looking down on the plain; he could see all the streams shining a way through the grainfields; driving bullocks along the road; he could hear them call as they passed to other men working in the fields; he could hear—

"Hi, you!" cried his jailer for the third time. "Not so much noise in there!"

Bunder-Runder came back with a bound, and sat cross-legged, smiling up at the eye which looked in on him through the hole in the door.

"High and mighty and merciful, I beg pardon," said Bunder-Runder, respectfully; "I forgot myself; I did not remember where I was. It is a beautiful day, is it not?"

The jailer grunted and withdrew, and Bunder-Runder was off again. He came back to his cell to sleep, quite tired, but most wonderfully refreshed. Truly, as he had said, it had been a beautiful day.

After that the days grew more and more beautiful. In and out went his thoughts; they never left him alone. He was always forgetting himself, and sang without knowing it.

His jailer reported him to the governor.

"Bunder-Runder," he said, "is always making more noise than he has any right to. From the way he sings, Sahib, you would think he was at a festival or at a wedding or at a rich uncle's funeral. I can't cure him of it; I've left him without light and I've left him without food, and still he goes on. It's not reasonable unless he is planning some way by which to escape."

The governor seemed to think as the jailer did; he caused Bunder-Runder to be brought before him, and examined him up and down, and could discover nothing. He caused his cell to be searched, and, to make doubly sure, had him transferred to another. But despite it all, the singing of Bunder-Runder went on, and some days it was as though he were burying not one rich uncle, but ten.

In a way that is what Bunder-Runder was doing. He was burying one after another all the injuries that life had done him in the days when he was at liberty, and from the grave of every injury and injustice that he buried a little kindness sprang up to life and came to keep him company. Bunder-Runder's cell became full of these little kindnesses. They sat round him and under him, they leaned over him, they laughed and jested, pushing him this way and that. Every morning when he woke they pushed him into the open. He left his cell behind, passing through the thin walls, and followed their leading away over the shining plains and into the lives of people he knew and of others he had never known, and of others still who had not yet been born.

He began to make a poem about them all in his own head; he must not write it down. That occupied him; day by day it grew larger, filling his mind. He sat very silent; his jailer no more complained of him.

"His spirit is properly broken," said he to the governor; "he has become good." And the governor gave him a good-conduct mark.

In the course of three years Bunder-Runder earned a lot of good-conduct marks, but he did not know of it. The poem was nearly finished; that was all he cared about.

It was a very beautiful poem, all about children—children of tender years, children in the spring of youth, in the full strength of manhood, and in the decline of age; for he had found out that secret which keeps alive the common child in us all. When the governor of the prison came and spoke to him, Bunder-Runder heard him—under his beard and inside that fat, red face of his—babbling like a child; and putting it into his poem as soon as the governor's back was turned, he swung his head this way and that and laughed: for the babbling of the governor's voice was as sweet to him as the sound of a brook that runs down to empty itself into the great river and into the sea. It wanted only that: the poem was done.

Out in the world everything had begun to spring; flowers and the young green fields of rice and music in the living heart; and from every tree, a little shaken by the wind, came fragrance to catch the breath and a twinkle of leaves to make delight to the eye. Bunder-Runder was there in the midst of it all; oh, yes, he was there. His poem was finished now, and he stood on the ridge of hills looking out over the villages of the plains, and in every village, he knew, a festival was going on, and people were rejoicing, perhaps not knowing why. But he knew that it was because the eternal child in Nature was looking once more into men's eyes as unspoiled as ever, as clear and shining and pure as in the days of old. For hundreds and thousands of years wrong and cruelty had been trying to possess and cover the earth; but it had failed, and Nature was as much a child as she had ever been.

Bunder-Runder, with his finished poem in his heart, followed his thoughts from village to village; and everywhere he went he found a home waiting for him. He had not to speak: the meaning of his poem was in his face; people came and looked at him, then ran to tell others, and word of him went before. Everywhere he went that day whole villages came out to meet him. The children and the young women threw garlands upon him as he passed. He became a wagon of flowers; a wonderful scent filled his brain; he ceased to see the faces that thronged about him or hear the voices of the people. Forward and forward he moved till he came to a deep sleep.

In the evening, just before sunset, the jailer opened the door of Bunder-Runder's cell. He looked in; then, without looking again, he ran fast, fast to fetch the governor. He was almost too frightened to speak; but what he did say was enough to make the governor understand that the prison rules were being broken. So the governor put on an angry countenance and came with him to the door of Bunder-Runder's cell.

Inside sat Bunder-Runder very still, his legs crossed, his hands resting upon his feet; and all about him hung garlands of flowers, breathing incense very strange. The cell was full of their fragrance.

"Number 109," said the governor, "where did you get those flowers?"

Bunder-Runder did not answer.

"Go and give him a shake," said the governor. "He is asleep."

"Sahib, I dare not," replied the jailer.

So the governor went and did it himself. At the governor's touch Bunder-Runder bowed softly forward, his face to the ground; and suddenly all the garlands of flowers that were upon him faded away, leaving only their fragrance behind.

The governor turned and ran out of the cell, for he too was afraid. Bunder-Runder was just as harmless now that he was dead as ever he had been in life, and yet the governor was afraid. That is often the way. People are afraid of things they do not understand.

The cell where Bunder-Runder lived those three years making his poem has been many times washed and disinfected; but there is still something the matter with it, and it is almost, useless, for when a prisoner is put into it he sings.

Lord Dunsany (1878–1957)

A TALL, BLUFF MAN who was a big-game hunter, a champion chess player, a soldier, a politician, and a peer of the realm hardly seems to have the right credentials for a writer of fantasy. But that's exactly what Edward John Moreton Drax Plunkett, Eighteenth Baron Dunsany, was. Writing in *The Encyclopedia of Fantasy* in 1997, John Clute remarked that Dunsany "was instrumental in creating the essential autonomous venues within which modern fantasy could be told." These venues were not only an adult world of faerie, and that none-too-clear overlap between our world and another, but also separate secondary worlds where heroes and villains led their bizarre and often uncertain lives. Dunsany's stories rarely conclude with "happy ever after." Quite the opposite. He recognised the realities of existence, even in a fantasy world.

Dunsany enjoyed the Irish literary world which, in the 1890s, was seeing a Celtic revival in the hands of W. B. Yeats, George Russell ("Æ"), and George Moore, and he may have been encouraged by Æ in his consideration of the deities of another world; but the key inspiration came when he saw a performance of the play *The Darling of the Gods* by David Belasco and John Luther Long at Her Majesty's Theatre in early 1904. The play is set in an idealized version of Japan, complete with its gods, and ends in a celestial heaven. Dunsany's imagination set to work creating an Old Testament-style volume that explored the mythology of a world through its deities. The result appeared as *The Gods of Pegana* in 1905, the first of over ninety books Dunsany would see published in his lifetime. The stories were illustrated by Sidney H. Sime, whose partnership with Lord Dunsany led to some of the most atmospheric stories and images in fantasy.

The pieces in *The Gods of Pegana* are scarcely stories, but more like fables, or simply incidents, and it is their sum total that produces the desired effect. Many of Dunsany's stories are brief, although he could write at great length if he wished, as he did successfully with the novels *The King of Elfland's Daughter* (1924), *The Charwoman's Shadow* (1926), *The Curse of the Wise Woman* (1933), and others. He also wrote many plays, some of which, such as *A Night at an Inn* (1916), are occasionally performed. But it is his short stories that proved the most important and influential—and there were over 500 of them. The early collections contain what most regard as the best, *Time and the Gods* (1906), *The Sword of Welleran* (1908), *A Dreamer's Tales* (1910), and *The Book of Wonder* (1912)—best because they were unique, original and inspirational.

Because the pieces are brief, I have selected two to include in this anthology; they are related, because the protagonist in the second story is the son of the protagonist in the first. Not that that helps either of them.

TALES OF TWO THIEVES
The Distressing Tale of
Thangobrind the Jeweller

Lord Dunsany

When Thangobrind the jeweller heard the ominous cough, he turned at once upon that narrow way. A thief was he, of very high repute, being patronized by the lofty and elect, for he stole nothing smaller than the Moomoo's egg, and in all his life stole only four kinds of stone—the ruby, the diamond, the emerald, and the sapphire; and, as jewellers go, his honesty was great. Now there was a Merchant Prince who had come to Thangobrind and had offered his daughter's soul for the diamond that is larger than the human head and was to be found on the lap of the spider-idol, Hlo-hlo, in his temple of Moung-ga-ling; for he had heard that Thangobrind was a thief to be trusted.

Thangobrind oiled his body and slipped out of his shop, and went secretly through byways, and got as far as Snarp, before anybody knew that he was out on business again or missed his sword from its place under the counter. Thence he moved only by night, hiding by day and rubbing the edges of his sword, which he called Mouse because it was swift and nimble. The jeweller had subtle methods of travelling; nobody saw him cross the plains of Zid; nobody saw him come to Mursk or Tlun. O, but he loved shadows! Once the moon peeping out unexpectedly from a tempest had betrayed an ordinary jeweller; not so did it undo Thangobrind: the watchman only saw a crouching shape that snarled and laughed: "'Tis but a hyena," they said. Once in the city of Ag one of the guardians seized him, but Thangobrind was oiled and slipped from his hand; you scarcely heard his bare feet patter away. He knew that the Merchant Prince awaited his return, his little eyes open all night and glittering with greed; he knew how his daughter lay chained up and screaming night and day. Ah, Thangobrind knew. And had he not been out on business he had almost allowed himself one or two little laughs. But business was business, and the diamond that he sought still lay on the lap of Hlo-hlo, where it had been for the last two million years since Hlo-hlo created the world and gave unto it all things except that precious stone called Dead Man's Diamond. The jewel was often stolen, but it had a knack of coming back again to the lap of Hlo-hlo. Thangobrind knew this, but he was no common jeweller and hoped to outwit Hlo-hlo, perceiving not the trend of ambition and lust and that they are vanity.

How nimbly he threaded his way thought the pits of Snood!—now like a botanist, scrutinising the ground; now like a dancer, leaping from crumbling edges. It was quite dark when he went by the towers of Tor, where archers shoot ivory arrows at strangers lest any foreigner should alter their laws, which are bad, but not to be altered by mere aliens. At night they shoot by the sound of the strangers' feet. O, Thangobrind, Thangobrind, was ever a jeweller like you! He dragged two stones behind him by long cords, and at these the archers shot. Tempting indeed was the snare that they set in Woth, the emeralds loose-set in the city's gate; but Thangobrind discerned the golden cord that climbed the wall from each and the weights that would topple upon him if he touched one, and so he left them, though he left them weeping, and at last came to Theth. There all men worship Hlo-hlo; though they are willing to believe in other gods, as missionaries attest, but only as creatures of the chase for the hunting of Hlo-hlo, who wears Their halos, so these people say, on golden hooks along his hunting-belt. And from Theth he came to the city of Moung and the temple of Moung-ga-ling, and entered and saw the spider-idol, Hlo-hlo, sitting there with Dead Man's Diamond glittering on his lap, and looking for all the world like a full moon, but a full moon seen by a lunatic who had slept too long in its rays, for there was in Dead Man's Diamond a certain sinister look and a boding of things to happen that are better not mentioned here. The face of the spider-idol was lit by that fatal gem; there was no other light. In spite of his shocking limbs and that demoniac body, his face was serene and apparently unconscious.

A little fear came into the mind of Thangobrind the jeweller, a passing tremor—no more; business was business and he hoped for the best. Thangobrind offered honey to Hlo-hlo and prostrated himself before him. Oh, he was cunning! When the priests stole out of the darkness to lap up the honey they were stretched senseless on the temple floor, for there was a drug in the honey that was offered to Hlo-hlo. And Thangobrind the jeweller picked Dead Man's Diamond up and put it on his shoulder and trudged away from the shrine; and Hlo-hlo the spider-idol said nothing at all, but he laughed softly as the jeweller shut the door. When the priests awoke out of the grip of the drug that was offered with the honey to Hlo-hlo, they rushed to a little secret room with an outlet on the stars and cast a horoscope of the thief. Something that they saw in the horoscope seemed to satisfy the priests.

It was not like Thangobrind to go back by the road by which he had come. No, he went by another road, even though it led to the narrow way, night-house and spider-forest.

The city of Moung went towering by behind him, balcony above balcony, eclipsing half the stars, as he trudged away with his diamond. He was not easy as he trudged away. Though when a soft pittering as of velvet feet arose behind him he refused to acknowledge that it might be what he feared, yet the instincts of his trade told him that it is not well when any noise whatever follows a diamond by night, and this was one of the largest that had ever come to him in the way of business. When he came to the narrow way that leads to spider-forest, Dead Man's Diamond feeling cold and heavy, and the velvety footfall seeming fearfully close, the jeweller stopped and almost hesitated. He looked behind him; there was nothing there. He listened attentively; there was no sound now. Then he thought of the screams of the Merchant Prince's daughter, whose soul was the diamond's price, and smiled and went stoutly on. There watched him, apathetically, over the narrow way, that grim and dubious woman whose house is Night. Thangobrind, hearing no longer the sound of suspicious feet, felt easier now. He was all but come to the end of the narrow way, when the woman listlessly uttered that ominous cough.

The cough was too full of meaning to be disregarded. Thangobrind turned round and saw at once what he feared. The spider-idol had not stayed at home. The jeweller put his diamond gently upon the ground and drew his sword called Mouse. And then began that famous fight upon the narrow way in which the grim old woman whose house was Night seemed to take so little interest. To the spider-idol you saw at once it was all a horrible joke. To the jeweller it was grim earnest. He fought and panted and was pushed back slowly along the narrow way, but he wounded Hlo-hlo all the while with terrible long gashes all over his deep, soft body till Mouse was slimy with blood. But at

last the persistent laughter of Hlo-hlo was too much for the jeweller's
nerves, and, once more wounding his demoniac foe, he sank aghast
and exhausted by the door of the house called Night at the feet of
the grim old woman, who having uttered once that ominous cough
interfered no further with the course of events. And there carried
Thangobrind the jeweller away those whose duty it was, to the house
where the two men hang, and taking down from his hook the left-
hand of the two, they put that venturous jeweller in his place; so that
there fell on him the doom that he feared, as all men know though
it is so long since, and there abated somewhat the ire of the envious
gods.

And the only daughter of the Merchant Prince felt so little gratitude for this great deliverance that she took to respectability of the
militant kind, and became aggressively dull, and called her home the
English Riviera, and had platitudes worked in worsted upon her tea-
cosy, and in the end never died, but passed away in her residence.

TALES OF TWO THIEVES, cont.
The Bird of the Difficult Eye
Lord Dunsany

Observant men and women that know their Bond Street well will appreciate my astonishment when in a jeweller's shop I perceived that nobody was furtively watching me. Not only this, but when I even picked up a little carved crystal to examine it no shop-assistants crowded round me. I walked the whole length of the shop, still no one politely followed.

Seeing from this that some extraordinary revolution had occurred in the jewelry business I went with my curiosity well aroused to a queer old person, half demon and half man, who has an idol-shop in a by-way of the City and who keeps me informed of affairs at the Edge of the World. And briefly over a pinch of heathen incense that he takes by way of snuff he gave me this tremendous information: that Mr. Neepy Thang, the son of Thangobrind, had returned from the Edge of the World and was even now in London.

The information may not appear tremendous to those unacquainted with the source of jewelry; but when I say that the only thief employed by any West-end jeweller since famous Thangobrind's distressing doom is this same Neepy Thang, and that for lightness of fingers and swiftness of stockinged foot they have none better in Paris, it will be understood why the Bond-street jewellers no longer cared what became of their old stock.

There were big diamonds in London that summer and a few considerable sapphires. In certain astounding kingdoms behind the East strange sovereigns missed from their turbans the heirlooms of ancient wars, and here and there the keepers of crown jewels who had not heard the stockinged feet of Thang, were questioned and died slowly.

And the jewellers gave a little dinner to Thang at the Hotel Great Magnificent; the windows had not been opened for five years and there was wine at a guinea a bottle that you could not tell from

201

champagne, and cigars at half a crown with a Havana label. Altogether it was a splendid evening for Thang.

But I have to tell of a far sadder thing than a dinner at a hotel. The public require jewelry, and jewelry must be obtained. I have to tell of Neepy Thang's last journey.

That year the fashion was emeralds. A man named Green had recently crossed the Channel on a bicycle and the jewellers said that a green stone would be particularly appropriate to commemorate the event and recommended emeralds.

Now a certain moneylender of Cheapside who had just been made a peer had divided his gains into three equal parts; one for the purchase of the peerage, country-house and park, and the twenty thousand pheasants that are absolutely essential, and one for the upkeep of the position, while the third he banked abroad, partly to cheat the native tax-gatherer, and partly because it seemed to him that the days of the Peerage were few and that he might at any moment be called upon to start afresh elsewhere. In the upkeep of the position he included jewelry for his wife, and so it came about that Lord Castlenorman placed an order with two well-known Bond Street jewellers named Messrs. Grosvenor and Campbell to the extent of £100,000 for a few reliable emeralds.

But the emeralds in stock were mostly small and shop-soiled, and Neepy Thang had to set out at once before he had had as much as a week in London. I will briefly sketch his project. Not many knew it, for where the form of business is blackmail the fewer creditors you have the better (which of course in various degrees applies at all times).

On the shores of the risky seas of Shiroora Shan grows one tree only, so that upon its branches if anywhere in the world there must build its nest the Bird of the Difficult Eye. Neepy Thang had come by this information, which was indeed the truth, that if the bird migrated to Fairyland before the three eggs hatched out they would undoubtedly all turn into emeralds, while if they hatched out first it would be a bad business.

When he had mentioned these eggs to Messrs. Grosvenor and Campbell they had said, "The very thing": they were men of few words, in English, for it was not their native tongue.

So Neepy Thang set out. He bought the purple ticket at Victoria Station. He went by Herne Hill, Bromley and Bickley and passed

St. Mary Cray. At Eynsford he changed, and taking a footpath along a winding valley went wandering into the hills. And at the top of a hill in a little wood, where all the anemones long since were over, and the perfume of mint and thyme from outside came drifting in with Thang, he found once more the familiar path, age-old and fair as wonder, that leads to the Edge of the World. Little to him were its sacred memories that are one with the secret of earth, for he was on business, and little would they be to me if I ever put them on paper. Let it suffice that he went down that path going further and further from the fields we know, and all the way he muttered to himself, "What if the eggs hatch out and it be a bad business!" The glamour that is at all times upon those lonely lands that lie at the back of the chalky hills of Kent intensified as he went upon his journeys. Queerer and queerer grew the things that he saw by little World-End Path. Many a twilight descended upon that journey with all their mysteries, many a blaze of stars; many a morning came flaming up to a tinkle of silvern horns; till the outpost elves of Fairyland came in sight and the glittering crests of Fairyland's three mountains betokened the journey's end. And so with painful steps (for the shores of the world are covered with huge crystals) he came to the risky seas of Shiroora Shan and saw them pounding to gravel the wreckage of fallen stars, saw them and heard their roar, those shipless seas that between earth and the fairies' homes heave beneath some huge wind that is none of our four. And there in the darkness on the grizzly coast, for darkness was swooping slantwise down the sky as though with some evil purpose, there stood that lonely, gnarled and deciduous tree. It was a bad place to be found in after dark, and night descended with multitudes of stars, beasts prowling in the blackness gluttered* at Neepy Thang. And there on a lower branch within easy reach he clearly saw the Bird of the Difficult Eye sitting upon the nest for which she is famous. Her face was towards those three inscrutable mountains, far-off on the other side of the risky seas, whose hidden valleys are Fairyland. Though not yet autumn in the fields we know, it was close on mid-winter here, the moment as Thang knew when those eggs hatch out. Had he miscalculated and arrived a minute too late? Yet the bird was even now about to migrate, her pinions fluttered and

---

*See any dictionary, but in vain.

her gaze was toward fairyland. Thang hoped, and muttered a prayer to those pagan gods whose spite and vengeance he had most reason to fear. It seems that it was too late or a prayer too small to placate them, for there and then the stroke of mid-winter came and the eggs hatched out in the roar of Shiroora Shan or ever the bird was gone with her difficult eye, and it was a bad business indeed for Neepy Thang; I haven't the heart to tell you any more.

"'Ere," said Lord Castlenorman some few weeks later to Messrs. Grosvenor and Campbell, "you aren't 'arf taking your time about those emeralds."

H. P. Lovecraft (1890–1937)

H. P. LOVECRAFT, the noted writer of cosmic horror, was one of those who fell under the spell of Lord Dunsany. In a letter written in 1929, Lovecraft commented that Dunsany "influenced me overwhelmingly about a decade ago—my 'White Ship' period." He also wrote, "I know of no other writer who so magically opens up the enchanted sunset gates of secret & ethereal worlds." Lovecraft had attended a lecture given by Dunsany in New York in 1919 and rapidly consumed everything Dunsany had written.

It is more likely that Dunsany's work tapped into an imaginative vein that Lovecraft already appreciated: the more exotic works of Poe, William Beckford, and Bulwer-Lytton. Lovecraft had written "Polaris" before he read anything by Dunsany, yet the story bears comparison with the later Dunsanian tales. These include "The White Ship," "The Doom That Came to Sarnath," "The Cats of Ulthar," "The Quest of Iranon," and "Celephaïs," all written within the space of two years. "Celephaïs," apart from being one of the best tales, has the added significance that Lovecraft later returned to the events in the story, reworking them into his novella *The Dream-Quest of Unknown Kadath*.

Dunsany's importance to Lovecraft was not so much in the stories that Lovecraft came to write, but in his creation of a pantheon of godlike entities whose existence looms over and inevitably interferes with the world of humans.

Celephaïs

H. P. Lovecraft

In a dream Kuranes saw the city in the valley, and the seacoast beyond, and the snowy peak overlooking the sea, and the gaily painted galleys that sail out of the harbour toward distant regions where the sea meets the sky. In a dream it was also that he came by his name of Kuranes, for when awake he was called by another name.

Perhaps it was natural for him to dream a new name; for he was the last of his family, and alone among the indifferent millions of London, so there were not many to speak to him and to remind him who he had been. His money and lands were gone, and he did not care for the ways of the people about him, but preferred to dream and write of his dreams. What he wrote was laughed at by those to whom he showed it, so that after a time he kept his writings to himself, and finally ceased to write.

The more he withdrew from the world about him, the more wonderful became his dreams; and it would have been quite futile to try to describe them on paper. Kuranes was not modern, and did not think like others who wrote. Whilst they strove to strip from life its embroidered robes of myth and to show in naked ugliness the foul thing that is reality, Kuranes sought for beauty alone. When truth and experience failed to reveal it, he sought it in fancy and illusion, and found it on his very doorstep, amid the nebulous memories of childhood tales and dreams.

There are not many persons who know what wonders are opened to them in the stories and visions of their youth; for when as children we listen and dream, we think but half-formed thoughts, and when as men we try to remember, we are dulled and prosaic with the poison of life. But some of us awake in the night with strange phantasms of enchanted hills and gardens, of fountains that sing in the sun, of golden cliffs overhanging murmuring seas, of plains that stretch down to sleeping cities of bronze and stone, and of shadowy companies of heroes that ride caparisoned white horses along the edges of thick forests; and then we know that we have looked back through the ivory gates into that world of wonder which was ours before we were wise and unhappy.

Kuranes came very suddenly upon his old world of childhood. He had been dreaming of the house where he had been born; the great stone house covered with ivy, where thirteen generations of his ancestors had lived, and where he had hoped to die. It was moonlight, and he had stolen out into the fragrant summer night, through the gardens, down the terraces, past the great oaks of the park, and along the long white road to the village. The village seemed very old, eaten away at the edge like the moon which had commenced to wane, and Kuranes wondered whether the peaked roofs of the small houses hid sleep or death. In the streets were spears of long grass, and the window-panes on either side broken or filmily staring. Kuranes had not lingered, but had plodded on as though summoned toward some goal. He dared not disobey the summons for fear it might prove an illusion like the urges and aspirations of waking life, which do not lead to any goal. Then he had been drawn down a lane that led off from the village street toward the channel cliffs, and had come to the end of things to the precipice and the abyss where all the village and all the world fell abruptly into the unechoing emptiness of infinity, and where even the sky ahead was empty and unlit by the crumbling moon and the peering stars. Faith had urged him on, over the precipice and into the gulf, where he had floated down, down, down; past dark, shapeless, undreamed dreams, faintly glowing spheres that may have been partly dreamed dreams, and laughing winged things that seemed to mock the dreamers of all the worlds. Then a rift seemed to open in the darkness before him, and he saw the city of the valley, glistening radiantly far, far below, with a background of sea and sky, and a snow-capped mountain near the shore.

Kuranes had awakened the very moment he beheld the city, yet he knew from his brief glance that it was none other than Celephaïs, in the Valley of Ooth-Nargai beyond the Tanarian Hills where his spirit had dwelt all the eternity of an hour one summer afternoon very long ago, when he had slipt away from his nurse and let the warm sea-breeze lull him to sleep as he watched the clouds from the cliff near the village. He had protested then, when they had found him, waked him, and carried him home, for just as he was aroused he had been about to sail in a golden galley for those alluring regions where the sea meets the sky. And now he was equally resentful of awaking, for he had found his fabulous city after forty weary years.

But three nights afterward Kuranes came again to Celephaïs. As before, he dreamed first of the village that was asleep or dead, and of the abyss down which one must float silently; then the rift appeared again, and he beheld the glittering minarets of the city, and saw the graceful galleys riding at anchor in the blue harbour, and watched the gingko trees of Mount Aran swaying in the sea-breeze. But this time he was not snatched away, and like a winged being settled gradually over a grassy hillside til finally his feet rested gently on the turf. He had indeed come back to the Valley of Ooth-Nargai and the splendid city of Celephaïs.

Down the hill amid scented grasses and brilliant flowers walked Kuranes, over the bubbling Naraxa on the small wooden bridge where he had carved his name so many years ago, and through the whispering grove to the great stone bridge by the city gate. All was as of old, nor were the marble walls discoloured, nor the polished bronze statues upon them tarnished. And Kuranes saw that he need not tremble lest the things he knew be vanished; for even the sentries on the ramparts were the same, and still as young as he remembered them. When he entered the city, past the bronze gates and over the onyx pavements, the merchants and camel-drivers greeted him as if he had never been away; and it was the same at the turquoise temple of Nath-Horthath, where the orchid-wreathed priests told him that there is no time in Ooth-Nargai, but only perpetual youth. Then Kuranes walked through the Street of Pillars to the seaward wall, where gathered the traders and sailors, and strange men from the regions where the sea meets the sky. There he stayed long, gazing out over the bright harbour where the ripples sparkled beneath an unknown sun, and where rode lightly the galleys from far places over the water. And he gazed also upon Mount Aran rising regally from the shore, its lower slopes green with swaying trees and its white summit touching the sky.

More than ever Kuranes wished to sail in a galley to the far places of which he had heard so many strange tales, and he sought again the captain who had agreed to carry him so long ago. He found the man, Athib, sitting on the same chest of spice he had sat upon before, and Athib seemed not to realize that any time had passed. Then the two rowed to a galley in the harbour, and giving orders to the oarmen, commenced to sail out into the billowy Cerenarian Sea that leads to the sky. For several days they glided undulatingly over the water, till finally they came to the horizon, where the sea meets the sky. Here the galley paused not at all, but floated easily in the blue of the sky among fleecy clouds tinted with rose. And far beneath the keel Kuranes could see strange lands and rivers and cities of surpassing beauty, spread indolently in the sunshine which seemed never to lessen or disappear. At length Athib told him that their journey was near its end, and that they would soon enter the harbour of Serannian, the pink marble city of the clouds, which is built on that ethereal coast where the west wind flows into the sky; but as the highest of the city's carven towers came into sight there was a sound somewhere in space, and Kuranes awaked in his London garret.

For many months after that Kuranes sought the marvellous city of Celephaïs and its sky-bound galleys in vain; and though his dreams carried him to many gorgeous and unheard-of places, no one whom he met could tell him how to find Ooth-Nargai beyond the Tanarian Hills. One night he went flying over dark mountains where there were faint, lone campfires at great distances apart, and strange, shaggy herds with tinkling bells on the leaders, and in the wildest part of this hilly country, so remote that few men could ever have seen it, he found a hideously ancient wall or causeway of stone zigzagging along the ridges and valleys; too gigantic ever to have risen by human hands, and of such a length that neither end of it could be seen. Beyond that wall in the grey dawn he came to a land of quaint gardens and cherry trees, and when the sun rose he beheld such beauty of red and white flowers, green foliage and lawns, white paths, diamond brooks, blue lakelets, carven bridges, and red-roofed pagodas, that he for a moment forgot Celephaïs in sheer delight. But he remembered it again when he walked down a white path toward a red-roofed pagoda, and would have questioned the people of this land about it, had he not found that there were no people there, but only birds and bees and butterflies. On another night Kuranes walked up a damp stone spiral stairway endlessly, and came to a tower window overlooking a mighty plain and river lit by the full moon; and in the silent city that spread away from the river bank he thought he beheld some feature or arrangement which he had known before. He would have descended and asked the way to Ooth-Nargai had not a fearsome aurora sputtered up from some remote place beyond the horizon, showing the ruin and antiquity of the city, and the stagnation of the reedy river, and the death lying

upon that land, as it had lain since King Kynaratholis came home
from his conquests to find the vengeance of the gods.

So Kuranes sought fruitlessly for the marvellous city of Celephaïs
and its galleys that sail to Serannian in the sky, meanwhile seeing
many wonders and once barely escaping from the high-priest not
to be described, which wears a yellow silken mask over its face and
dwells all alone in a prehistoric stone monastery in the cold desert
plateau of Leng. In time he grew so impatient of the bleak intervals
of day that he began buying drugs in order to increase his periods of
sleep. Hasheesh helped a great deal, and once sent him to a part of
space where form does not exist, but where glowing gases study the
secrets of existence. And a violet-coloured gas told him that this part
of space was outside what he had called infinity. The gas had not heard
of planets and organisms before, but identified Kuranes merely as one
from the infinity where matter, energy, and gravitation exist. Kuranes
was now very anxious to return to minaret-studded Celephaïs, and
increased his doses of drugs; but eventually he had no more money
left, and could buy no drugs. Then one summer day he was turned
out of his garret, and wandered aimlessly through the streets, drifting
over a bridge to a place where the houses grew thinner and thinner.
And it was there that fulfilment came, and he met the cortege of
knights come from Celephaïs to bear him thither forever.

Handsome knights they were, astride roan horses and clad in shining armour with tabards of cloth-of-gold curiously emblazoned. So
numerous were they, that Kuranes almost mistook them for an army,
but they were sent in his honour; since it was he who had created
Ooth-Nargai in his dreams, on which account he was now to be
appointed its chief god for evermore. Then they gave Kuranes a horse
and placed him at the head of the cavalcade, and all rode majestically
through the downs of Surrey and onward toward the region where
Kuranes and his ancestors were born. It was very strange, but as the
riders went on they seemed to gallop back through time; for whenever they passed through a village in the twilight they saw only such
houses and villagers as Chaucer or men before him might have seen,
and sometimes they saw knights on horseback with small companies
of retainers. When it grew dark they travelled more swiftly, till soon
they were flying uncannily as if in the air. In the dim dawn they came
upon the village which Kuranes had seen alive in his childhood, and
asleep or dead in his dreams. It was alive now, and early villagers
curtsied as the horsemen clattered down the street and turned off

into the lane that ends in the abyss of dreams. Kuranes had previously entered that abyss only at night, and wondered what it would look like by day; so he watched anxiously as the column approached its brink. Just as they galloped up the rising ground to the precipice a golden glare came somewhere out of the west and hid all the landscape in effulgent draperies. The abyss was a seething chaos of roseate and cerulean splendour, and invisible voices sang exultantly as the knightly entourage plunged over the edge and floated gracefully down past glittering clouds and silvery coruscations. Endlessly down the horsemen floated, their chargers pawing the aether as if galloping over golden sands; and then the luminous vapours spread apart to reveal a greater brightness, the brightness of the city Celephaïs, and the sea coast beyond, and the snowy peak overlooking the sea, and the gaily painted galleys that sail out of the harbour toward distant regions where the sea meets the sky.

And Kuranes reigned thereafter over Ooth-Nargai and all the neighboring regions of dream, and held his court alternately in Celephaïs and in the cloud-fashioned Serannian. He reigns there still, and will reign happily for ever, though below the cliffs at Innsmouth the channel tides played mockingly with the body of a tramp who had stumbled through the half-deserted village at dawn; played mockingly, and cast it upon the rocks by ivy-covered Trevor Towers, where a notably fat and especially offensive millionaire brewer enjoys the purchased atmosphere of extinct nobility.

Edgar Rice Burroughs (1875–1950)

THE ACCEPTANCE of fantasy as a legitimate fiction genre was evident from the extent that it was appearing in the popular fiction magazines, both in the United Kingdom and the United States. Much of this was due to the popularity of the novels of H. Rider Haggard (1856–1925), whose adventure romances, such as *King Solomon's Mines* (1885), *She* (1886), and *Ayesha* (1905) sparked an interest in stories of lost worlds on Earth. Others who tapped into this vein were Rudyard Kipling (1865–1936) with his *Jungle Book* (1894), and Edgar Rice Burroughs, in his tales of Tarzan.

It may seem surprising to see Burroughs in this anthology because, besides Tarzan, he is more closely associated with science fiction, or more properly the scientific romance, with stories set on Mars (Barsoom), Venus (Amtor) and the center of the Earth (Pellucidar); but, in fact, before he began his Martian series, he had experimented with a fairy tale, and the start of his first Martian adventure retains overtones of fantasy.

Burroughs was not very successful at the various business ventures he attempted. He had been a door-to-door salesman, worked on a ranch, worked for a mining company, and had even served as an accountant, all unsuccessfully. He had tried to follow in his father's footsteps in the military, but after two years a heart murmur brought that to an end. He married in 1900, and by 1911 had two young children. Burroughs dabbled in poetry, including some written for his nephews, which he called *Snake River Cottontail Tales*; but around 1907, or perhaps slightly earlier, he wrote what he called an "historical fairy tale," *Minidoka: 937th Earl of One Mile Series M*. It's a rather disjointed work, as if Burroughs had made up different stories about the characters on various nights and then attempted to string them together. He did nothing more with it and put it aside; it only came to light again after his death. Even then, the work remained unpublished until 1998.

However, desperate for money, Burroughs tried again and this time sent the draft of an unfinished novel to the pulp magazine *The All-Story,* whose editor, Thomas Metcalf, encouraged Burroughs to complete it. It was published as "Under the Moons of Mars" in the issues from February to July 1912. The book version, published in 1917, was retitled *A Princess of Mars.*

Although Burroughs later introduced a variety of scientific and technological innovations in "Under the Moons of Mars," at the outset the story has all the trappings of fantasy. The hero, John Carter, has been out prospecting with a friend, who is killed by Indians. Carter escapes with his friend's body and seeks refuge. The following excerpt picks up the story.

Under the Moons of Mars

Edgar Rice Burroughs

I had gone but a short distance further when what seemed to be an excellent trail opened up around the face of a high cliff. The trail was level and quite broad and led upward and in the general direction I wished to go. The cliff arose for several hundred feet on my right, and on my left was an equal and nearly perpendicular drop to the bottom of a rocky ravine.

I had followed this trail for perhaps a hundred yards when a sharp turn to the right brought me to the mouth of a large cave. The opening was about four feet in height and three to four feet wide, and at this opening the trail ended.

It was now morning, and, with the customary lack of dawn which is a startling characteristic of Arizona, it had become daylight almost without warning.

Dismounting, I laid Powell upon the ground, but the most painstaking examination failed to reveal the faintest spark of life. I forced water from my canteen between his dead lips, bathed his face and rubbed his hands, working over him continuously for the better part of an hour in the face of the fact that I knew him to be dead.

I was very fond of Powell; he was thoroughly a man in every respect; a polished southern gentleman; a staunch and true friend; and it was with a feeling of the deepest grief that I finally gave up my crude endeavors at resuscitation.

Leaving Powell's body where it lay on the ledge I crept into the cave to reconnoiter. I found a large chamber, possibly a hundred feet in diameter and thirty or forty feet in height; a smooth and well-worn floor, and many other evidences that the cave had, at some remote period, been inhabited. The back of the cave was so lost in dense shadow that I could not distinguish whether there were openings into other apartments or not.

As I was continuing my examination I commenced to feel a pleasant drowsiness creeping over me which I attributed to the fatigue of my long and strenuous ride, and the reaction from the excitement of the fight and the pursuit. I felt comparatively safe in my present location as I knew that one man could defend the trail to the cave against an army.

I soon became so drowsy that I could scarcely resist the strong desire to throw myself on the floor of the cave for a few moments' rest, but I knew that this would never do, as it would mean certain death at the hands of my red friends, who might be upon me at any moment. With an effort I started toward the opening of the cave only to reel drunkenly against a side wall, and from there slip prone upon the floor.

II

A sense of delicious dreaminess overcame me, my muscles relaxed, and I was on the point of giving way to my desire to sleep when the sound of approaching horses reached my ears. I attempted to spring to my feet but was horrified to discover that my muscles refused to respond to my will. I was now thoroughly awake, but as unable to move a muscle as though turned to stone. It was then, for the first time, that I noticed a slight vapor filling the cave. It was extremely tenuous and only noticeable against the opening which led to daylight. There also came to my nostrils a faintly pungent odor, and I could only assume that I had been overcome by some poisonous gas, but why I should retain my mental faculties and yet be unable to move I could not fathom.

I lay facing the opening of the cave and where I could see the short stretch of trail which lay between the cave and the turn of the cliff around which the trail led. The noise of the approaching horses had ceased, and I judged the Indians were creeping stealthily upon me along the little ledge which led to my living tomb. I remember that I hoped they would make short work of me as I did not particularly relish the thought of the innumerable things they might do to me if the spirit prompted them.

I had not long to wait before a stealthy sound apprised me of their nearness, and then a war-bonneted, paint-streaked face was thrust cautiously around the shoulder of the cliff, and savage eyes looked into mine. That he could see me in the dim light of the cave I was sure for the early morning sun was falling full upon me through the opening.

The fellow, instead of approaching, merely stood and stared; his eyes bulging and his jaw dropped. And then another savage face appeared, and a third and fourth and fifth, craning their necks over the shoulders of their fellows whom they could not pass upon the narrow ledge. Each face was the picture of awe and fear, but for what reason I did not know, nor did I learn until ten years later. That there were still other braves behind those who regarded me was apparent from the fact that the leaders passed back whispered word to those behind them.

Suddenly a low but distinct moaning sound issued from the recesses of the cave behind me, and, as it reached the ears of the Indians, they turned and fled in terror, panic-stricken. So frantic were their efforts to escape from the unseen thing behind me that one of the braves was hurled headlong from the cliff to the rocks below. Their wild cries echoed in the canyon for a short time, and then all was still once more.

The sound which had frightened them was not repeated, but it had been sufficient as it was to start me speculating on the possible horror which lurked in the shadows at my back. Fear is a relative term and so I can only measure my feelings at that time by what I had experienced in previous positions of danger and by those that I have passed through since; but I can say without shame that if the sensations I endured during the next few minutes were fear, then may God help the coward, for cowardice is of a surety its own punishment.

To be held paralyzed, with one's back toward some horrible and unknown danger from the very sound of which the ferocious Apache warriors turn in wild stampede, as a flock of sheep would madly flee from a pack of wolves, seems to me the last word in fearsome predicaments for a man who had ever been used to fighting for his life with all the energy of a powerful physique.

Several times I thought I heard faint sounds behind me as of somebody moving cautiously, but eventually even these ceased, and I was left to the contemplation of my position without interruption. I could but vaguely conjecture the cause of my paralysis, and my only hope lay in that it might pass off as suddenly as it had fallen upon me.

Late in the afternoon my horse, which had been standing with dragging rein before the cave, started slowly down the trail, evidently in search of food and water, and I was left alone with my mysterious unknown companion and the dead body of my friend, which lay just within my range of vision upon the ledge where I had placed it in the early morning.

From then until possibly midnight all was silence, the silence of the dead; then, suddenly, the awful moan of the morning broke upon my startled ears, and there came again from the black shadows the sound of a moving thing, and a faint rustling as of dead leaves. The shock to my already overstrained nervous system was terrible in the extreme, and with a superhuman effort I strove to break my awful bonds. It was an effort of the mind, of the will, of the nerves; not muscular, for I could not move even so much as my little finger, but none the less mighty for all that. And then something gave, there was a momentary feeling of nausea, a sharp click as of the snapping of a steel wire, and I stood with my back against the wall of the cave facing my unknown foe.

And then the moonlight flooded the cave, and there before me lay my own body as it had been lying all these hours, with the eyes staring toward the open ledge and the hands resting limply upon the ground. I looked first at my lifeless clay there upon the floor of the cave and then down at myself in utter bewilderment; for there I lay clothed, and yet here I stood but naked as at the minute of my birth.

The transition had been so sudden and so unexpected that it left me for a moment forgetful of aught else than my strange metamorphosis. My first thought was, is this then death! Have I indeed passed over forever into that other life! But I could not well believe this, as I could feel my heart pounding against my ribs from the exertion of my efforts to release myself from the anaesthesis which had held me. My breath was coming in quick, short gasps, cold sweat stood out from every pore of my body, and the ancient experiment of pinching revealed the fact that I was anything other than a wraith.

Again was I suddenly recalled to my immediate surroundings by a repetition of the weird moan from the depths of the cave. Naked and unarmed as I was, I had no desire to face the unseen thing which menaced me.

My revolvers were strapped to my lifeless body which, for some unfathomable reason, I could not bring myself to touch. My carbine was in its boot, strapped to my saddle, and as my horse had wandered off I was left without means of defense. My only alternative seemed to lie in flight and my decision was crystallized by a recurrence of the rustling sound from the thing which now seemed, in the darkness of the cave and to my distorted imagination, to be creeping stealthily upon me.

Unable longer to resist the temptation to escape this horrible place I leaped quickly through the opening into the starlight of a clear Arizona night. The crisp, fresh mountain air outside the cave acted as an immediate tonic and I felt new life and new courage coursing through me. Pausing upon the brink of the ledge I upbraided myself for what now seemed to me wholly unwarranted apprehension. I reasoned with myself that I had lain helpless for many hours within the cave, yet nothing had molested me, and my better judgment, when permitted the direction of clear and logical reasoning, convinced me that the noises I had heard must have resulted from purely natural and harmless causes; probably the conformation of the cave was such that a slight breeze had caused the sounds I heard.

I decided to investigate, but first I lifted my head to fill my lungs with the pure, invigorating night air of the mountains. As I did so I saw stretching far below me the beautiful vista of rocky gorge, and level, cacti-studded flat, wrought by the moonlight into a miracle of soft splendor and wondrous enchantment.

Few western wonders are more inspiring than the beauties of an Arizona moonlit landscape; the silvered mountains in the distance, the strange lights and shadows upon hog back and arroyo, and the grotesque details of the stiff, yet beautiful cacti form a picture at once enchanting and inspiring; as though one were catching for the first time a glimpse of some dead and forgotten world, so different is it from the aspect of any other spot upon our earth.

As I stood thus meditating, I turned my gaze from the landscape to the heavens where the myriad stars formed a gorgeous and fitting canopy for the wonders of the earthly scene. My attention was quickly riveted by a large red star close to the distant horizon. As I gazed upon it I felt a spell of overpowering fascination—it was Mars, the god of war, and for me, the fighting man, it had always held the power of irresistible enchantment. As I gazed at it on that far-gone night it seemed to call across the unthinkable void, to lure me to it, to draw me as the lodestone attracts a particle of iron.

My longing was beyond the power of opposition; I closed my eyes, stretched out my arms toward the god of my vocation and felt myself drawn with the suddenness of thought through the trackless immensity of space. There was an instant of extreme cold and utter darkness.

III

I opened my eyes upon a strange and weird landscape. I knew that I was on Mars; not once did I question either my sanity or my wakefulness. I was not asleep, no need for pinching here; my inner consciousness told me as plainly that I was upon Mars as your conscious mind tells you that you are upon Earth. You do not question the fact; neither did I.

I found myself lying prone upon a bed of yellowish, moss-like vegetation which stretched around me in all directions for interminable miles. I seemed to be lying in a deep, circular basin, along the outer verge of which I could distinguish the irregularities of low hills.

It was midday, the sun was shining full upon me and the heat of it was rather intense upon my naked body, yet no greater than would have been true under similar conditions on an Arizona desert. Here and there were slight outcroppings of quartz-bearing rock which glistened in the sunlight; and a little to my left, perhaps a hundred yards, appeared a low, walled enclosure about four feet in height. No water, and no other vegetation than the moss was in evidence, and as I was somewhat thirsty I determined to do a little exploring.

Springing to my feet I received my first Martian surprise, for the effort, which on Earth would have brought me standing upright, carried me into the Martian air to the height of about three yards. I alighted softly upon the ground, however, without appreciable shock or jar. Now commenced a series of evolutions which even then seemed ludicrous in the extreme. I found that I must learn to walk all over again, as the muscular exertion which carried me easily and safely upon Earth played strange antics with me upon Mars.

Instead of progressing in a sane and dignified manner, my attempts to walk resulted in a variety of hops which took me clear of the ground a couple of feet at each step and landed me sprawling upon my face or back at the end of each second or third hop. My muscles, perfectly attuned and accustomed to the force of gravity on Earth, played the mischief with me in attempting for the first time to cope with the lesser gravitation and lower air pressure on Mars.

I was determined, however, to explore the low structure which was the only evidence of habitation in sight, and so I hit upon the unique plan of reverting to first principles in locomotion, creeping. I did fairly well at this and in a few moments had reached the low, encircling wall of the enclosure.

There appeared to be no doors or windows upon the side nearest me, but as the wall was but about four feet high I cautiously gained my feet and peered over the top upon the strangest sight it had ever been given me to see.

The roof of the enclosure was of solid glass about four or five inches in thickness, and beneath this were several hundred large eggs, perfectly round and snowy white. The eggs were nearly uniform in size being about two and one-half feet in diameter.

Five or six had already hatched and the grotesque caricatures which sat blinking in the sunlight were enough to cause me to doubt my sanity. They seemed mostly head, with little scrawny bodies, long necks and six legs, or, as I afterward learned, two legs and two arms, with an intermediary pair of limbs which could be used at will either as arms or legs. Their eyes were set at the extreme sides of their heads a trifle above the center and protruded in such a manner that they could be directed either forward or back and also independently of each other, thus permitting this queer animal to look in any direction, or in two directions at once, without the necessity of turning the head.

The ears, which were slightly above the eyes and closer together, were small, cup-shaped antennae, protruding not more than an inch on these young specimens. Their noses were but longitudinal slits in the center of their faces, midway between their mouths and ears.

There was no hair on their bodies, which were of a very light yellowish-green color. In the adults, as I was to learn quite soon, this color deepens to an olive green and is darker in the male than in the female. Further, the heads of the adults are not so out of proportion to their bodies as in the case of the young.

The iris of the eyes is blood red, as in Albinos, while the pupil is dark. The eyeball itself is very white, as are the teeth. These latter add a most ferocious appearance to an otherwise fearsome and terrible countenance, as the lower tusks curve upward to sharp points which end about where the eyes of earthly human beings are located. The whiteness of the teeth is not that of ivory, but of the snowiest and most gleaming of china. Against the dark background of their olive skins their tusks stand out in a most striking manner, making these weapons present a singularly formidable appearance.

Most of these details I noted later, for I was given but little time to speculate on the wonders of my new discovery. I had seen that the eggs were in the process of hatching, and as I stood watching the hideous little monsters break from their shells I failed to note the approach of a score of full-grown Martians from behind me.

Coming, as they did, over the soft and soundless moss, which covers practically the entire surface of Mars with the exception of the frozen areas at the poles and the scattered cultivated districts, they might have captured me easily, but their intentions were far more sinister. It was the rattling of the accoutrements of the foremost warrior which warned me.

On such a little thing my life hung that I often marvel that I escaped so easily. Had not the rifle of the leader of the party swung from its fastenings beside his saddle in such a way as to strike against the butt of his great metal shod spear I should have snuffed out without ever knowing that death was near me. But the little sound caused me to turn, and there upon me, not ten feet from my breast, was the point of that huge spear, a spear forty feet long, tipped with gleaming metal, and held low at the side of a mounted replica of the little devils I had been watching.

But how puny and harmless they now looked beside this huge and terrific incarnation of hate, of vengeance and of death. The man himself, for such I may call him, was fully fifteen feet in height and, on Earth, would have weighed some four hundred pounds. He sat his mount as we sit a horse, grasping the animal's barrel with his lower limbs, while the hands of his two right arms held his immense spear low at the side of his mount; his two left arms were outstretched laterally to help preserve his balance, the thing he rode having neither bridle or reins of any description for guidance.

And his mount! How can earthly words describe it! It towered ten feet at the shoulder; had four legs on either side; a broad flat tail, larger at the tip than at the root, and which it held straight out behind while running; a gaping mouth which split its head from its snout to its long, massive neck.

Like its master, it was entirely devoid of hair, but was of a dark slate color and exceeding smooth and glossy. Its belly was white, and its legs shaded from the slate of its shoulders and hips to a vivid yellow at the feet. The feet themselves were heavily padded and nailless, which fact had also contributed to the noiselessness of their approach, and, in common with a multiplicity of legs, is a characteristic feature of the fauna of Mars. The highest type of man and one other animal, the only mammal existing on Mars, alone have well-formed nails, and there are absolutely no hoofed animals in existence there.

Behind this first charging demon trailed nineteen others, similar in all respects, but, as I learned later, bearing individual characteristics peculiar to themselves; precisely as no two of us are identical although we are all cast in a similar mold. This picture, or rather materialized nightmare, which I have described at length, made but one terrible and swift impression on me as I turned to meet it.

Unarmed and naked as I was, the first law of nature manifested itself in the only possible solution of my immediate problem, and that was to get out of the vicinity of the point of the charging spear. Consequently I gave a very earthly and at the same time superhuman leap to reach the top of the Martian incubator, for such I had determined it must be.

My effort was crowned with a success which appalled me no less than it seemed to surprise the Martian warriors, for it carried me fully thirty feet into the air and landed me a hundred feet from my pursuers and on the opposite side of the enclosure.

I alighted upon the soft moss easily and without mishap, and turning saw my enemies lined up along the further wall. Some were surveying me with expressions which I afterward discovered marked extreme astonishment, and the others were evidently satisfying themselves that I had not molested their young.

They were conversing together in low tones, and gesticulating and pointing toward me. Their discovery that I had not harmed the little Martians, and that I was unarmed, must have caused them to look upon me with less ferocity; but, as I was to learn later, the thing which weighed most in my favor was my exhibition of hurdling.

While the Martians are immense, their bones are very large and they are muscled only in proportion to the gravitation which they must overcome. The result is that they are infinitely less agile and less powerful, in proportion to their weight, than an Earth man, and I doubt that were one of them suddenly to be transported to Earth he could lift his own weight from the ground; in fact, I am convinced that he could not do so.

My feat then was as marvelous upon Mars as it would have been upon Earth, and from desiring to annihilate me they suddenly looked upon me as a wonderful discovery to be captured and exhibited among their fellows.

The respite my unexpected agility had given me permitted me to formulate plans for the immediate future and to note more closely the appearance of the warriors, for I could not disassociate these people in my mind from those other warriors who, only the day before, had been pursuing me.

I noted that each was armed with several other weapons in addition to the huge spear which I have described. The weapon which caused me to decide against an attempt at escape by flight was what was evidently a rifle of some description, and which I felt, for some reason, they were peculiarly efficient in handling.

These rifles were of a white metal stocked with wood, which I learned later was a very light and intensely hard growth much prized on Mars, and entirely unknown to us denizens of Earth. The metal of the barrel is an alloy composed principally of aluminum and steel which they have learned to temper to a hardness far exceeding that of the steel with which we are familiar. The weight of these rifles is comparatively little, and with the small caliber, explosive, radium projectiles which they use, and the great length of the barrel, they are deadly in the extreme and at ranges which would be unthinkable on Earth. The theoretic effective radius of this rifle is three hundred miles, but the best they can do in actual service when equipped with their wireless finders and sighters is but a trifle over two hundred miles.

This is quite far enough to imbue me with great respect for the Martian firearm, and some telepathic force must have warned me against an attempt to escape in broad daylight from under the muzzles of twenty of these death-dealing machines.

The Martians, after conversing for a short time, turned and rode away in the direction from which they had come, leaving one of their number alone by the enclosure. When they had covered perhaps two hundred yards they halted, and turning their mounts toward us sat watching the warrior by the enclosure.

He was the one whose spear had so nearly transfixed me, and was evidently the leader of the band, as I had noted that they seemed to have moved to their present position at his direction. When his force had come to a halt he dismounted, threw down his spear and small arms, and came around the end of the incubator toward me, entirely unarmed and as naked as I, except for the ornaments strapped upon his head, limbs, and breast.

When he was within about fifty feet of me he unclasped an enormous metal armlet, and holding it toward me in the open palm of his hand, addressed me in a clear, resonant voice, but in a language, it is needless to say, I could not understand. He then stopped as though waiting for my reply, pricking up his antennae-like ears and cocking his strange-looking eyes still further toward me.

As the silence became painful I concluded to hazard a little conversation on my own part, as I had guessed that he was making overtures of peace. The throwing down of his weapons and the withdrawing of his troop before his advance toward me would have signified a peaceful mission anywhere on Earth, so why not, then, on Mars!

Placing my hand over my heart I bowed low to the Martian and explained to him that while I did not understand his language, his actions spoke for the peace and friendship that at the present moment were most dear to my heart. Of course I might have been a babbling brook for all the intelligence my speech carried to him, but he understood the action with which I immediately followed my words.

Stretching my hand toward him, I advanced and took the armlet from his open palm, clasping it about my arm above the elbow; smiled at him and stood waiting. His wide mouth spread into an answering smile, and locking one of his intermediary arms in mine we turned and walked back toward his mount. At the same time he motioned his followers to advance. They started toward us on a wild run, but were checked by a signal from him. Evidently he feared that were I to be really frightened again I might jump entirely out of the landscape.

He exchanged a few words with his men, motioned to me that I would ride behind one of them, and then mounted his own animal. The fellow designated reached down two or three hands and lifted me up behind him on the glossy back of his mount, where I hung on as best I could by the belts and straps which held the Martian's weapons and ornaments.

The entire cavalcade then turned and galloped away toward the range of hills in the distance.

IV

We had gone perhaps ten miles when the ground began to rise very rapidly. We were, as I was later to learn, nearing the edge of one of Mars' long-dead seas, in the bottom of which my encounter with the Martians had taken place.

In a short time we gained the foot of the mountains, and after traversing a narrow gorge came to an open valley, at the far extremity of which was a low table land upon which I beheld an enormous city.

Toward this we galloped, entering it by what appeared to be a ruined roadway leading out from the city, but only to the edge of the table land, where it ended abruptly in a flight of broad steps.

Upon closer observation I saw as we passed them that the buildings were deserted, and while not greatly decayed had the appearance of not having been tenanted for years, possibly for ages. Toward the center of the city was a large plaza, and upon this and in the buildings immediately surrounding it were camped some nine or ten hundred creatures of the same breed as my captors, for such I now considered them despite the suave manner in which I had been trapped.

With the exception of their ornaments all were naked. The women varied in appearance but little from the men, except that their tusks were much larger in proportion to their height, in some instances curving nearly to their high-set ears. Their bodies were smaller and lighter in color, and their fingers and toes bore the rudiments of nails, which were entirely lacking among the males. The adult females ranged in height from ten to twelve feet.

The children were light in color, even lighter than the women, and all looked precisely alike to me, except that some were taller than others; older, I presumed.

I saw no signs of extreme age among them, nor is there any appreciable difference in their appearance from the age of maturity, about forty, until, at about the age of one thousand years, they go voluntarily upon their last strange pilgrimage down the river Iss, which leads no living Martian knows whither and from whose bosom no Martian has ever returned, or would be allowed to live did he return after once embarking upon its cold, dark waters.

Only about one Martian in a thousand dies of sickness or disease, and possibly about twenty take the voluntary pilgrimage. The other nine hundred and seventy-nine die violent deaths in duels, in hunting, in aviation and in war; but perhaps by far the greatest death loss comes during the age of childhood, when vast numbers of the little Martians fall victims to the great white apes of Mars.

The average life expectancy of a Martian after the age of maturity is about three hundred years, but would be nearer the one-thousand mark were it not for the various means leading to violent death. Owing to the waning resources of the planet it evidently became necessary to counteract the increasing longevity which their remarkable skill in therapeutics and surgery produced, and so human life has come to be considered but lightly on Mars, as is evidenced by their dangerous sports and the almost continual warfare between the various communities.

There are other and natural causes tending toward a diminution of population, but nothing contributes so greatly to this end as the fact that no male or female Martian is ever voluntarily without a weapon of destruction.

As we neared the plaza and my presence was discovered we were immediately surrounded by hundreds of the creatures who seemed anxious to pluck me from my seat behind my guard. A word from the leader of the party stilled their clamor, and we proceeded at a trot across the plaza to the entrance of as magnificent an edifice as mortal eye has rested upon.

The building was low, but covered an enormous area. It was constructed of gleaming white marble inlaid with gold and brilliant stones which sparkled and scintillated in the sunlight. The main entrance was some hundred feet in width and projected from the building proper to form a huge canopy above the entrance hall. There was no stairway, but a gentle incline to the first floor of the building opened into an enormous chamber encircled by galleries.

On the floor of this chamber, which was dotted with highly carved wooden desks and chairs, were assembled about forty or fifty male Martians around the steps of a rostrum. On the platform proper squatted an enormous warrior heavily loaded with metal ornaments, gay-colored feathers and beautifully wrought leather trappings ingeniously set with precious stones. From his shoulders depended a short cape of white fur lined with brilliant scarlet silk.

What struck me as most remarkable about this assemblage and the hall in which they were congregated was the fact that the creatures were entirely out of proportion to the desks, chairs, and other furnishings; these being of a size adapted to human beings such as I, whereas the great bulks of the Martians could scarcely have squeezed into the chairs, nor was there room beneath the desks for their long legs. Evidently, then, there were other denizens on Mars than the wild and grotesque creatures into whose hands I had fallen, but the evidences of extreme antiquity which showed all around me indicated that these buildings might have belonged to some long-extinct and forgotten race in the dim antiquity of Mars.

Our party had halted at the entrance to the building, and at a sign from the leader I had been lowered to the ground. Again locking his arm in mine, we had proceeded into the audience chamber. There were few formalities observed in approaching the Martian chieftain. My captor merely strode up to the rostrum, the others making way for him as he advanced. The chieftain rose to his feet and uttered the name of my escort who, in turn, halted and repeated the name of the ruler followed by his title.

At the time, this ceremony and the words they uttered meant nothing to me, but later I came to know that this was the customary greeting between green Martians. Had the men been strangers, and therefore unable to exchange names, they would have silently exchanged ornaments, had their missions been peaceful—otherwise they would have exchanged shots, or have fought out their introduction with some other of their various weapons.

My captor, whose name was Tars Tarkas, was virtually the vice-chieftain of the community, and a man of great ability as a statesman and warrior. He evidently explained briefly the incidents connected with his expedition, including my capture, and when he had concluded the chieftain addressed me at some length.

I replied in our good old English tongue merely to convince him that neither of us could understand the other; but I noticed that when I smiled slightly on concluding, he did likewise. This fact, and the similar occurrence during my first talk with Tars Tarkas, convinced me that we had at least something in common; the ability to smile, therefore to laugh; denoting a sense of humor. But I was to learn that the Martian smile is merely perfunctory, and that the Martian laugh is a thing to cause strong men to blanch in horror.

The ideas of humor among the green men of Mars are widely at variance with our conceptions of incitants to merriment. The death agonies of a fellow being are, to these strange creatures provocative of the wildest hilarity, while their chief form of commonest amusement is to inflict death on their prisoners of war in various ingenious and horrible ways.

The assembled warriors and chieftains examined me closely, feeling my muscles and the texture of my skin. The principal chieftain then evidently signified a desire to see me perform, and, motioning me to follow, he started with Tars Tarkas for the open plaza.

Now, I had made no attempt to walk, since my first signal failure, except while tightly grasping Tars Tarkas' arm, and so now I went skipping and flitting about among the desks and chairs like some monstrous grasshopper. After bruising myself severely, much to the amusement of the Martians, I again had recourse to creeping, but this did not suit them and I was roughly jerked to my feet by a towering fellow who had laughed most heartily at my misfortunes.

As he banged me down upon my feet his face was bent close to mine and I did the only thing a gentleman might do under the circumstances of brutality, boorishness, and lack of consideration for a stranger's rights; I swung my fist squarely to his jaw and he went down like a felled ox. As he sunk to the floor I wheeled around with my back toward the nearest desk, expecting to be overwhelmed by the vengeance of his fellows, but determined to give them as good a battle as the unequal odds would permit before I gave up my life.

My fears were groundless, however, as the other Martians, at first struck dumb with wonderment, finally broke into wild peals of laughter and applause. I did not recognize the applause as such, but later, when I had become acquainted with their customs, I learned that I had won what they seldom accord, a manifestation of approbation.

The fellow whom I had struck lay where he had fallen, nor did any of his mates approach him. Tars Tarkas advanced toward me, holding out one of his arms, and we thus proceeded to the plaza without further mishap. I did not, of course, know the reason for which we had come to the open, but I was not long in being enlightened. They first repeated the word "sak" a number of times, and then Tars Tarkas made several jumps, repeating the same word before each leap; then, turning to me, he said, "sak!" I saw what they were after, and gathering myself together I "sakked" with such marvelous success that I cleared a good hundred and fifty feet; nor did I this time, lose my equilibrium, but landed squarely upon my feet without falling. I then returned by easy jumps of twenty-five or thirty feet to the little group of warriors.

My exhibition had been witnessed by several hundred lesser Martians, and they immediately broke into demands for a repetition, which the chieftain then ordered me to make; but I was both hungry and thirsty, and determined on the spot that my only method of salvation was to demand the consideration from these creatures which they evidently would not voluntarily accord. I therefore ignored the repeated commands to "sak," and each time they were made I motioned to my mouth and rubbed my stomach.

Tars Tarkas and the chief exchanged a few words, and the former, calling to a young female among the throng, gave her some instructions and motioned me to accompany her. I grasped her proffered arm and together we crossed the plaza toward a large building on the far side.

My fair companion was about eight feet tall, having just arrived at maturity, but not yet to her full height. She was of a light olive-green color, with a smooth, glossy hide. Her name, as I afterward learned, was Sola, and she belonged to the retinue of Tars Tarkas. She conducted me to a spacious chamber in one of the buildings fronting on the plaza, and which, from the litter of silks and furs upon the floor, I took to be the sleeping quarters of several of the natives.

The room was well lighted by a number of large windows and was beautifully decorated with mural paintings and mosaics, but upon all there seemed to rest that indefinable touch of the finger of antiquity which convinced me that the architects and builders of these wondrous creations had nothing in common with the crude half-brutes which now occupied them.

Sola motioned me to be seated upon a pile of silks near the center of the room, and, turning, made a peculiar hissing sound, as though signaling to someone in an adjoining room. In response to her call I obtained my first sight of a new Martian wonder. It waddled in on its ten short legs, and squatted down before the girl like an obedient puppy. The thing was about the size of a Shetland pony, but its head bore a slight resemblance to that of a frog, except that the jaws were equipped with three rows of long, sharp tusks.

V

Sola stared into the brute's wicked-looking eyes, muttered a word or two of command, pointed to me, and left the chamber. I could not but wonder what this ferocious-looking monstrosity might do when left alone in such close proximity to such a relatively tender morsel of meat; but my fears were groundless, as the beast, after surveying me intently for a moment, crossed the room to the only exit which led to the street, and lay down full length across the threshold.

This was my first experience with a Martian watch dog, but it was destined not to be my last, for this fellow guarded me carefully during the time I remained a captive among these green men; twice saving my life, and never voluntarily being away from me a moment.

While Sola was away I took occasion to examine more minutely the room in which I found myself captive. The mural painting depicted scenes of rare and wonderful beauty; mountains, rivers, lake, ocean,

meadow, trees and flowers, winding roadways, sun-kissed gardens—
scenes which might have portrayed earthly views but for the different
colorings of the vegetation. The work had evidently been wrought by
a master hand, so subtle the atmosphere, so perfect the technique; yet
nowhere was there a representation of a living animal, either human
or brute, by which I could guess at the likeness of these other and
perhaps extinct denizens of Mars.

While I was allowing my fancy to run riot in wild conjecture on
the possible explanation of the strange anomalies which I had so
far met with on Mars, Sola returned bearing both food and drink.
These she placed on the floor beside me, and seating herself a short
ways off regarded me intently. The food consisted of about a pound
of some solid substance of the consistency of cheese and almost
tasteless, while the liquid was apparently milk from some animal. It
was not unpleasant to the taste, though slightly acid, and I learned
in a short time to prize it very highly. It came, as I later discovered,
not from an animal, as there is only one mammal on Mars and that
one very rare indeed, but from a large plant which grows practically
without water, but seems to distill its plentiful supply of milk from
the products of the soil, the moisture of the air, and the rays of the
sun. A single plant of this species will give eight or ten quarts of milk
per day.

After I had eaten I was greatly invigorated, but feeling the need of
rest I stretched out upon the silks and was soon asleep. I must have
slept several hours, as it was dark when I awoke, and I was very cold.
I noticed that someone had thrown a fur over me, but it had become
partially dislodged and in the darkness I could not see to replace it.
Suddenly a hand reached out and pulled the fur over me, shortly
afterwards adding another to my covering.

I presumed that my watchful guardian was Sola, nor was I wrong.
This girl alone, among all the green Martians with whom I came in
contact, disclosed characteristics of sympathy, kindliness, and affection; her ministrations to my bodily wants were unfailing, and her
solicitous care saved me from much suffering and many hardships.

As I was to learn, the Martian nights are extremely cold, and as
there is practically no twilight or dawn, the changes in temperature
are sudden and most uncomfortable, as are the transitions from brilliant daylight to darkness. The nights are either brilliantly illumined
or very dark, for if neither of the two moons of Mars happen to be
in the sky almost total darkness results, since the lack of atmosphere,

or, rather, the very thin atmosphere, fails to diffuse the starlight to any great extent; on the other hand, if both of the moons are in the heavens at night the surface of the ground is brightly illuminated.

Both of Mars' moons are vastly nearer her than is our moon to Earth; the nearer moon being but about five thousand miles distant, while the further is but little more than fourteen thousand miles away, against the nearly one-quarter million miles which separate us from our moon. The nearer moon of Mars makes a complete revolution around the planet in a little over seven and one-half hours, so that she may be seen hurtling through the sky like some huge meteor two or three times each night, revealing all her phases during each transit of the heavens.

The further moon revolves about Mars in something over thirty and one-quarter hours, and with her sister satellite makes a nocturnal Martian scene one of splendid and weird grandeur. And it is well that nature has so graciously and abundantly lighted the Martian night, for the green men of Mars, being a nomadic race without high intellectual development, have but crude means for artificial lighting; depending principally upon torches, a kind of candle, and a peculiar oil lamp which generates a gas and burns without a wick.

This last device produces an intensely brilliant far-reaching white light, but as the natural oil which it requires can only be obtained by mining in one of several widely separated and remote localities it is seldom used by these creatures whose only thought is for today, and whose hatred for manual labor has kept them in a semi-barbaric state for countless ages.

After Sola had replenished my coverings I again slept, nor did I awaken until daylight. The other occupants of the room, five in number, were all females, and they were still sleeping, piled high with a motley array of silks and furs. Across the threshold lay stretched the sleepless guardian brute, just as I had last seen him on the preceding day; apparently he had not moved a muscle; his eyes were fairly glued upon me, and I fell to wondering just what might befall me should I endeavor to escape.

I have ever been prone to seek adventure and to investigate and experiment where wiser men would have left well enough alone. It therefore now occurred to me that the surest way of learning the exact attitude of this beast toward me would be to attempt to leave the room. I felt fairly secure in my belief that I could escape him should he pursue me once I was outside the building, for I had begun to take great pride in my ability as a jumper. Furthermore, I could see from the shortness of his legs that the brute himself was no jumper and probably no runner.

Slowly and carefully, therefore, I gained my feet, only to see that my watcher did the same; cautiously I advanced toward him, finding that by moving with a shuffling gait I could retain my balance as well as make reasonably rapid progress. As I neared the brute he backed cautiously away from me, and when I had reached the open he moved to one side to let me pass. He then fell in behind me and followed about ten paces in my rear as I made my way along the deserted street.

Evidently his mission was to protect me only, I thought, but when we reached the edge of the city he suddenly sprang before me, uttering strange sounds and baring his ugly and ferocious tusks. Thinking to have some amusement at his expense, I rushed toward him, and when almost upon him sprang into the air, alighting far beyond him and away from the city. He wheeled instantly and charged me with the most appalling speed I had ever beheld. I had thought his short legs a bar to swiftness, but had he been coursing with greyhounds the latter would have appeared as though asleep on a door mat. As I was to learn, this is the fleetest animal on Mars, and owing to its intelligence, loyalty, and ferocity is used in hunting, in war, and as the protector of the Martian man.

I quickly saw that I would have difficulty in escaping the fangs of the beast on a straightaway course, and so I met his charge by doubling in my tracks and leaping over him as he was almost upon me. This maneuver gave me a considerable advantage, and I was able to reach the city quite a bit ahead of him, and as he came tearing after me I jumped for a window about thirty feet from the ground in the face of one of the buildings overlooking the valley.

Grasping the sill I pulled myself up to a sitting posture without looking into the building, and gazed down at the baffled animal beneath me. My exultation was short-lived, however, for scarcely had I gained a secure seat upon the sill than a huge hand grasped me by the neck from behind and dragged me violently into the room. Here I was thrown upon my back, and beheld standing over me a colossal ape-like creature, white and hairless except for an enormous shock of bristly hair upon its head.

VI

The thing, which more nearly resembled our earthly men than it did the Martians I had seen, held me pinioned to the ground with one huge foot, while it jabbered and gesticulated at some answering creature behind me. This other, which was evidently its mate, soon came toward us, bearing a mighty stone cudgel with which it evidently intended to brain me.

The creatures were about ten or fifteen feet tall, standing erect, and had, like the green Martians, an intermediary set of arms or legs, midway between their upper and lower limbs. Their eyes were close together and non-protruding; their ears were high set, but more laterally located than those of the Martians, while their snouts and teeth were strikingly like those of our African gorilla. Altogether they were not unlovely when viewed in comparison with the green Martians.

The cudgel was swinging in the arc which ended upon my upturned face when a bolt of myriad-legged horror hurled itself through the doorway full upon the breast of my executioner. With a shriek of fear the ape which held me leaped through the open window, but its mate closed in a terrific death struggle with my preserver, which was nothing less than my faithful watch-thing; I cannot bring myself to call so hideous a creature a dog.

As quickly as possible I gained my feet and backing against the wall I witnessed such a battle as it is vouchsafed few beings to see. The strength, agility, and blind ferocity of these two creatures is approached by nothing known to earthly man. My beast had an advantage in his first hold, having sunk his mighty fangs far into the breast of his adversary; but the great arms and paws of the ape, backed by muscles far transcending those of the Martian men I had seen, had locked the throat of my guardian and slowly were choking out his life, and bending back his head and neck upon his body, where I momentarily expected the former to fall limp at the end of a broken neck.

In accomplishing this the ape was tearing away the entire front of its breast, which was held in the vise-like grip of the powerful jaws. Back and forth upon the floor they rolled, neither one emitting a sound of fear or pain. Presently I saw the great eyes of my beast bulging completely from their sockets and blood flowing from its nostrils. That he was weakening perceptibly was evident, but so also was the ape, whose struggles were growing momentarily less.

Suddenly I came to myself and, with that strange instinct which seems ever to prompt me to my duty, I seized the cudgel, which had fallen to the floor at the commencement of the battle, and swinging it with all the power of my earthly arms I crashed it full upon the head of the ape, crushing his skull as though it had been an eggshell.

Scarcely had the blow descended when I was confronted with a new danger. The ape's mate, recovered from its first shock of terror, had returned to the scene of the encounter by way of the interior of the building. I glimpsed him just before he reached the doorway and the sight of him, now roaring as he perceived his lifeless fellow stretched upon the floor, and frothing at the mouth, in the extremity of his rage, filled me, I must confess, with dire forebodings.

I am ever willing to stand and fight when the odds are not too overwhelmingly against me, but in this instance I perceived neither glory nor profit in pitting my relatively puny strength against the iron muscles and brutal ferocity of this enraged denizen of an unknown world; in fact, the only outcome of such an encounter, so far as I might be concerned, seemed sudden death.

I was standing near the window and I knew that once in the street I might gain the plaza and safety before the creature could overtake me; at least there was a chance for safety in flight, against almost certain death should I remain and fight however desperately.

It is true I held the cudgel, but what could I do with it against his four great arms? Even should I break one of them with my first blow, for I figured that he would attempt to ward off the cudgel, he could reach out and annihilate me with the others before I could recover for a second attack.

In the instant that these thoughts passed through my mind I had turned to make for the window, but my eyes alighting on the form of my erstwhile guardian threw all thoughts of flight to the four winds. He lay gasping upon the floor of the chamber, his great eyes fastened upon me in what seemed a pitiful appeal for protection. I could not withstand that look, nor could I, on second thought, have deserted my rescuer without giving as good an account of myself in his behalf as he had in mine.

Without more ado, therefore, I turned to meet the charge of the infuriated bull ape. He was now too close upon me for the cudgel to prove of any effective assistance, so I merely threw it as heavily as I could at his advancing bulk. It struck him just below the knees, eliciting a howl of pain and rage, and so throwing him off his balance that he lunged full upon me with arms wide stretched to ease his fall.

Again, as on the preceding day, I had recourse to earthly tactics, and swinging my right fist full upon the point of his chin I followed it with a smashing left to the pit of his stomach. The effect was marvelous, for, as I lightly sidestepped, after delivering the second blow, he reeled and fell upon the floor doubled up with pain and gasping for wind. Leaping over his prostrate body, I seized the cudgel and finished the monster before he could regain his feet.

As I delivered the blow a low laugh rang out behind me, and, turning, I beheld Tars Tarkas, Sola, and three or four warriors standing in the doorway of the chamber. As my eyes met theirs I was, for the second time, the recipient of their zealously guarded applause.

My absence had been noted by Sola on her awakening, and she had quickly informed Tars Tarkas, who had set out immediately with a handful of warriors to search for me. As they had approached the limits of the city they had witnessed the actions of the bull ape as he bolted into the building, frothing with rage.

They had followed immediately behind him, thinking it barely possible that his actions might prove a clew to my whereabouts and had witnessed my short but decisive battle with him. This encounter, together with my set-to with the Martian warrior on the previous day and my feats of jumping placed me upon a high pinnacle in their regard. Evidently devoid of all the finer sentiments of friendship, love, or affection, these people fairly worship physical prowess and bravery, and nothing is too good for the object of their adoration as long as he maintains his position by repeated examples of his skill, strength, and courage.

Sola, who had accompanied the searching party of her own volition, was the only one of the Martians whose face had not been twisted in laughter as I battled for my life. She, on the contrary, was sober with apparent solicitude and, as soon as I had finished the monster, rushed to me and carefully examined my body for possible wounds or injuries. Satisfying herself that I had come off unscathed she smiled quietly, and, taking my hand, started toward the door of the chamber.

Tars Tarkas and the other warriors had entered and were standing over the now rapidly reviving brute which had saved my life, and whose life I, in turn, had rescued. They seemed to be deep in argument, and finally one of them addressed me, but remembering my ignorance of his language turned back to Tars Tarkas, who, with a word and gesture, gave some command to the fellow and turned to follow us from the room.

There seemed something menacing in their attitude toward my beast, and I hesitated to leave until I had learned the outcome. It was well I did so, for the warrior drew an evil looking pistol from its holster and was on the point of putting an end to the creature when I sprang forward and struck up his arm. The bullet striking the wooden casing of the window exploded, blowing a hole completely through the wood and masonry.

I then knelt down beside the fearsome-looking thing, and raising it to its feet motioned for it to follow me. The looks of surprise which my actions elicited from the Martians were ludicrous; they could not understand, except in a feeble and childish way, such attributes as gratitude and compassion. The warrior whose gun I had struck up looked enquiringly at Tars Tarkas, but the latter signed that I be left to my own devices, and so we returned to the plaza with my great beast following close at heel, and Sola grasping me tightly by the arm.

I had at least two friends on Mars; a young woman who watched over me with motherly solicitude, and a dumb brute which, as I later came to know, held in its poor ugly carcass more love, more loyalty, more gratitude than could have been found in the entire five million green Martians who rove the deserted cities and dead sea bottoms of Mars.

A. Merritt (1884–1943)

THE POPULARITY of Edgar Rice Burroughs's stories encouraged others to contribute stories of scientific romance and fantasy to pulp magazines, particularly *The Argosy, The All-Story,* and *The Cavalier,* all titles published by the firm of Frank A. Munsey. These stories did not offer scientific accuracy, instead using the ever-increasing knowledge and understanding arising from research as the basis for rather more fantastic adventures. While some writers did prefer to include a degree of plausibility in their fiction, others simply built upon the wonders of science to make their worlds more fantastic and exotic. The master of this genre, second only to Edgar Rice Burroughs in popularity, was Abraham Merritt.

Merritt was a newspaper journalist who became the assistant editor of Hearst's *American Weekly* in 1912, taking over as full editor in 1934 and remaining there until his death. *The American Weekly* was one of Hearst's most profitable papers and work on it kept Merritt busy, so that writing fiction was only a sideline, and an occasional one at that. Yet Merritt managed to complete eight novels and several short stories. Two of his novels were filmed: *Seven Footprints to Satan* (1927) in 1929 and *Burn, Witch, Burn!* (1932) as *The Devil Doll* in 1936, but these are the least exotic of Merritt's books. His highly imaginative novels of lost worlds and exotic life-forms were *The Moon Pool* (1919), *The Ship of Ishtar* (1926), *The Face in the Abyss* (1931), and *Dwellers in the Mirage* (1932).

Before his novels, Merritt wrote several short stories, the first of which was the tale that follows: "Through the Dragon Glass," published in *All-Story Weekly* (November 24, 1917).

Through the Dragon Glass

A. Merritt

Herndon helped loot the Forbidden City when the Allies turned the suppression of the Boxers into the most gorgeous burglar-party since the days of Tamerlane. Six of his sailormen followed faithfully his buccaneering fancy. A sympathetic Russian highness whom he had entertained in New York saw to it that he got to the coast and his yacht. That is why Herndon was able to sail through the Narrows with as much of the Son of Heaven's treasures as the most accomplished labourer in Peking's mission vineyards.

Some of the loot he gave to charming ladies who had dwelt or were still dwelling on the sunny side of his heart. Most of it he used to fit up those two astonishing Chinese rooms in his Fifth Avenue house. And a little of it, following a vague religious impulse, he presented to the Metropolitan Museum. This, somehow, seemed to put the stamp of legitimacy on his part of the pillage—like offerings to the gods and building hospitals and peace palaces and such things.

But the Dragon Glass, because he had never seen anything quite so wonderful, he set up in his bedroom where he could look at it the first thing in the morning, and he placed shaded lights about it so that he could wake up in the night and look at it! Wonderful? It is more than wonderful, the Dragon Glass! Whoever made it lived when the gods walked about the earth creating something new every day. Only a man who lived in that sort of atmosphere could have wrought it. There was never anything like it.

I was in Hawaii when the cables told of Herndon's first disappearance. There wasn't much to tell. His man had gone to his room to awaken him one morning—and Herndon wasn't there. All his clothes were, though. Everything was just as if Herndon ought to be somewhere in the house—only he wasn't. A man worth ten millions can't step out into thin air and vanish without leaving behind him the probability of some commotion, naturally. The newspapers attended to the commotion, but the columns of type, boiled down to essentials, contained just two facts—that Herndon had come home the night before, and in the morning he was undiscoverable.

I was on the high seas, homeward bound to help in the search, when the wireless told the story of his reappearance. They had found him on the floor of his bedroom, shreds of a silken robe on him, and his body mauled as though by a tiger. But there was no more explanation of his return than there had been of his disappearance. The night before he hadn't been there—and in the morning there he was. Herndon, when he was able to talk, utterly refused to confide in his doctors. I went straight through to New York, and waited until the men of medicine decided that it was better to let him see me than to have him worry any longer about not seeing me.

Herndon got up from a big invalid chair when I entered. His eyes were clear and bright, and there was no weakness in the way he greeted me, nor in the grip of his hand. A nurse slipped from the room.

"What was it, Jim?" I cried. "What on earth happened to you?"

"Not so sure it was on earth," he said. He pointed to what looked like a tall easel hooded with a heavy piece of silk covered with embroidered Chinese characters. He hesitated for a moment and then walked over to the closet. He drew out two heavy bore guns, the very ones, I remembered, that he had used in his last elephant hunt.

"You won't think me crazy if I ask you to keep one of these handy while I talk, will you, Ward?" he asked rather apologetically. "This looks pretty real, doesn't it?"

He opened his dressing gown and showed me his chest swathed in bandages. He gripped my shoulder as I took without question one of the guns. He walked to the easel and drew off the hood.

"There it is," said Herndon.

And then, for the first time, I saw the Dragon Glass! There has never been anything like that thing! Never! At first all you saw was a cool, green, glimmering translucence, like the sea when you are swimming under water on a still summer day and look up through it. Around its edges ran flickers of scarlet and gold, flashes of emerald, shimmers of silver and ivory. At its base a disk of topaz rimmed with red fire shot up dusky little vaporous yellow flames.

Afterward you were aware that the green translucence was an oval slice of polished stones. The flashes and flickers became dragons. There were twelve of them. Their eyes were emeralds, their fangs

were ivory, their claws were gold. They were scaled dragons and each
scale was so inlaid that the base, green as the primeval jungle, shaded
off into a vivid scarlet, and the scarlet into tips of gold. Their wings
were of silver and vermilion, and were folded close to their bodies.
But they were alive, those dragons. There was never so much life in
metal and wood since Al-Akram, the sculptor of ancient Ad, carved
the first crocodile, and the jealous Almighty breathed life into it for
a punishment!

And last you saw that the topaz disc that sent up little yellow
flames was the top of a metal sphere around which coiled a thirteenth
dragon, thin and red, and biting its scorpion-tipped tail.

It took your breath away, the first glimpse of the Dragon Glass. Yes,
and the second and third glimpse, too—and every other time you
looked at it.

"Where did you get it?" I asked, a little shakily.

Herndon said evenly: "It was in a small hidden crypt in the Imperial Palace. We broke into the crypt quite by"—he hesitated—"well,
call it by accident. As soon as I saw it I knew I must have it. What do
you think of it?"

"Think!" I cried. "Think! Why, it's the most marvellous thing that
the hands of man ever made! What is that stone? Jade?"

"I'm not sure," said Herndon. "But come here. Stand just in front
of me." He switched out the lights in the room. He turned another
switch, and on the glass opposite me three shaded electrics threw
their rays into its mirror-like oval.

"Watch!" said Herndon. "Tell me what you see!"

I looked into the glass. At first I could see nothing but the rays
shining further, further—into infinite distances, it seemed. And
then—"Good God!" I cried, stiffening with horror. "Jim, what hellish
thing is this?"

"Steady, old man," came Herndon's voice. There was relief and a
curious sort of joy in it. "Steady; tell me just what you see."

I said: "I seem to see through infinite distances—and yet what I see
is as close to me as though it were just on the other side of the glass.
I see a cleft that cuts through two masses of darker green. I see a claw,
a gigantic, hideous claw that stretches out through the cleft. The claw
has seven talons that open and close—open and close. Good God,
such a claw, Jim! It is like the claws that reach out from the holes in
the lama's hell to grip the blind souls as they shudder by!"

"Look, look further, up through the cleft, above the claw. It widens. What do you see?"

I said: "I see a peak rising enormously high and cutting the sky like a pyramid. There are flashes of flame that dart from behind and outline it. I see a great globe of light like a moon that moves slowly out of the flashes: there is another moving across the breast of the peak; there is a third that swims into the flame at the furthest edge—"

"The seven moons of Rak," whispered Herndon, as though to himself. "The seven moons that bathe in the rose flames of Rak which are the fires of life and that circle Lalil like a diadem. He upon whom the seven moons of Rak have shone is bound to Lalil for this life, and for ten thousand lives."

He reached over and turned the switch again. The lights of the room sprang up.

"Jim," I said, "it can't be real! What is it? Some devilish illusion in the glass?"

He unfastened the bandages about his chest. "The claw you saw had seven talons," he answered quietly. "Well, look at this."

Across the white flesh of his breast, from left shoulder to the lower ribs on the right, ran seven healing furrows. They looked as though they had been made by a gigantic steel comb that had been drawn across him. They gave one the thought they had been ploughed.

"The claw made these," he said as quietly as before. "Ward," he went on, before I could speak, "I wanted you to see—what you've seen. I didn't know whether you would see it. I don't know whether you'll believe me even now. I don't suppose I would if I were in your place—still—"

He walked over and threw the hood upon the Dragon Glass. "I'm going to tell you," he said. "I'd like to go through it—uninterrupted. That's why I cover it.

"I don't suppose," he began slowly—"I don't suppose, Ward, that you've ever heard of Rak the Wonder-Worker, who lived somewhere back at the beginning of things, nor how the Greatest Wonder-Worker banished him somewhere outside the world?"

"No," I said shortly, still shaken by what I had seen.

"It's a big part of what I've got to tell you," he went on. "Of course you'll think it rot, but—I came across the legend in Tibet first. Then I ran across it again—with the names changed, of course—when I was getting away from China. I take it that the gods were still fussing

around close to man when Rak was born. The story of his parentage
is somewhat scandalous. When he grew older, Rak wasn't satisfied
with just seeing wonderful things being done. He wanted to do them
himself, and he—well, he studied the method. After a while the Greatest Wonder-Worker ran across some of the things Rak had made, and
he found them admirable—a little too admirable. He didn't like to
destroy the lesser wonder-worker because, so the gossip ran, he felt
a sort of responsibility. So he gave Rak a place somewhere—outside
the world—and he gave him power over every one out of so many
millions of births to lead or lure or sweep that soul into his domain so
that he might build up a people—and over his people Rak was given
the high, the low, and the middle justice.

"And outside the world Rak went. He fenced his domain about
with clouds. He raised a great mountain, and on its flank he built a
city for the men and women who were to be his. He circled the city
with wonderful gardens, and he placed in the gardens many thing,
some good and some very—terrible. He set around the mountain's
brow seven moons for a diadem, and he fanned behind the mountain
a fire which is the fire of life, and through which the moons pass eternally to be born again." Herndon's voice sank to a whisper. "Through
which the moons pass," he said. "And with them the souls of the
people of Rak. They pass through the fires and are born again—and
again—for ten thousand lives. I have seen the moons of Rak and
the souls that march with them into the fires. There is no sun in the
land—only the new-born moons that shine green on the city and on
the gardens."

"Jim," I cried impatiently. "What in the world are you talking
about? Wake up, man! What's all that nonsense got to do with this?" I
pointed to the hooded Dragon Glass.

"That," he said. "Why, through that lies the road to the gardens of
Rak!"

The heavy gun dropped from my hand as I stared at him, and
from him to the glass and back again. He smiled and pointed to his
bandaged breast.

He said: "I went straight through to Peking with the Allies. I had an
idea what was coming, and I wanted to be in at the death. I was among
the first to enter the Forbidden City. I was as mad for loot as any of
them. It was a maddening sight, Ward. Soldiers with their arms full
of precious stuff even Morgan couldn't buy; soldiers with wonderful
necklaces around their hairy throats and their pockets stuffed with

jewels; soldiers with their shirts bulging treasures the Sons of Heaven had been hoarding for centuries! We were Goths sacking imperial Rome. Alexander's hosts pillaging that ancient gemmed courtesan of cities, royal Tyre! Thieves in the great ancient scale, a scale so great that it raised even thievery up to something heroic.

"We reached the throne-room. There was a little passage leading off to the left, and my men and I took it. We came into a small octagonal room. There was nothing in it except a very extraordinary squatting figure of jade. It squatted on the floor, its back turned toward us. One of my men stooped to pick it up. He slipped. The figure flew from his hand and smashed into the wall. A slab swung outward. By a—well, call it a fluke, we had struck the secret of the little octagonal room!

"I shoved a light through the aperture. It showed a crypt shaped like a cylinder. The circle of the floor was about ten feet in diameter. The walls were covered with paintings, Chinese characters, queer-looking animals, and things I can't well describe. Around the room, about seven feet up, ran a picture. It showed a sort of island floating off into space. The clouds lapped its edges like frozen seas full of rainbows. There was a big pyramid of a mountain rising out of the side of it. Around its peak were seven moons, and over the peak—a face!

"I couldn't place that face and I couldn't take my eyes off it. It wasn't Chinese, and it wasn't of any other race I'd ever seen. It was as old as the world and as young as tomorrow. It was benevolent and malicious, cruel and kindly, merciful and merciless, saturnine as Satan and as joyous as Apollo. The eyes were as yellow as buttercups, or as the sunstone on the crest of the Feathered Serpent they worship down in the Hidden Temple of Tuloon. And they were as wise as Fate.

"'There's something else here, sir,' said Martin—you remember Martin, my first officer. He pointed to a shrouded thing on the side. I entered, and took from the thing a covering that fitted over it like a hood. It was the Dragon Glass!

"The moment I saw it I knew I had to have it—and I knew I would have it. I felt I did not want to get the thing away any more than the thing itself wanted to get away. From the first I thought of the Dragon Glass as something alive. Just as much alive as you and I are. Well, I did get it away. I got it down to the yacht, and then the first odd thing happened.

"You remember Wu-Sing, my boat steward? You know the English Wu-Sing talks. Atrocious! I had the Dragon Glass in my stateroom.

I'd forgotten to lock the door. I heard a whistle of sharply indrawn breath. I turned, and there was Wu-Sing. Now, you know that Wu-Sing isn't what you'd call intelligent-looking. Yet as he stood there something seemed to pass over his face, and very subtly change it. The stupidity was wiped out as though a sponge had been passed over it. He did not raise his eyes, but he said, in perfect English, mind you: 'Has the master augustly counted the cost of his possession?'

"I simply gaped at him.

"'Perhaps,' he continued, 'the master has never heard of the illustrious Hao-Tzan? Well, he shall hear.'"

"Ward, I couldn't move or speak. But I know now it wasn't sheer astonishment that held me. I listened while Wu-Sing went on to tell in polished phrases the same story that I had heard in Tibet, only there they called him Rak instead of Hao-Tzan. But it was the same story.

"'And,' he finished, 'before he journeyed afar, the illustrious Hao Tzan caused a great marvel to be wrought. He called it the Gateway!' Wu-Sing waved his hand at the Dragon Glass. 'The master has it. But what shall he who has a Gateway do but pass through it? Is it not better to leave the Gateway behind—unless he dare go through it?'

"He was silent. I was silent, too. All I could do was wonder where the fellow had so suddenly got his command of English. And then Wu-Sing straightened. For a moment his eyes looked into mine. They were as yellow as buttercups, Ward, and wise, wise! My wind rushed back to the little room behind the panel. Ward—the eyes of Wu-Sing were the eyes of the face that brooded over the peak of the seven moons!

"And all in a moment, the face of Wu-Sing dropped back into its old familiar stupid lines. The eyes he turned to me were black and clouded. I jumped from my chair.

"'What do you mean, you yellow fraud!' I shouted. 'What do you mean by pretending all this time that you couldn't talk English?'

"He looked at me stupidly, as usual. He whined in his pidgin that he didn't understand; that he hadn't spoken a word to me until then. I couldn't get anything else out of him, although I nearly frightened his wits out. I had to believe him. Besides, I had seen his eyes. Well, I was fair curious by this time, and I was more anxious to get the glass home safely than ever.

"I got it home. I set it up here, and I fixed those lights as you saw them. I had a sort of feeling that the glass was waiting—for something. I couldn't tell just what. But that it was going to be rather important, I knew—"

He suddenly thrust his head into his hands, and rocked to and fro. "How long, how long," he moaned, "how long, Santhu?"

"Jim!" I cried. "Jim! What's the matter with you?"

He straightened. "In a moment you'll understand," he said. And then, as quietly as before: "I felt that the glass was waiting. The night I disappeared I couldn't sleep. I turned out the lights in the room; turned them on around the glass and sat before it. I don't know how long I sat but all at once I jumped to my feet. The dragons seemed to be moving! They were moving! They were crawling round and round the glass. They moved faster and faster. The thirteenth dragon spun about the topaz globe. They circled faster and faster until they were nothing but a halo of crimson and gold flashes. As they spun, the glass itself grew misty, mistier, mistier still, until it was nothing but a green haze. I stepped over to touch it. My hand went straight on through it as though nothing were there. I reached in—up to the elbow, up to the shoulder. I felt my hand grasped by warm little fingers. I stepped through—"

"Stepped through the glass?" I cried.

"Through it," he said, "and then—I felt another little hand touch my face. I saw Santhu! Her eyes were as blue as the cornflowers, as blue as the big sapphire that shines in the forehead of Vishnu, in his temple at Benares. And they were set wide, wide apart. Her hair was blue-black, and fell in two long braids between her little breasts. A golden dragon crowned her, and through its paws slipped the braids. Another golden dragon girded her. She laughed into my eyes, and drew my head down until my lips touched hers. She was lithe and slender and yielding as the reeds that grow before the Shrine of Hathor that stands on the edge of the Pool of Djeeba. Who Santhu is, or where she came from—how do I know? But this I know—she is lovelier than any woman who ever lived on earth. And she is a woman! Her arms slipped from about my neck and she drew me forward. I looked about me. We stood in a cleft between two great rocks. The rocks were a soft green, like the green of the Dragon Glass. Behind us was a green mistiness. Before us the cleft ran only a little distance. Through it I saw an enormous peak jutting up like a pyramid, high, high into a sky of chrysoprase. A soft rose radiance pulsed at its sides, and swimming slowly over its breast was a huge globe of green fire. The girl pulled me gently towards the opening. We walked on silently, hand in hand.

"Quickly it came to me—Ward, I was in the place whose pictures had been painted in the room of the Dragon Glass! We came out of the cleft and into a garden. The Gardens of Many-Columned Iram, lost in the desert because they were too beautiful, must have been like that place. There were strange, immense trees whose branches were like feathery plumes and whose plumes shone with fires like those that clothe the feet of Indra's dancers. Strange flowers raised themselves along our path, and their hearts glowed like the glow-worms that are fastened to the rainbow bridge to Asgard. A wind sighed through the plumed trees, and luminous shadows drifted past their trunks. I heard a girl laugh, and the voice of a man singing.

"We went on. Once there was a low wailing far in the garden, and the girl threw herself before me, her arms outstretched. The wailing ceased, and we went on. The mountain grew plainer. I saw another globe of green fire swing out of the rose flashes at the right of the peak. I saw another shining into the glow at the left. There was a curious trail of mist behind it. It was a mist that had tangled in it a multitude of little stars. Everything was bathed in a soft green light— such a light as you would have if you lived within a pale emerald.

"We turned and went along another little trail. The little trail ran up a little hill, and on the hill was a little house. It looked as though it was made of ivory. It was a very odd little house. It was more like the Jain pagodas at Brahmaputra than anything else. The walls glowed as though they were full of light. The girl touched the wall, and a panel slid away. We entered, and the panel closed after us.

"The room was filled with a whispering yellow light. I say whispering because that is how one felt about it. It was gentle and alive. A stairway of ivory ran up to another room above. The girl pressed me towards it. Neither of us had uttered a word. There was a spell of silence upon me. I could not speak. There seemed to be nothing to say. I felt a great rest and a great peace—as though I had come home. I walked up the stairway and into the room above. It was dark except for a bar of green light that came through the long and narrow window. Through it I saw the mountain and its moons. On the floor was an ivory head-rest and some silken cloths. I felt suddenly very sleepy. I dropped to the cloths, and at once was asleep.

"When I awoke the girl with the cornflower eyes was beside me! She was sleeping. As I watched, her eyes opened. She smiled and drew me to her—

"I do not know why, but a name came to me. 'Santhu!' I cried. She smiled again, and I knew that I had called her name. It seemed to me that I remembered her, too, out of immeasurable ages. I arose and walked to the window. I looked toward the mountain. There were now two moons on its breast. And then I saw the city that lay on the mountain's flank. It was such a city as you see in dreams, or as the tale-tellers of El-Bahara fashion out of the mirage. It was all of ivory and shining greens and flashing blues and crimsons. I could see people walking about its streets. There came the sound of little golden bells chiming.

"I turned towards the girl. She was sitting up, her hands clasped about her knees, watching me. Love came, swift and compelling. She arose—I took her in my arms—

"Many times the moons circled the mountain, and the mist held the little tangled stars passing with them. I saw no one but Santhu; no thing came near us. The trees fed us with fruits that had in them the very essence of life. Yes, the fruit of the Tree of Life that stood in Eden must have been like the fruit of those trees. We drank of green water that sparkled with green fires, and tasted like the wine Osiris gives the hungry souls in Amenti to strengthen them. We bathed in pools of carved stone that welled with water yellow as amber. Mostly we wandered in the gardens. There were many wonderful things in the gardens. They were very unearthly. There was no day or night. Only the green glow of the ever-circling moons. We never talked to each other. I don't know why. Always there seemed nothing to say.

"Then Santhu began to sing to me. Her songs were strange songs. I could not tell what the words were. But they built up pictures in my brain. I saw Rak the Wonder-Worker fashioning his gardens, and filling them with things beautiful and things—evil. I saw him raise the peak, and knew that it was Lalil; saw him fashion the seven moons and kindle the fires that are the fires of life. I saw him build his city, and I saw men and women pass into it from the world through many gateways.

"Santhu sang—and I knew that the marching stars in the mist were the souls of the people of Rak which sought rebirth. She sang, and I saw myself ages past walking in the city of Rak with Santhu beside me. Her song wailed, and I felt myself one of the mist-entangled stars. Her song wept, and I felt myself a star that fought against the mist, and, fighting, break away—a star that fled out and out through immeasurable green space—

"A man stood before us. He was very tall. His face was both cruel and kind, saturnine as Satan and joyous as Apollo. He raised his eyes to us, and they were yellow as buttercups, and wise, so wise! Ward, it was the face above the peak in the room of the Dragon Glass! The eyes that had looked at me out of Wu-Sing's face! He smiled on us for a moment and then—he was gone!

"I took Santhu by the hand and began to run. Quite suddenly it came to me that I had enough of the haunted gardens of Rak; that I wanted to get back to my own land. But not without Santhu. I tried to remember the road to the cleft. I felt that there lay the path back. We ran. From far behind came a wailing. Santhu screamed—but I knew the fear in her cry was not for herself. It was for me. None of the creatures of that place could harm her who was herself one of its creatures. The wailing drew closer. I turned.

"Winging down through the green air was a beast, an unthinkable beast, Ward! It was like the winged beast of the Apocalypse that is to bear the woman arrayed in purple and scarlet. It was beautiful even in its horror. It closed its scarlet and golden wings, and its long gleaming body shot at me like a monstrous spear.

"And then—just as it was about to strike—a mist threw itself between us! It was a rainbow mist, and it was—cast. It was cast as though a hand had held it and thrown it like a net. I heard the winged beast shriek its disappointment. Santhu's hand gripped mine tighter. We ran through the mist.

"Before us was the cleft between the two green rocks. Time and time again we raced for it, and time and time again that beautiful shining horror struck at me—and each time came the thrown mist to baffle it. It was a game! Once I heard a laugh, and then I knew who was my hunter. The master of the beast and the caster of the mist. It was he of the yellow eyes—and he was playing with me—playing with me as a child plays with a cat when he tempts it with a piece of meat and snatches the meat away again and again from the hungry jaws!

"The mist cleared away from its last throw, and the mouth of the cleft was just before us. Once more the thing swooped—and this time there was no mist. The player had tired of the game! As it struck, Santhu raised herself before it. The beast swerved—and the claw that had been stretched to rip me from throat to waist struck me a glancing blow. I fell—fell through leagues and leagues of green space.

"When I awoke I was here in this bed with the doctor men around me and this—" He pointed to his bandaged breast again. "That night when the nurse was asleep I got up and looked into the Dragon Glass, and I saw—the claw, even as you did. The beast is there. It is waiting for me!"

Herndon was silent for a moment.

"If he tires of the waiting he may send the beast through for me," he said. "I mean the man with the yellow eyes. I've a desire to try one of these guns on it. It's real, you know, the beast is—and these guns have stopped elephants."

"But the man with the yellow eyes, Jim," I whispered—"who is he?"

"He," said Herndon—"why, he's the Wonder-Worker himself!"

"You don't believe such a story as that!" I cried. "Why, it's—it's lunacy! It's some devilish illusion in the glass. It's like the—the crystal globe that makes you hypnotize yourself and think the things your own mind creates are real. Break it, Jim! It's devilish! Break it!"

"Break it!" he said incredulously. "Break it? Not for the ten thousand lives that are the toll of Rak! Not real? Aren't these wounds real? Wasn't Santhu real? Break it! Good God, man, you don't know what you say! Why, it's my only road back to her! If that yellow-eyed devil back there were only as wise as he looks, he would know he didn't have to keep his beast watching there. I want to go, Ward; I want to go and bring her back with me. I've an idea somehow, that he hasn't—well, full control of things. I've an idea that the Greatest Wonder-Worker wouldn't put wholly in Rak's hands the souls that wander through the many gateways into his kingdom. There's a way out, Ward; there's a way to escape him. I won a way from him once, Ward. I'm sure of it. But then I left Santhu behind. I have to go back for her. That's why I found the little passage that led from the throne-room. And he knows it, too. That's why he had to turn his beast on me. And I'll go through again, Ward. "And I'll come back again—with Santhu!"

★

But he has not returned. It is six months now since he disappeared for the second time. And from his bedroom, as he had done before. By the will that they found—the will that commanded that in the event of his disappearing as he had done before and not returning within a week, I was to have his house and all that was within it—I came into possession of the Dragon Glass. The dragons had spun again for Herndon, and he had gone through the gateway once more. I found only one of the elephant guns, and I knew that he had had time to take the other with him.

I sit night after night before the glass, waiting for him to come back through it—with Santhu. Sooner or later they will come. That I know.

H. G. Wells (1866–1946)

LIKE EDGAR RICE BURROUGHS, H. G. Wells might seem an unusual choice for this anthology. Along with Jules Verne, he is considered to be the father of science fiction based on his novels *The Time Machine* (1895), *The Island of Dr. Moreau* (1896), *The Invisible Man* (1897), *The War of the Worlds* (1898), and *The First Men in the Moon* (1901), among others. But Wells wrote quite a few fantasies, as well. "The Man Who Could Work Miracles" (1898), a wish-fulfilment tale, is perhaps the best known, but there are also "Mr. Skelmersdale in Fairyland" (1901), an updated but still somewhat traditional story of an imagined visit to fairyland; "The Magic Shop" (1903), about a store that sells genuine magic tricks; "The Beautiful Suit" (1909), which bestows perfection on its wearer; and novels such as *The Wonderful Visit* (1895), in which an angel visits Earth.

Even *The Time Machine* can be seen as an outgrowth of the fairy tale motif, despite all the scientific trappings. An inventor creates a machine that takes him into a distant future that seems at first to be an idyllic Eden, but is actually a place where evil lurks. *The Time Machine* is really a fairy tale for the scientific age. And that's what Wells achieved: He brought the ideas and images of fantasy up to date for the modern reader—at least at the time during which he wrote—the 1890s and the Edwardian age. Because Wells was such a skillful writer, producing stories that were relevant to the common reader, his works scarcely age. The following tale, first published in 1906, is a typical example; it takes the idea that Goethe expressed in "The New Paris" and reworks it for the modern reader, with an extra twist.

The Door in the Wall

H. G. Wells

One confidential evening, not three months ago, Lionel Wallace told me this story of the Door in the Wall. And at the time I thought that so far as he was concerned it was a true story.

He told it me with such a direct simplicity of conviction that I could not do otherwise than believe in him. But in the morning, in my own flat, I woke to a different atmosphere, and as I lay in bed and recalled the things he had told me, stripped of the glamour of his earnest slow voice, denuded of the focussed shaded table light, the shadowy atmosphere that wrapped about him and the pleasant bright things, the dessert and glasses and napery of the dinner we had shared, making them for the time a bright little world quite cut off from every-day realities, I saw it all as frankly incredible. "He was mystifying!" I said, and then: "How well he did it! . . . It isn't quite the thing I should have expected him, of all people, to do well."

Afterwards, as I sat up in bed and sipped my morning tea, I found myself trying to account for the flavour of reality that perplexed me in his impossible reminiscences, by supposing they did in some way suggest, present, convey—I hardly know which word to use—experiences it was otherwise impossible to tell.

Well, I don't resort to that explanation now. I have got over my intervening doubts. I believe now, as I believed at the moment of telling, that Wallace did to the very best of his ability strip the truth of his secret for me. But whether he himself saw, or only thought he saw, whether he himself was the possessor of an inestimable privilege, or the victim of a fantastic dream, I cannot pretend to guess. Even the facts of his death, which ended my doubts forever, throw no light on that. That much the reader must judge for himself.

I forget now what chance comment or criticism of mine moved so reticent a man to confide in me. He was, I think, defending himself against an imputation of slackness and unreliability I had made in relation to a great public movement in which he had disappointed me. But he plunged suddenly. "I have" he said, "a preoccupation—"

"I know," he went on, after a pause that he devoted to the study of his cigar ash, "I have been negligent. The fact is—it isn't a case of ghosts or apparitions—but—it's an odd thing to tell of, Redmond—I am haunted. I am haunted by something—that rather takes the light out of things, that fills me with longings . . ."

He paused, checked by that English shyness that so often overcomes us when we would speak of moving or grave or beautiful things. "You were at Saint Athelstan's all through," he said, and for a moment that seemed to me quite irrelevant. "Well"—and he paused. Then very haltingly at first, but afterwards more easily, he began to tell of the thing that was hidden in his life, the haunting memory of a beauty and a happiness that filled his heart with insatiable longings that made all the interests and spectacle of worldly life seem dull and tedious and vain to him.

Now that I have the clue to it, the thing seems written visibly in his face. I have a photograph in which that look of detachment has been caught and intensified. It reminds me of what a woman once said of him—a woman who had loved him greatly. "Suddenly," she said, "the interest goes out of him. He forgets you. He doesn't care a rap for you—under his very nose . . ."

Yet the interest was not always out of him, and when he was holding his attention to a thing Wallace could contrive to be an extremely successful man. His career, indeed, is set with successes. He left me behind him long ago; he soared up over my head, and cut a figure in the world that I couldn't cut—anyhow. He was still a year short of forty, and they say now that he would have been in office and very probably in the new Cabinet if he had lived. At school he always beat me without effort—as it were by nature. We were at school together at Saint Athelstan's College in West Kensington for almost all our school time. He came into the school as my co-equal, but he left far above me, in a blaze of scholarships and brilliant performance. Yet I think I made a fair average running. And it was at school I heard first of the Door in the Wall—that I was to hear of a second time only a month before his death.

To him at least the Door in the Wall was a real door leading through a real wall to immortal realities. Of that I am now quite assured.

And it came into his life early, when he was a little fellow between five and six. I remember how, as he sat making his confession to me with a slow gravity, he reasoned and reckoned the date of it. "There was," he said, "a crimson Virginia creeper in it—all one bright, uniform crimson in a clear amber sunshine against a white wall. That came into the impression somehow, though I don't clearly remember how, and there were horse-chestnut leaves upon the clean pavement outside the green door. They were blotched yellow and green, you know, not brown nor dirty, so that they must have been new fallen. I take it that means October. I look out for horse-chestnut leaves every year, and I ought to know.

"If I'm right in that, I was about five years and four months old."

He was, he said, rather a precocious little boy—he learned to talk at an abnormally early age, and he was so sane and "old-fashioned," as people say, that he was permitted an amount of initiative that most children scarcely attain by seven or eight. His mother died when he was born, and he was under the less vigilant and authoritative care of a nursery governess. His father was a stern, preoccupied lawyer, who gave him little attention, and expected great things of him. For all his brightness he found life a little grey and dull I think. And one day he wandered.

He could not recall the particular neglect that enabled him to get away, nor the course he took among the West Kensington roads. All that had faded among the incurable blurs of memory. But the white wall and the green door stood out quite distinctly.

As his memory of that remote childish experience ran, he did at the very first sight of that door experience a peculiar emotion, an attraction, a desire to get to the door and open it and walk in.

And at the same time he had the clearest conviction that either it was unwise or it was wrong of him—he could not tell which—to yield to this attraction. He insisted upon it as a curious thing that he knew from the very beginning—unless memory has played him the queerest trick—that the door was unfastened, and that he could go in as he chose.

I seem to see the figure of that little boy, drawn and repelled. And it was very clear in his mind, too, though why it should be so was never explained, that his father would be very angry if he went through that door.

Wallace described all these moments of hesitation to me with the utmost particularity. He went right past the door, and then, with his hands in his pockets, and making an infantile attempt to whistle, strolled right along beyond the end of the wall. There he recalls a number of mean, dirty shops, and particularly that of a plumber and decorator, with a dusty disorder of earthenware pipes, sheet lead ball taps, pattern books of wall paper, and tins of enamel. He stood pretending to examine these things, and coveting, passionately desiring the green door.

Then, he said, he had a gust of emotion. He made a run for it, lest hesitation should grip him again, he went plump with outstretched hand through the green door and let it slam behind him. And so, in a trice, he came into the garden that has haunted all his life.

It was very difficult for Wallace to give me his full sense of that garden into which he came.

There was something in the very air of it that exhilarated, that gave one a sense of lightness and good happening and well being; there was something in the sight of it that made all its colour clean and perfect and subtly luminous. In the instant of coming into it one was exquisitely glad—as only in rare moments and when one is young and joyful one can be glad in this world. And everything was beautiful there . . .

Wallace mused before he went on telling me. "You see," he said, with the doubtful inflection of a man who pauses at incredible things, "there were two great panthers there . . . Yes, spotted panthers. And I was not afraid. There was a long wide path with marble-edged flower borders on either side, and these two huge velvety beasts were playing there with a ball. One looked up and came towards me, a little curious as it seemed. It came right up to me, rubbed its soft round ear very gently against the small hand I held out and purred. It was, I tell you, an enchanted garden. I know. And the size? Oh! it stretched far and wide, this way and that. I believe there were hills far away. Heaven knows where West Kensington had suddenly got to. And somehow it was just like coming home.

"You know, in the very moment the door swung to behind me, I forgot the road with its fallen chestnut leaves, its cabs and tradesmen's carts, I forgot the sort of gravitational pull back to the discipline and obedience of home, I forgot all hesitations and fear, forgot discretion, forgot all the intimate realities of this life. I became in a moment a very glad and wonder-happy little boy—in another world. It was a world with a different quality, a warmer, more penetrating and mellower light, with a faint clear gladness in its air, and wisps of sun-touched cloud in the blueness of its sky. And before me ran this long wide path, invitingly, with weedless beds on either side, rich with untended flowers, and these two great panthers. I put my little hands fearlessly on their soft fur, and caressed their round ears and the sensitive corners under their ears, and played with them, and it was as though they welcomed me home. There was a keen sense of home-coming in my mind, and when presently a tall, fair girl appeared in the pathway and came to meet me, smiling, and said "Well?" to me, and lifted me, and kissed me, and put me down, and led me by the hand, there was no amazement, but only an impression of delightful rightness, of being reminded of happy things that had in some strange way been overlooked. There were broad steps, I remember, that came into view between spikes of delphinium, and up these we went to a great avenue between very old and shady dark trees. All down this avenue, you know, between the red chapped stems, were marble seats of honour and statuary, and very tame and friendly white doves . . .

"And along this avenue my girl-friend led me, looking down—I recall the pleasant lines, the finely-modelled chin of her sweet kind face—asking me questions in a soft, agreeable voice, and telling me things, pleasant things I know, though what they were I was never able to recall . . . And presently a little Capuchin monkey, very clean, with a fur of ruddy brown and kindly hazel eyes, came down a tree to us and ran beside me, looking up at me and grinning, and presently leapt to my shoulder. So we went on our way in great happiness. . . ."

He paused.

"Go on," I said.

"I remember little things. We passed an old man musing among laurels, I remember, and a place gay with paroquets, and came through a broad shaded colonnade to a spacious cool palace, full of pleasant fountains, full of beautiful things, full of the quality and promise of heart's desire. And there were many things and many people, some that still seem to stand out clearly and some that are a little vague, but all these people were beautiful and kind. In some way—I don't know how—it was conveyed to me that they all were kind to me, glad to have me there, and filling me with gladness by their gestures, by the touch of their hands, by the welcome and love in their eyes. Yes—"

He mused for awhile. "Playmates I found there. That was very much to me, because I was a lonely little boy. They played delightful games in a grass-covered court where there was a sun-dial set about with flowers. And as one played one loved. . . .

"But—it's odd—there's a gap in my memory. I don't remember the games we played. I never remembered. Afterwards, as a child, I spent long hours trying, even with tears, to recall the form of that happiness. I wanted to play it all over again—in my nursery—by myself. No! All I remember is the happiness and two dear playfellows who were most with me. . . . Then presently came a sombre dark woman, with a grave, pale face and dreamy eyes, a sombre woman wearing a soft long robe of pale purple, who carried a book and beckoned and took me aside with her into a gallery above a hall—though my playmates were loth to have me go, and ceased their game and stood watching as I was carried away. "Come back to us!' they cried. "Come back to us soon!' I looked up at her face, but she heeded them not at all. Her face was very gentle and grave. She took me to a seat in the gallery, and I stood beside her, ready to look at her book as she opened it upon her knee. The pages fell open. She pointed, and I looked, marvelling, for in the living pages of that book I saw myself; it was a story about myself, and in it were all the things that had happened to me since ever I was born. . . .

"It was wonderful to me, because the pages of that book were not pictures, you understand, but realities."

Wallace paused gravely—looked at me doubtfully.

"Go on," I said. "I understand."

"They were realities—yes, they must have been; people moved and things came and went in them; my dear mother, whom I had near forgotten; then my father, stern and upright, the servants, the nursery, all the familiar things of home. Then the front door and the busy streets, with traffic to and fro: I looked and marvelled, and looked half doubtfully again into the woman's face and turned the pages over, skipping this and that, to see more of this book, and more, and so at last I came to myself hovering and hesitating outside the green door in the long white wall, and felt again the conflict and the fear.

"'And next?' I cried, and would have turned on, but the cool hand of the grave woman delayed me.

"'Next?' I insisted, and struggled gently with her hand, pulling up her fingers with all my childish strength, and as she yielded and the page came over she bent down upon me like a shadow and kissed my brow.

"But the page did not show the enchanted garden, nor the panthers, nor the girl who had led me by the hand, nor the playfellows who had been so loth to let me go. It showed a long grey street in West Kensington, on that chill hour of afternoon before the lamps are lit, and I was there, a wretched little figure, weeping aloud, for all that I could do to restrain myself, and I was weeping because I could not return to my dear play-fellows who had called after me, "Come back to us! Come back to us soon!" I was there. This was no page in a book, but harsh reality; that enchanted place and the restraining hand of the grave mother at whose knee I stood had gone—whither have they gone?"

He halted again, and remained for a time, staring into the fire.

"Oh! the wretchedness of that return!" he murmured.

"Well?" I said after a minute or so.

"Poor little wretch I was—brought back to this grey world again! As I realised the fulness of what had happened to me, I gave way to quite ungovernable grief. And the shame and humiliation of that public weeping and my disgraceful homecoming remain with me still. I see again the benevolent-looking old gentleman in gold spectacles who stopped and spoke to me—prodding me first with his umbrella. "Poor little chap," said he; "and are you lost then?"—and me a London boy of five and more! And he must needs bring in a kindly young policeman and make a crowd of me, and so march me home. Sobbing, conspicuous and frightened, I came from the enchanted garden to the steps of my father's house.

"That is as well as I can remember my vision of that garden—the garden that haunts me still. Of course, I can convey nothing of that indescribable quality of translucent unreality, that difference from the common things of experience that hung about it all; but that—that is what happened. If it was a dream, I am sure it was a day-time and altogether extraordinary dream . . . H'm!—naturally there followed a terrible questioning, by my aunt, my father, the nurse, the governess—everyone . . .

"I tried to tell them, and my father gave me my first thrashing for telling lies. When afterwards I tried to tell my aunt, she punished me again for my wicked persistence. Then, as I said, everyone was forbidden to listen to me, to hear a word about it. Even my fairy tale books were taken away from me for a time—because I was "too imaginative." Eh? Yes, they did that! My father belonged to the old school . . . And my story was driven back upon myself. I whispered it to my pillow—my pillow that was often damp and salt to my whispering lips with childish tears. And I added always to my official and less fervent prayers this one heartfelt request: "Please God I may dream of the garden. Oh! take me back to my garden! Take me back to my garden!"

"I dreamt often of the garden. I may have added to it, I may have changed it; I do not know . . . All this you understand is an attempt to reconstruct from fragmentary memories a very early experience. Between that and the other consecutive memories of my boyhood there is a gulf. A time came when it seemed impossible I should ever speak of that wonder glimpse again."

I asked an obvious question.

"No," he said. "I don't remember that I ever attempted to find my way back to the garden in those early years. This seems odd to me now, but I think that very probably a closer watch was kept on my movements after this misadventure to prevent my going astray. No, it wasn't until you knew me that I tried for the garden again. And I believe there was a period—incredible as it seems now—when I forgot the garden altogether—when I was about eight or nine it may have been. Do you remember me as a kid at Saint Athelstan's?"

"Rather!"

"I didn't show any signs did I in those days of having a secret dream?"

He looked up with a sudden smile.

"Did you ever play North-West Passage with me? . . . No, of course you didn't come my way!"

"It was the sort of game," he went on, "that every imaginative child plays all day. The idea was the discovery of a North-West Passage to school. The way to school was plain enough; the game consisted in finding some way that wasn't plain, starting off ten minutes early in some almost hopeless direction, and working one's way round through unaccustomed streets to my goal. And one day I got entangled among some rather low-class streets on the other side of Campden Hill, and I began to think that for once the game would be against me and that I should get to school late. I tried rather desperately a street that seemed a cul de sac, and found a passage at the end. I hurried through that with renewed hope. "I shall do it yet," I said, and passed a row of frowsy little shops that were inexplicably familiar to me, and behold! there was my long white wall and the green door that led to the enchanted garden!

"The thing whacked upon me suddenly. Then, after all, that garden, that wonderful garden, wasn't a dream!". . .

He paused.

"I suppose my second experience with the green door marks the world of difference there is between the busy life of a schoolboy and the infinite leisure of a child. Anyhow, this second time I didn't for a moment think of going in straight away. You see . . . For one thing my mind was full of the idea of getting to school in time—set on not breaking my record for punctuality. I must surely have felt SOME little desire at least to try the door—yes, I must have felt that . . . But I seem to remember the attraction of the door mainly as another obstacle to my overmastering determination to get to school. I was immediately interested by this discovery I had made, of course—I went on with my mind full of it—but I went on. It didn't check me. I ran past tugging out my watch, found I had ten minutes still to spare, and then I was going downhill into familiar surroundings. I got to school, breathless, it is true, and wet with perspiration, but in time. I can remember hanging up my coat and hat . . . Went right by it and left it behind me. Odd, eh?"

He looked at me thoughtfully. "Of course, I didn't know then that it wouldn't always be there. School boys have limited imaginations. I suppose I thought it was an awfully jolly thing to have it there, to know my way back to it, but there was the school tugging at me. I expect I was a good deal distraught and inattentive that morning, recalling what I could of the beautiful strange people I should presently see again. Oddly enough I had no doubt in my mind that they would be glad to see me . . . Yes, I must have thought of the garden that morning just as a jolly sort of place to which one might resort in the interludes of a strenuous scholastic career.

"I didn't go that day at all. The next day was a half holiday, and that may have weighed with me. Perhaps, too, my state of inattention brought down impositions upon me and docked the margin of time necessary for the detour. I don't know. What I do know is that in the meantime the enchanted garden was so much upon my mind that I could not keep it to myself.

"I told—What was his name?—a ferrety-looking youngster we used to call Squiff."

"Young Hopkins," said I.

"Hopkins it was. I did not like telling him, I had a feeling that in some way it was against the rules to tell him, but I did. He was walking part of the way home with me; he was talkative, and if we had not talked about the enchanted garden we should have talked of something else, and it was intolerable to me to think about any other subject. So I blabbed.

"Well, he told my secret. The next day in the play interval I found myself surrounded by half a dozen bigger boys, half teasing and wholly curious to hear more of the enchanted garden. There was that big Fawcett—you remember him?—and Carnaby and Morley Reynolds. You weren't there by any chance? No, I think I should have remembered if you were . . .

"A boy is a creature of odd feelings. I was, I really believe, in spite of my secret self-disgust, a little flattered to have the attention of these big fellows. I remember particularly a moment of pleasure caused by the praise of Crawshaw—you remember Crawshaw major, the son of Crawshaw the composer?—who said it was the best lie he had ever heard. But at the same time there was a really painful undertow of shame at telling what I felt was indeed a sacred secret. That beast Fawcett made a joke about the girl in green—."

Wallace's voice sank with the keen memory of that shame. "I pretended not to hear," he said. "Well, then Carnaby suddenly called me a young liar and disputed with me when I said the thing was true. I said I knew where to find the green door, could lead them all there in ten minutes. Carnaby became outrageously virtuous, and said I'd have to—and bear out my words or suffer. Did you ever have Carnaby twist your arm? Then perhaps you'll understand how it went with me. I swore my story was true. There was nobody in the school then to save a chap from Carnaby though Crawshaw put in a word or so. Carnaby had got his game. I grew excited and red-eared, and a little frightened, I behaved altogether like a silly little chap, and the outcome of it all was that instead of starting alone for my enchanted garden, I led the way presently—cheeks flushed, ears hot, eyes smarting, and my soul one burning misery and shame—for a party of six mocking, curious and threatening school-fellows.

"We never found the white wall and the green door . . ."

"You mean?—"

"I mean I couldn't find it. I would have found it if I could.

"And afterwards when I could go alone I couldn't find it. I never found it. I seem now to have been always looking for it through my school-boy days, but I've never come upon it again."

"Did the fellows—make it disagreeable?"

"Beastly . . . Carnaby held a council over me for wanton lying. I remember how I sneaked home and upstairs to hide the marks of my blubbering. But when I cried myself to sleep at last it wasn't for Carnaby, but for the garden, for the beautiful afternoon I had hoped for, for the sweet friendly women and the waiting playfellows and

the game I had hoped to learn again, that beautiful forgotten game
. . .

"I believed firmly that if I had not told—. . . I had bad times after
that—crying at night and woolgathering by day. For two terms I
slackened and had bad reports. Do you remember? Of course you
would! It was *you*—your beating me in mathematics that brought me
back to the grind again."

For a time my friend stared silently into the red heart of the fire.
Then he said: "I never saw it again until I was seventeen.

"It leapt upon me for the third time—as I was driving to Padding-
ton on my way to Oxford and a scholarship. I had just one momentary glimpse. I was leaning over the apron of my hansom smoking
a cigarette, and no doubt thinking myself no end of a man of the
world, and suddenly there was the door, the wall, the dear sense of
unforgettable and still attainable things.

"We clattered by—I too taken by surprise to stop my cab until we
were well past and round a corner. Then I had a queer moment, a
double and divergent movement of my will: I tapped the little door
in the roof of the cab, and brought my arm down to pull out my
watch. "Yes, sir!' said the cabman, smartly. "Er—well—it's nothing,'
I cried. "*My* mistake! We haven't much time! Go on!" and he went
on . . .

"I got my scholarship. And the night after I was told of that I sat
over my fire in my little upper room, my study, in my father's house,
with his praise—his rare praise—and his sound counsels ringing in
my ears, and I smoked my favourite pipe—the formidable bulldog
of adolescence—and thought of that door in the long white wall.
"If I had stopped," I thought, "I should have missed my scholarship, I
should have missed Oxford—muddled all the fine career before me!
I begin to see things better!" I fell musing deeply, but I did not doubt
then this career of mine was a thing that merited sacrifice.

"Those dear friends and that clear atmosphere seemed very sweet
to me, very fine, but remote. My grip was fixing now upon the world.
I saw another door opening—the door of my career."

He stared again into the fire. Its red lights picked out a stubborn
strength in his face for just one flickering moment, and then it vanished again.

"Well," he said and sighed, "I have served that career. I have done—
much work, much hard work. But I have dreamt of the enchanted

garden a thousand dreams, and seen its door, or at least glimpsed its door, four times since then. Yes—four times. For a while this world was so bright and interesting, seemed so full of meaning and opportunity that the half-effaced charm of the garden was by comparison gentle and remote. Who wants to pat panthers on the way to dinner with pretty women and distinguished men? I came down to London from Oxford, a man of bold promise that I have done something to redeem. Something—and yet there have been disappointments . . .

"Twice I have been in love—I will not dwell on that—but once, as I went to someone who, I know, doubted whether I dared to come, I took a short cut at a venture through an unfrequented road near Earl's Court, and so happened on a white wall and a familiar green door. "Odd!" said I to myself, "but I thought this place was on Campden Hill. It's the place I never could find somehow—like counting Stonehenge—the place of that queer day dream of mine." And I went by it intent upon my purpose. It had no appeal to me that afternoon.

"I had just a moment's impulse to try the door, three steps aside were needed at the most—though I was sure enough in my heart that it would open to me—and then I thought that doing so might delay me on the way to that appointment in which I thought my honour was involved. Afterwards I was sorry for my punctuality—I might at least have peeped in I thought, and waved a hand to those panthers, but I knew enough by this time not to seek again belatedly that which is not found by seeking. Yes, that time made me very sorry . . .

"Years of hard work after that and never a sight of the door. It's only recently it has come back to me. With it there has come a sense as though some thin tarnish had spread itself over my world. I began to think of it as a sorrowful and bitter thing that I should never see that door again. Perhaps I was suffering a little from overwork—perhaps it was what I've heard spoken of as the feeling of forty. I don't know. But certainly the keen brightness that makes effort easy has gone out of things recently, and that just at a time with all these new political developments—when I ought to be working. Odd, isn't it? But I do begin to find life toilsome, its rewards, as I come near them, cheap. I began a little while ago to want the garden quite badly. Yes—and I've seen it three times."

"The garden?"

"No—the door! And I haven't gone in!"

He leaned over the table to me, with an enormous sorrow in his voice as he spoke. "Thrice I have had my chance—*thrice*! If ever that door offers itself to me again, I swore, I will go in out of this dust and heat, out of this dry glitter of vanity, out of these toilsome futilities. I will go and never return. This time I will stay . . . I swore it and when the time came—*I didn't go*.

"Three times in one year have I passed that door and failed to enter. Three times in the last year.

"The first time was on the night of the snatch division on the Tenants'' Redemption Bill, on which the Government was saved by a majority of three. You remember? No one on our side—perhaps very few on the opposite side—expected the end that night. Then the debate collapsed like eggshells. I and Hotchkiss were dining with his cousin at Brentford, we were both unpaired, and we were called up by telephone, and set off at once in his cousin's motor. We got in barely in time, and on the way we passed my wall and door—livid in the moonlight, blotched with hot yellow as the glare of our lamps lit it, but unmistakable. "My God!" cried I. "What?" said Hotchkiss. "Nothing!" I answered, and the moment passed.

"'I've made a great sacrifice,' I told the whip as I got in. 'They all have,' he said, and hurried by.

"I do not see how I could have done otherwise then. And the next occasion was as I rushed to my father's bedside to bid that stern old man farewell. Then, too, the claims of life were imperative. But the third time was different; it happened a week ago. It fills me with hot remorse to recall it. I was with Gurker and Ralphs—it's no secret now you know that I've had my talk with Gurker. We had been dining at Frobisher's, and the talk had become intimate between us. The question of my place in the reconstructed ministry lay always just over the boundary of the discussion. Yes—yes. That's all settled. It needn't be talked about yet, but there's no reason to keep a secret from you . . . Yes—thanks! thanks! But let me tell you my story.

"Then, on that night things were very much in the air. My position was a very delicate one. I was keenly anxious to get some definite word from Gurker, but was hampered by Ralphs' presence. I was using the best power of my brain to keep that light and careless talk not too obviously directed to the point that concerns me. I had to. Ralphs' behaviour since has more than justified my caution . . . Ralphs, I knew, would leave us beyond the Kensington High Street, and then I could surprise Gurker by a sudden frankness. One has sometimes to resort to these little devices. . . . And then it was that in the margin of my field of vision I became aware once more of the white wall, the green door before us down the road.

"We passed it talking. I passed it. I can still see the shadow of Gurker's marked profile, his opera hat tilted forward over his prominent nose, the many folds of his neck wrap going before my shadow and Ralphs" as we sauntered past.

"I passed within twenty inches of the door. "If I say good-night to them, and go in," I asked myself, "what will happen?" And I was all a-tingle for that word with Gurker.

"I could not answer that question in the tangle of my other problems. "They will think me mad," I thought. "And suppose I vanish now!—Amazing disappearance of a prominent politician!" That weighed with me. A thousand inconceivably petty worldlinesses weighed with me in that crisis."

Then he turned on me with a sorrowful smile, and, speaking slowly; "Here I am!" he said.

"Here I am!" he repeated, "and my chance has gone from me. Three times in one year the door has been offered me—the door that goes into peace, into delight, into a beauty beyond dreaming, a kindness no man on earth can know. And I have rejected it, Redmond, and it has gone—"

"How do you know?"

"I know. I know. I am left now to work it out, to stick to the tasks that held me so strongly when my moments came. You say, I have success—this vulgar, tawdry, irksome, envied thing. I have it." He had a walnut in his big hand. "If that was my success," he said, and crushed it, and held it out for me to see.

"Let me tell you something, Redmond. This loss is destroying me. For two months, for ten weeks nearly now, I have done no work at all, except the most necessary and urgent duties. My soul is full of inappeasable regrets. At nights—when it is less likely I shall be recognised—I go out. I wander. Yes. I wonder what people would think of that if they knew. A Cabinet Minister, the responsible head of that most vital of all departments, wandering alone—grieving—sometimes near audibly lamenting—for a door, for a garden!"

I can see now his rather pallid face, and the unfamiliar sombre fire that had come into his eyes. I see him very vividly to-night. I sit recalling his words, his tones, and last evening's Westminster Gazette still lies on my sofa, containing the notice of his death. At lunch to-day the club was busy with him and the strange riddle of his fate.

They found his body very early yesterday morning in a deep excavation near East Kensington Station. It is one of two shafts that have been made in connection with an extension of the railway southward. It is protected from the intrusion of the public by a hoarding upon the high road, in which a small doorway has been cut for the convenience of some of the workmen who live in that direction. The doorway was left unfastened through a misunderstanding between two gangers, and through it he made his way. . . .

My mind is darkened with questions and riddles.

It would seem he walked all the way from the House that night—he has frequently walked home during the past Session—and so it is I figure his dark form coming along the late and empty streets, wrapped up, intent. And then did the pale electric lights near the station cheat the rough planking into a semblance of white? Did that fatal unfastened door awaken some memory?

Was there, after all, ever any green door in the wall at all?

I do not know. I have told his story as he told it to me. There are times when I believe that Wallace was no more than the victim of the coincidence between a rare but not unprecedented type of hallucination and a careless trap, but that indeed is not my profoundest belief. You may think me superstitious if you will, and foolish; but, indeed, I am more than half convinced that he had in truth, an abnormal gift, and a sense, something—I know not what—that in the guise of wall and door offered him an outlet, a secret and peculiar passage of escape into another and altogether more beautiful world. At any rate, you will say, it betrayed him in the end. But did it betray him? There you touch the inmost mystery of these dreamers, these men of vision and the imagination.

We see our world fair and common, the hoarding and the pit. By our daylight standard he walked out of security into darkness, danger and death. But did he see like that?

A CATALOG OF SELECTED
DOVER BOOKS
IN ALL FIELDS OF INTEREST

A CATALOG OF SELECTED DOVER
BOOKS IN ALL FIELDS OF INTEREST

100 BEST-LOVED POEMS, Edited by Philip Smith. "The Passionate Shepherd to His Love," "Shall I compare thee to a summer's day?" "Death, be not proud," "The Raven," "The Road Not Taken," plus works by Blake, Wordsworth, Byron, Shelley, Keats, many others. 96pp. 5³⁄₁₆ x 8¼.   0-486-28553-7

100 SMALL HOUSES OF THE THIRTIES, Brown-Blodgett Company. Exterior photographs and floor plans for 100 charming structures. Illustrations of models accompanied by descriptions of interiors, color schemes, closet space, and other amenities. 200 illustrations. 112pp. 8⅜ x 11.   0-486-44131-8

1000 TURN-OF-THE-CENTURY HOUSES: With Illustrations and Floor Plans, Herbert C. Chivers. Reproduced from a rare edition, this showcase of homes ranges from cottages and bungalows to sprawling mansions. Each house is meticulously illustrated and accompanied by complete floor plans. 256pp. 9⅜ x 12¼.
0-486-45596-3

101 GREAT AMERICAN POEMS, Edited by The American Poetry & Literacy Project. Rich treasury of verse from the 19th and 20th centuries includes works by Edgar Allan Poe, Robert Frost, Walt Whitman, Langston Hughes, Emily Dickinson, T. S. Eliot, other notables. 96pp. 5³⁄₁₆ x 8¼.   0-486-40158-8

101 GREAT SAMURAI PRINTS, Utagawa Kuniyoshi. Kuniyoshi was a master of the warrior woodblock print — and these 18th-century illustrations represent the pinnacle of his craft. Full-color portraits of renowned Japanese samurais pulse with movement, passion, and remarkably fine detail. 112pp. 8⅜ x 11.   0-486-46523-3

ABC OF BALLET, Janet Grosser. Clearly worded, abundantly illustrated little guide defines basic ballet-related terms: arabesque, battement, pas de chat, relevé, sissonne, many others. Pronunciation guide included. Excellent primer. 48pp. 4³⁄₁₆ x 5¾.
0-486-40871-X

ACCESSORIES OF DRESS: An Illustrated Encyclopedia, Katherine Lester and Bess Viola Oerke. Illustrations of hats, veils, wigs, cravats, shawls, shoes, gloves, and other accessories enhance an engaging commentary that reveals the humor and charm of the many-sided story of accessorized apparel. 644 figures and 59 plates. 608pp. 6⅛ x 9¼.
0-486-43378-1

ADVENTURES OF HUCKLEBERRY FINN, Mark Twain. Join Huck and Jim as their boyhood adventures along the Mississippi River lead them into a world of excitement, danger, and self-discovery. Humorous narrative, lyrical descriptions of the Mississippi valley, and memorable characters. 224pp. 5³⁄₁₆ x 8¼.   0-486-28061-6

ALICE STARMORE'S BOOK OF FAIR ISLE KNITTING, Alice Starmore. A noted designer from the region of Scotland's Fair Isle explores the history and techniques of this distinctive, stranded-color knitting style and provides copious illustrated instructions for 14 original knitwear designs. 208pp. 8⅜ x 10⅞.   0-486-47218-3

Browse over 9,000 books at www.doverpublications.com

ALICE'S ADVENTURES IN WONDERLAND, Lewis Carroll. Beloved classic about a little girl lost in a topsy-turvy land and her encounters with the White Rabbit, March Hare, Mad Hatter, Cheshire Cat, and other delightfully improbable characters. 42 illustrations by Sir John Tenniel. 96pp. 5³⁄₁₆ x 8¼. 0-486-27543-4

AMERICA'S LIGHTHOUSES: An Illustrated History, Francis Ross Holland. Profusely illustrated fact-filled survey of American lighthouses since 1716. Over 200 stations — East, Gulf, and West coasts, Great Lakes, Hawaii, Alaska, Puerto Rico, the Virgin Islands, and the Mississippi and St. Lawrence Rivers. 240pp. 8 x 10¾. 0-486-25576-X

AN ENCYCLOPEDIA OF THE VIOLIN, Alberto Bachmann. Translated by Frederick H. Martens. Introduction by Eugene Ysaye. First published in 1925, this renowned reference remains unsurpassed as a source of essential information, from construction and evolution to repertoire and technique. Includes a glossary and 73 illustrations. 496pp. 6½ x 9¼. 0-486-46618-3

ANIMALS: 1,419 Copyright-Free Illustrations of Mammals, Birds, Fish, Insects, etc., Selected by Jim Harter. Selected for its visual impact and ease of use, this outstanding collection of wood engravings presents over 1,000 species of animals in extremely lifelike poses. Includes mammals, birds, reptiles, amphibians, fish, insects, and other invertebrates. 284pp. 9 x 12. 0-486-23766-4

THE ANNALS, Tacitus. Translated by Alfred John Church and William Jackson Brodribb. This vital chronicle of Imperial Rome, written by the era's great historian, spans A.D. 14-68 and paints incisive psychological portraits of major figures, from Tiberius to Nero. 416pp. 5³⁄₁₆ x 8¼. 0-486-45236-0

ANTIGONE, Sophocles. Filled with passionate speeches and sensitive probing of moral and philosophical issues, this powerful and often-performed Greek drama reveals the grim fate that befalls the children of Oedipus. Footnotes. 64pp. 5³⁄₁₆ x 8 ¼. 0-486-27804-2

ART DECO DECORATIVE PATTERNS IN FULL COLOR, Christian Stoll. Reprinted from a rare 1910 portfolio, 160 sensuous and exotic images depict a breathtaking array of florals, geometrics, and abstracts — all elegant in their stark simplicity. 64pp. 8⅜ x 11. 0-486-44862-2

THE ARTHUR RACKHAM TREASURY: 86 Full-Color Illustrations, Arthur Rackham. Selected and Edited by Jeff A. Menges. A stunning treasury of 86 full-page plates span the famed English artist's career, from *Rip Van Winkle* (1905) to masterworks such as *Undine, A Midsummer Night's Dream,* and *Wind in the Willows* (1939). 96pp. 8⅜ x 11. 0-486-44685-9

THE AUTHENTIC GILBERT & SULLIVAN SONGBOOK, W. S. Gilbert and A. S. Sullivan. The most comprehensive collection available, this songbook includes selections from every one of Gilbert and Sullivan's light operas. Ninety-two numbers are presented uncut and unedited, and in their original keys. 410pp. 9 x 12. 0-486-23482-7

THE AWAKENING, Kate Chopin. First published in 1899, this controversial novel of a New Orleans wife's search for love outside a stifling marriage shocked readers. Today, it remains a first-rate narrative with superb characterization. New introductory Note. 128pp. 5³⁄₁₆ x 8¼. 0-486-27786-0

BASIC DRAWING, Louis Priscilla. Beginning with perspective, this commonsense manual progresses to the figure in movement, light and shade, anatomy, drapery, composition, trees and landscape, and outdoor sketching. Black-and-white illustrations throughout. 128pp. 8⅜ x 11. 0-486-45815-6

Browse over 9,000 books at www.doverpublications.com

THE BATTLES THAT CHANGED HISTORY, Fletcher Pratt. Historian profiles 16 crucial conflicts, ancient to modern, that changed the course of Western civilization. Gripping accounts of battles led by Alexander the Great, Joan of Arc, Ulysses S. Grant, other commanders. 27 maps. 352pp. 5⅜ x 8½. 0-486-41129-X

BEETHOVEN'S LETTERS, Ludwig van Beethoven. Edited by Dr. A. C. Kalischer. Features 457 letters to fellow musicians, friends, greats, patrons, and literary men. Reveals musical thoughts, quirks of personality, insights, and daily events. Includes 15 plates. 410pp. 5⅜ x 8½. 0-486-22769-3

BERNICE BOBS HER HAIR AND OTHER STORIES, F. Scott Fitzgerald. This brilliant anthology includes 6 of Fitzgerald's most popular stories: "The Diamond as Big as the Ritz," the title tale, "The Offshore Pirate," "The Ice Palace," "The Jelly Bean," and "May Day." 176pp. 5⅜ x 8½. 0-486-47049-0

BESLER'S BOOK OF FLOWERS AND PLANTS: 73 Full-Color Plates from Hortus Eystettensis, 1613, Basilius Besler. Here is a selection of magnificent plates from the *Hortus Eystettensis*, which vividly illustrated and identified the plants, flowers, and trees that thrived in the legendary German garden at Eichstätt. 80pp. 8⅜ x 11. 0-486-46005-3

THE BOOK OF KELLS, Edited by Blanche Cirker. Painstakingly reproduced from a rare facsimile edition, this volume contains full-page decorations, portraits, illustrations, plus a sampling of textual leaves with exquisite calligraphy and ornamentation. 32 full-color illustrations. 32pp. 9⅜ x 12¼. 0-486-24345-1

THE BOOK OF THE CROSSBOW: With an Additional Section on Catapults and Other Siege Engines, Ralph Payne-Gallwey. Fascinating study traces history and use of crossbow as military and sporting weapon, from Middle Ages to modern times. Also covers related weapons: balistas, catapults, Turkish bows, more. Over 240 illustrations. 400pp. 7¼ x 10⅛. 0-486-28720-3

THE BUNGALOW BOOK: Floor Plans and Photos of 112 Houses, 1910, Henry L. Wilson. Here are 112 of the most popular and economic blueprints of the early 20th century — plus an illustration or photograph of each completed house. A wonderful time capsule that still offers a wealth of valuable insights. 160pp. 8⅜ x 11. 0-486-45104-6

THE CALL OF THE WILD, Jack London. A classic novel of adventure, drawn from London's own experiences as a Klondike adventurer, relating the story of a heroic dog caught in the brutal life of the Alaska Gold Rush. Note. 64pp. 5³⁄₁₆ x 8¼. 0-486-26472-6

CANDIDE, Voltaire. Edited by Francois-Marie Arouet. One of the world's great satires since its first publication in 1759. Witty, caustic skewering of romance, science, philosophy, religion, government — nearly all human ideals and institutions. 112pp. 5³⁄₁₆ x 8¼. 0-486-26689-3

CELEBRATED IN THEIR TIME: Photographic Portraits from the George Grantham Bain Collection, Edited by Amy Pastan. With an Introduction by Michael Carlebach. Remarkable portrait gallery features 112 rare images of Albert Einstein, Charlie Chaplin, the Wright Brothers, Henry Ford, and other luminaries from the worlds of politics, art, entertainment, and industry. 128pp. 8⅜ x 11. 0-486-46754-6

CHARIOTS FOR APOLLO: The NASA History of Manned Lunar Spacecraft to 1969, Courtney G. Brooks, James M. Grimwood, and Loyd S. Swenson, Jr. This illustrated history by a trio of experts is the definitive reference on the Apollo spacecraft and lunar modules. It traces the vehicles' design, development, and operation in space. More than 100 photographs and illustrations. 576pp. 6¾ x 9¼. 0-486-46756-2

A CHRISTMAS CAROL, Charles Dickens. This engrossing tale relates Ebenezer Scrooge's ghostly journeys through Christmases past, present, and future and his ultimate transformation from a harsh and grasping old miser to a charitable and compassionate human being. 80pp. 5³⁄₁₆ x 8¼.　0-486-26865-9

COMMON SENSE, Thomas Paine. First published in January of 1776, this highly influential landmark document clearly and persuasively argued for American separation from Great Britain and paved the way for the Declaration of Independence. 64pp. 5³⁄₁₆ x 8¼.　0-486-29602-4

THE COMPLETE SHORT STORIES OF OSCAR WILDE, Oscar Wilde. Complete texts of "The Happy Prince and Other Tales," "A House of Pomegranates," "Lord Arthur Savile's Crime and Other Stories," "Poems in Prose," and "The Portrait of Mr. W. H." 208pp. 5³⁄₁₆ x 8¼.　0-486-45216-6

COMPLETE SONNETS, William Shakespeare. Over 150 exquisite poems deal with love, friendship, the tyranny of time, beauty's evanescence, death, and other themes in language of remarkable power, precision, and beauty. Glossary of archaic terms. 80pp. 5³⁄₁₆ x 8¼.　0-486-26686-9

THE COUNT OF MONTE CRISTO: Abridged Edition, Alexandre Dumas. Falsely accused of treason, Edmond Dantès is imprisoned in the bleak Chateau d'If. After a hair-raising escape, he launches an elaborate plot to extract a bitter revenge against those who betrayed him. 448pp. 5³⁄₁₆ x 8¼.　0-486-45643-9

CRAFTSMAN BUNGALOWS: Designs from the Pacific Northwest, Yoho & Merritt. This reprint of a rare catalog, showcasing the charming simplicity and cozy style of Craftsman bungalows, is filled with photos of completed homes, plus floor plans and estimated costs. An indispensable resource for architects, historians, and illustrators. 112pp. 10 x 7.　0-486-46875-5

CRAFTSMAN BUNGALOWS: 59 Homes from "The Craftsman," Edited by Gustav Stickley. Best and most attractive designs from Arts and Crafts Movement publication — 1903–1916 — includes sketches, photographs of homes, floor plans, descriptive text. 128pp. 8¼ x 11.　0-486-25829-7

CRIME AND PUNISHMENT, Fyodor Dostoyevsky. Translated by Constance Garnett. Supreme masterpiece tells the story of Raskolnikov, a student tormented by his own thoughts after he murders an old woman. Overwhelmed by guilt and terror, he confesses and goes to prison. 480pp. 5³⁄₁₆ x 8¼.　0-486-41587-2

THE DECLARATION OF INDEPENDENCE AND OTHER GREAT DOCUMENTS OF AMERICAN HISTORY: 1775-1865, Edited by John Grafton. Thirteen compelling and influential documents: Henry's "Give Me Liberty or Give Me Death," Declaration of Independence, The Constitution, Washington's First Inaugural Address, The Monroe Doctrine, The Emancipation Proclamation, Gettysburg Address, more. 64pp. 5³⁄₁₆ x 8¼.　0-486-41124-9

THE DESERT AND THE SOWN: Travels in Palestine and Syria, Gertrude Bell. "The female Lawrence of Arabia," Gertrude Bell wrote captivating, perceptive accounts of her travels in the Middle East. This intriguing narrative, accompanied by 160 photos, traces her 1905 sojourn in Lebanon, Syria, and Palestine. 368pp. 5⅜ x 8½.　0-486-46876-3

A DOLL'S HOUSE, Henrik Ibsen. Ibsen's best-known play displays his genius for realistic prose drama. An expression of women's rights, the play climaxes when the central character, Nora, rejects a smothering marriage and life in "a doll's house." 80pp. 5³⁄₁₆ x 8¼.　0-486-27062-9

Browse over 9,000 books at www.doverpublications.com

DOOMED SHIPS: Great Ocean Liner Disasters, William H. Miller, Jr. Nearly 200 photographs, many from private collections, highlight tales of some of the vessels whose pleasure cruises ended in catastrophe: the *Morro Castle, Normandie, Andrea Doria, Europa,* and many others. 128pp. 8⅜ x 11¼. 0-486-45366-9

THE DORÉ BIBLE ILLUSTRATIONS, Gustave Doré. Detailed plates from the Bible: the Creation scenes, Adam and Eve, horrifying visions of the Flood, the battle sequences with their monumental crowds, depictions of the life of Jesus, 241 plates in all. 241pp. 9 x 12. 0-486-23004-X

DRAWING DRAPERY FROM HEAD TO TOE, Cliff Young. Expert guidance on how to draw shirts, pants, skirts, gloves, hats, and coats on the human figure, including folds in relation to the body, pull and crush, action folds, creases, more. Over 200 drawings. 48pp. 8¼ x 11. 0-486-45591-2

DUBLINERS, James Joyce. A fine and accessible introduction to the work of one of the 20th century's most influential writers, this collection features 15 tales, including a masterpiece of the short-story genre, "The Dead." 160pp. 5³⁄₁₆ x 8¼. 0-486-26870-5

EASY-TO-MAKE POP-UPS, Joan Irvine. Illustrated by Barbara Reid. Dozens of wonderful ideas for three-dimensional paper fun — from holiday greeting cards with moving parts to a pop-up menagerie. Easy-to-follow, illustrated instructions for more than 30 projects. 299 black-and-white illustrations. 96pp. 8⅜ x 11. 0-486-44622-0

EASY-TO-MAKE STORYBOOK DOLLS: A "Novel" Approach to Cloth Dollmaking, Sherralyn St. Clair. Favorite fictional characters come alive in this unique beginner's dollmaking guide. Includes patterns for Pollyanna, Dorothy from *The Wonderful Wizard of Oz,* Mary of *The Secret Garden,* plus easy-to-follow instructions, 263 black-and-white illustrations, and an 8-page color insert. 112pp. 8¼ x 11. 0-486-47360-0

EINSTEIN'S ESSAYS IN SCIENCE, Albert Einstein. Speeches and essays in accessible, everyday language profile influential physicists such as Niels Bohr and Isaac Newton. They also explore areas of physics to which the author made major contributions. 128pp. 5 x 8. 0-486-47011-3

EL DORADO: Further Adventures of the Scarlet Pimpernel, Baroness Orczy. A popular sequel to *The Scarlet Pimpernel,* this suspenseful story recounts the Pimpernel's attempts to rescue the Dauphin from imprisonment during the French Revolution. An irresistible blend of intrigue, period detail, and vibrant characterizations. 352pp. 5³⁄₁₆ x 8¼. 0-486-44026-5

ELEGANT SMALL HOMES OF THE TWENTIES: 99 Designs from a Competition, Chicago Tribune. Nearly 100 designs for five- and six-room houses feature New England and Southern colonials, Normandy cottages, stately Italianate dwellings, and other fascinating snapshots of American domestic architecture of the 1920s. 112pp. 9 x 12. 0-486-46910-7

THE ELEMENTS OF STYLE: The Original Edition, William Strunk, Jr. This is the book that generations of writers have relied upon for timeless advice on grammar, diction, syntax, and other essentials. In concise terms, it identifies the principal requirements of proper style and common errors. 64pp. 5⅜ x 8½. 0-486-44798-7

THE ELUSIVE PIMPERNEL, Baroness Orczy. Robespierre's revolutionaries find their wicked schemes thwarted by the heroic Pimpernel — Sir Percival Blakeney. In this thrilling sequel, Chauvelin devises a plot to eliminate the Pimpernel and his wife. 272pp. 5³⁄₁₆ x 8¼. 0-486-45464-9

Browse over 9,000 books at www.doverpublications.com